"DO IT NOW, GARY."

In response, the Canadian demolitions expert jammed his thumb on the button of the explosive device. An electrical charge raced to the fuel tank of the abandoned trailer. The explosion was small, but it instantly blew apart the tank and ignited the gasoline.

An orange fireball mushroomed toward the sky, and the large vehicle toppled on its side. The premature afternoon twilight caused by the heavy cloud cover had pitched a blanket of shadows across the area and made the violent fury of the roaring flames stand out eerily.

Katz heard the distant clamor of loudspeakers and knew the terrorists were alerted. The muscles in his jaw tightened, and he motioned to his men to charge toward the castle wall. There was no time to waste.

The terrorists were holding the President!

PHOENIX FORCE

FIRE STORM

GAR WILSON

A GOLD EAGLE BOOK FROM

WORLDWIDE®

TORONTO • NEW YORK • LONDON • PARIS
AMSTERDAM • STOCKHOLM • HAMBURG
ATHENS • MILAN • TOKYO • SYDNEY

First edition November 1988

ISBN 0-373-62201-5

Special thanks and acknowledgment to
William Fieldhouse for his contribution to this work.

1

Yakov Katzenelenbogen saw the cruise ship through the lens of his Bushnell binoculars. The beautiful luxury ocean liner resembled a great ivory sculpture as it floated across the blue-green waters of the Mediterranean Sea. It was a symbol of high-priced, idyllic travel for tourists enjoying the vacation of a lifetime.

But Katz knew the ship was no longer on a pleasure cruise. The crew and passengers had found themselves in the middle of a nightmare. The ship had been seized by a band of well-armed, well-organized terrorists within half an hour after leaving port in Greece. Katz did not know any other details except the terrorists had already killed at least one hostage. The United States Navy had sent a pair of helicopters from a base at southernmost Italy to recon the situation. The terrorists had immediately taken a middle-aged American tourist from among the hostages and had shot him in the back of the head, then had thrown the dead man overboard in clear view of the reconnaissance choppers. A terrorist delivered a warning on the ship radio. The Americans were told to get the helicopters out of the area immediately or more hostages would be killed. The spokesman further warned that no aircraft or vessel of any nationality had better come within view of the cruise ship.

Katzenelenbogen and the other members of Phoenix Force had learned about the hijacked cruise ship while they had been trying to get a lead on a terrorist bombing of the American embassy in Cairo. With the help of the Egyptian National Security Service, Phoenix Force had set out into the Mediterranean aboard an innocent-looking fishing boat equipped with a powerful high-speed engine.

"Cut the engine!" Katz ordered as he lowered the binoculars. "We're heading straight toward the cruise ship. Or perhaps I should say the ship is headed toward *us*."

"I hope you know what you're doing, Mr. Kenver," Ahmed Salamar said grimly. The Egyptian security officer spoke English in a singsong manner with an accent that sounded vaguely British. Salamar did not seem very happy to be on board the little fishing boat with the five strange foreigners. "Those crazy blighters claim they'll start killing hostages if anyone gets near that ship."

"Yes, Captain," Katz replied in a calm, even voice. "But even fanatics aren't going to start killing hostages if all they see is a little fishing vessel with three men on board. That would be like throwing away all their aces before they even know how many players are in the game. No, my friend. They won't start executing hostages the moment they see us. They need as many bargaining chips as possible when they reach their destination."

"We can't be certain where that might be," Salamar declared.

"I think it's safe to assume the ship is heading for Libya," Katz replied. "Your country certainly wouldn't welcome such hijackers, especially after the *Achille Lauro* incident of October 1985."

"The Egyptian government didn't willingly assist those terrorists, Mr. Kenver," Salamar said, bristling at the remark. "We've been trying to cooperate with you and your comrades since you arrived in Cairo. My very presence with you on this vessel is—"

"We don't have much time," Katz informed him. "Everyone, get ready. When they spot us, we'd better not seem the least bit suspicious."

Katz pushed up the right sleeve of his dark blue cotton shirt. His right arm had been amputated at the elbow. The Phoenix Force commander unfastened the leather straps of the prosthesis attached to the stump. Salamar wondered how he had lost the arm.

"We're ready back here," Rafael Encizo called out from the stern of the fishing vessel. "Going overboard with all our little gizmos."

The Cuban warrior was clad in a black wet suit with an air tank strapped to his back and swim fins on his feet. The snug rubber suit clung closely to his form and revealed the smooth bulk of muscular limbs and a firm torso. Although in his late forties, Encizo was in better physical condition than most men half his age. The Cuban lowered a diver's face mask over his dark, handsome features and stuck the regulator's mouthpiece between his teeth.

Calvin James, a tall, athletically trim black man, also outfitted with diving gear, stood next to Encizo. James was a former SEAL, a member of the navy's elite Sea, Air and Land team. A veteran of the Vietnam War, James had done plenty of underwater operations even before he joined Phoenix Force. He lowered a large waterproof rubber bag into the water and prepared to climb over the handrail.

"I hate to say this," James commented, "but we didn't get much time to test out those sea sleds. If those suckers malfunction, we'll have one hell of a time trying to swim into position, man. It won't be so good for you guys on this tub, too."

"I wish you hadn't said that," Gary Manning said with a sigh as he strapped on an air tank.

"I kind of wish I hadn't thought of it, either," the black commando admitted.

Manning, the Canadian, was a big man with the build of a lumberjack. He was the unit demolitions expert and a superb rifle marksman, but was less comfortable underwater than Encizo and James. The Cuban and the black warrior from Chicago were top-notch frogmen. Manning's experience in underwater operations was considerably less, and he preferred to stay on dry land as much as possible.

"I'm not so thrilled about doing this to begin with," the Canadian muttered as he hooked a rubber bag with special gear onto his diving belt. "Now, you have to start coming up with remarks about what could go wrong."

"That's a refreshing change," David McCarter said cheerfully. "You're complaining about somebody else instead of me."

"You just haven't said much since we left Egypt," Manning replied gruffly.

"I haven't been whining about getting my feet a bit wet, either," McCarter said with a wolfish grin.

A tall, lean Briton originally from the East End of London, McCarter was a former sergeant in the Special Air Service, and he thrived on excitement.

"Easy for you to say," Manning told the Briton. "You get to stay on the boat. For a while, anyway."

"Things might get a bit dicey here, too, mate," McCarter reminded him, patting the yellow life jacket that he wore like a vest. A 9 mm Browning Hi-Power autoloader pistol rode in shoulder leather. "At least I rather hope it will."

"Now I understand why they talk about mad dogs and Englishmen," Manning said, shaking his head. "Okay, we're out of here. You take care because you're sitting ducks if any of those terrorists have rocket launchers or a mounted machine gun."

"Let's move," Calvin James urged as he climbed over the rail. Manning nodded and headed for the stern to join James and Encizo.

Katz placed his single hand at the small of his back and felt the grips of the SIG-Sauer P227 pistol hidden under his vest. Satisfied that it was within easy reach, he moved toward the stem, his empty right sleeve flapping in the salt-laced wind.

"Getting closer," McCarter commented as the cruise ship approached the fishing vessel. "I wonder how many terrorists are on board."

"Probably more of them than there are of us," Katz answered. "Will you tie a knot in this sleeve? Knot it right under the stump. I want them to see, beyond any doubt, that I have only one arm."

"Trying to lull them into a false sense of security?" Salamar inquired, wishing that he could find some reason to feel more secure as the ship drew closer.

"Anything that works," the Israeli replied as McCarter knotted the sleeve. He nodded his thanks to the Briton.

The cruise ship was more than 250 feet long, with three deck levels. The legend was printed in Greek in large red Cyrillic letters, but modern Greek was not one of the languages Yakov Katzenelenbogen spoke fluently. Actually he had a very limited knowledge of about three hundred words in Greek. *"Tha'lasah Venus,"* Salamar said and translated the name right away. "The *Sea Venus*. Is that the hostage ship?"

"I don't think there's any room for doubt," Katz remarked as he stared at the two figures aft of the cruise ship.

The pair were dressed in white short-sleeved shirts, black trousers and *keffiyeh* Arab headdress. In their hands were Soviet-made AK-47 assault rifles. They peered down at the fishing vessel from behind dark glasses. Another man approached the pair. He was taller than the terrorists in the *keffiyehs* and appeared to have a lighter complexion. His shaggy brown hair showed under a straw Panama hat pushed back on his head. The three men conversed briefly, then the two riflemen aimed their weapons at the boat.

"Yah-sass!" Katz shouted, waving his arm overhead. He repeated the greeting, one of the few Greek expressions in his limited vocabulary. *"Yah-sass!"*

"Fi-yehte!" a terrorist shouted back and triggered his Kalashnikov rifle.

A burst of 7.62 mm rounds tore into the water near the fishing vessel. The bullets splashed and globs of water spit up from the sea. McCarter instinctively ducked behind the cabin and reached inside his life jacket for the Browning. He managed to stop himself from drawing the pistol and blowing their cover as harmless fishermen. To control himself the British ace sucked air through his clenched teeth. He was not accustomed to being shot at without returning the favor.

Salamar also dived for cover when the shots were fired. Katz ducked and nearly threw himself to the deck, but he fought his reflexes and remained on his feet in clear view of the enemy. He held his arms high to allow the terrorists to see that his right arm ended at the elbow and his only hand was empty. The terrorists ceased fire. Katz hoped this was because they did not see any reason to waste ammunition—not because they were waiting for one of their comrades to show up with an RPG rocket launcher to blast the boat out of the water.

"Ahmed," Katz rasped to the Egyptian, "talk to these trigger-happy morons. Tell them we've got engine trouble. We don't care what they're doing and we don't want to get involved. Tell them as soon as we can repair our engines we'll be on our way."

"Should I talk to them in Arabic or Greek?" Salamar asked, slowly stepping aft and joining Katz on the deck.

"Greek first," the Phoenix commander answered. "Poor Greek with some Arabic mixed in. Let them lead the conversation, including what language they want to use. They'll be less suspicious if they think you're an Arab fisherman who happens to speak a little Greek, not a fellow who speaks both Arabic and Greek fluently. Whatever you do, don't say anything in English."

Salamar nodded in agreement and called out to the cruise ship in halting Greek. The terrorists shouted something in return. Katz and McCarter had no idea what the gunmen said, but it did not sound encouraging. The big orange sun seemed to burn hotter, and the sea breeze appeared to die as they waited a few painfully long seconds to hear the translation.

"They ordered us to get out," Salamar explained.

"Did you tell them we have engine problems?" Katz asked.

"I don't think they care," the Egyptian replied. "They're simply demanding that we get away somehow. How we do this doesn't concern them. If we don't do it, they say they'll blow this boat to bits."

"Maybe this plan wasn't so good after all," McCarter commented. "What do we do now?"

"We still have to get closer," Katz stated. "The tide is in our favor. We'll drift toward the ship, but unfortunately they're still moving. They might pass right by us."

"What about your friends?" Salamar demanded. "How long will it take them to get into position?"

"We can't wait for them," Katz replied. "Michaels, get into the hold and start the flood."

"Right," McCarter answered to his cover name. "When I open it up, this boat will start to sink quickly. You blokes better be ready when it happens."

The Briton headed into the cabin. He took a scuba tank, face mask and fins from a shelf and grabbed a waterproof bag containing an Ingram M-10 machine pistol and a belt with ammo pouches for four 32-round magazines for the Ingram and two extra magazines for his Browning pistol. He stripped off his life preserver and slipped out of the shoulder holster rig. Opening the waterproof bag, he stuffed the holster, harness and gun inside it. He sealed the rubber container and carried it, along with the diving equipment, into the hold.

"Bleedin' water sports," McCarter muttered as he donned the air tank.

The British commando moved to a trapdoor in the boat's hull. Phoenix Force had gotten the boat from the Egyptian authorities. It had been used formerly by a group of seafaring smugglers. They had equipped the fishing vessel with the souped-up engine and the trapdoor, which had probably provided a means of disposing of illegal merchandise in a hurry or of retrieving smuggled items attached under the hull. Phoenix Force had another use for the secret door.

McCarter pulled back the bolt and allowed the water pressure to push the door open. The trapdoor was roughly five feet square, and it was a sizable entrance for the warm Mediterranean water to gush into the belly of the vessel. Within seconds, the water reached McCarter's ankles.

"Come on, now," the Briton muttered impatiently as he watched the water level rise. "We haven't got all day."

RAFAEL ENCIZO, Calvin James and Gary Manning jetted through the water beneath the surface of the Mediterranean. They clung to the handlebars of the sea sleds as the streamlined underwater devices cut through the sea. Columns of bubbles trailed from the propellers of the torpedo-shaped sleds like the tails of three aquatic comets.

The undersea world of the Mediterranean was magnificent and fascinating. The water was still mostly clean and clear despite the industrial waste of various European and Middle

Eastern countries, but the three Phoenix Force commandos had
no time to pause and view the natural wonders of the Mediterranean. They rode the sea sleds beneath the massive belly of the
cruise ship, then located the starboard side of the luxury liner.
It was the opposite side from the terrorists' view of the fishing
vessel.

Encizo was in charge of the trio. The Cuban's experience in
underwater operations was even greater than that acquired by
Calvin James with the SEALs in Vietnam. He brought his sled
to a halt and allowed it to drift. Then he grabbed a waterproof
bag from the contraption before it began to sink, hooked the
bag to his diving belt and paddled up to the surface.

James followed the Cuban's example and abandoned his sea
sled. The black warrior seized a waterproof bag and a spear gun
from the sled before he headed for the surface. Manning remained with his sled a few moments longer. He turned the
handlebars to aim the sled toward the port quarter of the cruise
ship. The Canadian demolitions expert switched on a timer that
controlled the detonator of a small C-4 plastic explosives charge
in the bottom of the sled. Then he let the sled go. It moved beneath the hull of the *Sea Venus*, but as there was no pilot op-
erating it, the device slowed down and gradually began to sink.

Manning made certain his waterproof bag was securely attached to his belt before he joined the other two Phoenix pros
at the surface. The trio floated along the starboard side of the
big luxury vessel. The smooth white metal hull was moving past
the three commandos at fifteen knots. They couldn't delay
acting or the vessel would be out of reach. Encizo removed
from his bag a large round plastic disk that resembled a giant
suction cup. A fifty-foot nylon rope extended from the disk. He
slapped the cup onto the hull of the ship. The disk was, in fact,
a sort of high-tech suction cup. The sucker disk clung to the
smooth surface and four metal spikes inside the cup snapped
into the metal skin to secure a firm viselike grip.

James and Manning grabbed the line and let the ship tow
them through the sea. Encizo held on to the disk with one hand
while he removed another device from his bag. It looked like an
oversize suitcase handle with checkered rubber grips and suction cups on each end. Encizo reached up and jammed the

handle into the hull. The cup clung to the surface, and spikes bit into metal for a claw grip. Encizo kicked off his diving fins, gripped the handle and hauled himself up from the water. He groped about with his naked foot until he secured a hold on the first disk. He removed another handle with sucker cups and planted it roughly three feet above the handle already in place.

Encizo pulled himself up to the next rung and found a foothold on the other handle. He repeated the procedure with a third handle, gradually climbing higher as he built a crude ladder up the side of the ship. It was a difficult, physically demanding task, but Encizo had attempted the exercise before during a training session with a ship moving almost twenty knots. After the *Achille Lauro* hijacking in '85, Phoenix Force had considered how they might have handled a similar situation. Now they would see if the plan worked in a genuine crisis as well as it had in training.

At last Encizo reached the top and grabbed the handrail. He had placed nine handles up the side of the ship, each roughly one yard apart. He glanced down and saw Calvin James making his way up the rungs. Though James was burdened with another bagful of gear and the spear gun, which hung from a leather strap at his wrist, he was making steady progress.

"Halte!" a voice snarled above Encizo's head. *"Bewegen Sie nicht!"*

Encizo did not understand much German, but he had a pretty good idea what the command had been, even before he turned to see the muzzle of a submachine gun pointed at his head. A tall, lean man with dark blond hair, bright blue eyes and pockmarked cheeks stood on the deck by the handrail with the subgun in his fists. Encizo recognized the weapon. It was a Walther MPL, a 9 mm parabellum submachine that fires 550 rounds per minute. Encizo had handled the Walther MPL on a mission in Turkey, and he knew what the blow-back action chattergun could do at close quarters.

There was another terrorist next to the German. He was short and heavyset, with a dark olive complexion and a mass of curly black hair. The second man's weapon was a compact submachine gun that resembled a British Patchett gun. He stared at Encizo with astonishment.

"*¿De dónde viniste usted?*" he demanded, clearly confused. To Encizo's ears, the accent of his Spanish was European rather than Latin American. "Where did you come from?"

"*¿No puede usted ver?*" Encizo replied, tilting his head down to indicate the ocean below. As much as the words, the gesture implied, "Can't you see?"

The Spanish terrorist frowned and stepped to the handrail. Encizo still stood on the outside of the rail, his hands gripping the top bar. The German gunman stood a few steps back from the Cuban, his Walther subgun still pointing at Encizo's head. The Spanish thug leaned over the rail and stared down at Calvin James.

Suddenly, the Spaniard dropped his weapon and stumbled backward. He uttered an ugly liquid gurgle as a pointed red finger jutted from the back of his neck. His body twitched and his knees folded, then he collapsed on the deck. The shaft of a harpoon wobbled under his chin. James's aim had been true with the spear gun, and he had skewered the man's neck.

"*Mein Gott!*" the German terrorist exclaimed as he stared at his dying comrade in apparent shock.

Encizo took advantage of the distraction. He vaulted over the handrail and lashed a foot into the German's subgun. The kick sent the Walther chopper flying from the terrorist's grasp. Encizo landed nimbly on the deck. He ignored the ache in his foot and quickly lashed a back-fist blow to his opponent's face.

The terrorist fell against the rail. A ribbon of blood oozed from his nostril, but the broken nose didn't deter him. He promptly swung his booted foot into Encizo's abdomen, making the Cuban gasp, then slammed a karate chop across Encizo's collarbone. The Phoenix pro doubled up from the assault, and the German swung his arm to deliver a finishing blow.

Suddenly Rafael Encizo drove his fist between the man's legs. The fierce uppercut made the terrorist gasp in breathless agony and clutch himself with one hand while attempting an awkward attack with the other. Encizo easily blocked the swing with a forearm and delivered a punch on the point of the chin. The man's head snapped back from the blow. Encizo quickly ducked and rammed his shoulder into his opponent's stomach. He scooped up the man's legs, hauled him onto his shoulder and straightened his knees. Then he tossed the German over the handrail.

The terrorist had been still trying to get his breath and barely uttered a sound as he plunged thirty feet and splashed into the ocean below. Encizo glanced around the decks. He did not see any more terrorists. He gathered up the fallen MPL submachine gun and scanned the handrails of the decks above, but there was no sign of the enemy.

Calvin James reached the handrail and climbed over it to join Encizo on the main deck. The black commando had discarded the spear gun, but still had his bag of equipment. They moved to the cabin section and crouched under a porthole. The Cuban held the Walther subgun ready while James opened his bag.

"You know, that body almost landed on me when you threw it overboard," James whispered. He glanced at the corpse of the terrorist he had speared through the throat. "Better give that one an impromptu burial at sea. Hope we don't drop it on Gary."

"We have to get rid of the body," Encizo agreed as he unhooked his waterproof bag from his belt. It was empty except for the last of the gadgets he'd used in climbing. James carried the Cuban's firearms in his bag. "So far we've been lucky. Only two terrorists appear to have been starboard. The others are probably busy guarding hostages, running the ship or watching the fishing boat sink."

"That's entertainment," James remarked as he extracted a Beretta Model 12 submachine gun from his bag. A nine-inch silencer was attached to the barrel. James pulled back the folding stock and locked it in place. He reached inside the bag for the other weapons and magazines.

A door to the cabins opened less than six feet from Encizo's left elbow. A skinny, rat-faced terrorist with a *keffiyeh*, his eyes obscured by a pair of dark glasses, emerged. The Arab carried a Skorpion machine pistol, a compact Czech weapon that was a favorite of terrorists throughout the world.

Encizo swiftly drew a Cold Steel Tanto from a sheath strapped to his right ankle. He leaped up from the deck and

pounced on the terrorist before the startled gunman could react
to the attack. Encizo grabbed the terrorist's lower face with his
left hand and jammed the Y of his hand, between thumb and
forefinger, into the Arab's mouth. He slashed the six-inch blade
of the Tanto across the back of the fist clenched around the
Skorpion's pistol grip.

Blood spilled from flesh as the ultrasharp knife cut through
muscles, arteries and veins. The man's scream was muffled by
Encizo's hand, and the Skorpion machine pistol fell from
trembling fingers. Encizo pushed the Arab against the doorframe and thrust the knife upward. The thick steel blade
pierced the solar plexus, and the sharp point powered up into
the heart, making the terrorist convulse violently as Encizo
pinned him to the doorway. Blood spilled over the Cuban's
wrist, and the dying man bit into the hand that gagged him.
Encizo felt the body go limp in his grasp, felt the life ebb from
his opponent. He lowered the corpse to the deck.

"Here you go, man," James whispered as he handed a
Heckler & Koch MP-5 subgun to the Cuban. James barely
glanced at the slain Arab. He had no doubt the man was dead.

Encizo gladly accepted his favorite make of submachine gun.
The H&K was compact, sturdy and reliable for close quarters
combat—better than the Walther MPL, in Encizo's opinion,
because the MP-5 was lighter, fired either semi- or full-auto and
had a greater round-per-minute rate. A silencer was attached to
the eight-inch barrel, and James had already slid a thirty-round
magazine into the weapon. The Cuban pulled back the cocking knob, chambered the first round and switched on the safety
catch.

He looked inside the door to the cabins. The corridor within
seemed deserted. So far, their luck was holding. Meanwhile,
James had loaded his Beretta subgun and slipped into a Jackass Leather shoulder holster rig with a Beretta 92 autoloading
9 mm pistol under one arm and a G-96 Jet-Aer fighting dagger
under the other. The Cuban reached into the bag and found his
shoulder holster rig with a Heckler & Koch P-9S pistol in
leather. Both men removed their diving belts, the last of their
frogman gear except for the wet suits, and buckled utility belts
around their waists. Ammo pouches with spare magazines hung

from the belts. They also carried some modified concussion grenades, flare guns and two-way radios. Calvin James was supplied with a special first-aid kit. The unit medic had included the usual first-aid items in the kit, along with a few vials of drugs that he hoped he would not have to use.

Gary Manning climbed up the rungs of the improvised ladder, swung over the handrail and landed on the deck next to the corpse of the Spanish terrorist. He placed his waterproof bag on the deck and stripped off his face mask, then glanced down at the corpses.

"You guys have been busy," he remarked in a soft voice.

"Yeah," Encizo replied. "Want to help us dump some deadweight?"

Manning responded by reaching down and grabbing the Spaniard's body, then easily picked it up and tossed it over the side. James gathered up the dead Arab terrorist and hauled him to the rail. Manning seized the dead man's ankles, and they hurled him overboard, as well.

"Three down," Manning commented as he opened his bag. "Wonder how many are left to go?"

"Hard to say," Encizo replied, "but I doubt if more than a dozen terrorists could have sneaked onto this ship and smuggled in weapons."

"They seem to have managed quite a bit of firepower," James commented as he gathered up the fallen Skorpion. "And they have weapons made on both sides of the Iron Curtain. Kind of unusual."

"They're unusual in more ways than that," Encizo added. He slipped the Walther's sling over his shoulder and held the H&K in his hands ready for action. "The nationalities of these bastards seem pretty varied, too. Arabs, Germans, Spanish and God knows what else."

"We've come across European terrorists with Arab comrades before," Manning reminded him as he opened his bag and removed an Israeli Uzi with silencer attached. "Remember the Vatican mission? There were Iranians, Syrians, Basque separatists and some Japanese *ninja* assassins that time."

"This is still pretty weird," Encizo insisted.

Manning loaded the Uzi subgun and donned a shoulder holster with a Walther P-5 pistol in leather. He buckled on a utility belt similar to those worn by his partners. Manning's gear also included a pack at the small of his back containing C-4 plastic explosives and a pouch near the belt buckle with detonators.

"Our partners' distraction trick must be working pretty well," he remarked, "but it won't be long before the terrorists lose interest."

"What about the diversion you set up?" Encizo asked.

"About twenty seconds left to go," Manning replied, glancing at his wristwatch. "And we'd better be ready when the fireworks start."

SIX OF THE TERRORISTS had gathered by the handrail at the bow of the ship to watch the fishing boat go under. They had been suspicious of the little vessel until they saw it start to sink and heard panicked shouts for help. They saw the one-armed man and the Egyptian dart about on the deck in apparent panic. The third crew member had disappeared below deck, probably trying to stop the leaks in the hold.

The terrorists were amused by the incident. They felt very powerful as they watched the helplessness of the men on the fishing boat. The irony of the situation also appealed to the observers. The fishing boat had wandered off course, developed engine trouble and started to sink in plain view of a large ship that was perfectly able to save them. Under ordinary circumstances, the crew of the *Sea Venus* would have certainly rescued the unlucky fishermen, but they had been unfortunate enough to have their boating accident when the terrorists had taken control of the cruise ship. Fate had surely spit in the faces of those fishermen.

Water eventually rose from the hold and flooded the deck of the little boat. The Egyptian and his companion splashed about in the mess and vanished from view as the boat tipped aft and started to sink into the sea. The terrorists laughed and applauded the sight. At last the boat sank below the surface. There was no sign of the three men who went down with it.

"Au revoir," an Arab terrorist said with a smile. He spoke French because it was a language understood by the majority of his comrades.

"The entertainment is over, *camarades*. We still have much to do. I'm going to check the radio room. Stay alert. The next boat may not be so amusing. *Comprenez vous?"* Sergio Coombo, the group leader of the terrorist unit declared.

"Yes, Lieutenant," another goon replied. "But I don't think the Americans or anyone else will try to stop us from reaching Libya. They worry too much about showing the world how civilized they can be. They are so concerned with trying to win the approval of other nations that they fail to take action until it is too late."

"What you think does not matter," Colombo told him. "We can't afford to assume anything nor to underestimate our opponents. They may still attempt to stop us before we reach Libya."

"How?" the terrorist asked with a smile. "They'll wait for us to get rid of the hostages and hope they can catch us later. That's how the Americans always handle such things."

"Just do as you're told," Colombo said crossly. He was a former member of the Italian Red Brigade. He remembered when he had believed his organization was invincible, and then had come the series of mass arrests of Brigade followers that proved how wrong that notion had been. "Keep your eyes open and report—"

The explosion interrupted Colombo. It was not a threatening roar that shook the cruise ship, but it startled the terrorists nonetheless. Gallons of water spewed up from the sea with a deep-voiced bellow. Something had blown up underwater, a little less than half a mile from the stern. Several terrorists rushed along the decks on every level to stare at the area where the explosion occurred.

"Now what in hell would that be about?" a red-haired terrorist with an Irish brogue wondered aloud as he leaned over the rail on the second-level deck. An American-made M-16 rifle was canted on his broad shoulder.

"Maybe the fishing boat engine exploded," another terrorist suggested. He was a short, wiry black man who spoke French with an uncertain hesitation between each word.

"The boat didn't go down in that area," an Arab gunman replied grimly. He turned to Colombo. *"Que veut dire ceci?"*

"I don't know what it means," the Italian terrorist confessed. He instinctively caressed the steel frame of his Skorpion machine pistol. He found some comfort in the familiar feel of the weapon and the sense of being in control it gave him. "Let us not make any hasty conclusions one way or the other. Perhaps debris from the boat drifted into an old underwater mine left undiscovered since World War II. Or it could be some sort of weapon malfunction of an enemy submarine. It is difficult to say what it was, but it didn't present any immediate danger. Watch for any sign of a periscope or floating debris. If anything looks suspicious, come get me in the radio room."

Colombo headed for the cabin section and galloped up a flight of stairs to the second-level deck. The black African and a dour-faced European terrorist marched across the deck toward the starboard. The African stared at the ocean as if he expected to spot a sea serpent. His European companion sighed and shook his head.

"What are you doing, B'Mau? What are you looking for?" he asked wearily.

"I tell you I heard splashing in this direction," the African insisted. "I don't know what it was, Colbert, but it must have been pretty large to make enough noise for me to hear it at the front of the ship."

"It is called the bow of the ship," Colbert muttered. "And the noise could not have been that loud or others would have heard it, too."

"But I tell you . . ." B'Mau began, frustration in his voice.

"Camarades!" a voice called to them from an entrance to the cabin section. *"Entrez, s'il vous plaît!"*

They turned and saw a man in the doorway. He was large, well-built with broad shoulders and a brawny chest, but they could not see him well enough to identify him, for it was dark in the corridor within.

"Qui êtes-vous?" Colbert demanded, the 9 mm Steyr sub-machine gun clenched tightly in his fists. "Who are you? What do you want?"

"I must show you what I've found!" came the reply in rapid French. "I need help to move it. Come!"

B'Mau eagerly rushed to the entrance. Colbert was less enthusiastic and slightly suspicious of a comrade who wanted to show them something yet seemed reluctant to show himself. Colbert stood back while the African entered. B'Mau stepped out of view, and Colbert sighed, relieved that his concerns seemed needless.

Then Gary Manning appeared at the doorway with his Uzi pointed at the French terrorist. Colbert gasped with astonishment and nearly swung his Steyr toward the door. He resisted the impulse, aware the other man could shoot him before he could hope to complete such a rash move.

"Entrez," Manning declared, "or I'll chop you in half."

Colbert raised his hands to shoulder level and walked forward. A black hand shot out from the doorway and yanked him across the threshold. Colbert was startled and immediately thought B'Mau had helped set him up. Then he discovered that the hand belonged to a different black man, taller and stronger than B'Mau. Calvin James jammed the silencer attached to his Beretta subgun under the Frenchman's jaw.

"I'll take that," James informed him as he relieved Colbert of his weapon.

B'Mau stood with his hands on a wall, feet apart and the muzzle of Encizo's H&K submachine gun pointed at the back of his head. The Cuban barely glanced at Colbert and did not bother to say a word. Encizo did not speak French so he let the other two Phoenix pros handle the question-and-answer segment.

"Qu'est-ce que c'est?" Colbert asked fearfully as he was shoved facefirst into a wall.

"We ask the questions and you answer them," Manning told him. "Where are the hostages? Tell me or I'll stick this gun between your legs and blow your testicles off."

"I can make him talk," James declared. He held the G-96 knife close to Colbert's face and placed the five-inch, double-edged blade in front of the terrorist's eyes. "I enjoy making people talk."

"The hostages are in the theater," Colbert announced in a quavering voice. "The tourists, the passengers, are held there. Most of the crew are held prisoner in the captain's mess on the boat deck."

"We'll see to the passengers first," Manning declared. "You're going to take us to the theater. Try any tricks and we'll kill you."

"What will we do with this turkey?" James asked, pointing the top of his dagger at B'Mau.

"You will not kill me, *monsieur*?" the African pleaded. "I am black like you. We are brothers of the skin. *Oui?*"

"Shut up." James snorted with disgust. "There are two kinds of assholes that really piss me off—morons who are prejudiced against people just because of the color of their skin and slime balls like you who try to use race for a cop-out. If you really had any pride in being black, you wouldn't be with these hijackers in the first place."

"You are a Daddy Tom nigger," B'Mau spit angrily.

"What the hell is a Daddy Tom?" James asked, more amused than angered by the slur. "Uncle Tom's brother? Where are you from, dumb butt? Niger? The Congo? Zaire?"

B'Mau hissed an obscenity, and James corrected the fractured phrases. "Can't you get anything right? I'm sure this dude is from some African country, but he won't tell me which one or maybe he's too stupid to remember. The accent is from the west coast or central Africa, but I can't place it for sure."

"Africans, Europeans and Arabs working together?" Encizo remarked. "What kind of terrorist outfit is this?"

"The kind that will kill a shipload of people if we don't stop them," Gary Manning said grimly. "Hopefully everything is going as we planned—the terrorists are a little confused without being really alarmed, and they're looking for possible trouble to come from the direction of the explosion. It seems to be working so far, but we won't be able to fool them for long."

"If we're going to pull this off we'd better move," Encizo added. "That's the problem with handling a mission cowboy style. The strategy has to be very simple, and it has to be something one does very quickly. The longer it takes, the more likely something will go wrong.''

"Well, we've got a choice of guides to show us the way to the hostages," James remarked. He glanced at B'Mau. "But we only need one. Trying to keep both of these suckers in line would be too much risk in a combat situation. I guess that means we put Daddy Tom under wraps for a while."

"Can you sedate him for about half an hour, Cal?" Manning asked, aware that James frequently carried some Thorazine for such occasions.

"Sure," James replied as he held his hands out, palms up in a wide gesture.

His right arm suddenly swung forward, and the hand closed into a rock-hard fist. Knuckles crashed into the point of B'Mau's jaw. The African's head snapped back. His skull rapped against the wall and his eyes rolled up into his head. B'Mau's knees buckled and he slumped unconscious to the floor.

"My pleasure," James stated with a grin.

2

The two terrorists at the entrance of the ship's theater were bored. They stood by the twin doors with submachine guns held at port arms and their eyes wide open in a show of vigilance, but they were less than enthusiastic about their current duty. Three guards were also posted inside the theater with the hostages. The prisoners could not get out, and it seemed impossible that anyone could attack the ship without creating a monstrous battle on the decks outside. No one could sneak on board the *Sea Venus* while it was still moving and get past the guards patrolling the decks.

"I think Colombo goes to extremes with security," one of the gunmen complained. He was a young German who had received his original training in terrorism from the Second June Movement, an organization that had never been noted for patience or finesse.

"*Ja*," his companion, an ex-member of the German Red Army Faction agreed wearily. "The Italian is just trying to impress the colonel with all this security business. He is worried about making a good impression. This is his first big assignment in command."

"I wish the colonel had put Koerner in charge instead," the other man commented, fishing in his shirt pocket for a pack of cigarettes. "He is far more experienced and he is a German. I do not trust Italians. They are too apt to surrender when things get difficult. Look at how they behaved during World War II."

"What do you know about such things, Klaus?" his companion laughed. "Only what they teach you in the history books, and those things are written by liars. Colombo is doing all right. Nothing has gone wrong so far and—"

The conversation was interrupted by the arrival of two men at the end of the corridor. The Germans were astonished to see Colbert, a Frenchman whom they had always regarded as incompetent, with a stranger in a black wet suit. He was a big fellow with lots of muscles and a belt with ammo pouches around his waist and a shoulder holster with a pistol still sheathed under his arm. But the man held his arms high, and Colbert had his Steyr submachine gun pointed at his back.

"Donnerwetter!" rasped the Second June Movement graduate. "Where did he come from?"

"I saw him come in from the quarterdeck," Colbert replied. "I don't know how he got here, but he certainly isn't one of us. Have you noticed any more strangers roaming about the corridors?"

"Nein," the other German terrorist replied with a frown. "You know this man still has a pistol in a shoulder holster? You should have searched him."

"I know he has a gun," Colbert said with a sneer. He jabbed the muzzle of his subgun into the small of Gary Manning's back. "But my gun is ready to blast his backbone in two. I would like him to try to reach for that pistol. If he lowers his hands, I will cheerfully send this bastard to hell."

"Suddenly the French mouse is a brave lion," the first German muttered in his native language, shaking his head in disbelief.

"There's something wrong here," his companion commented. He reached for a walkie-talkie on his belt. "I'm going to report this to Colombo. Take the pistol from the prisoner. Colbert is an idiot to allow an opponent to keep a weapon. Let's not be so foolish with—"

Gary Manning suddenly hurled himself to the floor, and Colbert immediately followed the Canadian's example. The French terrorist dropped on his belly and pushed the Steyr submachine gun aside as if the gun was suddenly too hot to handle. The two Germans fumbled with their weapons, caught off guard by the unexpected actions.

Neither sentry saw Rafael Encizo and Calvin James at the end of the corridor. The Phoenix pair had waited at the mouth of the passage while Manning and Colbert pretended to be captor and captive, the true roles reversed for the act in front of the two terrorists. Of course, Colbert's submachine gun was not loaded, and the Frenchman had known James and Encizo were behind him with weapons ready in case he tried to alert the sentries. The two commandos waited until Manning and Colbert dived to the floor, which left the German sentries confused and distracted. It also gave Encizo and James clear targets.

The Phoenix pair quickly aimed their weapons and opened fire. Actually they had had no choice. The terrorists had to be taken out quickly and ruthlessly. Bullets coughed from the silencers attached to James's Beretta M-12 and Encizo's H&K machine pistol. Nine-millimeter slugs slammed into the chests of the two German gunmen. Each terrorist received a well-placed 3-round delivery of death, and each fell lifeless to the floor. Taking at least one high-velocity 115-grain hollow-nose bullet directly in the heart, they suffered the type of cardiac failure CPR, or even open-heart surgery, could not help.

"Glad you guys didn't fall asleep back there," Manning commented as he rose from the floor, the Walther P-5 pistol in his fist.

"The performance wasn't too boring," James replied.

"You did all right, Colbert," Manning told the French terrorist as he removed a strip of red plastic from a pouch on his belt. "We'll see to it that your cooperation is acknowledged, if we all live through this and you get to stand trial."

"I didn't like betraying my comrades," Colbert said with a sigh, but he did not seem terribly upset about the death of the two terrorists. "I didn't have any choice, of course. They would have done the same in my place. *C'est la vie!*"

"Not if we get killed," the Canadian replied gruffly. He found Colbert's lack of loyalty toward his comrades disgusting. Manning realized his reasoning was a bit illogical since Colbert was helping them carry out their mission, but the Frenchman's amoral attitude and callousness about turning on his own people still rubbed the Canadian the wrong way.

"God, what an asshole," James growled, shaking his head.

Manning nodded in agreement and hastily bound Colbert's wrists together at the small of his back with the plastic riot cuffs. He shoved the terrorist into a corner and used another set of riot cuffs to bind his ankles. Colbert did not attempt to protest or resist.

"Stay down," the Canadian warned him. "You'll be less apt to catch a stray round when the shooting starts. Don't get any silly notions about crawling away, or hopping out of here. You won't get far bound up like this, and we'll be very unhappy with you if we have to hunt you down. We can be very unpleasant when we're unhappy."

"I understand, *monsieur*," Colbert assured him. "I will cause no problems. I am on your side now. *Oui?*"

"I doubt that." Manning snorted. "Just do what you're told, Colbert."

James handed Manning his Uzi submachine gun. Encizo stood by the door and listened for any sounds that might suggest someone had heard the sputtering, muffled reports of silenced weapons or the low groans of the terrorists before they died. The Cuban could make out a number of voices, mixed together into an unintelligible but confused and frightened-sounding murmur.

Encizo heard an angry voice yell something in Greek, followed by another voice shouting in English. "Shut your mouths!" The Cuban stiffened when he felt the door move next to him. He stood back as it opened, letting the barrel of a Kalashnikov rifle poke through the gap.

Quickly grabbing the gun barrel with both hands, the Cuban commando pulled with all his might and turned slightly, adding the motion of his body to the force of his pull. A startled Arab terrorist plunged through the doorway and hurtled abruptly into the corridor.

Moving into the fray, Calvin James pounced and chopped the stock of the Beretta M-12 across the wrists of the Arab gunman before the disoriented terrorist could react to the unexpected threat. The AK-47 clattered on the floor, and James quickly rammed the barrel of his subgun into the terrorist's belly. The Arab doubled up with a gasp, and Manning slammed a knee under the dazed man's jaw. The blow crashed the man's teeth together forcibly and his head snapped back from the knee kick. The man moaned softly and collapsed.

Gary Manning bolted through the doorway while James took care of the Arab gunman. The Canadian ducked his head low as he dashed across the threshold in a semicrouch. Encizo raised the stock of his MP-5 to a shoulder and covered his partner from the doorway.

More than a hundred hostages were seated in the theater. The tourists cried out in fear and ducked low in the theater seats. The houselights were turned up high, but the hostages still appeared as huddled shapes among the backrests of their chairs. But not everybody sought cover fearfully. A tall terrorist with shoulder-length blond hair was guarding the west wing of the theater with a Soviet-made PPSh-41 submachine gun. He swung his weapon at Manning and tried to get a clear target as the Canadian hit the carpet in a shoulder roll and tumbled toward the east wall. Another terrorist, a fat black man, stood at the edge of the stage with an Israeli Galil in one hand and a grenade in the other.

The man who was about to blast Manning failed to notice Rafael Encizo until the Cuban opened fire. The silencer-equipped H&K machine pistol spit out a muffled 3-round burst. The blond terrorist cried out and fell backward against the wall, and the Russian subgun slipped from his fingers as he stared down at the trio of 9 mm bullet holes in his chest. His eyes widened with surprise, then he glanced up at Encizo, blinked once and slumped to the carpet in a dead heap.

"Merde alors!" the black terrorist exclaimed as he raised the grenade to his mouth and tried to yank out the pin with his teeth. Simultaneously he attempted to brace the Galil rifle against his hip and aim the weapon at Encizo.

The Cuban ducked and dived to the carpet as the gunman opened fire. Half a dozen 5.56 mm rounds tore a diagonal line of holes across the double doors and surrounding plaster. The gunshots roared deafeningly within the confines of the theater. The terrorist waved the Galil about in a threatening manner as he continued his attempt to utilize the grenade.

Gary Manning dashed down an aisle and aimed his Uzi at the gunman on the stage. The Canadian wished he had a more familiar weapon in his hands, preferably a FN FAL NATO assault rifle. He favored rifles because of the superior accuracy and range of such long arms, but Manning had needed a more compact close-quarters weapon for the raid on the *Sea Venus*. He was more than competent with an Uzi, but he could not perform any precision marksmanship with the submachine gun—especially with a silencer, which reduces accuracy and the muzzle velocity of the projectiles.

He selected an easy target and squeezed the trigger. Three 9 mm parabellums ripped into the bulging stomach of the black terrorist. The man's mouth fell open in dumbstruck agony. The grenade tumbled from his hand, the pin still in the explosive egg. He clasped his bullet-torn stomach with the empty hand and tried to swing the Galil around to return fire at Manning.

The Canadian elevated the aim of his Uzi and triggered it again. Another round slammed into the enemy gunman. One slug sizzled into his open mouth, ripping a bloodied exit hole at the nape of his neck. A 115-grain projectile struck the man between the nose and lips. The upper jawbone cracked and splinters were driven up into his brain. The third round smashed through the bridge of his nose and drilled through his skull.

The black man toppled forward and fell from the lip of the stage to hit the floor like a large slab of mishandled beef. There was not enough life left in the body to manage a single twitch. Manning dashed to the stage and scooped up the dead man's hand grenade. He sighed with relief when he discovered the pin was still securely in place.

"Thank God pulling the pins out of these things with one's teeth is easier to do in the movies than in real life," he remarked as he hooked the grenade on his belt.

Calvin James entered the theater, his Beretta subgun held ready. Encizo signaled with a raised hand, his thumb and forefinger formed in the "okay" circle. The black commando nodded and lowered his weapon.

Several hostages raised their heads and glanced about, astonished to discover the terrorists had been taken out by the strangers dressed in black rubber wet suits. Excited voices erupted in Greek, English, French and Italian. Some literally jumped up from their seats and cheered. A few women and a couple of the men wept with relief.

There was a generalized chorus of "We've been rescued!"

"Not yet," Manning told them.

"I knew somebody would come for us!" a middle-aged woman declared as she clutched her husband's arm. "Didn't I tell you they'd come, George?"

"Thank God, we're safe!" somebody else cried out with joy.

"Everybody quiet down!" Encizo ordered, but his order was drowned out by the rising babble.

"Hey! Shut up and listen!" Calvin James bellowed.

The crowd fell silent, giving Encizo a chance to be heard. "You folks aren't safe yet," he announced. "Stay calm. We still have some enemies to deal with before this thing is over."

"And they probably heard the shots when that guy fired a rifle without a silencer," Manning remarked, tilting his head toward the stage.

"Terrorists can be so inconsiderate," James remarked as he headed out the door. "They'll be heading down here any second now, and we'd better be ready for them."

"What?" a passenger demanded, his tone on the verge of panic.

"Just be quiet and listen," Manning insisted.

Encizo followed James out of the theater. Manning wished he had reached the door first. Now, he had to handle the civilians alone. The Canadian demolitions expert did not relish the task. More than a hundred frightened people, people who had thought they were saved from the jaws of the dragon only to learn they were in even greater danger, were not going to be easy to reason with.

Manning could not explain the cold hard fact that Phoenix Force regarded the safety of the hostages as the second most important part of their mission. The first priority was to stop the terrorists. The commando unit would do its collective best to protect the passengers and crew of the *Sea Venus*, but the greatest concern was still to prevent the terrorists from getting away with their crimes.

Every time a band of terrorists succeeds it encourages more fanatics and criminals to carry out similar operations against innocent people. Every time terrorists are rewarded for their actions it serves as a message to others that such behavior will go unchallenged. That also suggests to decent people everywhere that they can be victimized and nothing will be done about it.

"The best thing you can do right now is stay here out of the line of fire," Manning told the crowd. "We can't protect you from flying bullets in a full-scale firefight. We'll have our hands full just taking care of ourselves."

"You don't care what happens to us!" a woman screamed. "You've just made things worse!"

"Shut up, lady!" a balding man with a bulldog face snapped. "Let this fella talk."

"She's right!" objected a young man dressed in a bright, flower-print shirt, and white shorts. His haircut must have cost at least fifty bucks, Manning thought. The youth continued, "We'd been kidnapped before, but they didn't intend to kill us...."

"You seem to forget what they did to my husband." A middle-aged woman with red-rimmed eyes and features lined with sorrow spoke. "They murdered him in cold blood just to serve as an example. You think they'll hesitate to do the same to any of us if they feel like it?"

"They only did that because they thought the choppers were an attempt to rescue us," the youth stated.

"Everybody shut up, damn it!" Manning shouted. "There's no time for debate. If you want to throw accusations and bitch about what should or shouldn't be done, do it later. Right now, I'm telling you people to stay put. If any of you know how to use an automatic weapon, you might take the guns from the dead terrorists. But don't touch those weapons if you don't know how to use them. That's how people get shot by accident, because somebody was panicky with a gun or didn't know what he or she was doing with the damn thing."

"I was in Vietnam, fella," Bulldog Face declared. "I know how to use an assault rifle, and I've handled Commie guns like the AK before, too."

"Great," Manning said with a nod, eager to get out of the theater and join up with his teammates again. "So you're in charge of looking after these people."

"Huh?" the man replied with dazed surprise.

"If you can get some others who have experience with automatic weapons, arm them with the terrorists' guns and post them at the entrance," Manning instructed. "But don't come out and go after the enemy. You only fight them as a last resort. If they get past us, then you'll have to protect yourselves. Put somebody outside to listen for enemies in the passages. If they hear a bunch of guys coming this way, get ready for trouble, but make sure you don't shoot any of my team. Okay?"

"I got it," the man said with a nod.

"If they get past us," Manning continued, "try to drive them back and evacuate the theater. Don't have everybody bunched together in one spot. They'll cut you down with automatic fire or lob in a grenade. Spread the people throughout the cabins and play it by ear if worse comes to worst."

"They're fanatics!" the young man with the expensive hairstyle declared. "They'll blow up the ship before they surrender!"

"They don't seem all that eager to die for whatever cause they believe in," Manning answered. "We've taken a couple of prisoners, one of whom spilled his guts to save himself. I don't think these guys are keen on suicide. By the way, you'll find two prisoners tied up in the corridor. Don't hurt them. Just stick them in a corner and keep them quiet. Most of them seem to understand French so find passengers who speak that language to communicate with them. Good luck."

"Hey, wait a minute—" the bulldog-faced man began as he watched Manning bolt for the door.

The Canadian ignored him. The passengers would have to sit tight and wait. Manning heard gunshots from the decks above. His partners were locked in combat with the enemy, and he couldn't afford to stay in the theater guarding the civilians when Phoenix Force needed him on the battlefield.

THE BATTLE WAS indeed in progress. Terrorists throughout the ship had heard the shooting in the theater and scrambled in all directions. Some ran to the bow or headed aft to see if they were under attack. Others rushed to the boat deck to try to find Colombo. The rest headed for the cabin sections to investigate the shooting. Most of them naturally assumed one or more of the hostages had tried to escape from the theater. Since they heard only one long burst from an automatic weapon, it seemed likely one of the guards had fired on the prisoners or at least fired a warning shot with the weapon on full-auto.

But Sergio Colombo was worried. The guards in charge of the hostages in the theater had walkie-talkies, yet no one had reported the incident to the radio room. Also, the Italian terrorist noticed the number of men teeming about on the decks seemed slightly less than he expected. Maybe he could not see enough of the ship from the boat deck, but instinctively he suspected something had gone seriously wrong. He decided to contact the colonel.

Suddenly, he heard screams from the lower starboard deck. Colombo peered over the boat deck rail and stared down at a figure in dripping-wet clothing that stood by the rail with a black rubber bag in one hand and a box-shaped compact machine pistol in the other. A nine-inch silencer was attached to the stubby barrel of the weapon. Two dead terrorists lay sprawled across the deck near the stranger's bare feet.

"Oh, bugger!" David McCarter growled through his teeth as he looked up at Colombo and raised his M-10. "Party's hot now!"

He triggered the Ingram machine pistol. A volley of 9 mm rounds rasped from the silenced weapon, and bullets rang sourly against the metal handrail of the boat deck. Colombo gasped in alarm and threw himself backward. Sparks appeared across the rail and he heard the whine of ricochets. The Italian terrorist moaned softly as a terrible pain traveled up his left hand to make his entire arm tremble.

He glanced down at his hand. The ring finger had been severed at the second knuckle and the tip of the little finger had been hacked off by the same bullet.

Colombo grabbed his Skorpion machine pistol and prepared to crawl to the rail to return fire, but his disciplined mind fought back his rage before he could carry out the rash scheme.

He recognized the clothes worn by the gunman. The man was one of the three "fishermen" who had supposedly gone down with the sinking boat. It had been a trick, and the insolence of such tactics astonished him. Then he realized that was exactly why the trick had worked.

Somehow, the man on the boat, and probably his two companions as well, had managed to reach the ship and climb aboard. How they did it was not important. What mattered was that the *Sea Venus* was under siege.

David McCarter fired another short burst at the boat deck and dashed to the cabin section to duck under the overhang of the deck platform above. This put him out of view of the bloke he had fired at on the top deck. McCarter was not sure if he had hit him, but he was positive he hadn't put him completely out of action.

An Asian gunman suddenly charged onto the starboard deck with an old French MAT-49 submachine gun in his fists. He gasped with surprise when he saw McCarter and quickly tried to aim his weapon at the Briton. The ex-SAS sergeant squeezed off a 3-round burst. All three 9 mm slugs caught the Asian in the center of the face. The terrorist's features underwent a sudden transformation, but he didn't care. He was already dead.

Two more terrorists appeared. One, an attractive woman with long jet-black hair, her face contorted by fury, swung a French MAB pistol at McCarter. Her partner, a skinny man with a large hawk-bill nose and small dark eyes, nearly tripped over the corpse of the Asian gunman. He staggered slightly, regained his balance and pointed a Spanish CETME submachine gun at McCarter.

The British ace immediately triggered his M-10. The bolt snapped forward with a metal crunch, but the Ingram did not fire. McCarter glanced down at the M-10 and saw a brass cartridge casing jammed in the path of the bolt. He grabbed the cocking knob and tried to yank back the bolt in the hope of clearing the chamber, although he knew he could not accomplish the task before the two terrorists would blow him away.

The harsh cough of a silenced weapon erupted, and the female terrorist suddenly fell backward with a line of bullet holes stitched across her chest. She fired the MAB pistol as she fell and pumped a harmless 9 mm slug into the overhang above. The parabellum whined against the metal edge and hurtled off to sink finally into the middle of the Mediterranean.

The male gunman swung about to see Yakov Katzenelenbogen poised on the outside of the handrail. The Israeli braced an Uzi submachine gun across the rail, his left fist on the pistol grip and the stump of his right arm over the rail. The terrorist pointed his CETME at Katz, but the Phoenix Force commander triggered his weapon first. A trio of 9 mm slugs smashed into the gunman's upper chest and throat. Two rounds shattered the manubrium bone above the sternum and the other drilled through the windpipe and smashed cervical vertebrae before tearing an exit wound at the nape of his neck as big as a quarter. The CETME subgun dropped from the man's grasp. His corpse collapsed next to it.

"Thanks, mate," McCarter told Katz as he removed the magazine from his Ingram machine pistol and cleared the chamber. "Wouldn't have beat the clock that time without you."

The "clock" McCarter referred to was the SAS Regiment memorial clock at Hereford, England. The names of Special Air Service commandos killed in action are carved into the clock. To an SAS veteran, "to beat the clock" meant that one's name would not be added to the list.

"That damn Ingram is going to get you killed, David," Katz commented as he climbed over the rail. He also had a waterproof bag hooked to his belt. The Israeli padded barefoot across the deck to McCarter's position.

"We got some gents upstairs to worry about," McCarter stated, reloading his M-10. He jacked the bolt to chamber the first round. "They know we're here. Seems from the activity on board they know about our mates, as well."

"Seems likely," Katz agreed. He opened his bag and removed a utility belt. The SIG-Sauer pistol was in a holster on the belt, and several ammo pouches contained spare magazines for his weapons.

A metal sphere the size of a baseball landed on the deck. McCarter immediately recognized the object as a grenade.

Someone had dropped it from the boat deck above their position. The Briton dashed forward and swung a bare foot to the grenade. The kick sent it flying toward the bow. McCarter simultaneously turned and fired his Ingram at the boat deck.

"Oh, Christ!" a redheaded terrorist exclaimed as he clutched the handrail with one fist and clamped his other hand over his bullet-torn stomach. "Me bleedin' guts is on fire!"

McCarter jumped back to the overhang, not a moment too soon as a burst of automatic gunfire blasted a salvo of bullets in his direction. Several slugs splintered wood from the deck where the Briton had been a split second earlier.

The grenade exploded. The blast seemed to rock the *Sea Venus*. The screams of at least two terrorists came from the bow of the ship when the grenade exploded near their position. The gun-shot Irish terrorist tumbled over the rail above and crashed to the deck in front of McCarter and Katz. The man was unconscious and in a state of shock as he bled freely across the wooden surface.

Ahmed Salamar climbed up the makeshift ladder that Encizo had installed on the side of the hull. Katz and McCarter had also used that route to get aboard the *Sea Venus*. The Egyptian security officer grabbed the handrail and hauled himself onto the deck. Water dripped from his soaked clothing, and a diving mask was still strapped around his face. He staggered forward, nearly exhausted from the effort, a waterproof bag swinging from his belt.

Katz shouted a warning in Arabic to Salamar, and to starboard the alerted Egyptian glimpsed a pair of terrorist gunmen advancing from aft. He dived to the deck and slid to join Katz and McCarter. The enemies' weapons snarled and more bullets ripped into the boards of the deck. Katz and McCarter returned fire. The silenced weapons sputtered like deranged automobile exhaust pipes. Flame spit from the muzzles, and the two terrorists performed a grisly dance of destruction before their bodies crumpled to the deck.

"Are you all right?" Katz asked Salamar.

The Egyptian replied with a nod, "Yes, thanks to Allah . . . and to you, Mr. Kenver or whatever your real name is."

Katz smiled understandingly. "Don't mention it. Catch your breath. We've got a lot of work to do, Ahmed."

The security man from Cairo was impressed by the stamina of the Phoenix pair. Katz was especially remarkable because he was at least twenty years older than Salamar, yet the Phoenix commander had seemed to handle the difficult underwater journey on the sea sled after the boat sank and the climb up the side of the ship far better than the Egyptian. The mysterious commando team was indeed something special.

Katz had buckled his utility belt around his waist and removed the prosthesis from his waterproof bag. The artificial limb had survived the trip without damage. He slipped the harness over the stump of his right arm and flexed muscles to operate the controls. The trident hooks of the prosthetic hand opened and closed like the steel talons of a mechanical bird of prey. Katz nodded with satisfaction and buckled the straps. He had to use his teeth, as well as the fingers of his left hand.

"Can I help you with that?" Salamar asked.

"He doesn't need help," McCarter informed him as he slipped into the shoulder holster rig with his Browning Hi-Power snug under his left arm. "Get your own goodies out of your bag. We've got to move, or they'll cut us to pieces with a cross fire or lob multiple grenades in our direction."

Salamar did not argue. The Briton was right about Katz. The Israeli had no trouble adjusting the prosthesis on the stump of his arm. The Egyptian removed from his bag a gun belt with a holstered pistol, a Sterling submachine gun and a walkie-talkie.

"Let's go upstairs," Katz announced as he braced the Uzi across his prosthesis, "and see if we can't make things a bit less hostile up there."

"That's sort of what I was thinking," McCarter declared as he pulled the pin from a concussion grenade.

He held the grenade for two seconds and leaned forward to lob the blaster in a high arch overhead. The grenade sailed up to the boat deck and over the handrail. Alarmed voices announced its arrival an instant before it exploded. The ship trembled from the concussion blast, and shattered glass and bits of debris showered down from the upper deck.

"Now!" Katz commanded as he dashed aft and headed for the stairwell to the boat deck.

Three terrorists appeared at the stern. A black woman with her hair teased into an exaggerated flaming Afro, a man with an Arab *keffiyeh* on his sleek dark head and a stocky gunman with a blond beard and mustache confronted the Israeli.

Although all three carried automatic weapons, they lacked the experience and training of the superprofessional Phoenix commander. Katz immediately fired a quick salvo from his Uzi. A diagonal slash of 9 mm rounds raked the enemy. The blond man's head snapped back and crimson flowed from two bullet holes in his face. Blood dripped from his beard as he tottered slightly and fell abruptly to the deck.

Salamar followed Katz and fired his Sterling at the remaining terrorists. The woman cried out as bullets punched into her chest and drove her body backward into a railing. Salamar hit her with another volley. The impact sent her body tumbling over the rail to plunge into the ocean below.

The Arab terrorist was startled by Salamar's gunfire and swung his Russian subgun toward the Egyptian. Katz triggered his Uzi and hit the terrorist with three parabellums in the left rib cage. The gunman spun about from the force of the multiple high-velocity bullets. Pink foam bubbled from his open mouth. Salamar fired his Sterling a split second later and blasted three rounds between the terrorist's shoulder blades. The man's body twitched in a wild convulsion, and his lifeless form wilted to the deck as Katzenelenbogen headed for the stairs.

The Israeli charged up the steps, the barrel of his Uzi leading the way. A figure appeared at the head of the stairs and pointed a black pistol, similar to a German P.08 Luger, at the Phoenix Force commander. Katz fired his Uzi, and the 115-grain projectiles delivered instant cardiac obliteration. The gunman tumbled forward, the pistol still unfired in his fist.

Katz stepped aside and allowed the corpse to topple down the steps past him before continuing up the stairs to the boat deck. Salamar followed the Israeli, but glimpsed two terrorists advancing from the bow of the ship. He swung his weapon toward the pair. They stopped abruptly and doubled up in mutual agony. The weapons fell from their fingers and they clutched their abdomens as if stricken by simultaneous stomachaches. That was indeed the case. David McCarter had shot them both in the belly.

"Keep going, damn it!" the Briton shouted at Salamar as he jogged to the foot of the stairs.

Salamar did not argue, but galloped up the steps after Katz. McCarter paused to extract the spent magazine from his Ingram and hastily shoved a fresh magazine into the well at the M-10's pistol grip. The British ace quickly sprayed the two wounded terrorists with 9 mm slugs until they folded up into bloody heaps.

"God," McCarter muttered with a shake of his head. "What a bloody mess." He dashed up the stairs behind Salamar.

Katz had reached the boat deck and fired a burst of Uzi rounds at somebody he spotted along the starboard. The gunman jumped for cover at a cabin doorway, and Katz scrambled for shelter behind a thick canopy post. He ejected the spent magazine from his Uzi and reached for a replacement from an ammo pouch on his belt.

Salamar reached the head of the stairs just in time to notice a wide-eyed, female terrorist about to point a French MAT chattergun at Katz's back. The woman's yellow hair swung wildly in the wind to form a fiery halo around her oval head. Salamar saw the hatred in her eyes, the vicious snarl plastered across a wide mouth that might otherwise have appealed to him. The Egyptian fired his Sterling and pumped the last three rounds into her.

The gunman at the cabin door fired back at Salamar with a Beretta 93-R machine pistol. The Egyptian cried out as a slug tore through his upper right arm. He dropped his Sterling and huddled down at the top step, trying to curl up into an invisible human ball.

The enemy with the Beretta exposed himself for less than a second, but it was enough time for Yakov Katzenelenbogen to draw his SIG-Sauer autoloader and quickly aim the pistol at the terrorist. He thumbed off the ambidextrous safety catch and fired two rounds. The terrorist's head snapped back, and a couple of projectiles punched through to the man's brain.

"How badly is Ahmed hurt?" Katz called out to McCarter as he returned his SIG-Sauer to its holster and finished reloading his Uzi.

"Caught one in the biceps," McCarter replied as he knelt beside the wounded Egyptian. "Bullet went clean through the muscle. I've seen worse, but it's not a ruddy nick."

"I am all right," Salamar declared, gasping in pain. His face was covered by a film of cold sweat. "Go on. Get the rest of them before they kill the hostages...."

"Let's find some cover for him," Katz announced.

He glanced about the boat deck. There were no opponents within immediate view, but he heard voices from both fore and aft. The report of automatic weapons revealed that the other Phoenix Force commandos were engaged in combat with terrorists on the lower deck. Katz wondered if Encizo, Manning and James were all still alive. He pushed the notion from the forefront of his mind. Such speculation could only make him less effective in combat. There was nothing he could do for the Phoenix Force warriors who were fighting the terrorists on the lower deck. At least not right then and there. He had to concentrate on the circumstances he faced at that very moment, the enemies he was immediately concerned with. Worrying about the others would only reduce his ability to do his job and jeopardize the lives of his teammates and the hostages, as well as his own life.

Katz moved to the nearest cabin door and pointed the Uzi at the doorknob. He fired a 3-round burst into the wood and metal around the lock. The latch shattered, and Katz kicked the door open. He dropped to one knee and braced the Uzi along the doorframe to point it inside the cabin. It was a first-class cabin, larger than most, with a kitchenette and well-stocked bar in addition to sofa, chairs and breakfast table. The Israeli entered and quickly checked the rest of the quarters. He found no one hiding behind the furniture or in the closets. A check in the bedroom and small bathroom confirmed that the cabin was empty.

McCarter approached, helping Salamar to the door. The Egyptian appeared pale and strained by the pain of his wound. His right sleeve was dyed crimson from the steady flow of blood. Katz nodded to inform McCarter that the quarters were safe, and the Briton hauled the wounded security officer into the cabin and lowered him onto the sofa.

"There isn't much we can do for you right now, Ahmed," Katz told the Egyptian. "We'll be back for you after we take care of the terrorists."

"I understand," Salamar replied weakly. "I'll be all right. Just give me my submachine gun in case the bastards try to come for me."

"All right," Katz assured him. He turned to McCarter. "Tie a tourniquet around that arm to keep him from bleeding and give him his weapon."

"Right," the Briton agreed. "What do we do then?"

"We have to split up," the Israeli answered. "I'll go aft. You head to the bow and take out any opponent who doesn't surrender. Even if they surrender, terminate if you even half suspect it might be a trick. We can't play by the Geneva convention here. There are far more terrorists on board than we expected. Too many to take chances with."

"I'd like to know what the hell is going on here," McCarter admitted. "I've never seen such a mixed lot of terrorists. Black, white, Asian, male, female, Arabs, Irish, and who knows what the rest of these blokes might be...."

"They're the enemy," Katz replied. "Right now, that's all we need to know. When this is over, we can figure out if they're international terrorists assembled by some global outfit or invaders from Mars. Now, take care of Ahmed and take the bow. I'm going aft."

"Allah be with you both," Salamar said.

"And may He be with you, my friend," Katz replied.

The Phoenix commander stepped from the cabin. He glanced in both directions before he headed aft, his Uzi held ready. A salvo of submachine gunfire erupted from the deck below, and although the bullets danced near him, he ducked but kept moving.

Katz glanced at the stairwell and saw two men charging up the steps. He stayed low and extended his left arm with the Uzi in his single fist. Katz had been an amputee for more than two decades and his left arm had developed formidable muscular power to compensate for the lack of his right. He pointed the submachine gun at the pair without exposing himself and triggered the weapon.

The automatic weapon recoiled fiercely in his grasp, but Katz managed to hold the Uzi fairly steady and fired a volley of parabellums down at the advancing gunmen. Screams greeted that maneuver, and the deadly hail sent the pair hurtling back down the stairs.

Katz saw something move from the corner of an eye and whirled to face the bow of the boat deck. David McCarter gazed back at him and nodded, then headed toward the bow as Katz continued to move aft. He began to approach the edge of the cabin section. What waited around the corner was difficult to determine. All Katz saw was an innocent sun deck with some chaise longues and a couple of patio tables. But what wasn't visible was what worried the Israeli.

He allowed the Uzi to hang from the strap on his shoulder and removed a concussion grenade from his belt. The Phoenix commander inserted a prosthesis hook in the ring of the grenade pin, jerked the steel ''hand'' back and pulled the pin. He tossed the grenade at the deck and dropped to one knee, Uzi braced across his artificial arm.

A figure rushed across the sun deck. The wind whipped the man's green windbreaker and lashed his long black hair into a streak at the back of his head. A Walther submachine gun dangled from his shoulder by a long leather strap. Katz glimpsed the terrorist's face as the man raced after the grenade. The gunman's Asian features revealed desperation as he tried to get into position to get rid of the immediate menace.

Katz fired, and the Uzi rounds slammed into the gunman's torso. The terrorist cried out as the force of the high-velocity slugs sent him tumbling over a lounge chair. Katz ducked his head and guarded his ears with his shoulders a split second before the grenade exploded.

The concussion blast shook the boat deck. Two lounge chairs, a table and the Asian terrorist were swept over the railing of the sun deck. Another enemy gunman staggered from around the corner of the cabin section, but he did not present much threat to Katz. The man had discarded his weapon to hold his hands to the sides of his skull. His face was a mask of agony, and blood trickled from his nostrils and mouth. Both eardrums had been ruptured by the blast and the pain drove him to his knees.

"Terrorism wasn't a very wise career move," Katz informed the disabled opponent as he moved in on him.

The Israeli swung a kick to the terrorist's face. His bare heel slammed into the point of the the man's jaw. He uttered a feeble groan and fell unconscious. Katz stepped over the vanquished opponent and moved around the corner of the cabin section. The sun deck was deserted. He walked to the port side of the boat deck and discovered the door to the captain's mess stood open.

Two white-uniformed men were struggling with a terrorist they had managed to pin across the threshold, trying to disarm their opponent. They failed to coordinate their efforts well enough to take the gun away from the enemy, and it was evident that the tangle of arms and legs could give way to a potentially deadly situation.

Katz peered inside the captain's mess. Tables and chairs had been knocked over during a fight with the terrorists who had been guarding the officers and crew. The prisoners had obviously taken advantage of the distraction caused by the sound of the battle, and they had jumped their two guards and brought them down by sheer weight of numbers.

Two other crewmen had pinned the second terrorist guard to the floor of the mess and were hammering away at the man's face and body with their fists.

The terrorist inside the mess was under control so Katz turned his attention to the Arab gunman involved in the clumsy wrestling match at the threshold. The Phoenix commander drew his SIG-Sauer pistol, bent over and pressed the muzzle to the terrorist's forehead. The man's eyes seemed to bulge with surprise and fear.

Katz greeted him in a calm voice and continued talking to him in Arabic. "Peace be with you. Surrender your weapons or your peace will be eternal."

The terrorist quickly agreed and released his MAT-49.

The two men at the door subdued the terrorist and dragged him inside the mess. The crew stared at Katz as if an angel had suddenly appeared before them.

"Does anyone speak English?" Katz inquired. *"Parlez-vous français? Sprechen Sie Deutsch?"*

"I speak English," a heavyset man with a balding pate and black scrub-brush mustache announced. "We also have men who speak French and German and even Arabic if you like. My name is Captain Paitoos. Who are you?"

"A friend," Katz replied. "That's what's important at the moment. Will you keep these two clowns under wraps while I see how my teammates are doing against the rest of the hijackers?"

"This is my ship," Paitoos declared. "We'll help fight them. We're responsible for the passengers on board."

"We'll look after the passengers," Katz assured him. "You can best help by staying here and keeping your crew out of the line of fire."

"We'd rather fight," the captain insisted.

"Fighting terrorists isn't your job," Katz told him. "Your people had a hard time just taking care of these two. I doubt that any of your crew is really trained to do this sort of thing. Let us do our job and then we'll let you get back to yours, Captain."

"Be careful," Paitoos said gruffly. "There are a hell of a lot of those bastards on board."

"We've noticed," Katz assured him.

DAVID McCARTER approached the radio room. Sergio Colombo had just completed a hastily sent message on the ship radio and told the terrorist communications expert to switch the radio off. The Italian ringleader peered out a porthole and saw the Briton an instant before McCarter fired a burst of 9 mm rounds through the filmsy wood door.

Colombo dived to the floor. Bullets splintered wood and sizzled into the small commo section. The terrorist radioman screamed as high-velocity slugs tore into his chest, making him slump against the radio. The headset slipped off his skull as he twitched his last.

McCarter kicked the door open. Colombo fumbled with his Skorpion machine pistol. His injured left hand was bandaged and clumsy. Before Colombo could raise his weapon from the floor, McCarter aimed his weapon and squeezed the trigger.

The Ingram did not fire. Another spent cartridge casing was jammed in the path of the bolt.

"Bloody hell," McCarter rasped as Colombo aimed the Czech subgun at him.

McCarter tossed the jammed Ingram M-10 at Colombo and threw himself sideways, out the door, just as the Skorpion snarled. McCarter landed on the deck, his hand already on the grips of the Browning Hi-Power in shoulder leather under his arm.

Colombo growled an obscenity as he charged across the threshold, eager to finish off his opponent.

McCarter lay on his back, knees bent, feet apart and head and shoulders raised. The Browning was clenched in both hands. His arms were extended between his knees. Colombo glanced down at the Phoenix commando. His mouth fell open with surprise and he tried to swing the Skorpion at McCarter's prone position.

The Browning roared and sent death flying at Colombo, piercing his chest and making him stagger backward, but he held on to the Skorpion. McCarter fired another round. The second Browning messenger crashed into Colombo's forehead, right above and between his eyes. The Italian terrorist folded up lifelessly, his eyes open to stare into the mystery realm of death.

McCarter rose to his feet, discovering that his knees felt a bit unsteady and his heart still beat violently inside his heaving chest—the familiar combination of fear and excitement, but this time the fear level had been stronger than usual. Damn close call, McCarter realized.

"David!" a voice called from behind McCarter.

The Briton whirled around, startled by the unexpected voice. He raised the muzzle of his Browning toward the sky as he recognized Rafael Encizo. McCarter was embarrassed that his partner had managed to sneak up on him. He hoped Encizo did not notice that he was a bit rattled at the moment.

"You got the guys in the radio room?" Encizo inquired. He glanced around McCarter and peered inside. "Guess you did. They were the last of the lot. We got a few prisoners and the rest are dead."

"All our mates okay?" the Briton asked tensely.

"Yeah," the Cuban confirmed. "So are the hostages. Katz told me Salamar stopped a bullet, but he ought to be okay. Calvin will take a look at him and do what he can until help arrives. Speaking of which, we'd better radio the Italians, the Greeks or the U.S. Navy and give them the good news."

"There was something really strange about this business, Rafael," McCarter remarked. "This wasn't a typical hijacking, you know."

"We'll figure it out later," Encizo replied with a shrug.

3

Martin Koerner stood before his commander with an uncomfortable air, then plunged into what he had to say. "We have confirmation about the mission in the Mediterranean. Unfortunately, it is not good news."

"That does not surprise me, Major," Colonel Skull replied in fluent German. "Colombo's last transmission stated our people were under siege. I take it the mission failed, *ja?*"

"A sweep of radio frequencies detected a message to the American naval base in Italy," Koerner explained grimly. "It stated that the hijackers of the *Sea Venus* had been neutralized, and they requested medical assistance for wounded personnel, and that a representative from the United States embassy be on hand to discuss the status of the terrorists' crimes. I suspect this means whoever launched the raid on the *Sea Venus* works for the Americans."

"And they want to interrogate the prisoners before turning them over to the Greek or Italian authorities or whoever they decide gets jurisdiction over them," Skull commented with a slight nod. "Very clever. The American Navy will apprehend the prisoners and take them to the military base in Italy. Then the Greeks, Italians, Americans and possibly the French and British will spend a day or two arguing about who gets to prosecute the hijackers. Meantime, the mystery group will be busy interrogating the prisoners. No doubt they'll use some sort of truth serum. There wouldn't be time to use sleep deprivation or conventional interrogation methods to break down the prisoners. Torture would be crude and unreliable, and easy to prove, too. Truth serum. They're professionals so they'll use scopolamine.''

"I agree, Colonel," Koerner said solemnly. "The Iraqis will learn about the outcome of this mission soon. It will be international news within an hour. What should we tell them?"

"I'll handle that, Major," Skull assured him, a thin smile on his narrow, bloodless lips.

Skull's face resembled the object he had chosen for his name. His face was lean, cheekbones sunken, the bony structure around his mouth prominent, and red-pink eyes set deep and close together. In addition, he was a true albino, with his skin and hair pale white due to lack of pigment. He had used his bizarre appearance to work in his favor, as a tool to make people afraid of him, and therefore make them easily controllable.

The man who called himself Colonel Skull had always been clever. That had been nature's compensation for giving him an appearance that always made him stand out in an unflattering way. He had been sickly and weak as a child. His pink-tinted eyes were weak and very sensitive to light. But he had a brilliant mind, and his genius allowed him to excel in all his studies. First he became an academic success, then he added cunning and manipulation to his capabilities. Ruthlessness had been easy to acquire after the other negative character traits had been purposely developed and cultivated. He was also outrageously daring and succeeded when others would not dream to venture into a scheme. That was exactly why he succeeded.

Skull rose from the armchair behind his desk. His height was another startling feature about him that disconcerted people. He was nearly seven feet tall.

As usual, Skull dressed in black. The stark contrast of his unnaturally pale skin and jet-black clothing contributed to his sinister, almost ghostly appearance. He stepped from behind his desk. The office was dimly lit. Only tinted green bulbs were used in the light fixtures, and a ghostly glow was cast across his skeletal face as he slowly stretched his body and limbs.

"When do you wish to see the Iraqis, *mein Herr*?" Koerner inquired. Martin Koerner had been one of Skull's top aides for nearly two years, but his commander was still an enigma to him.

Koerner was not an easy man to intimidate. The thirty-six-year-old son of a World War II Nazi war criminal, Koerner had been raised in a secret stronghold in the Mato Grosso in Brazil. His father and other fugitives from the war planned to raise their offspring to continue the struggle for the Third Reich. The next generation was instructed in military strategy, weapons, physical conditioning, language studies and national socialism. They were taught that Hitler was a great visionary, that the Aryan race was destined to rule the world and that one day the Nazi swastika banner would fly above the capital of every nation on the face of the earth.

Martin Koerner had no intention of wasting his life on such nonsense. When he left the stronghold in the jungle, he used his unique skills to pursue personal goals. He became a professional mercenary soldier. Intelligent, highly trained and disciplined, Koerner was very good at fighting other people's wars. He did not have much concern about which side might be right or wrong. Koerner was apolitical and amoral. All he really cared about was himself.

His life had changed dramatically when he met Colonel Skull. A brilliant strategist and daring planner, Skull's dreams of conquest were founded on the present, not the past of forty years ago. He intended to accomplish staggering goals in pursuit of personal wealth and power. No nonsense about honoring the memory of a long-dead dictator. No justifications by false claims of righteousness based on racial supremacy, duty to country or occult mumbo jumbo about fate and the spirits of one's ancestors. Compared to the Nazi rhetoric Koerner had been raised with, Skull's plans were refreshingly honest in their unabashed greed and frank ambition.

So Koerner had joined forces with Skull, and their private army had grown larger and richer ever since. Skull's ambitions had also grown. Koerner had never known the colonel to fail, until now. But Skull seemed to take the news in stride. Koerner had some doubts about the colonel's newest scheme. Skull's confidence was inspiring, but Koerner still wished his commander would reconsider their current mission.

"You may as well send the Iraqis in to see me now," Skull declared as he slowly moved his arms, first from side to side, then to form wide circles in the air.

"They may be upset, Colonel," Koerner warned. "Perhaps Major Hee and I should remain here with you."

"You and Major Hee have other duties to tend to, Martin," Skull informed him. Skull did not look at Koerner as he spoke. He had extended his arms, one hand placed over the other, and his eyes were focused on his hands. "You two are my most trusted officers. A lot of preparations still have to be made, and you and Hee are the only men who can handle such delicate matters. The Iraqis are our clients and I should see to them myself."

"Very well, Colonel," Koerner said with a sigh. "I'll send them in. Bear in mind, these Arabs can be an unstable lot."

"Arabs are no different than anyone else, Major," Skull commented as he stepped forward with his left foot and slowly pushed his hands into the air in front of him as if shoving back an invisible object. "People everywhere do what they believe to be in their own best interest. Don't worry. I can handle the clients. They aren't really any different than we are."

"All right, Colonel," Koerner agreed reluctantly, "but be careful."

"I always am, Martin," Skull replied. He raised one arm slowly and raised one leg simultaneously in a smooth coordinated motion. "You ought to know that by now."

"This new mission is bigger than anything we've done before," Koerner commented. "To be honest, it worries me. If anything goes wrong..."

"They can only kill us once," Skull said with a soft laugh. "You know, Martin, if you or any of the others want out of this, I won't hold it against you."

"Want out?" Koerner smiled. "You know me well enough to realize I might be worried about the risks involved in the operation, but I can't resist it, either. If it works, it will be unlike anything ever accomplished by any private paramilitary force in history. Making history and getting rich and powerful in the process is too tempting for me to resist, regardless of the risk."

"I thought so," Skull said with satisfaction.

Koerner left Skull's office, careful to close the door to prevent the harsh light from the corridor from pouring into his commander's room. Skull continued to perform a series of t'ai chi ch'uan exercises. He concentrated on every movement, his body, mind and spirit working as one. T'ai chi is perhaps the oldest of the Chinese martial arts, and serves as a form of meditation combined with movement and physical exercise. The albino found weight lifting and conventional calisthenics difficult due to his early years as a sickly child. The advantage of t'ai chi was that it required more mental concentration than muscular strength.

Skull had learned that energy wasted in anger was worthless, and he focused his anger and disappointment concerning the *Sea Venus* incident into the efforts of t'ai chi exercises. He kept the movements slow and controlled, gradually speeding up those of his hands and feet. His fists shot out like pistons, and clawed fingers struck the air. His feet slashed kicks at invisible opponents. His full concentration and the movement of his entire body were behind each blow. If only he could get his hands on the bastards responsible for the failure of his hijackers' operation!

He imagined lancing stiff fingers into the throats and solar plexus regions of his unknown opponents. A kick could crush the testicles of an antiterrorist commando into jelly. A tiger claw could tear the eyeballs from the troublesome cretin's sockets. Skull did not know who they were or what they looked like, so he pictured faces from his childhood. They said mocking things to him in German and French. Most were snotty schoolchildren and obnoxious teenagers. Skull imagined the delight of smashing in those smug grinning faces. All those young Swiss faces he had known in his youth would be so much more appealing to Skull if he could see their features contorted in agony, their lips trembling with pleas for mercy and their eyes wide with terror as they saw hideous slow death about to claim them.

Skull's mind's eye saw the face he hated most in all the universe, that of his father: the wealthy Swiss banker who was disgusted by his albino weakling son, the concerned parent who arranged private tutors for his loathsome child because he was ashamed of the sickly, pale creature he had sired, the loving husband who beat his wife in drunken rage and accused her of giving birth to "that thing."

Skull recalled overhearing talk by some of his father's friends and relatives who felt sorry for the man because he had to endure the terrible burden of raising a "handicapped child." Then his father—the heartless, selfish, wife-beating, child-abusing, drunken cheat and bully—would show a small, brave smile to his compassionate supporters and tell them it was "God's will."

The old man had been dead for two and a half decades, but his son's hatred lived on. What would his father think if he knew his offspring would one day claim the family inheritance, rob Daddy's precious bank and use the money to finance a private army composed of terrorists and international criminals? What would his dear, departed father think of the man who called himself Colonel Skull?

"Damn you to hell, you bastard," Skull growled at the memory of his father. He uttered the curse in all the languages he spoke as his hands slashed at the mental picture of his father's face. Yet he could never kill the ghost that haunted his memories.

"Bonjour, Colonel Crâne," a voice called from the door of the office. "Is this a bad time?"

"Non, Monsieur Saddoon," Skull replied as he straightened his clothing and moved to his desk. *"Entrez, s'il vous plaît."*

Nizar Saddoon and two associates entered the office. Saddoon was an important man in Iraq, the brother of the newly appointed chairman of the National Assembly of the Republic of Iraq. The Saddoon brothers had big plans for their country and even bigger ambitions for themselves. Nizar folded his fat fingers on his barrellike chest and squinted at Skull in the dim light.

"I can barely see, Colonel," Saddoon commented, speaking French because it was the only language he and Skull could communicate fluently in. "Can we have more light?"

"One moment," Skull replied as he took a pair of glasses from his desk and slipped them on his face. "I'll turn on the overhead light."

Skull switched on the only light in the room that was neither tinted nor less than sixty-watt power. It was not a bright bulb, but Skull still needed the dark, wraparound glasses when it was on. He sat behind his desk and gazed up at the three Iraqis.

"I trust you've been informed about what happened in the Mediterranean?" Skull inquired calmly. "It is disappointing news, but I wouldn't call it a setback."

Saddoon slumped into a chair across from Skull. "I don't understand," he began. "How did this happen? The hijacking seemed perfect. How did they stop the *Sea Venus* from reaching Libya?"

"I don't know," Skull confessed. "I can only guess what may have happened. Perhaps the Americans had a submarine in the area and managed to launch a raid with frogmen and commandos. I really don't know, Mr. Saddoon. It hardly matters. No one will associate the hijacking with you or your brother. So there really isn't any damage done."

"They certainly took some of your people prisoner," spoke another Iraqi who was known to Skull only as Jemal. He was a grim-faced Arab with a trim mustache and cold dark eyes. "I don't believe they will keep their mouths shut."

"I quite agree," Skull said with a thin smile. "But what can they say? Everyone on board that ship believed they were working for the Iranians. Let them talk. They'll say that they were headed to Libya to deliver the hostages to a Shiite Muslim terrorist organization known to be connected to Iran's so-called Islamic revolution. They'll blame Iran and they'll blame Khaddafi, but they still won't know anything about you or our ultimate mission."

"They know about *you*, Colonel," Jemal replied.

"*Et alors?*" Skull said with an exaggerated shrug. When he spoke French, he adopted French gestures. "So what? I've been in business for some time, gentlemen. I'm sure rumors about me have been floating about for years. A privately owned international terrorist army commanded by a tall ghostly figure known as Colonel Skull. It sounds exactly like the sort of exaggerated nonsense unbalanced radicals come up with when they have to say something, but they're trying to avoid the truth. Look at all the legends about Carlos the Jackal. Carlos was Ilyich Ramirez Sanchez, a Venezuelan Communist with a rather brief career in Europe. He was actually an incompetent drunkard and womanizer. The only reason he became a legend was because he was bold and foolish, not because he was successful. Yet, whenever a major terrorist operation occurs, people still wonder if Carlos might be involved. No one in any intelligence organization will believe stories about Colonel Skull any more than they'd believe that Carlos has made a return to active involvement in international terrorist operations.''

"I'm not so certain of that, Colonel," Saddoon commented. "But that will be your problem in the future. All that matters now is the security of our operation."

"Don't be concerned," Skull urged. "The purpose of the hijacking was simply to convince the world in general that Iran was conducting a new wave of large-scale terrorist operations. More fuel on the fires started by the Ayatollah's forces themselves. The Iranians have already been involved in so many terrorist actions in the past that it will be easy to convince people they were responsible for the *Sea Venus* hijacking. Half the population of the world regard the Iranians as dangerous fanatics. The idiots who run Iran have been foolish enough to make war with your country, make enemies with the United States and most of Western Europe. They even managed to alienate themselves from the majority of other Islamic nations after the bloody incident at the Pilgrimage in Mecca in 1987. Iran has become the perfect scapegoat.''

"You are clever with words, Colonel," remarked Rashid, Saddoon's other companion, with a sneer. He was a large man, built like a gorilla with a primitive face that looked like a throwback to the age of Neanderthal man. His small beady eyes glared from beneath a sloped brow. "But all your words do not change the fact that your people failed. How do we know they will not fail when the real mission begins? The mission at the summit meeting in Luxembourg?''

"Three points in reply to that," Skull said with a sigh as he slowly rose from his chair. "First, the Luxembourg mission has been carefully planned for several months. We've had to plan and alter plans and replan for different sites as the superpowers argued about where and when to have the next summit meeting. The hijacking of the *Sea Venus* was planned too quickly. There wasn't time to prepare for everything that might go wrong. The Luxembourg mission is entirely different. We've been able to prepare at length and consider every possible problem that might occur."

Skull strolled from his desk and peered down at the muscular Iraqi bodyguard through his dark glasses. "Second point, I and my top officers will personally supervise the entire operation. I'm putting everything on the line for the mission, including my own life. That's a strong motivation to make sure I carry out this mission with maximum efficiency."

"Your third point?" Rashid demanded.

"That is the simple fact that you, Rashid, are not qualified to even have an opinion in this matter, let alone voice it," Skull replied. "You are just a bodyguard. Brute strength with a gun and a nervous system designed to react rather than think. Mr. Saddoon ought to have your tongue cut out. You use it when it should remain still."

"You bloodless infidel freak," Rashid rasped as he stood before Skull, his thick shoulders arched back like an angered cat's. "I should break you in half for such insults."

"Rashid!" Saddoon snapped.

"He's a very poor bodyguard," Skull remarked. "He puts his personal pride above your safety. He talks too much and his temper is too short. You'd be better off without him, Mr. Saddoon. I can kill him if you like."

Rashid snarled something rude in Arabic and lunged at Skull, both hands going for the albino's throat. The terrorist commander stepped aside to avoid the attack and pivoted to push both hands into Rashid's left shoulder blade. The shove was very forceful with Skull's t'ai chi training behind it. Rashid's forward momentum was drastically increased, and he crashed into a wall, hard.

The bodyguard spun about to face Skull. He lashed a large fist at the colonel's pale face. Skull bent his knees and lowered his head beneath the path of the wild attack. Rashid's arm swung overhead like a deranged windmill. Skull suddenly shot up from the floor and thrust a hand into his opponent's face.

Two fingers stabbed deep into Rashid's eyes. The Iraqi screamed as blood spilled from the punctured orbs. Crimson blood and matter like egg white poured from the ravaged eye sockets. Skull stepped back and breathed deeply, his gaze fixed on the blinded Iraqi bodyguard. Saddoon gasped in horror and covered his mouth with a hand. Jemal reached inside his jacket for a pistol in shoulder leather, but stopped as he realized that wouldn't solve anything.

Skull moved forward, his entire body and energy concentrated into the tremendous blow he delivered to Rashid's solar plexus. The fist drove a powerful punch upward and sent a violent shock wave inside Rashid's chest cavity. The Chinese refer to "internal boxing," a blow delivered to drive inward and damage the internal organs of an opponent. Skull was a master of this technique.

Rashid's mouth opened. Blood spewed down his shirtfront. His heart and lungs had been ruptured by the punch. The bodyguard fell back into the wall and slumped to the floor. His eyeless sockets stared up at the other two Iraqis as if begging them to punish his murderer. Saddoon looked away and nearly vomited. Jemal shook his head and looked down at the floor. Rashid's body trembled in a final convulsion and then lay still, a dead lump of bloodied flesh.

"That was unnecessary, Skull," Jemal declared, still avoiding looking at Rashid's body. "You didn't have to kill him."

"You would have preferred if he was blind instead?" Skull asked, taking a handkerchief from a pocket to wipe the blood from his hands. "I think Rashid is better off dead. He was too stupid to adjust to blindness. Too stupid to be trusted in a mission as important as this one."

"Rashid was expendable," Saddoon declared, gathering his composure. He glared at Skull. "But you didn't need to kill him. I know you, Colonel. I know you well enough to realize you didn't do this simply to impress us with how lethal your martial arts skills have become. There was some other reason for this sacrifice?"

"Perhaps it is best to look at Rashid's death as an example of my commitment," Skull stated. "Anyone who endangers the success of this mission will be destroyed. I don't care if they are Europeans, Americans or Russians. I don't care if they are your people or members of my own command. I don't care if I have to kill one person or a million to accomplish this mission."

"Need I remind you my brother hired you, Colonel," Saddoon told Skull, but he was careful to keep any trace of challenge from his voice.

"Your brother needs me as much as I need him," Skull said in a firm tone. "If we succeed, we succeed together. If we fail, we *both* lose everything. You might survive for a while after your brother and I are dead, Mr. Saddoon, but not for long. Too many people will be out for a lot of blood if this fails. The superpowers of the East and the West, your government, the Iranian government, possibly others. There will be no place to hide if this doesn't work."

"I understand that," Saddoon assured him. "But I don't really understand why this is so vital to you. It must be more than the money."

"I have a lifetime of reasons," Skull replied. "Some of which you would never be able to appreciate."

"One thing is certain," Jemal commented grimly. "When this operation begins, there will be no turning back."

"*When* it begins?" Skull smiled. "It has already started."

4

Hal Brognola took the cigar from his mouth, looked at its well-chewed stump, then shoved it back into a corner of his mouth as though he hadn't really seen it and was acting in a dream. But the look with which he let his eyes roam around the Stony Man war room indicated a great deal of alertness.

The soft buzzing of the air conditioner merged with the clicking of the word processor hooked up to the computers at the opposite end of the room. Yakov Katzenelenbogen sat at the conference table and quietly waited for Brognola to speak.

"That sea rescue you guys pulled off was pretty impressive," Brognola remarked. He paused to look somewhat longingly at the glass ashtray on the polished wood table before him, then bit down on his cigar. "That's kind of what I expect from Phoenix Force. Of course, you were supposed to be hunting down the terrorists responsible for the embassy bombing in Cairo."

"We may have found them, Hal," Katz replied. "At least some of them. If you read the report, you'd notice that three of the terrorists from the *Sea Venus* hijacking revealed knowledge about the Cairo bombing that was not public information. We think both terrorist incidents were carried out by the same organization. What we put out of action at the *Sea Venus* hijacking might be just the tip of an international iceberg of terrorism."

"I read the report," Brognola assured him. He gestured with the cigar in his hand to point at the computers. "The Bear is checking on some data concerning the rumors about Colonel Skull and his alleged army of international terrorists."

"There was nothing 'alleged' about the terrorists we encountered on board that cruise ship, Hal," Katz informed him, taking out a pack of Camel cigarettes. "They were real, flesh-and-blood opponents. Well organized, well armed, and they represented at least nine different nationalities, at least four ethnic groups and both sexes. Now, I've never seen a terrorist organization quite like this before, and I've been doing this sort of thing for quite a few years."

"Longer than I have," the Fed admitted. "Even longer than Bolan. I agree there's something pretty strange going on."

Brognola had a lot of respect for the opinion of Yakov Katzenelenbogen. He and Mack Bolan had personally selected the Israeli supercommando to serve as the unit commander of Phoenix Force when they had first set up Stony Man operations. That time seemed a thousand years ago. So much had happened since the supersecret organization had been formed, but it had all started with Bolan, the man known to most of the world as "the Executioner," or the one-man war machine who took on the forces of organized crime and destruction in the world.

Brognola's job was to be the man in the middle, the link between Stony Man and the White House. He was responsible for assigning missions to the Stony Man operatives and gathering primary intelligence for each new assignment. When possible, Brognola supplied his people with assistance through contacts in various government organizations, including those of foreign nations. Brognola kept secrets, even from the President of the United States, who knew Phoenix Force existed and that it successfully carried out missions while generally maintaining a low profile, but did not know who they were or details concerning their assignments.

"Here's the file on Colonel Skull . . . if you can call it that," Aaron Kurtzman commented as he approached the conference table. "Not much more than a collection of rumors."

Kurtzman, also known as "the Bear," was the Stony Man computer wizard. He was an expert in tapping into the computer networks of the CIA, FBI, National Security Council and other intelligence organizations and police departments throughout the nation. The Bear had even managed to tap into a KGB computer center at the Soviet embassy in Washington, D.C.

The hum of the motor of Kurtzman's electronic wheelchair increased as he approached the table. He had been shot in the back and left for dead during an enemy raid on Stony Man headquarters. April Rose, Mack Bolan's love, had been killed during the assault. The Bear was paralyzed from the waist down, the damage to his spine irreversible. But he was still a fighter and still jockeyed a computer terminal better than anyone in the business.

"How long have you been getting these stories about Skull?" Katz inquired as he used the steel hooks of his prosthesis to flip open the file folder.

"For about three years," Kurtzman answered. "That's the first one on file, anyway. That report was printed in a British tabloid newspaper—the kind of publication that prints stories about werewolf cults in London and psychic predictions of the end of the world, UFOs landing in Scotland, members of the Royal Family being involved with strange aliens who've been living secretly in the Tower of London for centuries, that sort of thing."

"You see why we didn't take Colonel Skull very seriously?" Brognola asked Katz, tapping the ash from his cigar. "None of the rumors about this guy have been very convincing. He's supposed to look like something out of a horror film. A seven foot, pale white figure in black, who commands a secret army of terrorist mercenaries. Sounds like something from the old serials of the thirties."

"Some things that sound incredible turn out to be true," Katz declared as he leafed through the file. "A little man with a Charlie Chaplin mustache attempting to take over the world may have seemed pretty absurd before World War II. Nobody believed the Shah of Iran could be thrown out of power and replaced by an Islamic version of Rasputin. I wouldn't be too quick to dismiss Colonel Skull."

"You interrogated the terrorists from the *Sea Venus*?" the Fed inquired. "And they all mentioned Skull?"

"Not all," Katz replied. "Unfortunately, we only managed to take a few of the terrorists alive. There were quite a lot of them and they were well armed. Although they put up a decent fight, they didn't seem eager to literally die for anyone's cause. One French terrorist was quite willing to sell out his comrades to save his own skin, according to Gary, Rafael and Cal. Not one seemed to find suicide for final glory very attractive. In short, most were not political or religious fanatics, and they didn't seem to have much sense of loyalty. Rather like an international gang of sociopaths united to pull off the hijacking."

"I think that must be the result of the Interpol computer scan," Kurtzman declared as the teletext machine began to produce copies. "I've got a tap with the Justice Department that is patched into the Interpol main computer centers in Europe. They should have the identification of any terrorist who had been involved in previous operations that caught the attention of Interpol. I'll see what we've got."

Kurtzman turned his motorized chair around, working the control panel with experienced ease and rolled forward to the computers. Katz continued to examine the previous reports on Colonel Skull. Most were claims made by secondhand sources or criminals and political zealots with reputations as chronic liars.

"You used scopolamine on the terrorists?" Brognola asked.

"Calvin did," Katz confirmed. "As you know, he's had a lot of experience using truth serum on subjects. He's very good at administering the drug. Scopolamine can be dangerous. Use too much, and the subject will probably suffer a fatal heart attack. Too little, and he gets a bit dopey, but he can still lie. He can still resist the drug."

"Scopolamine doesn't work on everyone," Brognola reminded the Phoenix commander. "Some agents are trained with posthypnosis to relay false information under the influence of truth serum. Hard-core schizos can lie their heads off under the influence of scopolamine. They really don't *know* what the truth is."

"I'm aware of that, Hal," Katz assured him, "but I don't think those exceptions include the terrorists we interrogated in Italy. I believe they told us the truth. That means there really is a Colonel Skull, or someone is taking advantage of the rumors about this character to carry out real terrorist operations. As far as I can see, the problem is pretty much the same either way."

"In your report it states that they intended to take the hostages to a Shiite Muslim terrorist outfit in Libya," the Fed recalled. "A group associated with the Ayatollah's Islamic Jihad. Even if the Iranians hired Skull, this is still a case of state-sponsored terrorism. That's not good news for anyone, and it's bound to make matters worse in the Persian Gulf. The U.S. is just one skip and a jump away from war with Iran as it is. This incident is going to be fuel on the political fire any way you look at it."

"The terrorist group that attacked the U.S. embassy in Cairo is also supposedly part of Ach'dar Nar, the Shiite terrorist outfit in the Middle East that has supposedly expanded operations to include Southern Europe, as well. No one ever heard of Ach'dar Nar until now."

"Some of these outfits grow out of other groups," Brognola said with a sigh. "Hell, you know that as well as I do. Some terrorist organizations are just fronts for other outfits and a number of terrorists belong to more than one group."

"Yes, I know," Katz acknowledged with a weary nod. "We've seen lots of newly formed terrorist outfits on past Phoenix Force missions. Groups that were formed by bands of fanatics like the Tigers of Justice. Groups that turned out to be secretly run by the KGB or some other enemy intelligence outfit. Groups that were actually criminal organizations such as MERGE and TRIO. But we've never come across a terrorist operation with such a variety of nationalities. They didn't put them together overnight. I think the Ach'dar Nar is just a front for something else."

"Could be KGB," Brognola stated. "The Soviets could certainly organize something like this."

"They wouldn't have much reason to help Shiite Muslim terrorists connected with Iran," Katz mused. "Unless there's more to this than there appears to be."

Kurtzman returned to the table with a bundle of printout sheets on his lap. The wheelchair came to a halt and he placed the data on the table.

"Interpol evaluations of the terrorists involved in the *Sea Venus* hijacking," Kurtzman declared. "Lot of stuff here. Apparently, Interpol couldn't find anything on some of the terrorists, but they certainly came up with plenty on the others involved."

"Looks like we've got some real veteran bad guys here," Brognola remarked as he leafed through the reports. "Jesus! Irish Republican Army, Second June Movement, Red Brigade—both Italian and French Brigades—Baader-Meinhof Gang, Japanese Red Army..."

"The terrorists we interrogated mentioned all those and more," Katz stated. "According to them, the group also includes former SWAPO Communist troopers from Angola and other black Africans accustomed to carrying out ruthless jungle warfare against civilians. I doubt if Interpol has anything on them, but there may be mention of some individuals' former association with crime syndicates. Mafia in Italy and Sicily or perhaps the Corsican Union in France."

"That's right," Brognola confirmed as he continued examining the Interpol reports. "Okay, Yakov. Maybe there is something to these claims about Colonel Skull. What do you think we should do about it?"

"The interrogations didn't tell us much, really," Katz answered. "The terrorists were obviously low on the totem pole in Skull's organization. Or maybe I should say whoever *claims* to be Skull. Nonetheless, most of them agreed on two items of interest. The first was that Skull had set up a temporary headquarters off the coast of Greece. We can check that out, but I'm sure Skull will have already left and set up a new command base elsewhere. The other item is the notion shared by virtually all the terrorists that Skull plans a really big and important mission in Europe in the very near future. They weren't privy to details about the upcoming mission so they don't know what the target might be."

"And you think this is a genuine possibility," the Fed remarked. He was not asking a question. "That's why the rest of Phoenix Force is still in Europe?"

"McCarter came back with me," Katz corrected. "He's down at the firing range trying out some submachine guns. His

Ingram M-10 jammed twice during our raid on the *Sea Venus*.
It almost got him killed both times. So David has finally agreed
to get a different weapon. That M-10 has been his second-
favorite child for a long time. First place has to go to his
Browning Hi-Power. I don't think he'll ever give up that pistol. Of course, the Browning hasn't jammed in combat."

"But the other three of you are still in Europe," Brognola
said dryly. "Okay, I'll authorize it. You and McCarter go back
to Europe and join the rest of the team. I'll try to contact the
President and get everything cleared with the White House.
That is, unless something urgent has come up and the President
wants you guys to handle something else."

"You'd better contact him quickly, Hal," Kurtzman remarked. "He's going to be out of the country for a while for
that arms talk with the Soviets."

"Washington and the Kremlin finally agreed to a site for the
summit meeting to discuss treaties concerning nuclear arms?"
Katz inquired. "I guess I haven't been following the news much
lately. We were all a bit preoccupied while we were in Egypt and
then in Italy with the terrorists."

"Yeah," Brognola said with a pessimistic sigh. "The
President and the Soviet premier are going to have another chat
about arms controls. I can't claim that really thrills me. Both
sides say the other can't be trusted. They're probably right, too.
Each of the parties will claim they're more concerned about
arms reduction than the other. Then the mutual accusations will
come, along with statements about the need for more willingness to cooperate. These things also seem to turn out pretty
much the same regardless of who is involved or where the
meeting takes place. They never seem to accomplish much one
way or the other."

"Well, the U.S. and the Soviet Union haven't launched any
nuclear missiles at each other yet," Katz said with a shrug.
"Maybe the talks have something to do with that. Better to
launch accusations than nuclear warheads. There is a possibility the talks might do more good this time. I'm a bit suspicious
of the Soviet claims of *glasnost*, but most of my association
with Soviets has been confronting KGB agents. It's not the sort
of thing that inspires much trust."

"Would be nice if things worked out in Luxembourg," Brognola agreed. "That's where the summit meeting will be held, in Luxembourg."

5

Colonel Freddrick Mauser watched the plane descend to the runway. Red Cyrillic letters were painted across the sleek white body of the big TU-144 airliner. Mauser could not understand the writing, but he recognized it as Russian. The colonel felt uncomfortable as he watched the Soviet aircraft land. He was a professional soldier in the Luxembourg volunteer army. Since Luxembourg is a NATO nation, the colonel regarded the Soviets as being on the "other side," although Luxembourg had generally remained outside the arena of Cold War bickering.

The crowds at Findel Airport were enormous, far larger than airport security was accustomed to dealing with. Luxembourg had developed a healthy tourist industry, but foreign visitors did not usually gather in huge masses to watch the arrival of the leaders of the mightiest superpowers on the face of the earth. Diplomats from at least two dozen nations were present. Newspaper and television reporters and cameramen struggled to get a better viewing angle of the Soviet plane. The rest of the crowds comprised Luxembourgers and visitors from other countries.

It was a major news story, a political high point, a historical event and a once-in-a-lifetime opportunity to see this gathering of international leaders. It was also a nightmare for security personnel. Luxembourg was not accustomed to that sort of political circus. A country roughly the size of Rhode Island, Luxembourg was better known for its castles and storybook atmosphere than as a site for international conferences. Members of the European Community had held a summit meeting in Luxembourg Ville to discuss economic and social issues in

1985, but the current meeting was of a very different kind—the sort of conference that the entire world pays close attention to, the kind of summit meeting that creates enormous tension because it sets a stage where anything can go wrong.

Colonel Mauser was one of the top military intelligence officers in Luxembourg. Most of the time, his role was rather like that of a marriage counselor in a monastery. Luxembourg was hardly a hotbed of international intrigue. With both the President of the United States and the Soviet premier attending the summit meeting, security suddenly became a vital concern in the Grand Duchy of Luxembourg.

So far, things had gone smoothly. The President had arrived in Air Force One earlier that day. Crowds were present to greet his arrival, and most of the spectators cheered and welcomed the American leader. A handful of demonstrators waved protest signs written in French, German and English, criticizing the United States for involvement in the Persian Gulf and Central America, and for putting NATO missiles in Europe. Mauser had been rather glad that most of the protesters proved to be foreigners instead of native Luxembourgers. The majority were French, members of a Communist Party cell group with a reputation for bitching about anything connected with the United States, but not noted for violent behavior. Some of the other demonstrators were West German youths who belonged to the Green Party, an outspoken antinuke organization.

However, the President's arrival had been pleasant, and the demonstrators barely made a ripple in the official welcome arranged for the Americans. The prime minister of Luxembourg had greeted the President when he stepped off Air Force One. A couple of brief speeches were made at the airport before they departed for the palace where the grand duke waited with an elaborate reception for the statesmen.

Several Secret Service agents remained at the airport with the American secretary of state to wait for the Soviets to arrive. There were also some CIA agents among the crowd. The latter had been in Luxembourg for several days previously to help with security. The Soviet KGB had made similar arrangements. Mauser was less than thrilled about working with either group, especially the KGB. So far, there had not been any conflicts between the two spy networks, but Mauser could not help wondering how long that would last.

At least the Americans had agreed to move the President to the palace instead of insisting he remain at the airport to greet the premier when he stepped off the plane. That would have made the security problems greater at Findel Airport, an environment that afforded limited control. The secretary of state would meet the Soviet leader in order to follow proper protocol.

The Soviet TU-144 rolled to a halt on the runway. A ramp with stairs, appropriately lined with a red carpet, was rushed to the Russian VIP plane. The hatch opened and Soviet officials and KGB security personnel began their descent. Mauser regarded the Soviet officials as a grim lot, with stern faces that seemed incapable of smiling. Several Russians were in army uniforms. Probably GRU, Mauser thought, the Soviet military intelligence organization. The GRU was the second largest intelligence network in the world. The KGB was the biggest.

One of the uniformed figures looked impressive simply because of his formidable appearance. He stood more than six and a half feet tall. His muscles strained against the fabric of his green uniform. A handlebar-style mustache, not unlike that once worn by Stalin, extended from his upper lip like the horns of a steer. He wore the rank of major, but he could have passed for a heavyweight Olympic wrestler.

The Soviet premier finally appeared, and a band began to play the national anthem of the U.S.S.R. The premier smiled and waved. Unlike most of the previous Soviet leaders, he made a personal effort at public relations. The image of *glasnost* would not get much credibility if the premier himself failed to show some "openness."

The crowd cheered as the premier descended the ramp. The cheers were considerably less enthusiastic than they had been for the American President. Colonel Mauser also noticed that none of the antinuke demonstrators waved banners of protest when the Soviets arrived. He wondered if they did not object to Communist nations having nuclear weapons.

The U.S. secretary of state, a translator and several Secret Service agents approached the premier. Mauser and four other soldiers escorted the prime minister of Luxembourg as they marched forward to greet the Soviet visitors. The colonel paid little attention to the words exchanged by the politicians. He was busy scanning the crowds for any hint of danger. The plastic earphone in his left ear was a radio receiver so other security personnel could contact him in an emergency.

Everything continued to go smoothly. The premier, the prime minister and the secretary of state exchanged official greetings and moved to the motorcade waiting to take them to the palace. Colonel Mauser was among the group that would escort the VIPs to the next locale. He was relieved by how well things had gone so far and hoped the trend would continue.

No one noticed a small thin man dressed in a cheap, ill-fitting suit, who stood by a public telephone with the receiver to his ear. He appeared to be another one of the newspaper journalists who was calling his editor with an update of what was happening at the airport.

''Monsieur Albano?'' he said into the telephone.

''Oui,'' Colonel Skull replied.

''Everyone has arrived,'' the man declared simply.

''Including our friends from out of country?''

''Yes, sir,'' the man confirmed with a thin smile. ''I saw them both among the passengers. Everything seems to be as we'd expected....''

''Expect the unexpected,'' Skull informed him. ''Never take anything for granted and bear in mind small mistakes can be very costly. We can't afford any mistakes. Not now. I trust you understand.''

''Absolutely, sir,'' the agent assured him.

''Thank you for calling,'' Skull said and hung up.

SCOTT BERNELLI HAD BEEN a CIA case officer, attached to the United States embassy in Rome, for less than a year. An Italian-American who spoke Italian with a Florentine accent and English with a Jersey dialect, he was a college-bred Company man, one of the ''yuppies of espionage,'' who had far more experience in classrooms than in the field. The five mysterious operatives who had carried out the successful raid on the *Sea Venus* were unlike anyone he had encountered during his brief career with the Central Intelligence Agency.

Basically a desk jockey, the twenty-nine-year-old Bernelli nearly laughed when he was instructed to meet the five commandos at a safehouse on a side street by Via Torino, not far from the Piazzo de Repubblica. The safehouse appeared to be just a shoddy little shoe store, officially condemned and waiting to be torn down. Actually, it was a secret hideaway for the Company that even Bernelli had not known about.

The store was actually an ideal safehouse. Small and ugly, with boarded-up windows and locks on its doors, it was the sort of place no one looked at twice. It was unlikely to make anyone suspicious, and was located near two major subway stations and the central railroad station. Being close to the main transportation arteries enabled the residents of the safehouse to strike operations and quickly disappear among the crowds that were always clustered about the area day and night. The safehouse personnel could then disperse in separate directions. They might not try to take the train, though, if they wanted to go anywhere in a hurry. Mussolini had kept his promise to make the trains run on time, but Mussolini had been dead since 1945; some people claimed that the trains in Rome had never been on time since he died.

Bernelli sat on one of several folding chairs inside the safehouse. The walls were covered with faded wallpaper, with bare spots where chipped plaster showed through. The floors were uncarpeted with several loose boards. An air conditioner hummed quietly in a corner. Since none of the windows could be opened, the device served to freshen the air as much as to cool the building. Naked light bulbs were powered by a gasoline generator to avoid using the city electricity, for even the Italian government did not know about the safehouse. The CIA was paranoid under the best circumstances. Because Italy has the largest Communist party of any Western European nation, the precautions taken were greater than usual.

Yakov Katzenelenbogen and David McCarter had returned from the United States and rejoined the other members of Phoenix Force at the safehouse. Bernelli had been less than thrilled to see the pair return. He had hoped Mr. Kenver and Mr. Michaels would contact the other three on the radio transceiver and instruct them it was time to leave Italy. Bernelli was eager to get out of the safehouse and back to the U.S. embassy.

The CIA man could hardly believe these men were for real. They had stored an arsenal of assorted weapons at the safehouse, and on top of that, Katz and McCarter had brought even more guns back from the States by shipping the arms in a diplomatic pouch through the embassy. They looked as though they were prepared to go to war at a moment's notice. Bernelli wondered who these characters really were. A secret branch of Delta Force? Mercenaries? He even wondered if all of them were American citizens. They had top-priority authorization from the White House. He found that incredible. They outranked even the Company chief of operations and seemed to be able to pull the strings of the Italian intelligence outfits, as well. Was the President actually putting pressure on Rome to cooperate with the five supercommandos? What made them so damn special? That John Wayne-James Bond stunt with the *Sea Venus*?

"Well, Bernelli," Katz began as he helped himself to a cup of coffee and sat at a card table with Gary Manning and Calvin James. "You'll be glad to know we'll be leaving Rome in about one hour."

"I hope you have a nice trip, Mr. Kenver," the CIA man said with a forced smile.

"You, too, Bernelli," McCarter said with a grin. "Lucky day, mate. You get to go with us."

"What?" Bernelli was stunned by the news. "I'm stationed here in Rome. You can't make me pack up and run off at a moment's notice like this!"

"Yes we can," Katz corrected. "Check with your section chief if you don't believe us, but do it in a hurry. We have a flight to Luxembourg to catch."

"What are we going to Luxembourg for?" the CIA officer demanded. "And why do I have to go?"

"You know we questioned those terrorists and they claimed that Colonel Skull plans something big here in Europe," Man-

ning answered. "The summit arms talks with the President and
the Soviet premier are being held in Luxembourg. That's about
the biggest event taking place in Europe right now."

"Colonel Skull," Bernelli said and clucked his tongue with
disgust. "Sounds like something out of a comic book."

"Yeah," James remarked. "Sounds almost as silly as 'Big
Daddy' Idi Amin and 'Papa Doc' and 'Baby Doc' Duvalier.
From what Kenver and Michaels told us, reports about Skull
have been ignored for three years. Maybe that's because everybody had the same attitude you've got. Maybe that's something Colonel Skull has taken advantage of to continue
operations without any serious problems from you intelligence
guys, 'cause you're all too grown-up to believe such a weirdo
could actually be the head of a terrorist organization."

"You really believe this crap?" Bernelli asked with a sigh.

"I believe we really came across a group of terrorists on
board the *Sea Venus*," Gary Manning informed him. "They
seemed pretty real to me. The bullets they fired at us were real.
The hostage they killed is really dead. I'd say that's enough
reason to figure there might be some truth about Colonel
Skull."

"Hey, Michaels," Rafael Encizo said to McCarter, carefully maintaining their cover. "What kind of piece did you get
to replace the old M-10?"

"I'm still not sure there was anything wrong with the Ingram," the Briton muttered, opening a briefcase as he spoke.
"Could be the problem was just with the particular M-10 I used
during the raid on the *Sea Venus*. Hell, any gun can jam."

"This wasn't the first time you've had problems with an
Ingram machine pistol," Katz reminded him. "Its biggest
drawback in the past has been its limited range and accuracy.
That weapon was designed as a room cleaner and not for sustained combat. The Ingram had limited use, and I think your
new weapon will work much better in the greater variety of
circumstances one is apt to encounter in the field."

"Bloody pep talk for a firearm," McCarter snorted as he
removed a weapon from the case.

The gun was only a foot and a half long, blue-black with a
forward grip below the barrel. McCarter slid a long magazine

into the well just in front of the trigger guard. He placed the weapon on a table and hunted in an ice chest for a cold cola drink.

"KG-99?" Calvin James remarked as he examined the gun. "I remember handling some of these when they first came out. Interdynamics used to make 'em and then Intertec took over. To be honest, I wasn't that impressed with the gun."

"This one is an improved model," McCarter assured him as he popped the cap off a bottle of Coke. "It's also been converted to fire both semi- and full-auto. See the selector switch by the trigger guard? Not a standard feature in the KG-99s they sell at the gun shops. Magazine capacity is 36 rounds, and the barrel is five inches and threaded for a silencer. Pretty accurate up to twenty-five yards semiauto. A bit less accuracy with full-auto, of course."

"I always figured men who like guns so much must be trying to compensate for some kind of sexual shortcoming," Bernelli muttered sourly.

"Is this bloke really with the CIA?" McCarter asked, shaking his head. "The Company ought to stop hiring psychology majors straight out of college. Whatever happened to the good old days when they recruited people from military intelligence?"

"People knowledgeable about intelligence operations are also familiar with how CIA operates," Encizo supplied the answer. The veteran of the Bay of Pigs invasion did not have a terribly high opinion of the Company. "They're too smart to get involved with an outfit that can't keep secrets worth a damn. So the CIA winds up hiring inexperienced kids out of college."

"I resent that," Bernelli said stiffly.

"Good," Encizo replied. "You were supposed to."

"Change the conversation before tempers get out of control," Katz announced. "Mr. Bernelli, you've had very little experience in field operations. You'd do well not to open your mouth about things you know so little about."

"If I'm such a rank amateur why do you want me to go with you to Luxembourg?" the case officer inquired.

"We're not all that keen on taking you," Katz said bluntly, "but you have U.S. embassy credentials and diplomatic immunity, as well as being an operative for the Company. You can save us a lot of time and red tape with transporting our weapons and equipment to Luxembourg, as well as confirming that our White House authority is valid. That should help us get cooperation from CIA personnel in Luxembourg. I'm certain they've been involved in security measures for the President while he's in Luxembourg. That's basically what we want to see them about.''

''It's a waste of time,'' Bernelli said with a sigh. ''The security will be tighter than the skin on a bongo drum. CIA, Secret Service, National Security Agency and probably NATO intelligence and Interpol will be all over the place, not to mention the Soviet security provided by KGB and GRU, as well as whatever the Luxembourgers can come up with. Since there'll be diplomats from other European countries present, they'll have security people there, too. No terrorist outfit could get even a malaria-stricken mosquito into those arms talks. It's impossible.''

''And the *Titanic* was supposed to be unsinkable and bumblebees shouldn't be able to fly,'' Calvin James commented. ''Look, we're not going to ask too much from you, man. Just shut up and come along for the ride. Okay?''

''Do I have a choice?'' Bernelli asked, clearly disgusted.

''As a matter of fact—'' Katz paused to shrug eloquently ''—no.''

6

The first view of Luxembourg for Phoenix Force was from the windows of the Italian military transport plane twenty thousand feet in the sky. The scene of miniature castles down below perched atop rocky pedestals was picturesque, especially when framed by lacy wisps of clouds like the mists of a fable.

Luxembourg appeared to be a land from another time, a fairy-tale land that recalled childhood stories and whimsical daydreams of the days of knights and their noble deeds. Even the official name of the country—the Grand Duchy of Luxembourg—seemed to label the small European nation as something from another era.

Indeed, Luxembourg's history was long and colorful. It had been a part of the Roman Empire and was later ruled by Frankish conquerors and Charlemagne. Luxembourg was officially made a duchy in 1354. For three hundred years, France, Austria and Spain took turns dominating it, until in 1815, at the end of the Napoléonic Wars, the Congress of Vienna under the king of the Netherlands established Luxembourg as a grand duchy.

Luxembourg remained under control of the Netherlands until 1867, then German forces occupied the country during both world wars. But Luxembourg survived all these turmoils and finally emerged a strong and independent nation.

The plane landed at Findel Airport. Once again, Colonel Mauser was waiting on the runway to meet some visiting VIPs. The five men of Phoenix Force and Scott Bernelli descended the ramp with their baggage. Customs inspections were waived thanks to Bernelli's diplomatic immunity and CIA connections.

Mauser introduced himself to the group. "I understand you all speak English," he began, clearly less than thrilled about the meeting. "I've also been instructed, by the prime minister himself, that I am to cooperate with you in every way. Please accompany me to the bus provided for us, where we can discuss business confidentially while we travel to a place I know."

"Thank you, Colonel," Katz replied. "Sorry about the last-minute notice, but our project is extremely important."

"So is the security we have to maintain for the President of the United States and the Soviet premier during the arms talks," Mauser stated, leading the others to the bus.

"That's why we're here," Gary Manning assured him.

"That's what they say anyway," Bernelli muttered to himself as he watched Mauser open the side door of a blue-and-white tour bus.

Mauser and the six new arrivals climbed into the vehicle and sat in the seats at the rear. Mauser spoke briefly to the driver in Letzeburgesch, the "official" national language. Although Letzeburgesch is similar to German, Katz and Manning, who were fluent in German, understood not a word Mauser said to the man at the wheel.

The bus rolled forward. Colonel Mauser glanced at the luggage carried by Phoenix Force. The big aluminum suitcases and long metal cases probably contained special equipment. Possibly weapons. He frowned, wondering just who these strangers were.

"I am curious," the colonel said. "If you gentlemen are here to help protect the President, why didn't you arrive with the other security personnel?"

"We were involved with other business in the Mediterranean," Katz answered. "Perhaps you heard about the raid on the *Sea Venus*?"

"Of course." Mauser's eyebrows rose with surprise. "You gentlemen did that? Very impressive operation. How did you manage it?"

"Rather brilliantly, I thought," McCarter said with a grin. "Maybe we'll have some time later to exchange a few war stories. Can't share many details, I'm afraid. Top secret, for your eyes only and and all that rot."

"I think I understand." Mauser laughed. "We don't get a lot of high intrigue here in Luxembourg. I sometimes wonder if there's even a need for military intelligence in this country. Not that we have much of a military. The Luxembourg army consists of less than seven hundred soldiers."

"We've reason to believe the arms talks may be in extreme danger," Manning stated. "Some information we got from interrogating the terrorists from the *Sea Venus* suggests their leader plans a major operation in Europe. We think the meeting here might be the target."

"It's a very farfetched assumption, Colonel," Bernelli declared.

"We really don't need your help explaining this," Rafael Encizo told Bernelli, glaring at the CIA agent.

"I assume this fellow isn't a regular member of your team?" Mauser remarked. He tilted his head toward Bernelli.

"We're not totally convinced he's even on our side," Calvin James muttered. "But he's right that we don't have any proof Skull plans to hit the arms talks. We figure we'd better make sure."

"No offense, gentlemen," Mauser began, "but the security precautions that have already been taken are extraordinary. Frankly, I don't see how any terrorist organization could get near the conference."

"There's always a way to attack a target if the opponents are resourceful enough and have enough manpower and expertise to carry out their plan," Katz stated. "Colonel Skull may indeed have all of the above."

"Skull? *Totenkopf?*" Mauser asked with surprise. "I thought that fellow was a myth."

"You've heard of Skull before?" Bernelli inquired, obviously startled by the officer's comment.

"I recall some rumors," Mauser confirmed. "Supposedly Sûreté had been told Skull was hired by a Palestinian group to carry out some terrorist activity against synagogues and shops and businesses run by Jews in Paris and Nice. I don't think anyone took the stories very seriously."

"But they didn't find the terrorists responsible for those incidents, did they?" Manning remarked. "Who's involved in the security for the summit conference? American Secret Service, CIA, Soviet KGB and GRU, as well as your people?"

"Of course," Mauser said with a nod. "French Sûreté and the West German BND also have some people here, along with the British SIS and representatives of the Belgian National Security Service. I'm not too certain what other secret measures the Russians may have taken. I'm sure they've got more KGB personnel in Luxembourg Ville than I'm aware of. Possibly other Communist intelligence outfits have agents here, as well. East German, Czech or perhaps Bulgarians. The Soviets don't trust us much, and I must say the feeling is mutual."

"Do you know where the President and the premier are put up during their stay in Luxembourg?" Encizo asked thoughtfully.

"Separate hotels in the capital," Mauser answered. "Soldiers will be outside the hotels, agents and security people inside. Absolutely no one will be in either building without authorization. Everyone had to pass a security clearance to even set foot in either building. I wouldn't say it would be impossible to attack one of the hotels, but it would be extremely difficult. Even if terrorists somehow launched rockets at the buildings, the odds would be one in a thousand that any VIP types would be harmed."

"I imagine the grand duke is having a reception for them at the palace, correct?" Katz commented. "But I doubt the summit conference would be held there."

"Absolutely not," Mauser confirmed. "The Soviets would never agree to that. Luxembourg is a NATO nation. That puts us on the same side of the Cold War as the Americans. Besides, the duke is clearly regarded by the Communists as an aristocrat and the oppressor of the masses. The Soviets don't want the conference to be held in the palace. It would convey the impression they were giving in too much even before the talks begin."

"Do you know where they decided to hold the meetings, or haven't they figured that out yet?" Calvin James asked.

"It would be pretty hard for them to hold the talks without agreeing to a definite site in advance," Mauser replied dryly.

"Hey, when we're talking about politics I wouldn't assume anybody involved was showing much sense about how to handle a situation," James stated. "Common sense and politics don't often go hand in hand."

"You have a point," Mauser admitted with a smile. "However, they have agreed to conduct the conference at Strassmacher Castle. I don't suppose you gentlemen are familiar with it?"

"I can't even find it on the map," Bernelli announced as he scanned a map spread across his lap.

"I'm not surprised," Mauser answered. "It isn't a tourist spot like most castles in Luxembourg. Strassmacher is private property. However, the owners agreed to lease the castle to the local canton government, which in turn has offered the castle to the duke so he can supply it for the use of the President and the premier during the conference. I'm not certain who's scratching whose back or who's really paying the bills, but they managed to work things out among the government officials involved."

"There's some logic to selecting an obscure site that isn't much known to tourists," McCarter remarked, taking a pack of Player's cigarettes from his pocket. "This might be a silly and unnecessary question, but you blokes did check for electronic listening devices, underground tunnels, secret passages and all that sinister, exotic cloak-and-dagger stuff?"

"Secret passages?" Bernelli scoffed. "I think you've seen too many old movies."

"Actually, he has a point," Mauser stated. "You see, many of the castles had secret passages in case their owners needed to escape from invading forces that managed to break in. I think most of them were largely afraid of uprisings by their own subjects. We checked for passages. There were none. No tunnels, no electronic bugs, nothing like that. But both the Americans and the Soviets will also sweep the place from top to bottom before the talks begin."

"Security sounds pretty tight," Manning said. "Maybe it's more than Skull had planned for, or he could have a different target in mind."

"Or maybe the bogey man of international terrorism doesn't even exist." Bernelli snickered. "I think this is a waste of time and an unnecessary inconvenience for Colonel Mauser."

"I'm seriously considering whether or not I could remove your vocal cords by reaching down your throat," Calvin James commented, glaring at the CIA man. "Naw, it's just a day-dream, I guess."

"Bernelli's not worth it," Katz said, dismissing the Company man with a wave of his prosthesis. The Israeli wore an artificial hand at the end of the metal limb. A pearl-gray glove covered the five-finger device to present a more lifelike impression.

The CIA officer opened his mouth as if to protest, but de-cided to close it. He realized he was just there to help Phoenix Force cut through some red tape. He was also aware that Col-onel Mauser was impressed by the five mysterious commandos.

"It's not going to do any harm if we remain in Luxembourg during the summit meeting just in case," Katz declared. "That won't cause any problems for you, Colonel?"

"Absolutely not," Mauser assured him. "I still find it dif-ficult to imagine that any terrorist group could present a gen-uine threat under these circumstances, but I agree it is best not to take any chances. Perhaps, if nothing else, this will give you an opportunity to see my country."

The bus had traveled into the heart of Luxembourg Ville, the capital city of the small European nation. The quaint story-book atmosphere was still present. Ancient stone bridges, ca-thedral steeples and castles were visible in the distance. The houses in the city resembled large cottages. Lawns were neatly clipped, the streets devoid of litter, and the air was only slightly tainted by pollution.

Yet this image of Luxembourg was somewhat deceptive, for the country was more than a relic of the past. It is one of the top-twenty steel-producing countries in the world. Mining, manufacturing and banking thrive there. The Grand Duchy of

Luxembourg uses more electricity per capita than any other nation on earth—twice as much as the United States. The people enjoy a high standard of living, a stable economy and a low crime rate.

The notion that a grand duchy would have a repressive government does not apply to Luxembourg. The constitutional monarchy, established in 1868, provides for democratic government headed by a prime minister. Several political parties are active in Luxembourg and participate in elections. Although ninety-seven percent of the population is Catholic, there is no state religion and no restrictions on the right to practice one's faith. Illiteracy is virtually unknown in Luxembourg; in fact, most citizens understand at least two languages. The leading newspapers are printed in Letzeburgesch, German and French. Luxembourg television is transmitted in several languages and seen throughout Europe.

In many ways, Katz knew, the peaceful, the fairy-tale setting of Luxembourg was genuine. But even paradise is not immune to the destructive serpents of terrorism, he mused.

THEY FOUND Strassmacher Castle located along the Alzette River, about nineteen miles south of Luxembourg Ville. Surrounded by farmland, the castle stood in quiet majesty with great stone ramparts and towers. Telephone lines extended to the spires and electricity was fed into the castle by underground cables, yet Strassmacher was still a lasting monument of a past era.

The tranquillity of the setting was drastically altered by the arrival of the world leaders and their teams of diplomats, translators and security forces. Special Agent Edward Landon of the Secret Service and a CIA case officer named Jerome Duncan were in charge of supervising the security precautions and procedures for the President. Major Andrey Yasnev of the Soviet GRU was in charge of protecting the premier. Yasnev was the huge bear of a man with a Stalin-style mustache who had deplaned with the premier at the airport. His physical appearance was intimidating even without his field grade rank in the second largest intelligence network in the world. The

American intel personnel were very uncomfortable in the presence of Major Yasnev.

Yasnev was aware of that, of course. He frequently smiled at Landon and Duncan. They were smaller than the muscular Russian hulk and appeared to be scrawny weaklings in comparison. Yasnev spoke in a deep, booming voice. He snapped orders in Russian as he detailed duties to other Soviet agents. He offered meaningless pleasantries in English, always with a cat-who-got-the-canary grin plastered across his broad Slavic face.

"The weather is nice today, is it not?" Yasnev asked Landon, a slight smirk in his tone. "I wonder if the weather is always so nice in Luxembourg. Funny little country with funny little people, don't you think? Castle is very strange place for summit meeting. I suppose they could not find any place else in this strange little place."

Without waiting for Landon to reply, Yasnev turned to head toward some of his agents and began barking more orders. Agent Landon sensed there was something sinister about Yasnev, and he mentioned his suspicion to Duncan.

"The guy's a Russian spy," the CIA officer replied with a shrug. "They all seem sinister to me. Besides, the bastard looks like a circus strongman, and he always has that shit-eating grin."

"He doesn't smile like that when he talks to the other Russians," Landon insisted. "Yasnev only smiles when he talks to us. You know what I mean. Looks at you like he's looking *through* you. Like he's got some funny secret joke that he's waiting to pull on us."

"Look, Landon," Duncan said with a sigh. "Yasnev is an asshole. So what? I figure most Russians are assholes. He's a Commie military intelligence officer, and he'd probably like to snap our necks just for being Americans, but he's not going to pull anything here. The Reds won't do anything to make themselves look bad during this summit conference. Oh, they'll probably try to plant some bugs here and there, listen in on some conversations, maybe set up a camera or two if they think they can gather any intel on us while they're here. What the hell, Landon. We'll do the same thing if we get a chance."

"We're here to protect the President, Duncan," the Secret Service agent stated.

"*You're* here to protect the President," Duncan corrected, lighting a cigarette with the glowing end of the butt of a cigarette he was about to discard. "That's what the Service does. Me? I'm with the Company, pal. We're concerned with protecting national security. We keep a lid on information we need to keep secret and try to get information from the proverbial 'other side.' The Soviets are top dog of that other side. The KGB and the GRU are here, so the CIA is here, too. We'll protect the President, of course, but that's not our primary concern."

"That's great, Duncan," Landon remarked dryly. "Well, you have fun with your listening devices, miniature cameras and whatever else you cloak-and-dagger boys like to play with. I'm going to check on the President. He ought to be ready to enter the conference room by now."

"Tell him it's clean," the CIA officer declared, puffing on his cigarette as if he were afraid it might go out. "We scanned the room for bugs and made sure it was soundproof. KGB was in there, too, and scanned, as well, but they didn't plant anything."

"Did you?" Landon inquired with a raised eyebrow.

"Didn't get the chance," Duncan replied with a shrug.

Landon happily left Duncan in the dining hall of the castle. The Service agent would have enjoyed wandering about the ancient structure on his own, but duty came before sight-seeing. He thought it a pity that the heads of state could not conduct the meeting in the dining hall. The long antique table was beautifully hand carved with intricate designs and figures in the wooden rim and thick sturdy legs. The chairs had also been handmade with equal care, although the seats and backs had been repaired with modern leather.

Landon admired other items in the halls as he moved through Strassmacher Castle. Numerous fine paintings, landscapes and portraits of the Strassmacher clan, hung on the gray stone walls. The family crest was mounted above a huge fireplace in the great hall. A large bronze shield with a boar's head between the crossed blades of twin battle-axes hung between polished brass candlesticks. Landon wondered what the castle had been like four hundred years ago. What had the Strassmacher family been like? Benevolent rulers or callous dictators?

A great stone stairway extended to the floors above, where the bedrooms and library were located. The current owners had installed bathrooms with modern plumbing and a den complete with television, stereo and video tape player. The devices of the twentieth century seemed almost obscene to Landon in that place. Of course, he would not have cared to use an outhouse in the dead of winter or to rely on candles instead of electricity and horse-drawn wagons instead of automobiles. Still, Landon wished the castle had been left as a pure, uncorrupted monument to the past. Even a government agent is entitled to some romantic fancy.

The sight of American, Soviet and Luxembourgian personnel clad in dark business suits and modern uniforms further detracted from the charm of the castle. Landon was not certain which men were CIA, KGB, diplomats or castle staff members. They all seemed to wear the same type of clothing— single-breasted dark blue suit, white or pale blue shirt, dark necktie and black shoes. Everyone had a busy air, and no one appeared interested in exchanging many words with anyone else. A great way to start an arms talk, Landon thought. Nobody is willing to talk.

The Luxembourg military personnel and the GRU officers were the only individuals in actual uniform. The Luxembourgians seemed agreeable enough. The soldiers were an open display of the host nation's concern for the safety of its guests. They obviously favored their American allies over the Soviets. Luxembourg was a small nation, but there was no doubt which side of the Cold War they supported. Many of them spoke English and engaged in friendly conversations with anyone whom they thought to be an American. However, since most KGB agents also spoke English, the troopers on occasion ended up chatting with Soviets, who patiently played along with the conversations.

The obvious presence of the GRU had surprised Landon and many others who had been exposed to similar talks in the past. Soviet leaders did not usually arrive at conference sites with personnel clad in military uniform. It was also unusual for the GRU to be in charge of security, instead of the higher-ranking and far more powerful KGB. Landon suspected that Major Yasnev was actually under command of a KGB supervisor who chose to remain unacknowledged as one of the more anonymous men running about in business suits. Perhaps the uniformed GRU agents were intended to be another example of *glasnost*. Landon wondered how much of the Soviets' new "openness" was really for appearance rather than substance.

Major Yasnev was on the landing, halfway up the stairs, discussing something with another uniformed Russian. Landon gazed up at the GRU officer, still distrustful of him. The major noticed him and nodded, once again smiling at him with insufferable smugness.

"What a bastard, huh?" a voice commented softly.

Landon turned to see a lean blond man with a scrub-brush mustache. He recognized him as one of Duncan's CIA agents, a man named Mamer. He was a relatively inexperienced young Company player, probably chosen for the assignment because he spoke Luxembourgian fluently. After his recent conversation, Landon did not feel like talking to anyone from the CIA, but anybody who thought Yasnev was a jerk could not be all bad.

"I don't know about his ancestry," Landon replied, "but that Russian gives me the creeps, too."

"They can talk about disarmament until they are blue in the face, but I say you can never trust those Commies," Mamer stated. "Does the President really believe the premier will keep his word about the arms reductions they already agreed on last year? Let alone any new so-called mutual reductions?"

"I'm afraid I really don't know the President that well," Landon answered. "He hasn't told me many of his personal opinions. Speaking of the President, I have to go to him now. Conference is scheduled to begin in just ten minutes."

"These things are generally pretty dull," Mamer said with a shrug. "The only danger anybody really faces is the risk of being bored to death."

"I hope you're right," Landon told him. "I hope everything stays nice and dull for the entire conference."

7

"Hello, Mr. President," Special Agent Landon began as he joined the cluster of diplomats and heads of state in the parade field within the heart of Strassmacher Castle. "The conference room is ready for you, sir."

The President nodded his thanks. He was not sure what Landon's name was, but he recognized the Secret Service agent. There were so many of them that trying to keep up with which name belonged to which face was virtually impossible. He also had to try to keep track of the names of various officials and diplomats at the summit conference. Of course, the President was familiar with the Soviet premier and the Russian translator who accompanied him, but most of the others were either strangers or people who had been introduced in rapid succession.

Naturally, the secretary of state was present, and the Soviet minister of foreign affairs was not a total stranger, either, although the President had not spent much time with the man when he attended the previous arms talks in Washington, D.C. The European diplomats were all relatively new faces. The President had briefly met most of them at the grand duke's reception. The British, West German, Belgian and Italian representatives seemed pleasant enough, but the Communist country delegates hovered apart from the others. The Czech, East German, Hungarian and Polish officials were obviously waiting to take their cues from the premier.

The Soviets might preach *glasnost*, but they still pulled the strings of the puppet governments in most of the East European nations. The premier preferred to be addressed as the secretary-general of the U.S.S.R., but his position in the Soviet government remained the same whatever title he used. His authority was no greater or less than that of his most recent predecessors. The politburo was still the real ruling power of the Soviet Union and, naturally, continued to call the shots for the satellite nations. The premier represented the politburo more than he did the Soviet people or his own personal views on world politics.

But the premier was more than a mouthpiece for the real power of his country. He had genuine concern for the people of the U.S.S.R. and hoped to make improvements on a system of government that had an abysmal record for human rights and freedoms for its individual citizens. He was also a tough negotiator, although a clever public-relations strategist. Nonetheless, the premier was still more agreeable to deal with than any of the previous premiers. The question posed by many in the West about his trustworthiness was something only time could answer.

Landon noticed, not for the first time, how alike the participants appeared at summit conferences. The political leaders were all middle-aged or slightly older Caucasian males, well fed and dressed. They were well educated and worldly, but to an impartial observer it seemed that they had a streak of ruthlessness that was concealed by friendly banter and less than sincere professional smiles. The security personnel were identifiable only by the facts that most were younger men and most wore an earphone with a cord extending to a suit jacket. A bulge of fabric under an arm betrayed the location of a concealed handgun here and there, but otherwise the protectors were dressed in much the same manner as the VIPs. Few of the American Secret Service and CIA agents were black or Hispanic, and even fewer Soviet KGB and GRU agents appeared to be of Tartar or Mongolian descent.

None of the uniformed GRU agents and Luxembourgian troops accompanied the group as they crossed the parade field to the ramparts at the castle's west wing. The obvious military presence was still on display as Luxembourgians patrolled the field and stood sentry duty at the stone towers that flanked the great walls of Strassmacher Castle. Yet none of the uniformed figures would escort the VIPs to the actual conference room, more for the sake of appearances than any other reason. Although the press was not allowed within the walls of the castle and even helicopter-borne reporters were forbidden to fly directly over the site, the politicians still felt a need to present pleasant images for one another.

Ceremony and public gestures seemed to be a necessary part of all such events. Landon wondered how many issues discussed at the summit had already been decided in advance. He was not knowledgeable about such matters, yet he knew negotiators from the United States and the Soviet Union had met in private to discuss the terms of the conference months ago, long before the world leaders decided on a location and a date for their meeting. Had these faceless, unappreciated negotiators also put together the actual plans for new arms agreements, which it was hoped the President and the premier would sign before leaving the castle? Were these unknown wheeler-dealers the real heroes behind whatever success emerged from summit conferences?

The collection of international diplomats and world leaders reached the rampart and moved into the conference hall. The room was less regal than the den or the dining hall Landon had admired earlier, but was certainly better from a security point of view. The stone walls were reinforced and absolutely soundproof. About ten feet of solid brick and mortar separated the conference room from the outside of the castle. No rifle-microphone or laser-vibration amplifier could intrude on the conversation within. A direct hit by a tank shell would not penetrate that rock barrier. Within the walls of Strassmacher Castle, more than a hundred armed troops and security agents were entrusted with protecting the conference. Nearly a hundred more were located on the opposite side of the wall, posted to guard the castle from any threat approaching from outside the ancient stone fortress.

Four tractor-trailer rigs were positioned outside the castle, manned by American, Soviet and European personnel. They were equipped with long-range radios, field telephones and even radar scanners. Bilingual operators were stationed at radios, ready to receive reports of approaching vehicles or aircraft spotted by observation units posted in a ten mile radius. Maps were set up to track reported intruders, determine their progress and estimate the likelihood of a real threat.

The Luxembourgian military was even prepared to supply reinforcements in case of emergency. Borders could be blocked off within minutes. Heat-seeking missiles could be fired at enemy aircraft that presented a threat. Crack commandos were on standby to assist the security forces if an unexpected riot or violent demonstration suddenly occurred at the site of the summit conference. They had carefully planned for almost anything that could jeopardize the meeting and those involved.

Almost anything.

SPECIAL AGENT LANDON stood in the archway near the conference room when he heard a buzz signal in his earphone. He told the next-highest-ranking Service man to take over. As he headed for the parade field, Landon removed a radio transceiver from his belt and switched it on.

"Hey, Landon," Duncan's voice inquired from the earphone, "you read me?"

"Yeah, I read you," Landon spoke into the mouthpiece. "Duncan, right? What's up? You Company boys find a gopher you think might be a Commie or something?"

"Gee-whiz," Duncan remarked with exaggerated surprise. "You made a joke. Isn't that clever! Seriously, we've got visitors coming. I thought you'd like to know."

"Okay," Landon replied. "Where are you?"

"West wing by the staircase. I've got Major Yasnev with me, so don't get uptight when you see him. Okay?"

"Sure," Landon said with a sigh. "What could be more fun than chitchatting with you guys? I'll be there PDQ. Over and out."

Landon walked briskly, but not so quickly as to attract attention as he headed for the east wing. The Service man had to show his ID to a pair of zealous Luxembourgian troopers before they would allow him to enter the section. Landon finally found Duncan and Major Yasnev by the stairs in the great hall.

"Glad you could make it," Duncan said dryly. "You remember Major Yasnev?"

"Oh, yeah," Landon assured him, giving a quick nod at the GRU commander. "Now, what's this about visitors?"

"Colonel Mauser, the Luxembourgian intel boss, is on his way here with those five hotshot mystery men from the States," Duncan answered. "The ones with the special authorization from the President."

"I was sort of hoping they wouldn't make it," Landon admitted. "Whoever they are, they've got top authorization right out of the Oval Office. They can take over the whole operation if they want, and the President would give them his blessing to do it."

"You've got to be kidding!" Duncan snorted, then lit another cigarette. "They can take command from us and start running this show? Well, they can kiss my ass, too. We know what's going on here and they don't. By the way, a Company guy is with them. Case officer from another branch office. I'll have a talk with him and try to find out more about what the hell is going on here."

"Strange things happen in this business," Yasnev commented with a smug smile. "You forgot to mention our radio and radar equipment, Duncan."

"I was coming to that," Duncan assured him. "That's the other reason I called you. Major Yasnev tells me the GRU radio and tracking equipment they brought out here has malfunctioned, so he's got two tractor trailer rigs full of stuff headed for the castle."

"Wait a minute," Landon began, glaring at Yasnev. "This is pretty damn sudden. You're talking about bringing in two eighteen-wheelers loaded with tons of equipment that none of us have had a chance to inspect. Why can't you use some of the other radios and trackers that are already here? For crissake, we've got four rigs here already."

"That's true," Yasnev agreed. "But only three are loaded with functional equipment, and those are handled by you Americans and Europeans from NATO countries. To maintain security for the Soviet officials, I must insist Soviet technicians using our own equipment be present. I have inspected the equipment in advance and arranged for an emergency backup unit in case what we brought here malfunctioned. I suspected this might happen. Sadly, our Russian computers are not as reliable as those used by you Americans. Maybe we will catch up after we improve relations with Japan, eh?''

''Duncan?'' Landon asked, turning to the CIA agent for support.

''I don't like it, either,'' Duncan answered with a shrug. ''But this is a joint effort. We're supposed to be cooperating with each other during the summit meeting, the way you Secret Service people cooperated with the KGB when the premier visited Washington, D.C., for the meeting a while back.''

''Yeah, I was there at the time,'' Landon replied. ''KGB didn't pull anything like this. The wonderful secretary-general did that cute stunt on the street when he had his driver stop his Zim so he could run over to the crowd and shake hands like he thought he was running for office in the U.S. Good public-relations trick, clever way to get good press coverage, but it sure was a pain in the ass from a security point of view. If this is another publicity stunt, like hauling out a bus load of people to stand here and cheer when the VIPs come out so the premier can act like Santa Claus in the Macy's parade, you can forget it right now, Major. Better not be any reporters and cameramen inside those rigs, either, or you can just send them right back to Luxembourg Ville.''

''Your suspicions are amusing, Mr. Landon,'' Yasnev said with a smile. ''If you wish, you may accompany me to inspect the equipment in person when the trucks arrive. Is that not reasonable?''

''I've got to get back to the conference room,'' Landon replied. ''But I want some of my people to check inside those trailers before you park 'em here.''

''I have no objections to that,'' the GRU officer assured him. ''We all need a bit more trust in one another if we are to bring the Cold War to an end. Is this not true?''

''Hell, I'll help check it out myself,'' Duncan declared. ''I'll take Mamer along, too, in case we need somebody to translate the local dialect. Seems to me every Luxembourgian in the country speaks French, German or English anyway, but Mamer might still be useful before this blasted circus is over.''

"Okay," Landon agreed. "But I'm going to assign two of my people to it, anyway. As for you, Major, when your government tears down the Berlin Wall, that's when I'll believe the Cold War can come to an end."

Landon turned on his heel and headed back to the parade field. Yasnev watched him depart, then shook his head and smiled.

"He is hostile, that one," the major remarked.

"Maybe," Duncan replied, tossing his cigarette butt to the floor and crushing it under his heel. "But he's right about a couple of things. Bringing in two big trucks loaded with equipment we didn't know anything about isn't playing by the rules, Major. That's the kind of surprise that makes any intel guy uptight and a little worried. I'm not too thrilled about this, either, pal. I just hope you comrades don't have any more surprises lined up for us."

Major Yasnev looked at Duncan, smiled broadly and walked away. Duncan went to join the others—Duncan, Yasnev, Mamer and two Secret Service agents—outside, and less than five minutes later the two rigs arrived. The soldiers had been told to allow the rigs into the restricted area despite the fact the drivers could not show any authorization. They knew Major Yasnev by name and showed proof that he had in fact contracted their services in advance with the understanding that they would only be ordered to deliver the merchandise in an emergency.

The guards waved the trucks through, and both vehicles came to a halt near the already parked trailer rigs. A man dressed in gray coveralls emerged from the cab of one of the tractor rigs. He tugged on the brim of his cloth cap with one hand and carried a clipboard in the other.

"Bonjour, monsieur," he said to Yasnev.

"These gentlemen are Americans, *monsieur*," the GRU officer replied. "We should speak English so they understand."

"Yes," the man agreed with a nod. "I did not mean to be rude, gentlemen. My English is not very good, but I try very much to be more good at it. Yes?"

"I admire your efforts," Duncan declared. "We've got to check in the back of both these trailers before you can drop these units. You know this place is off limits to the public?"

"Yes, this I know," the workman confirmed with a nod. "But Monsieur Yasnev has the combination of numbers needed to unlock the doors. He must unlock the doors because I do not know the numbers."

"You didn't tell us you had the combination to the locks on the doors, Major," Duncan told Yasnev. "When the hell did you manage all this? You must have made some pretty quick arrangements here, considering the fact you arrived on the same plane with the premier...."

"I made many of these arrangements last week when I came to Luxembourg with some comrades to make special preparations before the meeting," Yasnev explained as he moved to the rear of the trailer. "You see something wrong with that, Mr. Duncan?"

"I just don't like these surprises, Major," the CIA man answered. "Never mind. Let's just get these things open so we can take a look inside and decide whether or not to let these rigs stay here."

"Of course," Yasnev said with a grin. "I do it in the spirit of *glasnost*, eh?"

The GRU officer reached for the combination lock on the right-hand door. Duncan noticed that the big metal doors had been custom-made and the dial to the lock was built into the door. It was not just an ordinary padlock that Yasnev had snapped onto the doors when he rented the trailer. The thing was built like a bank vault. One would probably have to use dynamite to force the doors open.

"Nice setup, huh?" Agent Mamer commented as he watched Yasnev turn the combination dial to the lock. "I bet this sucker cost you a few rubles."

"Not from my salary," Yasnev answered. "There. It is opened now."

The Russian pulled the right-hand door open, and Mamer grabbed the handle to the other door and pulled it back, as well. Duncan stared up at the black cloth curtain that covered the

mouth of the trailer and concealed whatever was inside. The
CIA case officer groaned with annoyance.

"I'll check it out, sir," Mamer volunteered as he started to
climb into the trailer. "Does one of your Secret Service
specialists want to check this out, too? Got to report back to
Landon one way or the other, man."

"Okay," one of the Service agents agreed, and followed
Mamer inside.

Mamer yanked back the curtain, but it was bolted at the
bottom and top. He managed to pull open a space along the
side and slithered inside. The Secret Service agent followed his
example, and both men disappeared from Duncan's view. The
CIA case officer felt the hairs on the back of his neck stiffen
along with an icy shiver that raced along his spine. Duncan's
long-neglected instincts signaled danger.

"What the hell is this, Yasnev?" he demanded as he turned
to glare at the Russian agent and opened his jacket to make
room to draw his pistol.

"I don't know what you mean," Major Yasnev replied with
raised eyebrows, his hands extended, the palms held up in a
gesture of helplessness.

Bullshit, Duncan thought. The big muscle-bound Russian
was about as helpless as a hungry grizzly bear and as clever as
a fox. Something was wrong about the whole damn business
with Yasnev and his goddamn trucks....

"Duncan?" Agent Mamer began as he stuck his head out
from behind the curtain. "I think you might want to take a look
at this for yourself."

Duncan sighed with relief when he saw that Mamer was all
right. Whatever was behind the curtain, it had not swallowed
up the CIA agent. Duncan naturally assumed the Secret Service agent who had accompanied Mamer was also unharmed.
He glanced at Yasnev. The Russian simply smiled and
shrugged.

"Uh, sir?" Mamer continued. "I really think you ought to
see this before you let the Russians set up here."

"Okay," Duncan agreed, throwing a sneer at Yasnev. "I'll
take a look. If I find anything that looks even slightly suspi-

cious, you'd better have some good answers to any questions that come up, Major.''

"Oh, I promise," Yasnev assured him.

Duncan climbed into the back of the trailer. Mamer again disappeared behind the black curtain. Duncan grunted, grabbed the apron of the heavy black veil and pulled. It would not move far. The bolts were solid and held it fast. Yet the Company case officer still opened a wide enough gap to slip through.

"Can you make it, sir?" Mamer's voice inquired.

The interior was dark, almost pitch-black. Duncan's eyes started to adjust just a little bit to the shadows, and he saw the shapes of dozens of figures standing within the long trailer section of the rig. He felt their presence more than he saw them. He also felt something with the tip of his shoe. Something sprawled on the floor of the trailer. Something warm and soft and . . . squishy.

Oh, God! Duncan thought with astonishment. It's a body!

"Fuck you, sir," Mamer whispered, inches from Duncan's ear.

The CIA case officer opened his mouth to scream a warning to the others outside, but a hard metal object suddenly jammed into the side of his skull. Duncan realized Mamer had hit him with something. Mamer! It was really Mamer, not one of the mystery figures inside the trailer. In a fragment of a second Duncan understood that Mamer had sold him out. In that split second it also dawned on him that the body at his feet belonged to the Secret Service agent who had followed Mamer inside the truck.

The explosion within his own head proved Duncan was right. A steel projectile burst through bone, cracking his skull like an eggshell. The deadly intruder sliced into Duncan's brain. The case officer still could not scream. A terrible instant of blinding, mind-shattering agony ended in the final black void of oblivion.

"I kind of enjoyed that one," Mamer whispered as he lowered Duncan's corpse to the floor and placed it beside the body of the slain Service agent.

Major Yasnev, the other Secret Service agent and the French-speaking workman stood waiting for a response from within the trailer. Yasnev sighed and started to climb into the back of the rig.

"Just a minute, Major," the Service agent began nervously. He reached for the radio attached to his belt. "I think you'd better wait—"

"You come with me," Yasnev replied as he swiftly reached down and grabbed the American by the lapel of his suit jacket.

The powerful Russian pulled with only one hand, yet he easily hauled the smaller man off his feet and lifted him up. The Secret Service agent gasped, disoriented by the sudden, abrupt action and the astonishment of being manhandled so easily by the Soviet muscle man.

Yasnev shoved his captive into the gap in the curtain. Hands seized the Secret Service man and pulled him inside. The agent forgot his radio and reached for his gun instead. Strong fingers locked around his wrist and prevented him from drawing the pistol from leather. He recognized Mamer's face despite the darkness. The CIA agent stood directly in front of him, their noses almost touching.

Mamer's hand descended, something that looked like a large metal pen clenched in the fist. The device was called a Double-L weapon in the trade, a special weapons gizmo for assassination. The "pen" fired on contact with the Service man's forehead. A steel needle pierced the man's skull. The weapon was "Double-L"—double lethal—because it delivered a deadly metal projectile and an equally lethal dose of cyanide poison. The result was virtually instant destruction of the man's brain.

"Very nice work so far," Yasnev whispered to Mamer.

"Thank you, Comrade," Mamer replied with a soft chuckle.

The two tractor trailer rigs pulled into a space between two others already parked outside the castle. Doors to the cabs opened. Uniformed figures emerged from the tractor cabs quietly and unnoticed. The other trailers effectively concealed the clandestine arrival of dozens of men clad in Luxembourgian and Russian uniforms. They filed out from a compartment linking the trailer section with the tractor. The soldiers calmly dispersed and slowly mingled with other troops in the area.

More people stepped from the truck cabs, like clowns in a trick circus car. Men dressed in dark suits, white shirts and ties. They were outfitted with earphones, and had no problem blending in with the security forces. The teams separated and moved toward the real security units. Men in Russian uniforms avoided the groups of real Soviet troops because the soldiers would certainly recognize a new face among their own ranks. Those clad in Luxembourgian uniforms followed the same rule and steered clear of the real troops of the host country. The men in suits had more variety in movement. So many intel agents, diplomats and security personnel were dressed in that manner that it was far more difficult to tell who was working for whom.

Major Yasnev and Agent Mamer easily entered the castle with four companions dressed in suits and three in Russian uniforms. They marched into the great hall, then separated into groups. Some headed upstairs or moved into other rooms within that wing of Strassmacher Castle. Two "Soviet soldiers" followed Yasnev and Mamer to the parade field.

Special Agent Landon saw them approach the conference hall. The Secret Service agent glanced at the two other Feds and three KGB agents who were posted outside the maximum-security meeting site. The Russians shrugged. The highest-ranking KGB officer stepped forward.

"Do not look at me in such a manner, Mr. Landon," the Russian insisted. "I do not know what Major Yasnev is doing any more than you do."

"Jesus," Landon muttered sourly.

Yasnev smiled broadly and walked forward to meet Landon and the KGB agent. Mamer stood behind the big GRU officer while the men in Soviet uniforms stood by with AK-47 assault rifles slung over their shoulders. Landon shook his head. Yasnev and his troopers were not assigned to that section of the castle, but he figured he would let the KGB man chew out Yasnev's arrogant butt.

"Everything is all right now," Yasnev announced. "Your men and Mr. Duncan inspected the trucks and had no complaints about what they found. Ask Mr. Mamer if you do not believe me."

"I'll call my people, if you don't mind," Landon replied, reaching for his radio. "They should have already reported back to me."

"There have been some radio problems because of the static created by the frequencies used by those big transceivers outside," Mamer stated.

"Comrade Yasnev," the KGB agent began grimly. "I'm afraid you have no authorization to be in this area. I am also not aware of any authorization to bring any vehicles or equipment to the castle site that has not already been put in place...."

Yasnev assumed a reassuring look. "It is not a problem for you to worry about. I do outrank you, *da*?"

"We are not discussing your rank, Major," the KGB agent replied stiffly. "Besides, KGB always has authorization above GRU."

"I don't like any of this," Landon declared, holding the radio transceiver in his fist. "I haven't been able to reach my men. I'm not just getting static. It's a high-pitched whine. Sounds like some sort of radio frequency jamming device."

"Oh, I don't think that's it," Mamer told him.

"Where the hell is Duncan?" Landon demanded, switching off his radio. "And where are the two men I sent with you?"

"They're still outside in one of the trailers," Yasnev answered with a slight laugh. "They were just dying to get a better look."

"I want a straight answer..." Landon began.

Suddenly, the unexpected roar of an explosion outside the castle walls startled Landon and cut his remark short. Other explosions followed in rapid succession. Some were within the Strassmacher Castle grounds while others occurred outside. Screams seemed to follow each explosion. Glass burst from windows, and flames shot out from the shattered openings. The reports of rifle shots were nearly drowned out by the explosions. Sentries in towers above the parade field suddenly collapsed with bullet holes in their heads.

Without warning, Yasnev swung a vicious uppercut to the KGB agent's jaw. His big fist smashed under the other Russian's jaw and slammed his teeth together hard. The blow lifted the KGB man off his feet and dumped him on the cobblestone pavement.

Landon was astonished and confused. He instinctively reached for his gun. Yasnev's left fist plowed into the chest of the Secret Service agent. Landon received the painful blow under the breastbone. He gasped and doubled up from the punch, badly winded and half paralyzed by the jarring force to his solar plexus. Yasnev's right hand swooped down, and he chopped the bottom of his fist across Landon's nape. The Service man's eyes filled with white light and his skull seemed to explode. Landon fell to all fours near Yasnev's feet.

The other Secret Service agents and KGB operatives were stunned by the sudden outbreak of violence all around them in general and by Yasnev's unprovoked attack in particular. None of them realized that the gunmen with Yasnev had pointed their Kalashnikovs at the security team until it was too late. The assault rifles snarled and blasted the American and Soviet protectors with merciless salvos of 7.62 mm slugs.

Bodies fell in a cluster of bleeding mounds near the thick metal doors of the conference hall. Mamer drew a .45 Colt pistol and calmly fired a single shot into the horrified face of the KGB man who sat on the ground before him. The two fake Russian troopers rushed to the doors and quickly removed packets of plastic explosives from the pouches on their belts.

Landon shook his head and tried to clear it before he attempted to rise. Yasnev suddenly grabbed him by the hair and yanked his head back. The big Russian wrapped a brawny arm around Landon's neck as he abruptly yanked the Service man to his feet.

Yasnev violently jerked his arms in opposite directions.

Landon's head was twisted forcibly and vertebrae cracked in protest. The Secret Service agent heard bone snap, felt the awesome pain and vaguely realized his spinal cord had been severed by bone splinters at the base of his skull. He knew he was dead a shred of a second before his brain ceased to function. Special Agent Landon's final thought was one of utter amazement.

The plastic explosives charges planted by the doors erupted with subdued fury. The blasts were not loaded with large portions of high explosives, but only enough to destroy the locks and hinges. The doors fell from the stone archway. Inside the conference room, the President of the United States, the Soviet premier, five officials from NATO countries and other participants in the summit talks stared into the muzzles of the gunmen's rifles.

Yasnev grinned as he drew his Makarov pistol from the holster on his belt. He stepped across the threshold and pointed his side arm directly at the chest of the American President.

"Your plans have been changed, gentlemen," Yasnev declared. "You are now our prisoners."

The President turned to face the Soviet premier, who shook his head and ordered his translator to explain that this was not something his government had arranged.

Yasnev kept his pistol trained on the President with one hand and tossed his service cap away with the other. A rifleman stepped forward and handed Yasnev a black beret, which the big Russian pulled onto his head. The President then noticed Mamer and the two gunmen had donned the same sort of headgear—a black beret with a white skull emblem.

"And may I ask just who has taken us prisoner?" the American leader inquired.

"Of course," Yasnev replied cheerfully. "The professional terrorist mercenary army of Colonel Skull."

8

The tour bus with the men of Phoenix Force, Colonel Mauser and Scott Bernelli had stopped at another roadblock along the way to Strassmacher Castle when the men in the bus heard the thunder of explosions and saw columns of black smoke drift from above the towers of the castle less than two miles away.

"Oh, my God!" Bernelli exclaimed, staring at the castle with astonishment. "This can't be happening!"

"Then we're all seeing the same mirage," Gary Manning said with annoyance. The Canadian was sick of listening to the young CIA agent's snotty remarks. "That sounds like separate charges, strategically placed for specific effects. In other words, the explosives are probably being used to take out certain targets without blowing the castle apart."

"Son of a bitch," Calvin James rasped, frustrated that they were close enough to see and hear the results of terrorism, yet not close enough to do anything about it. "We've got to get down there, damn it!"

"Bloody right," McCarter agreed, fists clenched in helpless rage. "Whatever Skull has planned, it's happening now."

"I know, I know," Mauser replied. His head bobbed nervously with each word. Terrorism was a new experience for the Luxembourgian officer, and he really was not prepared for the reality of the situation. "The troops at the blockade will radio ahead to clear us through the next roadblock. We'll be there as fast as this bus will allow."

"That may not be fast enough," Rafael Encizo said grimly. "If they planned one or more assassinations, they've probably already killed their victims by now."

"So we'll make sure they don't escape," Yakov Katzenelenbogen stated firmly. "What's done is done, and all we can do is handle the situation the way it is now, not the way it was five minutes ago. Mauser, tell your driver to make this bus move as if it was jet-propelled. Let's get our gear out. The fireworks have started without us, but that doesn't mean they're over yet."

The bus bolted across the road. Clouds of dust rose up from the tires as the speeding vehicle rushed toward Strassmacher Castle. Inside the bus, Phoenix Force had opened their aluminum luggage and cases. Mauser and Bernelli watched as the five commandos unloaded the tools of their trade.

Katz removed his jacket. He wore a gray turtleneck shirt with a shoulder holster rig complete with SIG-Sauer pistol in leather under his right arm. The Israeli removed an Uzi submachine gun from a case and slid a magazine into the metal well, then strapped a utility belt around his waist with ammo pouches already in place. He pulled off his black dress loafers and slid on a pair of canvas boots with rubber soles—Israeli paratrooper boots.

"Do you need any help with those laces?" Bernelli inquired, aware Katz had only one arm.

"I can manage," the Phoenix commando replied. "If you want to make yourself useful, check our walkie-talkies to make certain they all work and the frequency is set the same for each radio."

Gary Manning opened a rifle case to remove a FAL assault rifle with a Bushnell scope already mounted on the weapon. He raised the buttstock as he aimed the rifle and peered through the telescopic sights as he aimed the rifle at a window. The gun was empty, but Manning never neglected fundamental firearm safety. Satisfied that the scope did not need adjustments, the Canadian loaded a magazine into the rifle and chambered a round.

"Silencers?" Manning inquired, switching on the safety catch before he placed the rifle on the seat next to him and started to slip out of his jacket.

"We might need them," Katz replied. "If we don't, we can remove them when we reach the castle."

David McCarter had already attached a foot-long silencer to the threaded barrel of his KG-99 subgun. He removed his jacket now and patted the familiar Pacmyer grips of his Browning Hi-Power under his left arm. After buckling on a utility belt with extra magazines for both weapons, he opened another case, which contained a Barnett Commando crossbow with a leather quiver and strap and half a dozen bolts.

"Good grief," Bernelli exclaimed with surprise as he stared down at the unorthodox weapon. "What do you plan to do with that?"

"I strum the bowstring while I whistle the 'William Tell Overture,'" the British ace snorted. "What the hell do you think?"

The Barnett Commando model was a high-tech version of a centuries-old design. The crossbow had a skeletal metal stock and a cocking lever to enable one to cock the bow, reload and fire far faster than was possible with conventional crossbows. Mounted on the bow was a telescopic sight.

"I'm surprised people of your caliber would still use something like that," the CIA agent remarked. "I thought those things went out with flintlocks and tomahawks."

"Think again," McCarter told him as he carefully slid the bolts into the scabbard of the quiver. "A crossbow is as accurate as a rifle and a lot quieter than even the best silenced firearm. No muzzle-flash to give away one's position in the dark, either."

"But I thought arrows lacked the knockdown power of a bullet," Bernelli remarked.

"I'll be damned," Rafael Encizo said as he began to tie the laces of his combat boots. "You must have read something other than Company public relations pamphlets, after all."

Bernelli glared at the Cuban, but did not reply to the gibe. After being so smug about the impossibility of terrorism at the conference, the young case officer figured he did not have any right to object to Encizo's comment.

He noticed the hilt of a knife at the top of Encizo's boot. The sheath was inside the boot and held in place by a metal clip. Bernelli did not realize the knife handle was made of cast aluminum or that it was fashioned in the style of a fencing foil.

Encizo had carried such a knife for years. It was a Gerber Mark I fighting dagger with a five-inch double-edged steel blade.

The Cuban's Cold Steel Tanto was also sheathed in a belt scabbard in a cross-draw position. In addition, he carried a Heckler & Koch P-9S 9 mm autopistol on his hip and a Walther PPK in shoulder leather for backup. Propped against the seat beside him he also had an H&K MP-5 machine pistol with an extended magazine and a silencer attached. The Cuban veteran did not believe there was such a thing as being too well prepared for combat.

"Actually," McCarter remarked as he took the Barnett Commando model from its case, "a crossbow fires bolts or quarrels, not arrows. Now, these bolts have steel tips, and the projectile will penetrate with considerable force up to two hundred yards. You're right about the lack of knockdown power compared to a rifle slug from a large-caliber weapon, but these bolts kill almost instantly. The fiberglass shafts are hollow and contain enough cyanide to kill a Cape buffalo. If I can score a direct hit in the upper torso, back or anywhere in the neck or head, the bloke won't live long enough to even cry 'ouch.' "

"Hang around us long enough you learn all kinds of stuff, huh?" Calvin James commented as he assembled an M-16 assault rifle.

The black warrior attached an M-203 grenade launcher to the barrel's underside. The launcher would serve as a forward stock when the rifle was fired and could also be triggered to propel 40 mm cartridge-style grenades. James had shells for the M-203 in a pouch on his belt, as well as spare magazines for the 5.56 mm rifle and his Beretta pistol holstered under his left arm.

The Jet-Aer G-96 fighting dagger was clipped to the Jackass Leather rig under James's right arm. He also carried his everpresent medic kit at the small of his back. James had removed his dress shirt and wore a black T-shirt with matching trousers and boots. To complete his combat attire he slipped into a black field jacket with plenty of pockets.

"We're almost there," he remarked, screwing a silencer into the threaded muzzle of his M-16 as he glanced out the nearest window. Strassmacher Castle was getting closer by the second.

"I noticed that, too," Manning declared as he slipped into a backpack and adjusted it between his shoulder blades. The Canadian had donned a dark green field jacket and slid a number of pencil detonators and fuses into the pockets. "Where the hell is the grenade case?"

"You didn't pack the grenades?" McCarter asked with mock horror. "I thought you brought them along with the bloody tea set. Next you'll tell us you forgot the crumpets and digestive biscuits."

"Oh, that's cute, David," Manning muttered. He sorted through the remaining luggage to search for the case. "We're charging into the figurative jaws of death and you're helping to ease the tension by being a smart ass. How droll."

"What the hell are digestive biscuits?" James wondered out loud as he stood up and checked his gear one more time. "Some kind of cookies, right? Sounds like something you threw up."

"In England they don't know the difference," Manning said dryly. The Canadian had located the grenade case and opened it. "What can you expect from people who like warm beer? I've got the grenades—M-26 fragmentation, SAS flash-bang concussion, a couple of tear gas canisters and three smoke grenades."

"I got fraggers and tear gas shells for the 203," James stated. "Guess I'll take a couple of concussion grenades and maybe an M-26 just in case."

"What about Mr. Bernelli and I?" Colonel Mauser inquired. "Shouldn't we arm ourselves with more than our service pistols?"

"I'm not carrying a gun," Bernelli admitted sheepishly. "I've never cared much for them, but I'll—"

"You're not trained for this sort of thing, Bernelli," Katz told him in a firm voice. "This is no time for a crash course in antiterrorist combat tactics. Colonel Mauser, I think you'll be more good to us if you stay with your troops and concentrate on commanding them rather than getting personally involved in the fighting. No offense intended, but I think you'd help us more if you were handling the Luxembourgian soldiers from the sidelines than in the actual field of fire."

"I suppose you're right," Mauser admitted with a sigh. "You fellows have a lot more experience at this sort of thing than I do."

"It's pretty quiet out there," Encizo remarked as he added some grenades to his arsenal. "Everybody's standing around staring at the castle. Whatever's going on, it's already making my stomach knot up."

The other men of Phoenix Force understood what their Cuban teammate meant. More than a hundred security personnel were standing outside Strassmacher Castle and slowly backing away from the tractor trailer rigs parked near the entrance. The forest of soldiers and agents blocked the view, and Phoenix Force could not see what had convinced the summit security forces to back down.

"Oh, hell," James rasped. "Something really nasty is coming down."

The bus shrieked to a stop, brakes and tires protesting the abrupt halt. Heads turned toward the vehicle. A voice shouted, *"Wer ist da?"* and an assortment of Luxembourgian soldiers, Secret Service agents and KGB men rushed to the bus. They waved their hands in a frantic manner, their faces filled with desperation. Colonel Mauser unlatched his door. His fellow countrymen certainly recognized the field grade officer's rank but none came to attention or saluted.

"What are you doing?" Mauser demanded. "What is happening?"

"Colonel," a Service agent began. "We have a very critical situation here. I strongly advise you to leave."

Yakov Katzenelenbogen appeared next to Mauser. The Uzi hung from a shoulder strap by his left hand. A black field jacket concealed his shoulder holster rig, but the ammo pouches on his belt were still visible. The security personnel groaned when they saw the heavily armed Israeli.

"We do not need more guns here," a KGB agent declared in heavily accented English. "Shooting will only get us all killed."

"Tell me what this is about!" Katz snapped as he moved into the crowd.

"Who the hell are you?" a voice asked. "American? Russian? What?"

Katz ignored him and slowly moved through the mob of disoriented and frightened security forces. He finally managed to get close enough to the trailers to see what had caused near panic among so many professionals.

Several men stood by the rear of an open trailer, some in the uniform of the host country and others in Soviet outfits. They displayed an assortment of weapons, mostly of Soviet, Czech, Belgian or West German manufacture. All wore black berets with white skull emblems.

Major Martin Koerner was clad in a dress-blue Luxembourgian army uniform, complete with gold trimmings and field grade insignia. On his hips was a long pistol holster, and a radio transmitter, about twice the size of a pack of cigarettes, was in his hand. Next to the ex-Nazi was a bulky gray metal object that resembled a fire hydrant. It was braced on the steel rails of a forklift.

"New arrivals in the bus?" Koerner called out. "I don't care to repeat myself, but I'll explain this once more in English since most of you seem to understand it. At any rate, make sure they comprehend my meaning, or you can all anticipate going into oblivion in the form of a mushroom cloud."

Koerner raised his arm to make sure that everyone would see the transmitter in his hand. The terrorist subleader glimpsed Katz among the crowd. He noticed that the new arrival appeared to be older than the majority of the security personnel. Possibly a minor diplomat or aide, Koerner thought, failing to see Katz's Uzi because his view was obstructed.

"The device next to me is a bomb," Koerner declared. "It is a fairly primitive nuclear device, considering the state-of-the-art missiles and such they make these days. The bomb is a simple fission-system reactor, loaded with approximately six kilos of plutonium. It is sealed inside a lead reactor vessel and safely surrounded with lead and steel. The men who made this device are experts in such matters, and I assure you that this bomb is real and it will explode if I press this button."

Koerner's thumb was poised over a red button on the transmitter in his hand.

"This little remote control device will detonate an explosive inside the bomb," Koerner continued. "The radio signal will trigger the blast and start a chain reaction within the nuclear core. The plutonium will reach critical mass level and the explosion that follows will destroy virtually everything within one and a half to two kilometers in every direction. We'll be lucky, of course. Vaporized instantly. Others, perhaps more than a hundred kilometers away, will suffer the effects of fallout. Radiation sickness is a very ugly, slow and painful way to die. Depending on how the winds blow, clouds of plutonium dust could travel to Luxembourg Ville, or across the border to France, Germany or Belgium. Hundreds, probably thousands, will die."

The ex-Nazi lowered his arm and smiled.

"If any of you think you can simply have a marksman put a bullet between my eyes," Koerner continued, "then I warn you that three of my comrades are also armed with identical radio transmitters. They can detonate the nuclear weapon if I am killed. Stay back and follow orders. Failure to meet any of our demands will mean destruction for everyone here and tragedy and agonizing death for countless innocent people. Their lives mean nothing to us, and we are prepared to sacrifice our own lives to carry out this mission."

"I don't think you have to worry about whether or not you'll be taken seriously," Yakov Katzenelenbogen called out from the crowd. "What are your demands and what do you want with the President and the Soviet secretary-general?"

"You sound like you're accustomed to giving orders," Koerner commented, suddenly more interested in Katz than he had been before. "Good. Most men accustomed to giving orders also recognize when they must be followed. Our demands for now are quite simple. Three helicopters will be arriving soon. We'll be leaving in them. We've already taken over your communications here and sent out a warning to the military bases set up in the area. Americans and Russians are to contact their people as well and order them to make no attempt to stop us. We demand that you order the governments of France, West Germany and Belgium to allow the aircraft to cross their borders and land unmolested. Let them know that one of the aircraft will contain the nuclear device. Any attempt to shoot down one of our helicopters will be followed by very grave and terrifying consequences. Is that understood?''

"Everybody understands," Katz assured him. "Colonel Mauser, I think you ought to provide information about some of the problems involved in authorizing the helicopters to fly in a restricted area and then to cross the borders of other countries without proper clearance."

"Oh, of course, Mr. Kenver," Mauser replied as he moved to the front of the crowd. The colonel realized Katz wanted him to give the terrorists as much double-talk and complex bullshit as possible to stall for time. "You must realize it won't be easy to get the sort of cooperation you'll need for your purposes. The French, German and Belgian governments aren't going to jump up and follow orders regardless of what we ask."

"Tell them if they shoot down one of our helicopters there will be a one-in-three chance they will detonate a nuclear explosion over their territory," Koerner snapped. "You must convince them to cooperate. Otherwise, thousands of innocent people will die. So will the President of the United States and the Soviet secretary-general. In their case, I don't know if one could say they were innocent or not."

"What do you want with them?" Mauser asked. "If we knew what you wanted, we might be able to negotiate—"

"You'll know what we want you to know when we want you to know it," Koerner told him. "Don't try any games with us. We're holding all the cards. Even if you kill us, we'll win. Actually, the terms will not be unreasonable and may even appeal to your governments when we're prepared to present them. For now, you need only know that failure to obey our instructions will result in disaster."

Katz headed back to the tour bus to join the other members of Phoenix Force. He found Bernelli involved in a conversation with three other CIA officers. Several Secret Service and KGB agents were arguing with one another while at the same time trying to get information from Phoenix Force.

"We haven't been able to learn much," Rafael Encizo told Katz. "Apparently the terrorists arrived in two large trucks— two trailers loaded with Skull's men. A GRU officer in charge of Soviet security—Major Yasnev—actually authorized the

vehicles' entry. It seems he is in on this scheme with the terrorists, who were disguised as soldiers and KGB, CIA and Secret
Service. Nobody had any idea that something was wrong until
all hell broke loose."

"They took out all the communications," Gary Manning
added. "Blasted the hell out of everything except one trailer
filled with American security people. They gunned those fellows down with silenced weapons and took over the radios
themselves. The bastards also got to the conference room,
murdered the agents there and got to the VIPs inside. As far as
we know, the President, the premier and the others haven't been
harmed. Not yet, anyway."

"Do you Americans think we're fools?" A Soviet agent demanded. "This is all the work of the capitalist conspiracy
headed by the United States!"

"Bullshit, Vashnov!" a Secret Service agent replied. "Yasnev was part of this. Remember? A lot of our people have been
killed, including Landon and Duncan. If anybody deserved to
be suspected of working with these terrorists, it would be you
Reds. You guys are so used to killing your own people back in
Russia you wouldn't object to wasting a few of your own here."

"That's ridiculous," Vashnov said as he whirled to face
Phoenix Force. "What are these men doing here? Who are
they? They show up from nowhere, armed to the teeth and
giving orders—"

"We've got only one order for you, pal," Calvin James declared. "Back off and keep out of our way."

The KGB agent glared at James. "And what do you intend
to do about this situation . . . boy?"

James met his gaze without blinking. The Russian was nearly
as tall as James, and his broad Slavic face was filled with outrage. His dark eyes burned with unreasonable fury and his lips
twisted into a challenging sneer. Vashnov did not simply distrust Americans, he hated them. He was also a racist and clearly
did not intend to take any guff from a black man.

"We don't have time for this crap," James said with a sigh.
"You think what you want to think . . . or get as close to thinking as you can manage. Just don't get in the way."

"Since my superior officer is dead and Yasnev is inside the castle with the terrorists," Vashnov began as his chest puffed out like a pigeon's at mating time, "I am now in charge of all Soviet intelligence matters at this time."

"Lucky you," a short, heavyset man with a Texas accent remarked as he stepped around Vashnov to extend a hand to the Phoenix leader. "The name's Walters. I'm with the Company. Bernelli tells me you have White House authority. Reckon that puts you in charge."

"Pleased to meet you, Mr. Walters," Katz replied, extending his left hand to the Texan. "Did Bernelli tell you about Colonel Skull?"

"Yeah," the CIA agent confirmed. "I find that story sort of hard to swallow, but then what's happened here seems incredible to me. Never figured something like this would happen. You people have any ideas?"

"We're going in," Katz answered. "With a bit of luck, we might be able to rescue the hostages and take out the fellows with those radio detonators. That so-called nuclear device might be real."

"I got a look at it when the terrorist spokesman was yapping away about how they intend to blow us all to hell if we try anything," Gary Manning stated. "I looked at it through binoculars, but I still can't tell you if the damn thing is real or not. The top portion looks like a lid, bolted into position. The receiver to the radio detonator for any explosives inside has to be located there if the device really is a nuclear weapon. The body would be so heavily packed with lead and steel walls to contain the plutonium that a radio signal wouldn't reach it. They could have six kilos of plutonium inside that thing. Probably less, but even one kilo would be enough to worry about. He mentioned a reactor vessel and that suggests there are already rods in the plutonium to control the radioactive core. That means it's unstable and very dangerous. Crack the shell housing the plutonium and you've got a serious radiation leak to deal with even if the damn thing doesn't explode."

"We'd better assume the bomb is genuine," McCarter commented. "You reckon you can deactivate it if you can get your hands on it?"

"Not that hard if I can get the cap off and get to the radio detonator inside," Manning answered. "It's not really a sophisticated device, but it's not the sort of thing that leaves any room for mistakes."

"Wait a minute," Walters said urgently. "You can't just charge in there like the cavalry. What about them setting off the bomb? There doesn't appear to be a way to prevent them from doing that."

"We encountered some of Skull's people before," Katz countered calmly. "They're well trained, well organized and ruthless, but they aren't fanatics and they're not suicidal. They want us to believe they are, but that's just because the image of mad dogs ready to die for a demented cause would be in their favor right now. Skull's followers won't use that bomb unless they get to a point where they think that the game is already lost and that they won't have anything left to lose by killing us and a few thousand innocent people in the process."

"I don't know," Walters muttered and shook his head. "That's a mighty big assumption. What if you're wrong? We go storming in there and they might just trigger the bomb. I really don't want to be a part of setting off a nuclear disaster. Not even a fairly small one."

"We don't want that, either," Manning assured him. "That's why we must get in there. If they've got a nuclear bomb, we've got to deactivate it. We can't stand by and allow their helicopters to leave, either. Right now, we know where the bomb is and we have a general idea where they have the hostages. Our job would be ten times more difficult if they managed to fly out of here."

"The odds of rescuing the hostages and putting that bomb out of commission will be less favorable also," Encizo added. "This is going to be tricky. We don't want to encourage anyone to press any buttons or kill hostages while we're trying to take out the enemy."

"That's the reason my team goes in alone," Katz told Walters. "We don't want to startle the terrorists into drastic action. If only five men hit them, they'll be less apt to set off the bomb than if they think a large force is trying to overpower them."

"Just the five of you?" Walters looked stunned. "That's plain crazy. I mean, at this point we can only guess at their numbers. There might be fifty or sixty of them inside the castle."

"I don't believe this heroic gesture for a moment," Vashnov declared with a disgusted snort. "You five aren't afraid to go inside the walls of Strassmacher Castle because this entire affair is an elaborate stunt. Those terrorists are simply hoodlums hired by the CIA. You will go in, tell them to surrender and appear to have rescued your precious President and our secretary-general. Then we of the Soviet Socialist Republic are suppose to believe you have 'saved the day' as if this was some idiot Western from your Hollywood."

"God, you Russians are paranoid," Walters groaned. "And I thought some of our people were oversuspicious about seeing Communist conspiracies in every corner."

"Being a little paranoid is part of an intelligence officer's job," Katz said with a shrug. "I can understand that, Mr. Vashnov. You're wrong about this, of course, but I don't expect you to take our word for that. Right now, let's just concentrate on the mission. You can argue whatever you want later. We don't have time to let political dogma or absurd accusations interfere with our job."

"I've got an argument for you," a senior Secret Service agent stated. "Our job, speaking for the Secret Service, is to protect the President of the United States. I don't think much of letting him get in the middle of a damn gun battle between you commando types and the terrorists. You guys want to be big heroes? Find a situation that doesn't endanger the President."

"A private army of terrorists is holding him hostage and you don't think *that* puts his life in danger?" James inquired. "Get real, man. Maybe they don't intend to kill him right now, but every minute that he spends as a captive lessens his chance of coming out of this alive."

"The first thing to do in a hostage situation is attempt to establish a line of dialogue with the terrorists in order to negotiate for the release of the hostages," the Service man insisted. "That's what we should be trying to do instead of attempting this Green Beret bullshit."

"There isn't time to negotiate," McCarter stated. "Those choppers could be on their way while we're standing around here running a bloody debating society. Now, if you chaps want to discuss this until your tongues wear out, that's up to you. Just let us do our goddamn job, and you can file any complaints later."

"Hey, listen to me—" the Secret Service agent began, thrusting a finger at McCarter's face.

"We have authority over you," Katz cut him short in a flat, hard voice. "Whether you like it or not is beside the point. We're in command and you'll follow orders. It's really that simple. Understood?"

"You do not give orders to the KGB!" Vashnov snapped. "We will do what is best for our premier and you shall not stop us!"

"If you get in the way of our operation we might have to kill you," Katz told him bluntly. "Terrible waste since this time we're actually on the same side, but we'll do it if we have to."

"You dare threaten us!" Vashnov snarled, his eyes wide with fury.

"We're just being honest with you, buddy," James said with a grin. "You know about *glasnost*, right? Consider this part of a policy of openness."

9

Yakov Katzenelenbogen examined the blueprints to Strassmacher Castle provided by the Luxembourgian security forces. Colonel Mauser, Walters and a few others advised the Phoenix Force commander about the structure of the castle and the probable locations of the terrorists. It seemed likely that Skull's forces would set up observation posts and guard weak points in the castle in much the same manner as the security forces had.

"The man with the bomb and his crew have gone inside the castle," Mauser told Katz. "They took the bomb with them. By the way, I spoke with that fellow in German, which seems to be his native language, yet I couldn't place his accent. It wasn't any regional German accent I'm familiar with."

"I recognized his accent even in English," Katz replied. "It's a cross between Austrian and so-called High German taught in the expensive private schools in Germany before World War II. Some words have a strange Latin emphasis on vowels. That's because Spanish or Portuguese was his second language. He was probably raised with it. Such an odd combination is spoken by a unique breed of individuals born in South America to German refugees."

"You mean that son of a bitch is the son of a goddamn Nazi war criminal?" Walters asked in an astonished voice.

"Probably," Katz confirmed. "The men I've encountered in the past with that accent have all been members of ODESSA. To be exact, they were the descendants of Nazi SS and Gestapo fugitives who fled to Brazil or Paraguay after the war. I'd say the terrorist spokesman is probably the product of one of the Nazi strongholds in the jungles of South America.''

"Christ!" Walters rasped. "You mean these terrorists are a bunch of Nazis?''

"I don't think so," Katz answered with a shrug. He didn't even glance up from the blueprint as he spoke. "Judging from what we've been able to learn about Skull, he and his people are pretty much apolitical. I doubt that this is some elaborate scheme to resurrect the Third Reich or anything of that sort, but it's bigger than anything Skull has done in the past. I'm certain he has a very big goal in mind. Probably some kind of political ambitions involved, although I have no idea what they might be.''

Rafael Encizo and David McCarter entered the tour bus where Katz and the others had assembled to examine the prints. Encizo leaned over Katz's shoulder for a close look.

"Right here at the south wall," the Cuban declared, pointing at the plans, "there's a guard posted at the top and another in a tower nearby. He's got a walkie-talkie so he's got to be taken out before we can go over the wall. From the looks of the blueprints, this ought to be our best position to go in. The tower will block the view of the wall from the west, and the view from the east wing is largely obscured by the chapel steeple inside the walls. Of course, the guards in the towers will spot us if they're looking in our direction when we go over the top.''

"We're putting together preparations for a distraction," Katz stated. "Hopefully, the majority of the terrorists will be busy watching the fireworks while we make our move.''

"I hope it's a bloody good distraction," McCarter said with a sigh. "Otherwise, we might all wind up a bit dead before we make it inside the walls.''

Gary Manning stepped inside the bus and whistled sharply. The others turned to face him. The Canadian jerked his head toward the trailers outside.

"I rigged a pyro-charge to the gas tank of one of the abandoned vehicles," Manning announced. "Make sure everybody stays clear of the area. It won't blow until I hit the lever to the squib wired to it, but when that tanks blows there will be flaming gasoline jetting out at least twenty feet. Other debris might be thrown even farther.''

"All right.'' Katz handed the blueprints to Encizo. ''Now, for the last time: does everyone understand what to do?''

"Hell,'' Walters remarked with a shrug. ''Our job is easy. We'll just carry on and look surprised when the explosion occurs and then claim to know nothing, that it must have been a freak accident. You're the ones who are taking all the risks.''

"It won't be that easy,'' Katz warned him. ''The terrorists will be suspicious, and they are not inclined to believe you anyway. More than anything else, we need to distract the enemy long enough to get inside and hopefully stall them for a few minutes. Where is Vashnov? We have to contact the Soviets and explain what we're doing.''

"I saw Vashnov outside with some of the Soviet soldiers and some men in suits who must be other KGB,'' Manning stated. ''It looked like he was having his own council of war with the KGB and GRU. For what it's worth, it appeared a lot of the other Russians were arguing with Vashnov. I figure whatever that paranoid jackass wants to do, it won't be something we'll be too thrilled about.''

"We can't be too hard on Vashnov,'' Katz said with a slight sigh as he gathered up his Uzi. ''If we had been with the security forces when this occurred and a group of Soviet commandos suddenly arrived unannounced with high-security clearance from the Kremlin, we'd probably be suspicious, as well.''

"That bloke is more than just suspicious,'' McCarter stated. ''He's an extremist. Vashnov is convinced we're the villains here, and he's not about to change his mind. Probably looks under his bed every night to see if there's a capitalist hiding under it.''

"I guess both sides have people like that,'' Manning commented. ''East and West have certainly created a lot of distrust over the past four decades. We'll still have to tell Vashnov to keep his people back a safe distance before we set off the explosion.''

"Naturally,'' Katz agreed. ''Mr. Walters, perhaps you or Colonel Mauser will see to that? My team has to get in position. Time is not at our disposal.''

"Okay," Walters replied. "You know, we've contacted the governments of France, Belgium and the Federal Republic of Germany. They all agreed to letting the helicopters enter their airspace. Nobody wants to risk setting off a nuclear bomb. However, they will try to track any aircraft that enters their airspace from Luxembourg, and they'll attempt to find out where it lands and deal with the situation from there."

"Let's hope it doesn't get that far," Katz said. "Well, gentlemen, let's get to work."

DARK AND TOWERING storm clouds had assembled in the sky above Strassmacher Castle. The gloom contributed to the oppressive tension of the situation. The castle was no longer a charming remnant of past history. It was a sinister fortress, an evil lair guarded by terrorist trolls and a nuclear dragon. The enemy inside the stone walls was just part of the problem Phoenix Force faced as they knelt behind the tour bus, fully armed and ready for combat. Who the hostages were, the threat of a nuclear weapon and the likelihood that other terrorists would soon arrive via helicopters, all made the mission more sensitive and more desperate than even Phoenix Force was accustomed to dealing with.

"A thought occurred to me during that meeting inside the bus," McCarter commented as he worked his crossbow's cocking lever. "Want to hear it?"

"No," Gary Manning replied, one hand on his FAL assault rifle while the other held the squib detonator. "I don't think so."

"Just a minute," Calvin James said while he checked the forty-foot nylon rope attached to a grappling hook. "Maybe David thought of something encouraging. Something that would give us more confidence in the success of our mission."

"No," the Briton admitted. "It's nothing like that...."

"Screw you, then," James told him. "We don't need to hear it."

"Everybody should be clear of the danger zone by now," Encizo announced, checking his Seiko diver's watch. "Thirty seconds before fireworks start."

"We want everybody out there to look surprised," Katz declared as he adjusted the strap to the Uzi across his left shoulder. "So let's surprise them. Do it now, Gary."

The Canadian demolitions expert raised his eyebrows, smiled slightly and jammed his thumb on the button to the squib. The device sent an electrical charge through the wires attached to the blasting caps inserted in a four-ounce set charge under the fuel tank of one of the abandoned trailers outside the castle walls. The explosion was relatively small, but it instantly blew apart the tank and ignited the gasoline within.

An orange ball of flame burst from the trailer, and the force of the explosion sent the large vehicle toppling over on its side. Chunks of metal and flaming debris spewed from the wreckage. The premature afternoon twilight caused by the dark cloud cover had pitched a blanket of shadows across the area. The explosion was made even more spectacular set as it was against the surrounding darkness.

Alarmed shouts and curses came from both sides of the castle wall. Katz imagined some of their allies were less than thrilled that the explosion had been set off thirty seconds ahead of schedule. Perhaps some of the security personnel would have stinging eardrums for a while. That would be a small price indeed if the tactics helped Phoenix Force succeed in carrying out the raid.

The five commandos immediately charged from their hiding place and ran for the south wall even as the explosion continued to echo on the crisp wind. They saw terrorists running along the top of the castle walls, to stare down at the burning wreckage below. Several pointed their weapons at the security forces, but none opened fire. Colonel Mauser's voice bellowed from a bullhorn, telling the terrorists they were not under attack. Mauser claimed there had been an accident. A gas tank had apparently been punctured and somehow leaking petrol had been ignited. Perhaps someone had carelessly tossed away a burning cigarette and unintentionally set off the explosion. He repeated this story in English, German and French to make certain the enemy understood. The translations also served to further stall the terrorists for a few precious seconds.

David McCarter raised the skeletal stock of the Barnett crossbow to his shoulder as he ran, then the British ace pointed the weapon at the watchtower and dropped to one knee to steady his aim. He sighted through the telescope mount and quickly set the cross hairs on the upper torso of the terrorist sentry posted at the tower. The magnified view allowed McCarter to glimpse the man's astonished features. He saw the terrorist's mouth fall open, saw him raise a walkie-talkie to his face.

McCarter triggered the Barnett. The bowstring sang with a vibrating hum as the bolt streaked upward. The steel tip pierced the chest of the terrorist guard. Almost half the fiberglass shaft of the bolt sank into his flesh. The bolt had struck its target left of center. The sharp point had punctured the heart, and the hollow shaft split to discharge its load of cyanide. The sentry stiffened, twitched violently, then collapsed to the stone platform of the watchtower.

Gary Manning had also selected a target and shouldered his FAL to a ready position as he hastily centered the telescopic sight on the terrorist who patrolled the south wall. The enemy gunman glanced down at Manning. His face appeared vividly in the magnified lenses of the scope. Manning saw a young face filled with fear. It was not sinister. The expression seemed almost innocent and pitiful, twisted by terror.

But Manning already knew that most human monsters do not look like wild beasts or wild-eyed psychos. He squeezed the trigger when the cross hairs marked the enemy's forehead. Manning did not hesitate. He knew if he looked at that face for more than an instant, he would not be able to shoot. Gary Manning did not have the soul of a murderer. He hated killing a man in this manner, but circumstances demanded it. If the roles had been reversed, the terrorist would not have felt any remorse about snuffing out the Canadian commando's life.

The twelve-inch silencer attached to Manning's FAL rifle rasped as the bullet hissed from the muzzle. A 7.62 mm slug smashed into the terrorist's face and the projectile drilled a lethal hole right above and between his eyes. The bullet punched through his skull and blasted out another, larger hole at the back of his head. The impact snapped the sentry's head forward, and his body tumbled limply over the castle wall and plunged to the ground below. It landed with a bone-shattering thump only a few feet from Rafael Encizo and Calvin James.

"They used to talk about 'dropping out' in the sixties," James whispered as he glanced at the mangled, bloodied corpse. "No wonder it went out of style. Doesn't look so good to me."

James and Encizo both carried grappling hooks with nylon paratrooper lines attached. They looked up at the wall and estimated the distance as they began to swing the hooks in preparation for a throw.

"I guess he got high with the wrong people," Encizo whispered, picking up on James's gallows humor, as well as the sixties slang. "Coming down was bound to be a bummer."

The Cuban hurled his grappling hook. It sailed upward in a high arc, then the metal claws landed on the stone ridge along the top of the wall. Encizo heard the steel prongs scrape stone. It sounded loud enough to attract every terrorist inside Strassmacher Castle, yet he realized he was so sensitive to the noise level because he was listening for the hook to hit its target. The bullhorn bellowing and the crackling flames of the explosion would mask the noise unless a terrorist was located directly under the hook at the opposite side of the wall.

Encizo tugged on the rope hard to satisfy himself that it was secure. James threw his hook and yanked the line to pull the big steel prongs into a firm anchor on the stone ridge. Katz appeared next to the black commando and nodded his approval. Manning and McCarter joined them two seconds later.

"You think we are fools!" a voice bellowed from a bullhorn inside the walls of Strassmacher Castle. "Another so-called 'accident' and we'll kill the American secretary of state and the Soviet minister of foreign affairs! If you attempt to stop the helicopters, we'll set off the bomb and we will all die together! We're not bluffing! Defy us and you will surely find out we mean exactly what we say!"

This was the terrorists' reply to Mauser's claim that the exploding trailer had been an accident. Phoenix Force paid little attention to the booming voice from within the castle. Encizo and James climbed up the ropes first, hand over hand with their feet braced on the stone wall. The pair easily scaled the wall to the top and climbed over the edge to the catwalk on the opposite side of the barrier. James leaned over the edge and signaled for the others to come up.

McCarter and Manning climbed the rope next. The SAS-trained Briton was an accomplished mountaineer, and the rugged Canadian was equally adept. They scaled the wall, "walking up" as easily as most men on a ladder. McCarter pulled up one rope while Katz seized the other. The Israeli wound part of the line around his prosthesis and grabbed it with his other hand.

Manning saw Katz had a firm hold on the rope and started to pull the line up. Katz used his feet on the wall to assist his ascent, but he hardly needed to bother. Manning hauled up the line with Katz attached as if bringing in a fish.

Phoenix Force knelt along the catwalk at the top of the wall and stared down at Strassmacher Castle. A chapel with a steeple and bell tower was located directly in front of them, helping to conceal the commandos from the terrorists within. The parade field was empty, probably cleared for a landing pad for the helicopters. Lights were on in the stone structures within the castle. They knew that the conference had been held at the ancient quarters once used by knights stationed at the castle to protect the Strassmacher feudal lords. The main section of the castle had been regarded as too obvious a site, and the security personnel had chosen to set up their headquarters in the halls and rooms that had formerly been the home of royalty.

The terrorists would almost certainly have changed that arrangement in case the military and intelligence forces outside attempted a rescue. The two biggest questions for Phoenix Force were where were the terrorists holding the President, the premier and the other VIPs, and where was the bomb located? They could not attempt more than a vague guess from the catwalk on the wall.

McCarter fitted the prongs to a grappling hook on the ridge above the catwalk and lowered the rope. He grabbed the line in both hands, placed his feet on the wall and slowly climbed down the rope, the KG-99 strapped to one shoulder and the

Barnett crossbow on the other. Manning prepared to anchor the other hook to send down the second line.

A terrorist suddenly stepped from a door at the rear of the chapel. The man was in the host country's uniform and also had a black beret bearing the skull emblem. He carried a Belgian FAL slung to his shoulder. From the appearance of the man, he did not seem to be following up any suspicions. Perhaps he had just stepped outside for a breath of air, but he still saw David McCarter dangling from the rope, halfway from the ground.

The terrorist quickly pulled his FAL from his shoulder and slipped his arm from the sling. Suddenly, a large steel object crashed into the frame of his rifle and struck the weapon from his grasp. The man gasped with alarm and glanced at the grappling hook that had slammed into his rifle. Manning had hurled the hook from the catwalk above. The Canadian pulled sharply on the line and the hook rose swiftly. A long steel tine caught the terrorist in the small of the back.

Manning yanked forcibly and the hook snared the enemy gunman. The terrorist cried out briefly, but the powerful pull yanked him off his feet and propelled him forward. Manning turned sharply and swung the line. The terrorist was towed into the wall like a pendulum out of control and smashed into unyielding stone. He uttered a soft whimper and sagged limply, still impaled on the hook at the end of Manning's line.

By then, David McCarter reached the ground. He quickly unslung the KG-99 and rushed to the unconscious man to make sure he would not be a threat for quite a while. The Briton removed a plastic strip from the small of his back and quickly used it to bind the terrorist's wrists behind him, just to be certain. There was no need to gag him. The fellow would not regain consciousness for at least ten minutes, and by then Phoenix Force would have completed the raid and their presence would already be known.

Calvin James descended on the same rope McCarter had used. He slipped the sling of his M-16 from his shoulder and trained the rifle on the chapel door. Encizo climbed down the line next, followed by Katz. The Israeli ran the line across his prosthetic arm, braced between the thumb and forefinger of the artificial hand. Katz had a little difficulty climbing up ropes, but none going down them.

Finally, Manning descended the line and joined the other members of the team. He yanked on the rope and pulled the grappling hook free. It dropped to the grassy ground near his feet.

"I owe you, mate," McCarter whispered as he placed a hand on Manning's shoulder. "That bloke had me cold until you took him out."

"Since when did we keep count on that stuff?" the Canadian replied with a shrug.

Katz gestured for Manning to move to the right-hand corner of the chapel and for James to cover the left. He signaled for McCarter to stay put and pointed at Encizo, then jerked his head toward the door. The Cuban nodded and stepped forward. Katz braced the Uzi across his prosthesis and pointed the muzzle of the silencer at the doorway, then he stepped inside the chapel. Encizo stood at the doorway, the barrel of his H&K subgun held high, to cover the Israeli.

The door led to a dark room. Katz allowed his eyes to adjust to the dim light. He had entered a humble priest's quarters with a plain wooden table, two chairs, a cot and a chest of drawers. A door was ajar, and light streamed into the quarters from the room beyond.

Katz moved to the door and carefully peered around the edge. He was looking into the main chapel. The door was next to an altar atop a red-carpeted platform. An ornate brass crucifix was mounted on the wall above the hand-carved altar. A row of silver candlesticks and some brass collection plates were set on the altar. Two lecterns stood at the edge of the platform, a large, leather-bound Bible placed on each. Beyond the altar were a couple of confession booths, and several rows of pews bisected by a carpeted center aisle. Light poured into the chapel from the multicolored stained-glass windows along the walls.

There was a soft murmur of several voices. Katz saw three men seated in the pews, but he was certain there were more who were not in his immediate field of vision. One man was dressed in a Russian army uniform and the other two wore dark suits, but all wore the terrorist beret, which had become their badge of identity.

Encizo moved beside Katz at the doorway and peered out at the terrorists. He withdrew into the priest's quarters, looked at Katz and shook his head.

"I don't like it," Encizo whispered. "We can't tell how many of them are out there. Nice of the bastards to wear their little beanies so we know for sure they're Skull's men instead of hombres on our side."

"They probably put on the berets during the raid so they could identify one another among all the security personnel," Katz answered. "I suppose they're still wearing the berets so the helicopter pilots will feel safer when they try to land at the parade field."

"So how do we handle these characters? Take them out now or come back for them later?"

Katz raised his gloved prosthesis to his lips to signal silence. Encizo also heard the footsteps that had warned the Israeli of danger. Shadows danced along the light from the chapel as the steps drew closer. Two terrorists had decided to step up to the altar.

"Devlin?" a voice called out. "What are you doing in there? Thinking of joining the ruddy clergy?"

Encizo ducked behind the door, and Katz pressed his back to the wall by the doorway. A terrorist appeared at the threshold. He was about average height and build, and his accent was British although he was dressed in a Soviet uniform and carried a Kalashnikov rifle slung on his shoulder. He failed to notice Katzenelenbogen until the Israeli swung the prosthesis and slammed the edge of his steel hand under the man's heart.

The terrorist gasped, the breath knocked from his lungs by the unexpected and forcible blow. Katz quickly shoved his Uzi into the man's upper arm and shoulder to push him aside and rush out the doorway. Encizo emerged from behind the door and slammed the silencer-equipped barrel of his MP-5 across the collarbone of the dazed man. The enemy gunman doubled up from the blow with a groan that seemed to express astonishment as much as pain.

Encizo held the H&K subgun in one fist and gripped the edge
of the door with his other hand. He shoved it hard and sent the
door rapidly forward to slam into the bowed head of the
stunned terrorist. Wood and skull connected with a loud thud.
The terrorist collapsed to the floor. Encizo swung the door open
wide and jumped over the unconscious opponent to charge
through the opening to the altar platform.

Katz had exploded into action the moment his feet touched
the carpeted surface of the platform. Another terrorist, a big
heavyset man with a face that resembled a shovel with eyes,
stood by the altar. The brute glared at Katz and snarled something as he fumbled with the bolt of his M-3A1 submachine
gun, but Katz triggered his Uzi before the terrorist could even
chamber a round.

The silenced muzzle of the Uzi spit flame as the weapon
sputtered its muffled report. Katz hit the gunman with a 3-
round burst of 9 mm rounds. The impact kicked the terrorist
off his feet and dumped him on his back with a loud moan of
agony. The Phoenix Force commander barely glanced at the
fallen opponent as he swiftly swung his subgun toward the three
others he had previously spotted among the pews.

The trio were taken off guard by the sudden appearance of
Yakov Katzenelenbogen and his avenging Uzi. The Israeli did
not hesitate. There was no time to think about fair play or to
question the morality of shooting down opponents before they
could reach for a weapon. Too much was at stake. Too many
lives relied on the success of Phoenix Force's mission. Katz
pointed the Uzi at the three enemy gunmen and squeezed the
trigger.

The submachine gun sizzled with a salvo of muffled parabellums. Bullets ripped into the chest of one terrorist and
seemed to nail him to the backrest of a pew. The man's body
twitched wildly and deposited his Soviet-made PPSh-41 submachine gun in his lap. The terrorist died in a seated position,
head bowed and lifeless hands resting on the frame of the unfired weapon in his lap. Another enemy gunman managed to
drop to the floor in time to avoid the high-velocity hailstorm of
Uzi slugs. The third terrorist was less fortunate. He didn't duck
quite fast enough and lowered his head directly in the path of

a 9 mm projectile. The bullet drilled a fatal tunnel above his right eyebrow and sliced through his brain to open a gory exit wound at the back of his skull.

Katz saw movement via the corner of an eye and realized more terrorists lurked among the rows of pews. Two of Skull's mercenary killers had been spared the fury of the Israeli's attack, yet they had also been unprepared for such an unexpected and unannounced assault. The pair hastily readied their weapons. However, Rafael Encizo had emerged from the priest's quarters to join Katz on the platform.

Encizo and Katz had worked together in Phoenix Force for years. They had spent countless hours in training operations and actual combat together. The members of Phoenix Force knew one another as well as if they could climb inside one another's minds. They knew how the other man would react, and each instinctively acted to protect his partner and trusted him to be a backup in a crisis. Encizo knew that Katz would take out the clear and immediate threat first. Katz knew Encizo would be there to cover him if more danger appeared.

The Cuban's MP-5 erupted in a volley of silenced 9 mm rounds even as Encizo ran to the edge of the platform and jumped. Bullets crashed into the biceps and shoulder of one gunman. The impact spun the man around to receive two more parabellum slugs in the center of the chest. Blood spewed from the terrorist's upper body as he fell across the top of a pew bench and tumbled lifelessly to the floor.

The second gunman swung his Walther MPL subgun toward Encizo's position. The Cuban was no longer on the platform. The terrorist searched hastily for Encizo and tried to keep an eye on Katz at the same time, uncertain which opponent to fire at first. Unable to spot Encizo, the man swung his CAR-15 assault rifle toward Katz.

Encizo suddenly appeared above the backrest of the first-row pew in front of the altar. The Cuban commando snap-aimed his H&K and opened fire. A trio of 9 mm rounds plowed into the terrorist. A bullet sparked against the steel frame of the gunsel's CAR. Another round smashed into the hand fisted around the pistol grip of the assault rifle. Flesh and muscle were torn apart by the projectile. Bone and hard plastic shattered. The

terrorist cried out and dropped his weapon, his right hand a
bloodied mass—punctured by a bullet and sliced deeply by
sharp shards of plastic. Bone splinters jutted from torn skin.
The man grabbed his wounded hand and threw himself to the
floor, hoping the pews would provide adequate cover.

Katz had ducked behind a lectern for shelter and scanned the
chapel for signs of the remaining terrorists. A hunchbacked
figure appeared along the edge of the pews near the confession
booths. It was the terrorist who had managed to escape the Israeli's previous Uzi blasts. The remaining uninjured terrorist
was attempting to get into position to fire at Katz and Encizo
as soon as their attention was focused elsewhere. Katz pretended he had not noticed the shape and turned his head and
the Uzi in the general direction where the terrorist with the
crushed hand was hiding among the pews.

The gunman by the confessional rose and pointed his Skorpion machine pistol at Katz. The Israeli glimpsed the movement, expecting it, and suddenly swung the Uzi around. The
silenced subgun rasped a deadly salvo of 9 mm hornets. The
terrorist's head snapped back as a bullet smashed through his
upper teeth and cracked the upper jawbone. Two more parabellums slammed into his chest and hurled him backward.

A shadow suddenly fell across Katz. He turned and saw that
the big, heavyset terrorist had gotten to his feet and was staggering toward him. The brute's right arm dangled limply, blood
oozing from a bullet wound in his biceps. Crimson also stained
his shirtfront where two other bullets had drilled into his chest,
yet neither round had struck the heart. Pink froth bubbled
from his lips. A lung had been punctured, but the big bastard
was still alive. The fury in his eyes suggested he was still ready
to fight, too.

The Israeli swung the Uzi toward the wounded terrorist. The
mercenary thug lashed out with the M-3A1 subgun in his left
fist. He held it by the barrel and swung it like a club, as if his
mind had been turned into that of a primitive being due to the
pain and shock of the multiple bullet wounds. Complex mech-
anisms like triggers and metal sights were no longer within the
brute's comprehension. He wanted to bash in the Israeli's skull.
He wanted to feel Katz's life splatter out from shattered bone.

The enemy's submachine gun struck the Uzi instead. Metal clashed on metal and the force of the blow sent the Uzi hurtling from Katz's single hand. The Israeli jumped upright and seized the terrorist's wrist before the man could attempt another swing with the M-3. Katz rammed a knee for his opponent's groin, but managed to hit a thigh muscle instead.

The terrorist suddenly turned and shoved Katz with all his might. The man was bigger and stronger than the Israeli and was also powered by maniacal rage and desperation. The hulk drove Katz backward. He bellowed like a wounded beast as he charged with the M-3 still in his fist, and his forearm jammed against the Phoenix commander's chest.

They crashed into the altar. The candlesticks rocked unsteadily from the impact. The terrorist stayed on top of Katz and shoved him backward across the top of the altar. Crimson drool dripped from his lips and spotted the Israeli's jacket. The terrorist pinned Katz and pushed the submachine gun under the Phoenix pro's jaw. The barrel pressed across Katz's neck while the steel folding stock held down his right arm. The prosthesis was trapped. Katz flexed the muscles of his stump to try to free the artificial limb, but could barely move it.

The terrorist's terrible wet mouth smiled. More blood oozed from his lips, but the brute did not seem to care. His eyes gleamed as he stared down at Katz. The gun barrel continued to press into Katz's throat, not letting him breathe. He moved his left hand to his opponent's face and jammed two fingers under the eyes of the terrorist. The brute shot back his head, trying to shake off Katz's fingers before his eyeballs could be poked out of their sockets.

Katz continued to jab with his fingers as he tried to force his right shoulder against the frame of the subgun to gain some slack. The terrorist growled, but refused to let up on the pressure, then suddenly the thug shoved his wounded right arm into Katz's left forearm to push the Israeli's hand away from his face.

Katz's fingers touched something hard and round. He gripped the metal rim and realized the object was one of the brass collection plates. He swung his arm with all the strength he could muster and smashed the side of the plate into his opponent's skull. The terrorist's head recoiled from the blow, his eyes screwed shut, mouth twisted in pain. Katz hammered him again with the plate. The hard metal rim smashed into the man's right temple. The terrorist fell abruptly to his knees. The M-3 slipped away from the choke hold, and Katz easily shoved it aside with his prosthesis.

Katz stood, collection plate in his hand. The edge was stained with crimson. He glanced down at the terrorist. The big man groaned and slowly tried to rise. Blood streaked his face. Katz hit him with the brass plate once more and clipped him behind the ear. The man dropped facefirst to the carpet and did not stir. Katz sighed with relief and returned the collection plate to the altar. He took a deep breath and swallowed, glad to be able to do those things at ease.

Encizo had captured the remaining terrorist by simply rushing to the man's hiding place before the wounded man could manage to open a button-flap holster and attempt to draw a pistol awkwardly with only his left hand. Encizo had gambled the guy would not try to use the Walther MPL because the slide might have been damaged when a bullet ricocheted off it and the weapon might explode in the owner's face. The gamble had paid off. Encizo had him cold when he darted up the aisle and pointed his H&K chopper at the man's startled face.

"Give up or I kill you," the Cuban declared. "Either way, it's over for you. Which will it be?"

The terrorist held up one hand in surrender. The other hand was mangled and bloodied. Encizo herded him out from the pews and forced him to get on his belly. The Cuban pulled the man's arms behind his back and bound his wrists with riot cuffs.

The terrorist gasped. "The hand! Be easy with it, *monsieur*! The pain is very bad...."

"Pain can be worse," Katz told him. He decided to speak the man's native tongue, to be sure he was understood. "We can inflict terrible pain or simply kill you. We may do both if you don't cooperate. Get it?"

"Yes," the terrorist replied with a weary nod. "I understand, but I know very little."

"Where are the President, the premier and the other hostages?" Katz demanded as he scooped up a discarded black beret from the floor and examined the white skull emblem sewn onto the cloth. "You must know that."

"They're being held in the den in the east wing of the castle," the prisoner answered. "At least, that is where they were. Koerner may have moved them. I don't think he truly trusts anyone. Not even his own men."

"Koerner?" Katz inquired as he pulled the beret onto his head. "Is he in charge?"

"Until the colonel arrives," the terrorist replied.

"Skull is coming in one of the helicopters?" Katz asked with surprise.

"To supervise the operation personally," the captive confirmed. "Koerner is one of his top officers and advisers. His father was a Nazi general or something like that. The man was born into military training. Skull's other top aide is a Korean named Hee. That one is a former commando of some sort. Very dangerous man. Expert in karate and small arms. Skull's top bodyguard and enforcer."

"What about Skull himself?" Katz asked. "What sort of man is he? What does he hope to gain by this?"

"I don't know," the terrorist confessed. "No one knows anything about Skull. His nationality, his real name, what his plans are. Skull is death personified, the Grim Reaper in uniform. Some of us even doubt that he is a man at all. He's more like a brilliant computer in human form. Skull plans every move like a master chess player, guessing what his opponents will do, setting up men like pawns and outthinking his opponents every time."

"Nobody is right all the time," Katz commented. "Skull may have bitten off more than he can strategically chew this time."

"You would not feel so confident if you knew him," the terrorist insisted. "No one has ever beaten him. That's why we're part of his private army. Skull always wins in the end."

"We'll see," Katz replied. "What about that thing you people claim is a nuclear device? Is it really a bomb?"

"I don't know," the man admitted. "Koerner says it is. I believe it probably is genuine. Skull once abducted a team of French nuclear physicists and engineers. I don't know why he wanted them or what he did with the scientists. There was no ransom and three months after he kidnapped them, he had them executed. We think they were forced to work on building a nuclear weapon of some sort. At the time, we assumed this was a device to be sold to the Palestinians or the Libyans or perhaps even the Iranians. It is possible the bomb we have here is the one they built."

"Where is it now?" Katz demanded.

"I don't know," the prisoner answered, shaking his head slightly. "West wing, I think. None of us know anything beyond what is necessary to carry out orders. Koerner and Yasnev didn't tell me any details about the bomb."

"I just checked the front door," Encizo announced as he approached Katz and the prisoner. "I didn't see any terrorists near the chapel, and the men I saw at the opposite side of the parade field didn't appear to be interested or even vaguely suspicious of this building. I don't think anyone heard our silenced weapons. Either that, or they're being very cool about it. My guess is they don't know we've gotten inside yet."

"That won't last long," Katz commented. "They will notice the missing sentries, and pretty soon. These aren't the kind of people who make many mistakes. When they realize where we got across the wall, they'll easily guess where to find us if we stay here."

"Did the prisoner tell you anything useful?" Encizo inquired. He understood enough French to know what the conversation had been about.

"More than I knew before and not enough to help much," Katz answered. "Go get the others. We've got to get out of here before the enemy realizes their security has been breached."

"Right," Encizo agreed. He looked at the black beret on Katz's head. "Why are you wearing that thing? Part of a plan?"

"I'll explain it as soon as you bring the others to hear it," the Israeli replied. "Let's see if we can't surprise a chess master with a couple of moves he hasn't anticipated."

The sky above Strassmacher Castle continued to get gloomier, and light rain began to drizzle down on the ancient structure. But the sound of whirling metal thunder was not caused by the change in weather. Three helicopters had appeared in grim gray sky. The aircraft approached from the west and moved steadily toward the castle. Their lights looked like stars in the early darkness. The approaching trio of copters could have been an evil constellation that had descended to earth to visit some dreadful cosmic punishment upon mankind.

The terrorists within the walls of the castle stared up at the helicopters in the distance. So did the men of Phoenix Force. The five commandos stood outside the chapel. They had donned black berets and jackets taken from the terrorists already put out of action. A couple of the jackets had bullet holes and bloodstains, which would certainly appear suspicious to anyone who got a good look at them. Of course, the enemy would notice the unfamiliar faces beneath the headgear and the fact they all carried silencer-equipped weapons. The disguises would serve Phoenix Force if the real terrorists only glanced in their direction. Anyone giving them a second look would quickly realize they were infiltrators.

"Looks like the Luxembourgians decided to let the choppers through," Calvin James remarked as he tugged on the lapels of the oversize suit jacket he had taken from a slain terrorist. The black commando would have looked extremely suspicious in the military jacket of a Soviet or Luxembourgian soldier. "Can't say I blame them. Not with a bunch that's threatening to set off a plutonium bomb less than twenty miles from the nation's capital.''

"Hard to say what kind of choppers those are," McCarter commented. The Briton wore a Russian military tunic, unbuttoned to allow him to reach inside for his Browning in shoulder leather. "They look to be about the size of Bell transport craft. Each could probably haul about fifteen men. They could also be armed with machine guns or even rocket launchers."

"That's a cheerful thought," Gary Manning muttered. "One thing is for sure, we're running out of time fast."

"David, Cal and Rafael," Katz began, adjusting the buttons of the Soviet jacket he wore. "You three take the east wing. Koerner had the hostages in that section in the den. Rafael has the blueprints of the place. They may have been moved, and the bomb may be in there instead. Don't forget, that thing can be set off by a remote control unit. If you see anybody with one of those radio transmitters, take him out fast. Don't risk a thing. If you even suspect one of them has a remote, put a bullet between his eyes. Koerner has one, and I guess Yasnev probably has one, too, but it's hard to say where the rest of those remotes are or who has them."

"We are a motley bunch, and I hope nobody gives us a close look," Encizo said with a sigh. "None of these jackets even match the pants we're wearing."

"What the hell," McCarter snorted. "We have to make do. Let's hit it! That's why we're here."

Katz and Manning headed for the west wing. The pair made the most of shadows for camouflage and tried to avoid getting near any of the terrorists. McCarter, James and Encizo moved toward the east wing. The main section of the castle was larger and had more rooms and windows than the other portions of the fortress. Men were stationed at the windows. The three Phoenix warriors hoped the terrorists were still concentrating on the approaching aircraft.

Encizo was familiar with the blueprints and room locations since he had studied the information in greater detail than McCarter and James. The Cuban led the trio along a cobblestone pathway to a side entrance. A single sentry stood by the door and gazed up at the sky. McCarter gestured for his part-

ners to stay back and strolled to the door alone, glancing about
to be certain none of the enemy was paying much attention to
him. The Briton took a pack of Player's from a shirt pocket
and stuck a cigarette in his mouth as he approached the sentry.

"Hello, mate," he called out cheerfully as he drew closer.
"Got a light?"

The terrorist was surprised somewhat, but shook his head
and mumbled a few words in French.

McCarter switched to that language and repeated his re-
quest as he pointed at the cigarette dangling from his lips.

The sentry nodded, lowering his FAL rifle to reach into a
pocket for a lighter.

"Merci," the Briton replied and suddenly grabbed the man's
jacket with both hands.

Gripping the lapels, McCarter pulled the astonished terrorist forward, and drove a knee between the man's legs. The sentry gasped in agony, mouth open in a mute scream. McCarter
snapped his head forward, to butt his hard forehead into the
terrorist's skull. The guard fell backward, pushing open the
door in the process. Still holding the man's lapels, McCarter
followed him through the doorway.

The British ace snapped another well-placed head butt to the
sentry's face. His forehead crashed into the bridge of the other
man's nose, breaking cartilage on impact. The terrorist began
to sag. McCarter swung a right cross to the jaw. His knuckles
connected hard, and the sentry fell unconscious at his feet.

Four pairs of eyes stared at the Briton, as McCarter found
himself face-to-face with four surprised enemy gunmen. He and
the sentry had plunged through the door into a kitchen, complete with modern ovens, sinks, freezer unit and tables with
assorted pots, pans and utensils. The four terrorists held
weapons, but only one actually pointed a firearm at Mc-
Carter. The Phoenix pro had left his crossbow at the chapel,
but the KG-99 hung from a shoulder strap by his right hip and
the Browning Hi-Power was sheathed in shoulder leather under his left arm. McCarter realized he could not hope to reach
either weapon before the terrorists could blast him to eternity.

"Well," he began, gesturing at the unconscious man sprawled on the tile floor, "you blokes should have heard what he said about my mother...."

McCarter suddenly dropped to one knee and grabbed his KG-99 with both hands. The terrorist who had already trained his Sterling subgun at the Briton quickly lowered his weapon to point the muzzle at McCarter's head. The other three enemy triggermen also swung their firearms toward the Phoenix commando. McCarter saw the familiar face of death staring at him from four gaping black gun muzzles. The Briton's backbone quivered with icy fear, yet his pulse still quickened with excitement, and the thrill of danger kept pace with his terror of sudden violent death. He had already made his move. Right or wrong, he was committed to it and had to play it out. Aware that that moment might be his last, the Briton started to raise the barrel of his subgun.

The terrorist with the Sterling blaster suddenly staggered backward as his head exploded in a fountain of crimson and liquid brain tissue. The harsh coughing of a silenced automatic weapon accompanied the man's two-step shuffle. The terrorist started to fall as his comrades glanced at the door to see Calvin James at the entrance, M-16 rifle at his shoulder, smoke rising from the muzzle of the weapon's silencer.

The new opponent caught the terrorists off guard and distracted their attention from McCarter. The Briton triggered his KG-99. The compact subgun spit out a 3-round burst of silenced 9 mm slugs. Another terrorist rose on tiptoe as the parabellum messengers ripped into his face and forehead. The top of his skull burst open, and his weapon fell from lifeless fingers. He dropped dead next to another member of Skull's private army.

The horrified gunman barely glanced at his slain companion as he swung his weapon from James to McCarter. Three sizzling metal projectiles tore into his face before he could trigger his Skorpion chopper. A parabellum split his cheekbone and shattered bone at the hinge of his jaw. Other bullets caused further damage to the gray matter within his skull. He was dead before he could hear the whispered reports of the silenced weapon that had snuffed out his corrupt and misused young life.

Rafael Encizo knelt at the side of the doorway next to Calvin James, his H&K machine pistol braced to his shoulder. The metal stock still vibrated from the 3-round burst he had fired at the enemy trooper. The last terrorist hesitated for a split second, torn between McCarter and the two-man threat at the doorway. His indecision caused him to hold his fire too long to counterattack effectively.

McCarter's KG-99 hissed angrily and blasted a salvo of silenced 9 mm slugs into the upper torso of the remaining gunman. The terrorist staggered backward from the impact, blood staining his shirtfront. James triggered his M-16. A trio of 5.56 mm rounds smashed into the gunman's face. The opponent's nose vanished in a geyser of crimson, and a splotch of scarlet appeared from a bullet hole above his eyebrows. The terrorist collapsed with a bullet-ravaged body.

"That wasn't very subtle, David," Encizo whispered as he entered the kitchen.

"It worked out all right," the Briton replied. He knelt by the unconscious terrorist sentry and reached for a set of riot cuffs on his belt. "Got anything to gag this bastard with?"

Calvin James crossed the room to the next door. His decision was not made a moment too soon, for the door suddenly swung open, and a terrorist entered, a Makarov pistol in his fist. The gunman must have heard the muffled reports of silenced weapons in the kitchen and decided to investigate.

James quickly chopped the barrel of the M-16 across the terrorist's wrist. The pistol fell from the man's numb fingers as he cried out in surprise and pain. His cry was cut off abruptly as James rammed the buttstock of his rifle into the man's gut. The terrorist doubled up from the blow and James shoved him out of the way, toward McCarter and Encizo.

The terrorist staggered forward and stumbled into Encizo's rock-hard fist. The punch drove the man back into McCarter. The British ace swung the side of his hand across his opponent's nape. The terrorist fell forward only to receive a hard uppercut from Encizo that bounced his body back to McCarter. The Briton grabbed the man from behind and drove a knee to the tailbone. The terrorist groaned as a wave of pain traveled up his spine.

McCarter slipped his arms under the arms of his dazed opponent and clasped his hands together at the back of his neck. He held the man in a full nelson while Encizo swung a kick to the terrorist's battered abdomen. The man convulsed in McCarter's grasp. The Briton felt the terrorist's body begin to sag. It looked as though there was no more fight left in the man, but McCarter did not take any chances. Still holding the man in the full nelson, he hauled him around to face a refrigerator, thrust his arms forward and slammed the terrorist's forehead into the refrigerator. The skull met the hard surface with a loud banging slap. McCarter released his opponent and allowed him to drop unconscious to the floor.

"Two against one in our favor for a change," McCarter commented as he glanced about. "Where did Cal go?"

"He tossed us this fellow to bounce around and went out the door," Encizo answered, slipping his H&K subgun from his shoulder. "I'll go see if he needs any help. You tie up our beach ball. Make sure he doesn't roll away for a while."

JAMES HAD STEPPED from the kitchen to enter a narrow corridor. He held his M-16 ready in case more opponents waited for him, but the corridor was empty. It was a drab and ugly little hallway with ancient gray stone walls and a rough stone floor. A naked electric bulb hung from the ceiling, the only modern innovation to corrupt the centuries-old passage.

He noticed another door at the end of the corridor and moved toward it. James stood clear of the door and kicked it open. No gunshots or startled voices responded. He slipped around the corridor and entered the next room.

It was a dining hall with a long fancy table, antique hand-carved chairs and a big fireplace mounted in the wall near the table. The room appeared to be unoccupied. James approached the table and glanced down at a brass plate on the tabletop. A burning cigarette lay across the rim, with a long strip of ash extending from the butt.

A man appeared from the archway to the next room. He was blond and dressed in a suit and tie. He held a snub-nosed .38

revolver in his fist, but the weapon was pointed at the floor. James immediately raised the M-16 to aim it at the enemy gunman.

"Jesus," CIA agent Mamer rasped, glaring at James. "Don't point that thing at me. We're about to get out of here. Don't be so goddamn jumpy. Okay?"

"The choppers are here?" James inquired. Apparently the man thought he was one of Skull's flunkies. If James could deceive him for just a minute or two more, he might be able to get the guy to tell him where the hostages were.

"You deaf or something?" Mamer snorted. "Will you put that thing down before you shoot me by accident? We've got to go get the hostages now. Where are the others?"

"They're getting some guys in the kitchen," James answered truthfully. He lowered the barrel of his M-16. "Where did they move the hostages to? Still in the den?"

"Maybe you ought to check up your black ass, boy," Mamer sneered as he pointed his revolver at James's face. "Drop the rifle, or I'll blow your head off."

"I thought you were buying it for a minute there," James confessed as he let the M-16 drop to the floor.

"Skull has some darkies working for him," Mamer stated and stepped closer, "but he didn't send any with the guys in the trailer rigs."

"Sounds like discrimination to me," James said as he raised his hands to shoulder level. "Doesn't Skull believe in equal opportunity to participate in terrorist raids?"

"There aren't many coons in the Company or the Secret Service," Mamer replied. "And none at all in the KGB or Luxembourgian military. Skull just figured a black face wouldn't fit in too well. Personally, I just hate niggers, period, so you'd better tell me where the rest of your pals are and how many of you bastards got over the wall. I'm more than willing to kill you, baboon boy, so don't—"

Rafael Encizo suddenly showed up at the door to the corridor behind James, his MP-5 subgun in hand. Mamer saw the Cuban and realized the new arrival held his fire for fear of hitting James. Mamer hissed through clenched teeth and swung his revolver toward Encizo.

James quickly executed a karate snap kick. The toe of his boot struck Mamer's wrist hard. The .38 flew from the traitor's hand. James whipped a back fist to his opponent's face and sent Mamer staggering toward the fireplace. The corrupt CIA agent fell against the mantel and quickly grabbed a brass candlestick from the ledge.

Mamer whirled and attacked James, swinging the candlestick like a club. James stepped forward, blocked the attack with a forearm and grabbed the traitor's sleeve. His other hand snared Mamer's jacket lapel. James turned sharply and hurled Mamer over a hip. The CIA agent crash-landed on the tabletop. James held the guy's wrist above the candlestick with one hand and delivered a karate chop to his opponent's breastbone with the other. Mamer gasped breathlessly.

James swung his arm again and chopped a hard blow to the ulna nerve in Mamer's forearm. The candlestick fell from the CIA guy's grasp, but his other hand closed in a fist and hooked a solid punch to the side of James's jaw. The black warrior staggered from the blow and Mamer broke free. He rolled to the opposite side of the table and landed on his feet.

"Hold it!" Encizo warned, H&K subgun pointed at the terrorist.

Mamer froze, hands raised in surrender. Calvin James suddenly vaulted over the table and slammed both feet into Mamer's chest. The double kick drove him back into a wall. James immediately closed in and rammed a fist into his opponent's solar plexus. Mamer doubled up with a choked moan.

"That's for 'nigger,'" James told him and slammed a knee to Mamer's chest. The blow snapped him back into the wall. Mamer's skull bounced against the surface. "That's for 'baboon boy.'"

James seized Mamer's necktie with one hand and yanked hard. Mamer's head jerked forward, and James whipped an uppercut under the man's jaw. Mamer's teeth clashed together hard and his eyes rolled up into his head. The CIA agent began to slump toward the floor, and James grabbed him by the hair and the jacket front to haul him back to his feet.

"That's for being an American and a blasted traitor!" James announced as he swung his fist into the man's battered face.

Mamer crashed into the table and hit the floor, gone to the world. James charged forward and kicked him hard in the ribs. Encizo grabbed his partner's shoulder and pulled him back. "He's had enough, Cal," Encizo stated. "We still have other opponents to worry about."

"Yeah," James admitted with a shrug. "This guy just really ticked me off. He said they were going to move the hostages. Those choppers might be setting down by now so he might have told the truth."

David McCarter entered the dining hall. He took stock of the situation quickly and with evident approval.

"Just a lesson in manners that got carried away," James told him as he located his M-16 and gathered it up.

"The den is at the end of the next corridor," Encizo explained as he knelt by Mamer and strapped a pair of riot cuffs on the traitor's wrists. "That leads directly to the main hall and the door to the parade field. If they've got the hostages or the bomb in the building, they'll be moving them out that way now."

"Let's go," McCarter said eagerly, patting the frame of his KG-99.

"Wait a second," Encizo began as he felt an object in Mamer's jacket pocket. He reached inside and extracted a small radio transmitter. "Bingo! It's one of the remote control units to the bomb."

Encizo drew the Cold Steel Tanto knife from the sheath on his belt and used the tip of the blade to pop open the plastic back of the radio. He removed two nine-volt batteries and tossed them aside, then snapped the radio back together and slipped it into a jacket pocket.

"What are you keeping it for?" McCarter inquired.

"Might be useful," the Cuban answered. "Can't do any harm without batteries. I wonder who has the other units."

"We'll find out same way we found that one," the Briton remarked cheerfully.

"I just hope we don't find out after somebody used his to set off the goddamn bomb," James said grimly.

The three commandos moved into the corridor. It was empty. They headed for the next room and carefully pushed open the door. Encizo entered first, throwing himself in a shoulder roll across the carpeted surface. McCarter remained posted at the doorway, weapon pointed at the room, while James stood in the corridor to cover their backs.

They had found the den. The large comfortable room was decorated with antique paintings and furniture that suited Strassmacher Castle. Many were original items that had been handed down by the family. A modern bar, television set, stereo and VCR were among the more recent additions. So were nine men, who were seated on the leather sofa and chairs. They were all handcuffed and gagged, ankles bound together by a long chain that linked the prisoners together and kept them from acting as individuals. Padlocks ensured that the chains could not be wiggled out of or kicked off.

"Thank God," Encizo whispered. "We found the hostages!"

Yet even as he spoke, Encizo realized something was wrong. There were no guards posted by the prisoners. McCarter entered, scanning the den with care. The Briton and the Cuban glanced at the faces of the hostages and saw what was missing. The President of the United States and the Soviet premier were not among them. Encizo recognized the secretary of state. He approached the American cabinet member and pulled the gag from his mouth. The secretary of state seemed more confused than frightened. He did not speak, but raised his eyebrows in a mute question.

"Yes, Mr. Secretary," Encizo whispered. "We're here to rescue you. Do you know where the President and the premier have been taken?"

"They're taking them away in the helicopters," the secretary of state replied hoarsely. "They didn't want us. Said they didn't need that many hostages. We were left behind to deliver a message for the terrorists. I don't even understand it...."

"We'd better move it," Calvin James declared as he appeared next to Encizo. "By the time we get these men free Skull's boys will be flying the friendly skies over the border."

"You two go ahead," Encizo replied, taking a leather packet of picklocks from his gear. "I'll stay here and look after these gentlemen."

"Right," McCarter agreed quickly. "Let's go."

Encizo watched his partners rush out of the den to the main hall beyond. He looked at the bewildered faces of the hostages. The Soviet minister of foreign affairs was among them, but he was not sure who the others might be. Delegates from European nations, he figured, probably including translators. The Cuban suddenly realized they should have guessed the terrorists would not take all the hostages. Trying to haul so many prisoners along with the large number of mercenary terrorists would have been too great a load for the helicopters to handle. Skull would not make such a careless mistake.

"I'm not sure you should try to stop them," the secretary of state whispered. "They still have that bomb."

"We know," Encizo assured him as he selected two picklocks from his packet and inserted the instruments into the keyhole of a padlock. It was a simple single-tumbler lock and he easily picked it. The padlock clicked open. "We also know the risk will be even greater if the terrorists manage to get out of here."

"They may kill us all," the secretary remarked.

"It's possible," Encizo admitted, "but nobody lives forever anyway."

JAMES AND McCARTER moved to the great hall. Only two of the enemy stood at the foot of the stone stairwell leading to the next story. Neither man noticed the two Phoenix Force commandos. No other opponents lurked in the hall, although the two terrorists looked upward, which suggested there were probably more of them upstairs.

Through the open doors at the end of the hall, McCarter and James saw a helicopter on the parade field. The landing gear touched down on the cobblestones. Several figures moved near the chopper, which stirred a thick fog of dust, and the roar of the rotor blades seemed like the bellowing of an angry dragon.

McCarter held up a hand to James to signal that they should wait. The black commando nodded. He understood the Briton's logic. They could easily take out the two opponents at the foot of the stairs, but that would alert the others. They would have a better chance of reaching the door unnoticed by wait-

ing for the other terrorists to descend the stairs and mingle with
the group to shuffle outside. How to best handle the situation
at the parade field would depend on what they found when they
got there.

An explosion erupted somewhere outside. The building
trembled from the force of the blast. The two men at the stairs
exclaimed in alarm and immediately looked about, grabbing
their weapons nervously. One gunman's eyes widened when he
spotted James and McCarter.

"Hell," James rasped as he quickly snap-aimed his M-16 and
fired from the hip.

A trio of 5.56 mm slugs ripped a line of bullet holes in the
terrorist's chest. The man dropped his weapon and tumbled
backward. The other terrorist started to turn toward James, but
McCarter triggered his KG-99 and blasted a volley of missiles
into the gunman's upper torso and face. The second opponent's body twitched as it slid to the floor.

McCarter headed for the door, counting on James to cover
his move. The explosion still echoed throughout the confines
of Strassmacher Castle. The terrorists outside seemed confused and alarmed. Any sound warning of the advance of more
men was masked by the painful ringing in McCarter's ears, yet
he sensed danger with the battle-honed sixth sense developed
by years of experience with life-and-death situations.

Before he reached the exit, two terrorists charged down the
stone steps, weapons in hand. McCarter instantly whirled and
swung his KG-99 at the pair. They shouted something unintelligible in the babble of noises that filled the ancient structure.
Their guns' muzzles swung toward McCarter as he squeezed the
trigger.

The KG-99 snarled with the muffled voice of the silencer. The
Briton hosed the pair with a long 6-round burst. One terrorist
fell against a handrail and slid awkwardly along its length, then
sprawled across the steps to lie motionless.

The other gunman fell backward and landed on his behind.
He sat on the stairs like a drunkard, dazed and disoriented by
the high-velocity slugs that had smashed into his flesh. The
expression on his stunned features would have been comical if
the situation had not been so critical. The terrorist fired his

Soviet subgun. A burst of 7.62 mm rounds slashed through the air above McCarter's head as the Briton rushed alongside the stairwell.

McCarter's instincts to find cover also saved him from a burst fired by another gunman at the doors leading to the parade field. Obviously the man had noticed McCarter exchanging fire with the two gunmen on the stairs and realized the Briton was not working for Colonel Skull. The terrorist's H&K G-3 assault piece rattled out a salvo of avenging messengers, but the bullets only ricocheted and sparked against stone. McCarter dived to cover before the gunman could correct his aim.

Calvin James fired from the opposite side of the hall. The black warrior braced the M-16 to his shoulder and carefully aimed before he triggered his rifle. His actions took nearly one full second. A sliver of time, two blinks of an eye, yet an eternity in a kill-or-be-killed battlefield where a microsecond can mean life or death. The precious time was well spent. James fired his rifle and placed a trio of 5.56 mm rounds through the forehead of the gunman at the door. The opponent's face vanished in a crimson spray, and the terrorist fell backward to land among his comrades in the parade field.

The wounded gunman on the stairs started to turn his Russian PPSh-41 subgun toward James's position. McCarter thrust the barrel of his KG-99 between two supports of the handrail and fired a 3-round burst upward into the stomach and solar plexus of the terrorist. The man's belly opened up and a scarlet river streamed from his ravaged flesh. He uttered a single cry of agony, cut short as his heart ceased to function.

From the top of the stairs came a medley of voices demanding to know what was going on.

"Good question," Calvin James rasped as he swapped magazines to make certain his M-16 was fully loaded. "Wish I knew the answer."

YAKOV KATZENELENBOGEN and Gary Manning saw more of the parade field from their position than the other members of Phoenix Force. They also knew what had happened. Two of the enemy helicopters had landed on the parade field while the third hovered above Strassmacher Castle, apparently keeping track of the scene from an elevated point of view. Terrorists swarmed from the buildings within the castle walls, but in somewhat smaller numbers than previously expected because Phoenix Force had reduced their population by more than twenty.

Katz and Manning had encountered only three terrorists in the west wing, which had been badly damaged by explosions set off earlier by the terrorists. Two enemy troopers were dead and the third was unconscious, bound and gagged, when the choppers began to descend; the Phoenix pair had remained in position in the west wing and waited for a chance to move in before the enemy could load up the choppers. Since at that point the terrorists had not been alerted by gunshots or alarms, Katz figured they still had a go at rescuing the hostages and dismantling the bomb.

Then the plan went to pieces—literally. An explosion at the north wall tore a huge gap in the brick and mortar. The eruption immediately signaled danger to the terrorists and fully alerted them to expect trouble. Several uniformed figures suddenly charged through the opening in the north wall. In the billowing dust they looked like raiders from an alien planet with their heads covered by gas masks to protect them from the tear gas drifting about.

In a second, though, it became obvious that several of them were in Soviet Army uniforms and that they all carried assault rifles or submachine guns.

Katz clenched his teeth in anger. "Vashnov!" he rasped bitterly. "That KGB idiot must have put together this clumsy excuse for an attack. He probably thought the odds would be better if he waited until the choppers landed. That fool is just going to get his own people killed."

Katz's prediction proved accurate. Terrorists opened fire on the north wall, shredding the clouds of tear gas and dust with automatic fire. The Soviet attackers collapsed in silence, their cries muffled by the gas masks. The chopper hovering above the castle suddenly contributed to the carnage as a mounted machine gun erupted from the sliding doors at its carriage. More than a hundred high-velocity, rapid-fire bullets rained down on the north wall. Men were thrown back against the stone barrier, propelled by the force of multiple 7.62 mm rounds.

"Vashnov might be an idiot," Gary Manning remarked as he slipped the sling to his FAL assault rifle from his shoulder, "but he may unintentionally have done us a favor. This bullheaded raid is certainly distracting the terrorists."

"Right," Katz agreed with a sigh. "Not how we planned it, but it might work anyway. Let's go."

Katz and Manning headed toward the helicopters. The terrorists continued to concentrate on the Soviet raiders at the north wall. Some were also positioned at the door at the east wing and exchanged fire with McCarter and James inside the building. The others were clustered around the two choppers that had landed on the parade field and were being loaded with their human cargo.

Manning noticed a familiar-looking metal object being rolled up a short ramp to the carriage of a copter. At first glance, the bomb seemed to move forward on its own, as if it were a sinister version of R2D2. But the fireplug-shaped bomb was not a robot, only mounted on a mechanized trolley and assisted by two men who were bending into the task of pushing the steel shell forward. The Canadian demolitions expert moved closer to mingle with the group of terrorists huddled around the copter. If he could reach the bomb and examine it, he might be able to determine how to deactivate it.

The Canadian slithered in among the terrorists. The black beret and jacket disguise was actually more effective the closer he got to the busy crowd who were occupied by trying to load the bomb and deal with the opponents at the north wall and inside the castle's east wing. They scarcely noticed Manning. The Canadian pro's nostrils twitched as he got a whiff of the sour stink of tear gas. The Soviets had set off the canisters too far from the center of the parade field for the gas to be more than annoying, but the wind was blowing more of it in the direction of the helicopters. Many of the terrorists were already teary eyed, which was also in Manning's favor.

The Canadian felt cold fear crawl inside his stomach like a cat with icy paws, yet he also felt adrenaline rush through his body. Though the risk was very high, the gamble might pay off.

A sense of confidence floated inside Manning's mind, but he realized it was part of the high often caused by danger. It did not mean things were really going well enough to merit such confidence.

Manning stepped on the ramp and helped the two terrorists with the bomb. They shoved it up to the open cabin and rolled it inside the chopper. One of the men turned to Manning and displayed a wide grin. Manning smiled and nodded. The guy slapped him on the shoulder.

"*Très bien,*" he declared with satisfaction.

Manning replied with the correct acknowledgment, glad that French was his second language.

The two loaders stepped down from the ramp. Manning glanced about the interior of the aircraft. It was bigger than he had guessed when he'd spotted the choppers from a distance. There was room for twenty-five or thirty men easily. Indeed, at least fifteen were already on board, sitting along the benches in the cabin hull. Others may have been up front in the cockpit.

Manning turned his attention to the bomb. The dome appeared to be bolted and welded. He hoped his original theory was correct and the detonator was located in the dome, apart from the plutonium core within the heavy vessel. If he was right, disarming the weapon would not be difficult once he managed to get the dome off.

"You!" a voice snarled in thickly accented English. "What do you think you're doing?"

Major Yasnev stomped from the group of men at the hull. The Russian giant stared down at Manning and pointed a Kalashnikov rifle at him. Manning couldn't afford to start any shooting right then and kept the FAL pointed downward while he looked up at Yasnev with an expression that he hoped conveyed innocence.

"Nothing, *monsieur*," the Canadian replied with a Quebec accent and a broad shrug. "I simply wanted to be certain the bomb would stay rooted here instead of rolling back outside—"

"I do not recognize you!" Yasnev stated, stepping closer to jam the barrel of his AK-47 under Manning's jaw. "You weren't in the trailers with the others."

"No, I am an engineer and I came with the other helicopter," Manning lied smoothly. "Skull himself ordered me to examine the device as soon as it was brought on board."

"How strange." Manning heard a man's voice, deep and haunting with its slow tongue and lingering accent on each vowel. The man went on, "I don't recall giving such an order."

Manning turned toward the man who spoke. Colonel Skull stood by the cockpit. The Canadian felt a tremor along his spine as he stared into the merciless features of the sinister albino. Skull was dressed in a black uniform and cap, and the polished ivory buttons of his tunic gleamed in the subdued light. The thin colorless lips were pulled back tight across his teeth in a grim smile. Dark glasses covered Skull's pink-red eyes as he peered back at Manning.

"In fact," Skull continued, "I don't know who you are. Not yet. Yasnev, take his weapons."

"Why not kill him?" the Russian inquired.

"I want to talk to this man," Skull answered. "There's no time to explain, Major. Do as I say."

Yasnev suddenly slammed the stock of his AK-47 into Manning's FAL rifle and knocked the gun from the Canadian's grasp. The FAL clattered on the floor of the hull. The Russian abruptly punched the buttstock of his AK into Manning's belly. The Phoenix warrior gasped as the wind was driven from his lungs. Yasnev gripped his rifle between his fists like a bar and used it to shove Manning into the hull.

The Russian's face was less than an inch away from Manning's. Yasnev's teeth were clenched and his eyes glittered with sadistic pleasure. He slammed his knee into Manning's groin, and the Canadian howled in agony. Pain branched upward to twist his stomach and fill his nerves with shrieking hot lava. Yasnev smiled and slipped one hand inside Manning's jacket to reach for the Canadian's pistol in shoulder leather.

Manning reacted to the pain and rage. He drove both fists under Yasnev's ribs, the big middle knuckles braced to concentrate force into the hard, bony knobs. The Russian gasped from the unexpected blow. Manning shoved both arms into the frame of the Kalashnikov to push the weapon away and drive it back at Yasnev. He swung a hard right cross to Yasnev's face.

The Russian staggered back against the bomb. Manning tried to throw a kick at his opponent, but his legs would not respond. The pain in his groin was too great. Suddenly, a flash of a pale hand appeared at the corner of his eye. The hard edge struck him in the side of the jaw with surprising force. The Phoenix warrior's head filled with painful exploding lights as if fireworks had burst inside his cranium. He vaguely felt himself fall as his knees folded and he landed on all fours.

"No more nonsense," Colonel Skull commanded. "We haven't time for it."

Yasnev lashed out a boot and kicked Manning in the side of the head. The Canadian lost his hold on consciousness and he plunged into a black senseless pit.

THE HELICOPTER HOVERING above Strassmacher Castle continued to fire a steady stream of machine gun rounds as it rose higher. Bullets raked the security forces beyond the walls. American, European and Soviet victims were gunned down, and the wounded wet the dust with their blood while other agents and soldiers dived for cover behind the vehicles outside the great stone walls.

Yakov Katzenelenbogen was also forced to seek shelter. Two terrorists had noticed the one-armed Israeli and turned their weapons on him. Katz ducked behind a statue of a knight on horseback as they opened fire. Bullets rang against the stone horse and rider. Katz returned fire with his Uzi. One of the gunmen doubled up after being hit with a trio of parabellum rounds, while the other returned fire as he backed toward the choppers.

Both helicopters on the parade field began to lift off. Half a dozen terrorists had failed to get on board. They reached for the sleds of the landing gear, but the choppers did not slow down. Two men jumped off when they realized the effort was useless. Another held on to the sled as the chopper rose higher.

An explosion from the east blasted away part of the doorway and knocked several terrorists off their feet. Calvin James had fired a 40 mm grenade into the target with his M-203 launcher attached to the underside of the M-16 barrel. The black commando and David McCarter appeared at the threshold. Their automatic weapons snarled and hosed the terrorists in the parade field with lethal fury. Bodies convulsed from the tidal wave of bullets. Katz triggered his Uzi to create a cross fire and trap the remaining opponents in the deadly zigzag pattern of high-velocity rounds. The last terrorists were wiped out in a matter of seconds.

But the three enemy helicopters were climbing higher into the sky. The Phoenix Force warriors could do nothing but watch the aircraft ascend. Rain started to pelt down hard and fast from the dark, brooding sky. The desperate terrorist still hung on with his body dangling helplessly. At last he lost his grip on the sled and plunged more than five hundred feet to the ground below.

"Son of a bitch!" James snapped as he stared up at the sky. Rain drizzled down his face. He felt as if a slop pail were being tossed at him in derision. "They got away and they took the President and the premier with 'em!"

"And the bomb," McCarter added with a disgusted grunt. "Looks like Skull won this round."

"That's not all," Katz said grimly. "I think they've got Gary, too."

"Gary?" James stared at Katz with dismay. "He's still alive, isn't he?"

"I don't know," Katz admitted. "If he is alive, he might not stay that way for long. God knows what will happen now."

"I sure wish we did," McCarter commented.

11

Calvin James marched from the entrance of Strassmacher Castle with the M-16 canted over his shoulder. David McCarter followed, his KG-99 clenched in both fists. Both men's features showed a cold and determined rage. Yakov Katzenelenbogen jogged behind them, desperate to catch up with the pair. The Phoenix Force unit commander was well acquainted with the personalities of his men and knew how they would react to particular situations.

"Hold it!" Katz urged. "We don't have time to waste getting even with Vashnov!"

"It won't take long," James stated. "That stupid bastard screwed up our mission and I'm gonna rearrange his face for it."

"You punch him out and then I'll shoot the bastard," McCarter said with a nod. "That KGB moron got a lot of people killed with his idiotic stunt."

"We're not at war with the KGB," Katz reminded his partners. "Not this time anyway. We've got to try to work together."

"I know we worked with the KGB once before," James said with a weary sigh. "But Vashnov isn't Major Alekseyev and the situation is a hell of a lot different, Yakov."

"Vashnov won't be in charge after Rafael frees the Soviet minister of foreign affairs," Katz explained. "In fact, I think you two should go back and help him with the remaining VIPs instead of charging out of here to take out frustrations on Vashnov."

"All right," McCarter agreed reluctantly. "I'm feeling more inclined toward homicide right now than Calvin is, so I'll go. You blokes can play diplomat with those cloak-and-dagger types. But you should warn Vashnov to steer clear of me. I don't think I'll be able to look at that Russian rat's face without imagining a bull's-eye on his forehead.

"We'll do our best," Katz assured him.

McCarter headed back inside the walls of the castle and walked to the east wing while Katz and James turned toward the security forces. The scene wasn't new to Phoenix Force but was too well-known. Bullet-torn bodies lay sprawled on the ground, bloodied pools formed around the mangled corpses. Several other men had been wounded by the murderous spray of machine gunfire from the enemy helicopter.

American CIA and Secret Service agents were gathered in groups by the vehicles. Water leaked from bullet-punctured radiators, and windows and windshields had been shattered by the indiscriminate hailstorm of flying projectiles.

A variety of wounds were apparent, some to the torsos of the men; others had bullet-shattered limbs, with bleeding, pulped flesh and splintered bone. Luxembourgian troops had gathered near Colonel Mauser's tour bus. The soldiers were busy giving first aid to the wounded, while Mauser used the bus radio to contact observation points near the borders and to call Luxembourg Ville for medical assistance.

Vashnov had assembled what remained of the Soviet personnel. None of the GRU soldiers had escaped uninjured. Most had been killed during the hasty and inept attempt to charge through the north wall. Surviving GRU members lay moaning alongside a Zim limo. The KGB had fared somewhat better. Vashnov had purposely sent the GRU into the front lines of the abortive raid, preferring to put them in jeopardy than his fellow KGB comrades. Nonetheless, the KGB had also suffered losses and several survivors were injured.

Naturally, Vashnov had remained to the rear of the assault team and had avoided any serious risk while commanding the other Soviets during the raid. The KGB officer seemed unconcerned about the fate of his comrades. He folded his arms on his chest and glared at Katz, and James as the Phoenix pair walked toward the tour bus.

"Look at that son of a bitch," James muttered, returning Vashnov's hostile stare with an equally hard gaze. "He's acting as if this mess was our fault."

"Ignore him," Katz replied. "We've got more important matters to worry about than Vashnov's opinion."

"Yeah," James agreed. He glanced about at the wounded. "I'd better get out my medic kit and help these guys. I haven't seen a mess like this since Nam."

"They can certainly use your assistance," Katz said with a nod. "I'll talk to Mauser and the others. When David and Rafael get back, tell them to bring the VIPs to the bus. Maybe a chat with the Soviet minister of foreign affairs will take care of Vashnov for us. Hopefully, the secretary of state and the others can provide some useful information to allow us to catch up with the terrorists."

"What do you figure Skull will do with Gary?" James asked, wishing he had not asked because he already suspected what the answer would be.

"I don't know any more about that than you do, Cal," Katz admitted. "There's about a fifty-fifty chance Skull will keep him alive for questioning. How long he decides to conduct interrogations is hard to say. Unfortunately, there's not much we can do for Gary except continue with the mission. There's too much at stake here to put anything ahead of the success of the mission. Now that Skull has both the President and the Soviet premier, as well as the device that may indeed be a nuclear weapon, our mission is more critical than ever. We have to put our concern for Gary in the proper perspective—that is, keep in mind the priority of the hostages and what is involved when Skull continues to wield an atomic threat that might kill thousands of people before this is over."

"Yeah," James said with a weary nod. "Sometimes doing your duty really stinks. But I guess there's nothing we can do for Gary until we catch up with Skull, anyway."

James moved to the group of wounded Americans and shouted at a man with a canteen not to give water to anyone with an abdominal wound. Katz walked to the tour bus. Colonel Mauser emerged from the vehicle, accompanied by CIA agents Walters and Bernelli.

"We had nothing to do with that crazy attack on the wall," Walters declared quickly. His left arm was bleeding and twisted into an unnatural position. The man's face was contorted with pain and streaked with sweat, but he continued, "It was those damn Russkies. Vashnov and his cronies blasted the wall before we knew what happened—"

"There's nothing we can do about what's already happened," Katz cut him off, "except to pick up the pieces and go on. Colonel Mauser, have you contacted Luxembourg Ville?"

"Yes," Mauser confirmed. "Ambulances and medical units are already on their way. I also alerted headquarters. Tracking stations, in Luxembourg and surrounding countries, will be following the helicopters' progress by observation posts and radar. Don't worry, Mr. Kenver. Wherever they go, we'll find them."

"Don't count on it being that easy," Katz warned. "Skull was well prepared to get through security here at Strassmacher Castle. He's planned this for a long time. The fact he had agents among both the American and Soviet security people proves that. He'll know the choppers will be tracked in every way possible and must have something set up to mislead us. He's second-guessed us so far, and he'll certainly expect standard monitoring of the aircraft and probably prepare for whatever actions the Germans, Belgians or French attempt to stop his people."

Bernelli shook his head as if to clear it. "I can't believe this is happening."

"Summit conferences have gone pretty smoothly in the past, from a security point of view, anyway," Katz replied. "Everyone got a little careless. Personnel weren't screened closely enough. Emphasis was placed more on public relations and showing the world how the two superpowers could be chums. It was just another show, for all the facade of secrecy and restrictions imposed. Nobody thought anything could go wrong. Now it has."

"You said nothing could be done about what's already happened," Walters reminded him, clearly offended by Katz's remarks. "What the hell do we do now?"

"The terrorists didn't take all the hostages," Katz answered. The Israeli reached for the cigarettes in his shirt pocket, but realized the rain would make it difficult to smoke. "Unfortunately, the President and the premier are still held prisoner. My partners are bringing out the VIPs left behind. They'll also march out some of the terrorists we managed to take alive. You might send some people in to check the castle to see if there are any other wounded terrorists whom they may have overlooked."

"How many did you manage to take out?" Bernelli inquired. The young Company man clearly hoped the body count among the enemy would be higher than the number of security personnel casualties.

"Two dozen, maybe thirty," Katz said with a shrug. "It's hard to say for certain. About five or six are alive. We'll interrogate them and compare information. I strongly advise you to permit my associate to use scopolamine. He's very experienced in administering the drug."

"Truth serums aren't really approved of in my country," Mauser commented, "but we'll have to keep the media out of this for now, anyway. That may not be easy."

"We have an extraordinary situation, and it requires bending a few rules of proper conduct," Katz told him. "Besides, even if we don't use truth serums, the Soviets certainly will. Vashnov would set up a torture chamber if he thought he could get away with it. We can't keep the KGB uninvolved—after all, this concerns the Soviet Union, as well as the United States and Western Europe."

"Vashnov could ruin things again," Walters said angrily, gripping his injured arm tightly. "If he hadn't ordered his Siberian spud-pullers to go through that wall, you might have been able to take out the terrorists and rescue the President. Instead, Vashnov's stunt convinced the bastards to spray us down with machine gunfire just to keep us at bay."

"Forget Vashnov for now," Katz urged. "We have to get in touch with the CIA in the Federal Republic of Germany, France and Belgium. If the CIA isn't as successful as the National Security Association in any of those countries, then we'll link up with them. I know CIA and NSA have a sort of rivalry going, but I don't want that petty nonsense to get in our way. We'll also bring in U.S. Army Intelligence if they can be of assistance and I want the Grenzschutzgruppe-Neun on call. That's the West German antiterrorist unit better known as GSG-9. Colonel Ludwig Bohler has worked with my group in the past. He's a fine man, and GSG-9 is one of the best antiterrorist squads in the world."

"That's an awful lot to ask on short notice," Walters said, shaking his head.

"I'm not finished yet," Katz informed him. "La Sûreté nationale, French intelligence, must also be contacted."

"French intelligence is a contradictory term," Mauser muttered. Like many Luxembourgians, he was not very fond of his French neighbors.

"There's no time for bickering and silly bigotries of any sort," Katz insisted. "A nuclear bomb in the hands of terrorists may be crossing into France. Sûreté has a right to know about that."

"We don't know if the enemy are going to cross into France or Germany," Walters commented. "Isn't this sort of jumping the gun and letting the other countries get all stirred up about something that might not even involve them? Doesn't do a great deal for our image, either."

"Or the image of Luxembourg," Mauser added.

"Terrorism," Katz began, "especially terrorism on this scale, involves *everyone*. I would rather give a false alarm to the intelligence agencies in France, Germany and Belgium than wait till the last moment to warn them. We need their cooperation and can't expect it if we fail to share information that, after all, concerns their national security. As for images getting tarnished, I hope you'll forgive me if I don't see that as a vital issue at this time. The political ramifications of this event can be dealt with later."

"All right," Walters said with an exhausted sigh. The pain of his wounded arm and the blood loss were clearly taking their toll. "I'll have to go back to Luxembourg Ville and contact my section chief. I don't have enough clout to get all this stuff authorized. Most likely you'll have to talk to him, too.''

"In fact there isn't much we can do out here," Mauser added. The wail of sirens and headlights on the road signaled the ambulances were rapidly approaching. "Sounds like help is coming for the wounded. When it arrives, we can be on our way."

Enciso and McCarter emerged from the castle. Nine VIPs accompanied the two Phoenix warriors, including the American secretary of state and the Soviet minister of foreign affairs. Four terrorists were also escorted at the rear of the group. The prisoners were bruised and bloodied, but able to walk. Their hands were still cuffed behind their backs and McCarter kept his KG-99 trained on the captives as they marched from the entrance of the ancient structure.

Vashnov exclaimed and rushed toward the Soviet minister to find out how he was.

"You get the hell away from us, Vashnov!" McCarter snapped, nearly swinging his subgun toward the KGB officer.

"Take it easy," Katz urged as he came up to the group. He turned his attention to the minister and spoke to him in Russian.

The minister turned to Vashnov, who had tried to interfere and was nursing a ferocious scowl that looked ludicrous, given the situation that clearly demanded cooperation from all concerned.

"This is urgent. We need to talk to these gentlemen."

"I'm a bit confused," the American secretary of state admitted. "Are you with our people or what?"

"We'll explain what we can, Mr. Secretary," Katz assured him. "And we expect you to do likewise. *All* of you. The crisis we face is a joint one. One might compare its gravity to the threat of Nazis in World War II."

"I think I understand," the Soviet minister confirmed with a nod. "The Soviet Union and the United States joined forces during World War II to fight against a common enemy—the Nazis. If that is the case, we shall most certainly cooperate."

"Your side can start by replacing Vashnov with somebody else," McCarter growled. "Somebody who isn't brain damaged by an overdose of propaganda."

"Don't try to blame me for what happened here," Vashnov replied with an angry stare. "I acted according to the situation I was faced with."

"The KGB's only qualification for dealing with terrorists is helping to support their activities in the past," Encizo declared. The Cuban's generally well-controlled temper was beginning to get as frayed as McCarter's. "Oh, I nearly forgot the KGB style of antiterrorist tactics you people displayed in the Middle East after some Soviet advisers were kidnapped. Butchering the families of suspected terrorists is more your style than commando raids against armed opponents. Isn't it, Vashnov?"

"Gentlemen!" the secretary of state said quickly before the argument could escalate to an exchange of blows or even worse. "There is no need for this—"

"And no time," Katz insisted. "Come on. We've got a herculean task on our hands and not much time to deal with it."

"You sure got that right," the secretary of state confirmed. "Less than one week."

GARY MANNING BECAME aware of pain as he began to regain consciousness. His head throbbed, and there was a dull ache in his groin. A moan rose into his throat, but he instinctively suppressed it before it could slip from his lips. The Canadian commando's mind was still blurred and his memory slowly returned from a dense mental fog.

He was tempted to retreat back into the peaceful limbo of unconsciousness, but his mind was too disciplined to allow him to pursue that escape. Behind his closed eyes was a light show of moving strobes and tiny comets that flashed across his inner lids as the throbbing behind his eyeballs grew stronger. He did not attempt to open his eyes until his head cleared. The Phoenix warrior recalled events that had occurred before his senses had deserted him. He pretended to be still unconscious as he silently took inventory of his own body.

Manning did not detect any open cuts or puncture wounds. No bones seemed broken although he could not move his arms. The constriction at his wrists explained this. He was handcuffed, the wrists locked together at the small of his back. Manning's aching head was the only injury that troubled him. He knew it was possible he might have a concussion. The sound of the roaring engine and the chopping bellow of rotor blades mingled with a number of voices speaking several languages, mostly English and French. His hearing had evidently not been impaired, and he smelled sweat, oiled metal and fear. Of all emotions, fear had the strongest odor, a copper and saltwater stench, like that of a wet penny. Manning sensed other bodies nearby, but he could not tell if the fear was theirs or his.

"Are you all right?" a voice inquired. It was a man's voice, with a throaty quality, yet each word was clear and articulate—the voice of a man who had spent many years perfecting it for public speaking. "Can you hear me?"

The voice seemed familiar. Manning was sure he had heard it before, but he could not identify the owner. Slowly, he eased his eyelids open. His vision was slightly blurred, and the vague outline of a person's head appeared in the watery mist. Manning blinked and his sight cleared. The face before him was one he had seen often in the past. A famous face, recognized throughout the world. Manning's eyes widened with surprise as he stared at the President of the United States.

"Can you understand me?" the President asked, leaning toward Manning. "Will you be all right?"

"I...I think so," Manning answered hoarsely. His mouth tasted as if he had been sucking on an old sweat sock. "How are you, Mr. President?"

"I've felt more secure," the American politician replied. He even managed a slight grin. "I know you tried to rescue us. Are you an American? CIA? Delta Force?"

"I'd rather not go into that, sir," Manning stated as he glanced about at the others seated on the bench in front of him.

The middle-aged man beside the President was another familiar face, a round face that could have belonged to a high school principal. He was balding and wore a pair of glasses perched on the bridge of his stubby nose. The Soviet premier looked back at Manning and nodded.

"Hello," he said with a slight shrug. "Excuse me, please. I speak English not so good. I read it better."

"Sorry, I don't speak Russian," Manning replied. He noticed two other prisoners with the pair of world leaders, but he did not recognize them.

"Andrew Thornton," declared a thin man dressed in a gray suit with a houndstooth-checked tie, guessing that Manning wondered who he was. His features seemed small and delicate as if carefully placed on his face by surgeons armed with watchmakers' tools. "Member of Parliament, United Kingdom. I was representing Great Britain at the summit meeting. Lucky me. These chaps decided to bring me along."

"Klaus Weiss," a heavyset man with a broad face and baggy, tired eyes explained with a guttural Bavarian accent. "Federal Republic of Germany. I'm here for the same reason as Andrew."

"Everyone is getting to know everyone else?" a harsh voice asked in a sneering tone.

Yasnev stood near the prisoners, his thick arms folded across his chest. The Makarov pistol in his big fist looked like a toy squirt gun. His Stalin-style mustache bristled as he grinned at the captives.

"So the hero is awake now," Yasnev said, fixing his mocking gaze on Gary Manning. "How you feel, hero?"

"Put that gun away and take the cuffs off me, and I'll show you how I feel," Manning answered with a thin smile.

"I would like that," the renegade GRU agent declared. "I would like to break your neck, Yankee. Maybe later."

"Gives me something to look forward to," the Canadian replied mildly. "Where are you taking us?"

"You'll find out when the time comes," Colonel Skull declared as the terrorist leader appeared next to Yasnev. "Sorry for the discomfort you have to endure, but it really is necessary. However, it won't be much longer."

Skull still wore the black Gestapolike uniform and cap, as well as dark glasses although the lights inside the helicopter were dim. An Asian, clad in camouflage fatigues, stepped beside the terrorist colonel. The man was built like a concrete slab, five and a half feet tall and with the muscles of a pro-football player or a trimmer version of a sumo wrestler. His face could have been granite, as expressionless and inscrutable as the fabled reputation of the Far East. The man's almond-shaped eyes were hazel, unusual for an Oriental. Manning guessed him to be Korean.

"What do you expect to gain from this outrage?" the President demanded. "You must realize this action will result in the combined efforts of every intelligence agency of both the West and the Soviet Union to hunt you down. As well as every police department in Europe. You can't get away with this—"

"Do be quiet, Mr. President," Skull replied. "You're not running for office here, and I've never had much tolerance for politicians and their egotistic speeches. Right now, you are a hostage. You have no authority and no value except as a hostage. Fortunately, you and these other gentlemen are quite valuable to me alive and well. I intend to keep you that way, but that doesn't mean I have to let any of you ramble on with your annoying rhetoric."

"Sounds to me like you've decided to monopolize that market for yourself," Andrew Thornton commented.

The Korean stepped forward with surprising speed for such a bulky man. He seized Thornton's suit jacket with one hand and easily yanked him to his feet. The Korean's other hand rose in front of the Briton's startled face, fist clenched with the index finger extended. Thornton's features revealed raw terror as the Asian stared mercilessly into his eyes.

"Treat the colonel with respect," the Korean instructed, his voice flat and emotionless.

Suddenly, he swung his arm in a fast arc and drove the rigid index finger into Thornton's abdomen. The Briton's mouth opened into a black oval and his eyes squinted with pain. The Asian shoved him back to the bench. Thornton's body jack-knifed and he slumped to the floor, gasping for breath. Hand-cuffed and unable to hug his aching belly, he thrashed about like a fish on hot concrete and then stopped moving to gulp air with relief as the pain subsided.

"Major Hee," Skull announced, "I think you've made your point. Thank you."

The Korean nodded and returned to Skull's side. Major Hee was clearly a formidable opponent, Manning thought; the information might prove useful in the near future. The henchman's punishment of Thornton revealed precise knowledge of *atemi* pressure points and nerve centers, and the blow Hee delivered had been carefully controlled to inflict exactly the amount of pain he desired. He was a highly skilled martial artist, who could have just as easily killed Thornton with a single jab of his index finger.

"Let's try to avoid these unpleasantries," Skull stated. "If all goes well, every one of you will get to return to your home countries, slightly ruffled perhaps, but unharmed. That will, of course, depend on how cooperative your governments prove to be. Actually, our demands aren't unreasonable and, in fact, agreeing to them will be in the best interest of the United States, Western Europe and the Soviet Union."

"I hope you'll understand if I find that difficult to believe," the President replied. "Kidnappers and terrorists are hardly noted for humanitarian behavior. I witnessed an example of your idea of proper conduct back at the castle. Dozens of innocent people were butchered. Is that the form of politics we're supposed to welcome?"

"Da," the Soviet premier agreed, able to understand the basic meaning of the President's claim. "You are gangsters and killers."

Major Yasnev leaned forward and spit in the premier's face. The saliva stained the Soviet leader's glasses and dripped down his cheek. Unable to wipe it off, he could only glare angrily at the renegade GRU traitor.

"You gentlemen are rather amusing." Skull laughed lightly. "The United States and the Soviet Union have both participated in wars. Mr. President, you ordered troops to invade the small island country of Grenada and bombed the capital city of Libya when you considered it to be a matter of national security. The Soviet genocide activities in Afghanistan and Cambodia have been going on for more than a decade, not to mention the support of Marxist dictatorships in Africa, Central America, Eastern Europe, Southeast Asia . . . Need I continue? Violence is a political tool wielded by governments all the time. The men we killed at Strassmacher Castle were a mere handful compared to the lives destroyed by you noble statesmen and world leaders. You always have excuses when such actions serve the interest of your country. That's exactly why your governments will agree to my terms. It will, in fact, take care of a burden that has concerned all your nations for a number of years. You may eventually even thank us for what we're doing.''

''Do these justifications make it easier for you or is this all just for our sake?'' Manning inquired.

''I haven't forgotten you, our little warrior,'' Skull declared, turning his head toward Manning. ''You might wonder why you're still alive. You're not a head of state and you participated in an attack on my people that resulted in the deaths of quite a few of them. Yasnev here would love to tear your head off with his bare hands, and all the rest of my soldiers would be more than happy to throw you from this helicopter. I'd enjoy doing that myself.''

''You plan to have a bridge tournament and you need an extra player?'' Manning replied, trying to sound more calm than he felt.

''You mentioned 'Colonel Skull' when you tried to bluff your way around Yasnev,'' the terrorist leader stated. ''That means you somehow knew I was responsible for the operation at Strassmacher Castle. I want to know your source and what other details you might know.''

''You can't have everything you want, Skull,'' Manning told him. ''I don't think you'll find me very cooperative.''

''Oh, I'm sure you're a very tough fellow,'' Skull said with a nod. ''Very professional. The equipment we confiscated from you proved that. Plastic explosives, sophisticated detonators, high-quality firearms with threaded barrels for silencers, pocket transceiver and wire garrote. All very impressive. Not to mention your clever, if rather inadequate disguise, your fluent French and no doubt a number of other awesome skills. Yet, as a professional, you must surely realize that any man can be broken. Any man can be forced to talk. I have people who are very good at making tough men like you talk. Some of their methods are very unpleasant.''

''I can imagine,'' Manning said grimly, all too well aware of what Skull's people would be all too willing to do in the effort to break him down.

''Good,'' Skull replied with a grimace of a smile. ''That will give you something to think about before we start interrogations. You may decide to save yourself a great deal of discomfort and pain. I won't insult your intelligence by suggesting you can do anything to save your life, but a quick and fairly merciful death is better than a slow and painful one. Do consider that while you are still capable of rational thought.''

12

"You said we have less than a week to find the hostages," Katz reminded the secretary of state as they discussed the crisis in a conference room at the American embassy in Luxembourg Ville. "Would you please explain that deadline for us?"

"The terrorist spokesman, the one called Major Koerner," the secretary began, "told us we would only have one week. He also gave me a cassette tape that would explain the details. It's in my jacket pocket."

"I was also given such a tape," the Soviet minister of foreign affairs added. "Apparently, the one I received is in Russian instead of English."

"I'll get a tape player," Colonel Mauser declared. "This is just an audiotape, correct? Not video?"

"Yes, yes," the secretary confirmed. "Just a plain cassette tape recorder is all we need."

"Very well," the Luxembourgian officer replied and hurried from the room.

"Did you overhear any bits and pieces of conversations that might help us find Skull?" Rafael Encizo inquired. The Cuban had removed his jacket and was leaning back in his chair with the Walther PPK clearly visible in shoulder holster under his arm. "Any comments about going to other countries or plans of what they'd do when they got there?"

"No," the secretary answered. "Koerner was furious when one of the terrorists called him by name. That was about the only mistake they made. Yasnev or that CIA traitor, Mamer, were with us most of the time to supervise the others and make sure nobody got careless. I noticed your friends managed to take Mamer alive.''

"He's being interrogated along with the other terrorist prisoners," Katz stated. "My other two associates are helping with questioning. The prisoners will be given scopolamine to try to make certain we're getting the truth from them. We're doing all we can to get as much information as possible."

"I really think you should get someone else from the Company in here," Scott Bernelli admitted with an apologetic shrug. "I'm not experienced with this sort of thing. Hell, I didn't realize how green I really am until this happened."

"Walters is having a bullet removed from his arm," Katz reminded Bernelli. "Right now, you're the highest-ranking CIA official we've got. As for your lack of experience, none of us have had a situation like this before. Don't worry about your qualifications. A lot of people in authority aren't qualified."

"Speaking of a lack of qualifications," Encizo began as he turned to face the Soviet minister. "That's why Vashnov isn't here. You're going to see about getting a replacement for that extremist, aren't you? The man is a liability and can't be any help to us. He can only cause more problems."

"I realize you are unhappy with Vashnov," the minister replied. "Bear in mind, he was not in charge of any security forces until his superiors were killed by the terrorists. Indeed, one of his superiors was Major Yasnev, who proved to be a double agent working for the terrorists. Vashnov assumed you Americans were responsible and he acted according to what he believed to be true. He is not used to command and not skilled in such matters. Vashnov has done badly, but that's simply because he has had to cope with more than he was prepared to deal with."

"Uh-huh," Encizo said with a weary nod. "Well, either replace him or keep the KGB out of this. If Vashnov gets in our way again, he'll go back to Moscow in a pine box."

"I understand your frustration," the minister said with a sigh. "I hope you also understand that I do not control the KGB. Contacting them is difficult enough and issuing orders is even more difficult, since I have no direct authority over them. The Committee for State Security virtually operates as an organization separate from the mainstream of Soviet government.''

''Vashnov is out,'' Katz stated. ''So is the KGB unless they put someone else in his place.''

Mauser returned with a tape recorder. He placed the machine on the table near the secretary of state. Since everyone in the room understood English, it was logical to listen to the American's tape. The secretary took the tape from his pocket and inserted it into the recorder. A shrill whistle sang out from the machine.

''Greetings to the government of the United States of America and whatever officials of that state may be listening to this tape,'' a voice began. The words were clear, but had an odd robotlike singsong quality with a slight echo in the background.

''Why does it sound like that?'' the secretary wondered.

''The voice has been electronically altered,'' Katz answered. ''That's to prevent identifying the speaker by voiceprints or detecting any trace of accent or background sounds that might betray a location.''

''If you are listening to this,'' the voice continued, ''you know the situation. If all has gone according to plan, the President, the secretary-general of the Soviet Union and probably one or more NATO country delegates have been kidnapped by us. You also know that we have a nuclear weapon. A very nasty plutonium bomb. You must find this situation as baffling as it is uncomfortable.''

''That's an understatement,'' Bernelli muttered.

''Let me assure you,'' the message went on, ''we have no wish to harm the hostages or detonate the plutonium device. We will release the hostages, alive and unharmed, and leave the bomb at a safe location with instructions and tools needed to safely deactivate it. All this will be done if you carry out our demands as follows.''

The men in the conference room listened carefully, fascinated by the strange recording. Skull's confidence was staggering. He must have been absolutely positive his plan would succeed exactly as he conceived it. The scary part was the fact that the terrorist leader had guessed right so far.

"The United States government will announce plans to send three billion dollars in financial aid to the government of Iraq to assist it in its war against Iran," the voice declared. "In addition, you will send no less than two billion dollars' worth of weapons, medical supplies, ammunition, aircraft and other goods to be determined after the agreement has been made with the leaders of Iraq. NATO countries are to maintain friendly relations with Iraq. Their financial assistance will be appreciated, although no definite demands will be made of them. The facts that their delegates are vulnerable to abduction and that plutonium bombs may be detonated in their cities in the future should encourage them to cooperate."

The quality of amusement in the voice was clear despite the electronic distortion. The blackmailer was clearly enjoying himself.

"Now, before you get too upset, let me assure you the Soviet Union will have to meet similar demands. The Kremlin isn't as rich as Washington, so they'll only have to supply one billion dollars in financial aid. I might add, we will demand they pay this amount in gold instead of Russian rubles. American dollars are valuable everywhere, but the same isn't true about rubles. The Soviets will also be required to send no less than three billion dollars' worth of arms and other supplies. The Russians have more tanks than any other nation on earth and Iraq will need roughly one thousand more tanks when they invade Iran. The Soviets shouldn't mind. They've got plenty to spare."

"Iraq?" The Soviet minister knitted his brow. "What is this madness?"

"Actually, the entire business should please both the United States and the Soviet Union in the end," the voice continued. "Europe and the Middle East countries may also find the ultimate results of the venture to be most agreeable. What will happen after Iraq is given a new military edge to use against Iran will be the complete destruction of the Islamic Jihad government ruled by the Ayatollah. Ever since the Ayatollah seized power, Iran has been a problem to both the U.S. and the Soviets. Tehran has been stirring up Islamic revolutionaries, masterminding terrorist groups, creating sheer havoc in the Persian

Gulf. Many believe the Soviets invaded Afghanistan to turn it into a buffer zone to protect them from Iran. The Soviets also have the second largest population of Shiite Muslims in the world, another reason to find the Ayatollah's Shiite movement worrisome."

"Jesus," Bernelli whispered in amazement. "He makes this sound almost reasonable."

"Of course," the voice went on, "Western Europe and Japan will be glad to be able to do business with Iran without taking the chance of angering their American friends. Saudi Arabia will be pleased to have the Ayatollah's regime out of the way after that bloody riot at the Great Mosque. It should be a relief to Israel that at least one threat to their existence is gone. Kuwait and Oman will be able to operate their oil tankers without fear. Benefit will come to everyone in the end. Naturally, the new government of a united Iraq-Iran will charge a service fee for vessels using the Persian Gulf, but it's a small price to pay for everything you'll gain. Think of it, gentlemen. No more fretting about American ships being attacked in the gulf. No more costly armed escorts of Kuwaiti tankers. No more Ayatollah's Iran."

The Soviet minister glanced at the American secretary of state. For a minute they studied each other in an effort to gauge each other's reaction.

"The beauty of the arrangement is the fact neither the Soviets or the Americans can be blamed for bringing down the current regime in Iran," the voice stated. "Both nations are to assist in building Iraq, yet neither need send in advisers or troops. Iraq can take care of Iran from there. As I'm sure you realize, Iran's only advantages are the size of its manpower and its fanatic zeal. Iraq can easily compensate for that with more sophisticated weapons and what it lacks in manpower, it can compensate from other sources. The victory will be assured after Iraq gets the support previously mentioned."

Yakov Katzenelenbogen rose from his seat and began to pace. He put his hands behind his back and marched up and down the length of the room. The Phoenix Force commander was certain the voice on the tape belonged to Colonel Skull himself. A brilliant opponent, he realized. A man who could

murder your people, kidnap your leaders, threaten and blackmail you and still try to convince you he was really your friend.
The dreadful thing was history was full of successful politicians and leaders who had done exactly what Skull was attempting—and often they got away with it.

"Two very important matters to bear in mind," the voice
continued. "The first concerns the safety of the hostages. We
will try to protect them and keep them healthy, but we can't
promise they'll remain that way if you come hunting for us.
Mind you, I know you'll try, but if you get too close the results
will mean death for the hostages and thousands of innocent
Europeans when we send off the bomb. If all goes according to
plan and all our demands are met, we will release the hostages
and you fellows can claim you rescued them from terrorists
supported by Iran. It can be a shining example of how the U.S.
and the Soviet Union can work together in a crisis. That will
allow you to salvage your public image and save face with the
rest of the world."

"Son of a bitch thought of everything," Encizo remarked,
expressing reluctant admiration for a shrewd opponent.

"The second matter, and this is very important, is the delivery of the aid to Iraq," the voice stated. "It must be done exactly one week from this date. The weapons, supplies and
money must be received by Iraq precisely on the twenty-third
of this month. Not one day sooner or later. On the twenty-third
exactly. If you fail to do this, you will never see either the
President or the premier alive again. Also, since you have surely
already learned we have infiltrated your intelligence networks
in both the United States and the Soviet Union, you must also
realize we can easily carry out very sophisticated and destructive sabotage in your countries. Refuse our demands and we
will take action. The first will be the plutonium bomb you saw
here. It will explode somewhere in Europe. Perhaps in Paris or
Bonn. Perhaps in East Berlin or Warsaw. We are apolitical and
really don't care which side of the Iron Curtain suffers. This act
of retribution will be followed by other bombs in the U.S. and
the U.S.S.R. The price you will pay for failing to obey these
instructions will far exceed the few billion dollars it will cost
you to avoid these terrible consequences."

"My God," the secretary of state whispered.

"You might call this blackmail," the voice on the tape remarked. "Perhaps it is, but governments blackmail one another all the time. You Americans support numerous dictatorships to prevent communism from taking over in other countries. The choice you have now is very simple. Death, destruction and terror, or agree to our terms and in the end, the world will be a better and safer place. For everyone's sake, I hope you make the correct decision."

The men in the conference room sat quietly at the table. Katz continued to pace. The tape recorder went on running, but the rest of the tape was blank. The secretary of state switched off the machine. He looked at the Soviet minister, then turned toward Colonel Mauser.

"I imagine you're wishing we hadn't picked Luxembourg for the summit meeting," he remarked.

"I wish the terrorists had chosen a different target," Mauser admitted. "What do you gentlemen suggest we do now?"

"We can't make decisions about something this critical on our own," the secretary of state answered.

"I agree," the Soviet official stated. "We're not able to authorize such things as billion-dollar foreign aid or delivery of weapons—"

"Wait a minute," Encizo said, eyebrows raised. "You're not thinking of agreeing to these demands?"

"That isn't for us to decide," the Russian replied. "Nor is it up to you and your friends."

"One week," Katz mused. "Less time than that, really. That doesn't leave time for debates, senate committees or decrees by the politburo. How familiar are you with the leadership in Iraq? The Soviets have been manipulating that country for years."

"I resent the way you put that," the minister replied stiffly.

"Iraq is a socialist-military dictatorship," Katz said. "It isn't any state secret that the Soviets have been backing Iraq for years, so I assume you know more about the leaders in Iraq than the rest of us. Now, do you think the present heads of state in Iraq would resort to drastic action along these lines to try to secure money and weapons to use in the war with Iran?"

"I find it hard to believe that the Iraqi president or the chairman of the Federal Assembly would attempt such a plan," the minister of state answered. "The popular notion in Iraq is that the Iranian government under the Ayatollah is destined to fall apart because the Ayatollah has tried to turn back the clock and set back his nation in the process. Iraq believes Iran will crumble from within after the Ayatollah dies. There are already stories of widespread dissent within Iran. Many are very unhappy with the changes made by the Islamic regime. Of course, Iraq has been getting support from my country, and recently the United States reestablished diplomatic relations with Iraq. I certainly would not have guessed Iraq would jeopardize its relations with either of our countries simply to try to get an early and swift victory in Iran. Especially if such a plan involved such extreme action."

"Maybe your guess is wrong," the secretary of state commented.

"I don't think so," Katz declared. "Skull insisted on delivery of the financial aid, weapons and supplies to Iraq on the twenty-third. Not one day sooner or one day later. Why? What difference would one day make? Especially one day sooner?"

"It doesn't make any sense to me," Bernelli admitted.

"Not if the present leaders in Iraq hired Skull," Encizo stated. "But it does make sense if someone else is responsible for the terrorists. Someone who plans to take control of Iraq in exactly one week."

"You're suggesting there will be a revolution within Iraq?" the Soviet minister asked, eyes wide with surprise. "By whom? What sort of political force would take over?"

"I doubt that it would be a revolution in the general sense of that term," Katz explained. "Probably there's someone who ranks high in the government chain of command who'd be in line to rule the nation after the Iraqi president and perhaps some others died abruptly. My guess is the same man who hired Skull's army also plans to assassinate the present leaders of Iraq and take control."

"Probably make the assassinations appear to be terrorist hits by Iran," Encizo added. "Everything is falling in place now. The seemingly meaningless hijacking of the *Sea Venus* by

Skull's people was supposed to be terrorism supported by Iran.
It was just a performance to help stir up public opinion against
Iran in the United States and Western Europe. The attack on
Strassmacher Castle and the kidnappings is really Skull's doing
as part of this scheme, but he wants us to claim the Iranians are
responsible if he releases the President and the premier.''

"The Iranians are perfect fall guys," Bernelli commented.
"They've been involved in so much terrorism for real it would
be easy to convince the public they're also behind this."

"No one would be upset to see Iran fall," Mauser added his
opinion. "Except, perhaps, Khaddafi. If both the U.S. and the
U.S.S.R. supported Iraq, it would prevent either country from
getting much blame. Clever scheme. It lets everyone off the
fishhook, as you Americans might say."

"Most Americans would just say 'hook,'" Encizo explained. "Now we have a pretty good idea why this is happening, but we still have to concentrate on locating the terrorists
and rescuing the hostages."

"That may very well get the President killed," the secretary
of state insisted. "For now we need to keep a lid on the details
involved and consult with our governments. Military advisers,
CIA director, the treasury department, I'm not sure who
else."

"I must agree," the Soviet minister stated. "It's a time when
cool heads are needed rather than rash actions. We need to
black out the media and try to prevent anyone without authorization from learning what has happened."

"Well, the Germans, the French and the Belgians already
have a pretty good idea about most of it," Bernelli said with a
sigh. "They've been warned to expect the terrorist helicopters
to head for their territory."

"Who authorized that?" the Russian demanded.

"I did," Katz answered. "The terrorists aren't about to remain in Luxembourg. We can't hope to find them without the
assistance of the intelligence networks and possibly police departments of those neighboring countries."

"Damn it, Kenver!" the secretary of state snapped. "I would have thought you would have more concern for maintaining security—"

"We have to stop Skull," Katz stated. "And whatever has to be done to accomplish that, we're prepared to do it. You can't give in to this blackmail scheme. What will the demands be next year if Skull is rewarded for such an outrage? Do you think it will be the end of terrorism and international extortion? You can't keep it a secret. Maybe the general public will never know the details, but every government in the world will either learn about it or suspect what really happened."

"Yeah," Bernelli commented. "But it sure would be nice to get rid of the Ayatollah and his fanatic following. The idea is sort of appealing and I'm not so sure the American public wouldn't agree."

"The American public wouldn't agree to paying off blackmailers and terrorists," Encizo told him. "You think the guys who'll take over Iraq by committing murder and hiring terrorists to kidnap world leaders are going to turn out to be wonderful trade partners after they conquer Iran? If Skull wins, we lose. Don't kid yourself that there will be compensation to make it all worthwhile. That's what he wants us to believe."

"Your convictions are admirable," the secretary of state said with a helpless gesture with his open palms spread apart. "But these decisions are not up to us. *Any* of us."

"Then who is supposed to be responsible?" Katz demanded, turning sharply to fix his hard stare on the American and Soviet political leaders. "Government committees that take months to make decisions? Officials who spend more time trying to blame each other than trying to find solutions? Agencies and departments that try to hide problems or minimize their importance rather than facing them and doing something about them? You two can go back to Washington and Moscow and try to find out who will be responsible in the current situation. We'll concentrate on finding Colonel Skull and putting him out of the terrorist business for good."

"I'll pick a clean fight over dirty politics any day of the week," Encizo muttered as he rose from his chair.

"That's not a fair statement," the secretary of state declared. "I resent the implication—"

"I couldn't care less what you resent," the Cuban replied in a hard flat voice. "Just let us do our job. We'll let you guys do yours . . . if you can figure out what it's supposed to be."

The door opened and David McCarter appeared at the entrance. The Briton's face seemed a bit flushed as if he had bolted through the corridor. He would have had to show his identification to get past the Marine embassy guards at the end of the hall, but apparently he hadn't been slowed down for more than a second or two.

"Radar and visual observation tracking has located the enemy helicopters," McCarter announced. "The choppers have been identified as Krumbacher LMY-17 West German-design transport gunships. We used a chopper like that ourselves during a mission about five years ago."

"These details can wait," Katz told him. "Where were the choppers sighted?"

"They separated," McCarter answered. "One crossed the border into Belgium. Another headed for northern France, and the third is probably in West Germany by now."

"Do they have any idea which helicopter might carry the hostages or the bomb?" Mauser inquired.

"I don't think they'll be doing any skywriting to identify themselves," the Briton replied. He glanced at the disgruntled expressions of the secretary of state and the minister of foreign affairs. "What's wrong with you blokes? You look bloody constipated."

"Maybe they are," Encizo commented as he headed for the door. "Did you just get this information?"

"Less than a minute ago," McCarter confirmed. "Reckon the terrorists figured it would be harder for us to check out three leads instead of one. I suppose they're right at that, eh?"

"Your deductions can be staggering at times," Katz said dryly as he joined the others at the door. "Colonel Mauser? Bernelli? We need your help."

"What to do, what to do?" the secretary of state repeated the helpless litany as he and his Soviet counterpart sat at the table while Mauser and Bernelli followed the three Phoenix Force commandos into the hallway.

"You two are experts in world affairs and international politics," Katz replied. "I'm sure you'll think of something."

13

The rainstorm grew more fierce as the Krumbacher LMY-17 hovered above the treetops. The sky was black and streaked with rain. The windows were blurred and rippling with water as Gary Manning craned his neck to try to peer out. A flash of white light filled the window and thunder roared with an angry bestial voice that seemed to vibrate through the hull of the helicopter.

Major Yasnev pointed his Makarov pistol at Manning's forehead. The Canadian looked up at the Russian's hard, cruel features. Yasnev smiled so broadly the tips of his mustache threatened to poke him in the eyes. Without warning, Yasnev swatted his free hand across Manning's face. Manning grunted and slipped off the bench to land on his knees. One of the other prisoners gasped.

"You looking for something, Yankee?" Yasnev inquired.

"Just curious about the weather," the Canadian replied. His fists clenched at the small of his back in anger, the wrists still trapped by the steel grip of the handcuffs.

"It's raining," Yasnev sneered. "If lightning strikes the helicopter, you'll know it. Now, get back on the bench before I decide to kick your head in."

"There's no need for that sort of brutality," the President declared.

"It's okay," Manning said as he awkwardly rose without the use of his hands.

Yasnev lashed out with his booted foot and slammed a vicious kick to Manning's chest. The Canadian fell backward and landed on the bench, gasping breathlessly, his lungs like frozen and slivered ice. He inhaled deeply through his nostrils and exhaled through his mouth, trying to regulate his breath in an effort to control the pain. Yasnev chuckled and stepped back, pistol still pointed at the captive Phoenix Force pro.

"Good God," Thornton remarked in a stunned voice. "Are you all right?"

Manning tried to speak, but his voice came out in a weak croak.

"Schweinhund," Klaus Weiss hissed as he glared at Yasnev. "That coward is very brave with a man who cannot fight back."

"He is insult to Soviet people," the Soviet premier added bitterly.

"Shh!" Manning urged. His head rose sharply as he strained his ears. "What was that?"

"I can't hear anything but that bloody storm," Thornton replied with a slight quaver in his voice. "Is something wrong?"

Manning was not certain what the sound had been until he saw Yasnev awkwardly shuffle across the hull. The Russian nearly lost his balance when the chopper shifted abruptly. Yasnev grabbed a safety harness that hung near the sliding doors. Manning then felt the helicopter move downward. The engines sounded different. The chopper was beginning to descend.

"We'll be landing soon," Manning informed the others.

Terrorists hurried to benches and braced themselves for the landing. There were no safety belts in the Krumbacher. Major Hee marched from the front of the craft. The powerful Korean did not seem to have any trouble keeping his balance as he approached the hostages. The man held an Uzi submachine gun in one fist and gripped another harness near the sliding doors opposite Yasnev. The Korean stared at the prisoners with eyes that looked reptilian because of their lack of feeling. He gestured with the barrel of his Uzi.

"Stay put and do not talk," Hee warned. "Do exactly as you are told. I don't want to fire this weapon inside this craft. That would be dangerous for all of us. But I will do it if necessary. I would try to shoot you through the legs, of course, but such things are unpredictable in a moving aircraft. You understand, yes?''

Manning and the other prisoners nodded. Yasnev and Hee hardly needed the guns to keep handcuffed prisoners under control. Both men were physically strong, ruthless and highly trained opponents. The threat of the firearms was simply to discourage the hostages, Manning in particular, from trying to escape when the chopper landed. The terrorists need not have bothered. The Canadian knew he could not hope to take either the Russian brute or the Korean killer without the use of his hands.

The helicopter descended into a large flat clearing among the forest of oak trees. A powerful searchlight cast a beam from the belly of the chopper to illuminate the ground below. Several vehicles of various types and sizes waited just beyond the edge of the clearing. The vehicles were partly obscured, but several figures stood in the glare of headlights below. They were vague hooded forms, who stood around in the pelting rain as though they were willing to endure not only rain, but a veritable flood.

Thunder continued to bellow as the copter touched down on the moist ground. The heavy craft pressed the sleds of the landing gear into the damp earth. Yasnev and Hee kept the hostages covered with their weapons while the other terrorists hastily pulled open the sliding doors to rush from the chopper. Colonel Skull himself emerged from the cockpit. The terrorist leader wore a black raincoat with a hood pulled onto his cap. With his dark glasses fixed to his dead-white face, he rather resembled a fiend from a science fiction movie.

A Heckler & Koch MP-5A2 submachine gun hung from a strap over Skull's shoulder, but he did not place a hand near the trigger or threaten the hostages with the weapon. The terrorist mastermind tossed a bundle of drab green ponchos to the floor of the cabin near the prisoners.

''Major Hee,'' Skull began, ''please help our guests put on the rain gear. We don't want them to get soaked and possibly become ill during their time with us.''

The Korean nodded and gathered up the ponchos. Hee handed his Uzi to Yasnev before he moved to the hostages and began to slip the ponchos over the heads of the captives, one by

one. Manning wondered where the helicopter had landed, but
he knew there was no point in asking. The terrorists were not
likely to tell him and the question was apt to invite more physical abuse by Skull's henchmen.

"Before we leave," Skull stated, "I trust you understand that
trying to escape is a waste of time. This helicopter is surrounded by my men. Just come along quietly and do as you are
told. Major Yasnev, escort the premier and Mr. Thornton to
Captain Lacoste and help him get them into his vehicle. The
others will come with Major Hee and myself. We don't wish to
hurt anyone, so don't try any foolish heroics. It really won't do
you any good."

Rain streaked through the open sliding doors and headlights formed a ring around the helicopter. Yasnev pushed the
Soviet premier and Thornton outside and roughly escorted the
pair to the vehicles among the trees. Hee and Skull did not bully
Manning, the President and Weiss. The terrorists realized the
prisoners would not attempt to escape. At the moment, at least,
there was nowhere to escape to.

Manning's foot sunk into the muddy ground outside the
chopper. The wind was cold and clammy, whipping rain across
his exposed face. The poncho flapped in the wind, hanging
loosely from Manning's frame. The hood covered his head and
the rim blocked part of his vision, but he saw enough to know
Skull had told the truth. They were indeed surrounded by the
terrorist minions.

The President and Weiss shuffled beside Manning. All three
captives followed Skull while Major Hee brought up the rear.
Colonel Skull strode confidently across the muddy surface,
arrogantly in command and as sure of himself as any general
reviewing his troops.

"*Bonjour, Colonel,*" a voice called out above the howling
storm. "*Quel beau temps, non?*"

"*Ouvrez la porte!*" Skull snapped, not amused by the man's
sarcastic humor about the weather.

The terrorists obeyed their leader's command and opened the
rear doors of a large white trailer attached to a tractor rig. Skull
gestured for the captives to enter. Manning stepped to the
opening and saw two terrorists waiting inside. One reached

forward to seize Manning's poncho and help haul him inside while the other kept a French MAB pistol pointed at the Canadian's head.

The President and Klaus Weiss were assisted up in a similar manner, and were followed by Skull and Hee. The doors started to close, but a figure suddenly blocked them. Major Yasnev stood there, glaring into the trailer, then he climbed inside and the doors closed behind him.

"You should be with the premier and Thornton," Skull declared, his voice hard and cold. A single, low-watt light bulb in the ceiling cast a sickly red glow inside the rig. Skull's lean albino features suddenly looked as though he had been skinned.

"Lacoste is with them," Yasnev answered. "He speaks fluent Russian and English. Lacoste does not need me to translate for him, and he knows Belgium. I do not. There is nothing I can contribute to his needs, Colonel. It is best that I stay with you. Yes?"

"You disobeyed the colonel's order," Hee said, eyes narrowed to resemble knife slits in his hard face. "You could be shot for such insubordination."

"My decision was based on self-preservation," Yasnev stated with a sly smile. "I suspect my odds of survival will be better if I stay with Colonel Skull and his prize hostage. Don't forget, I was a field-grade officer in the GRU. I am fully aware of the fact that the politburo will be less apt to agree with your demands because you hold the Soviet secretary-general captive than those groveling American politicians, who will fret over the well-being of their beloved President. The politburo will simply appoint a new premier and tell *Pravda* and Tass to print whatever they feel is the most advantageous version of this entire affair. I know what sort of corruption breeds within the Kremlin. A Russian is born with a great love of his homeland. I would not have turned against it without good reason—"

"I'm not a priest and I don't want to hear your confession," Skull said curtly. "We haven't got time to argue. The helicopter has certainly been located by now. Radar, night-scanning devices, possibly heat sensors have been used to determine where we landed. Soldiers are no doubt already on their way to this forest. We don't want to be here when they arrive."

They felt the vehicle move forward and heard the engine growl and rumble. Manning sat quietly on the floor of the trailer. He watched Skull remove the dark glasses and saw the albino's pinkish-red eyes. Manning recalled reading that albinos generally had poor eyesight, highly sensitive to light. The dim tinted light within the trailer was probably all Skull's eyes could stand without the dark glasses.

"Why did you have the premier and Mr. Thornton separated from the rest of us and sent to Belgium?" Weiss inquired. "That must mean we're in France. Correct, Colonel?"

"Das ist nicht gut, mein Herr," Manning whispered. The Phoenix pro had also figured out they were probably in France and he suspected why Skull had separated the hostages. It was not wise to let Skull know anything that they observed. Manning added in German, "Don't say any more."

"Sprechen Sie Deutsch?" Skull inquired with a thin smile. "So do I. Let's speak English so everyone understands. I imagine you've already guessed I sent the premier and Thornton with Captain Lacoste to cross the border to Belgium, because one of the other helicopters landed in Belgium. Actually, the premier was originally supposed to be on that craft, but we were a bit rushed at Strassmacher Castle. If they happen to catch up with our people in Belgium, they may concentrate their investigations in that country for a while instead of looking for us in France. The discovery of the premier might convince them the search is worth pursuing."

"It is as I thought," Yasnev snickered. Skull's remarks proved that the Russian's reasons for insisting on staying with the terrorist leader had been valid.

"There's no way of being certain they won't catch up with us here," Skull reminded him.

"Oh, I realize that," Yasnev agreed, "but you still have the bomb. That plutonium device will be a strong deterrent if KGB or CIA locates us."

"If that device is genuine," the President began. "I hope you're wise enough to realize what that 'deterrent' can do."

"We do," Skull assured him. "That's exactly why we had one built. No government takes anyone seriously these days unless they have nuclear weapons. You ought to realize that more than anyone, Mr. President."

A violent roar erupted somewhere in the night beyond the metal walls of the trailer. The others might have thought it was simply thunder, but Gary Manning recognized the sounds as a man-made explosion. The demolitions expert was far too familiar with the noises of a chemical blast to mistake the sound for the natural grumble of a stormy sky.

"That may have been the helicopter," Skull mused, his ghoulish eyes wandering toward the ceiling. "Or perhaps a land mine. Difficult to say at this distance."

"You blew up the helicopter?" Weiss asked, confused.

"Of course," Skull confirmed. "It no longer served any useful purpose except as a distraction. The flaming gasoline will probably burn nicely even in the rain and attract any patrols that may be looking for us. Besides, I mentioned they might be using heat sensors to try to track us. The explosion and the burning fuel ought to make quite an impression on such equipment."

"What did you mean by land mines?" the President asked, his voice admirably calm under the stressful circumstances.

"A number of mines have been set up in the forest and on the roads to form an additional barrier for anyone who may be rushing about trying to find us," Skull answered. "Only need to blow up a few soldiers to make the rest reluctant to continue hunting us. It also gives a false impression about which way we're heading. In case you wondered, this vehicle and two others are registered as the property of a nuclear corporation. About one-fourth of all electrical power in France is supplied by nuclear power plants. These trucks are supposed to carry radioactive waste being transported to a dumping site. Not likely anyone will care to look inside even if we do encounter a roadblock or two."

"A lot of planning has gone into your scheme, Skull," Manning commented. "Men, equipment, vehicles, all the rest. Must have been very expensive, time-consuming and difficult. You probably expect to gain something pretty special from it."

"Naturally," Skull admitted. "No need to go into that. You have enough to think about without worrying about such matters."

"I can't help being worried when I'm held prisoner by a man who's willing to butcher and maim French troops with land mines just to serve as a distraction," the President stated, his eyes aflame with hot Irish anger. He was not a young man, but the fire in his gaze did not belong to a senile fossil without any fight left in him. "That doesn't bother you in the least, does it?"

"No," Skull admitted without a trace of guilt. "Soldiers die during wars. This is a sort of paramilitary operation and some people will naturally die in the process. The French soldiers should have realized that donning a uniform makes one a target. I didn't make those rules. They have existed for centuries. A number of my men have had to make the ultimate sacrifice. Before everything is over, we may all have to do likewise. I intend to win, of course, but I'll settle for a stalemate if no option is left."

"Stalemate?" Manning inquired. "You mean if your plan doesn't work you intend to kill us all and yourselves, as well?"

"You have a fine grasp of the situation, Mr..." Skull turned his gaze toward Manning, and his eyes appeared to be bleeding sockets in the red-tinted light. "What should we call you?"

"Well, I think 'Lucky' would be an inappropriate nickname under the circumstances," Manning replied with a sigh.

14

Yakov Katzenelenbogen was no stranger to Frankfurt. He recalled when he first visited the city with his father before World War II—before Hitler and the tidal wave of hatred and bloodshed that flooded across Europe beneath the banner of the swastika. Yakov was not certain how old he was when he saw Frankfurt through the eyes of a child. No more than eight or nine, he guessed. His father was a noted linguist and author, known and respected throughout the Continent as a superb translator and scholar. Professor Katzenelenbogen was a Jew and Jews were not well liked in Europe even before the Nazis rose to power, but he was a Jew with a useful talent and that made his status far more valuable—for a while.

Frankfurt had seemed larger to young Yakov when he visited it so long ago. God, he thought now as he gazed at the city from the window of the Mercedes. Almost half a century had passed since he saw Frankfurt as a small boy. The city had changed a great deal since those prewar days. Modern buildings had been erected and centuries-old structures had been destroyed by bombs during World War II. It saddened Katz to think of the suffering Frankfurt had endured during the last worldwide conflagration. The city had once been the home of Charlemagne and the great poet and dramatist Goethe. Gutenberg had set up his printing press in Frankfurt, and the city had once been the center of printing for all of Europe. Frankfurt had always been a progressive city, a hub of trade and education and free thinking. During Hitler's rule, it became an unofficial headquarters for German opposition to the Nazis.

The familiar cobblestone streets and columns of shops, taverns and restaurants packed closely together were a welcome sight for Katz. Cars, mopeds and buses hustled through the busy streets and people strolled along the sidewalks with various degrees of urgency. Most did not seem in a great hurry. Frankfurt was not a frantic city like Bonn or West Berlin. It still retained a quaint, comfortable quality. The morning sunlight seemed to caress the buildings with a gentle, lazy glow. Frankfurt was a city that looks best in the early morning and twilight, or draped in light foggy mist.

"You look tired, Yakov," Colonel Ludwig Bohler remarked. He was sitting next to Katz in the back seat of the Mercedes. "None of us will be getting much sleep until this is over. The situation is even worse than that time terrorists infiltrated a NATO missile site."

"It's as bad as anything I've faced in the past," Katz admitted. "I can't recall any situation that was worse or a mission that was more critical."

"That's quite a statement from you," Bohler said with a frown. "I know enough about your career to appreciate the gravity of the situation, given your scope of experience."

Bohler had worked with Katz on three previous occasions: once when the Israeli had still been with Mossad and twice since Katz had become unit commander of Phoenix Force. The muscular Nordic German officer knew more about the team's activities than most of the people who dealt with Phoenix Force, and in fact, he even knew the names of all five commandos. Yet, even Bohler had learned few details about the top-secret elite unit headed by the Israeli professional.

Katz liked Bohler and trusted him more than most individuals outside the Stony Man organization. The German colonel was one of the top officers in GSG-9. He had been with the special antiterrorist squad for more than a decade and had plenty of experience in fighting the twentieth-century barbarians who threatened the lives and freedoms of people throughout the world. Bohler knew the realities of terrorism all too well.

"One of the helicopters was tracked over the Rhineland area," Bohler explained. "Soldiers were dispatched to the site minutes after the craft landed, but the terrorists escaped in vehicles waiting for them in the forest. They blew up the helicopter and set land mines in the path of our troops. We lost half a dozen good men.''

"The same thing happened in northern France and Belgium,'' Katz stated. "The terrorists aren't taking any chances and they're quite ruthless about covering their tracks. Skull has no respect for human life...apparently not even the lives of his own men.''

"I'm astonished that a phantom terrorist leader has been able to assemble such a large private army and keep them together,'' Karl Hahn commented as he steered the Mercedes around a slow-moving beer truck. "If anyone other than you or one of your teammates had told me the story, I would be inclined to think Colonel Skull was a myth. BND has previously regarded him as such when stories were floating around concerning Skull in the past.''

Hahn had good reason to trust the opinion of Katz and the other members of Phoenix Force. The tough BND agent had worked with the elite commando unit several times in the past. Hahn had even substituted for Rafael Encizo while the Cuban warrior was hospitalized and recovering from a head wound. Karl Hahn had charged into the battlefields with Phoenix Force, and he knew they were the best, the very best in the world. It had been an honor to be part of the unit. Hahn respected Katz too much to question the veteran professional's word.

Katz had similar sentiments about Hahn and was glad to have the German commando working with him, especially since he had been forced to divide up Phoenix Force in order to cover Belgium, France and the Federal Republic of Germany simultaneously. Besides, with Manning held prisoner, Phoenix Force was short a member and Hahn had experience as a replacement team member. Hahn was very capable in the field. A former GSG-9 antiterrorist, he had training and experience in fighting the modern-day savages. His BND intelligence background made him equally adept in the clandestine operations often involved in Phoenix missions. Hahn was also an electronics expert and computer whiz. He was skilled in small arms combat and hand-to-hand warfare and had a unique talent for using ordinary objects as deadly weapons in an emergency.

"Skull is all too real," Katz assured him. "Don't underestimate him because he's not with KGB or some other established intel outfit."

"If you take him seriously, so will I," Hahn replied with a firm nod. "You say that Skull has a wide variety of nationalities among his private army. Does that include Japanese and black Africans?"

"It seems he's an equal-opportunity employer," the Phoenix commander answered wryly. "All the terrorists at Strassmacher Castle were Caucasians, but a much wider racial variety took part in the hijacking of the *Sea Venus*—Arabs, blacks, Asians. Why do you ask?"

"Because I think BND might have a lead for us," Hahn announced with a sly smile as he glanced over his shoulder at the back seat.

A traffic signal stopped the Mercedes by a brothel. Prostitution is legal in Germany. Women dressed in seductive costumes sat at picture windows and tried to convince passersby to enter. Morning trade was not very good and the prostitutes knew it. They didn't waste much energy trying to attract customers, although one enterprising woman waved at the Mercedes and gestured for the car to pull over.

"Good God," Colonel Bohler remarked with surprise. "BND managed to find a clue already? The terrorists only arrived last night and no one else has any idea where they might be."

"It could be a coincidence," Hahn admitted. "However, just four days ago, two Japanese and three black men—who spoke French and claimed to be from the republic of Zaire—rented an abandoned farm in the Rhineland. They claimed to be members of some sort of Afro-Asian agriculture organization concerned with advanced methods of farming or something like that. I'll have to check the records. Not a matter I was personally involved with."

"Why was BND interested in something like that?" Katz asked, hoping the lead would have some substance.

"These fellows offered to try out some crop growing methods or whatever they call it," Hahn explained, casting an interested glance at the brothel as the Mercedes rolled on up the street. "If the efforts failed, they agreed to pay the property owners for damaged land and soil and if they succeeded they promised to split the profits on the crops fifty-fifty. Sounded like a good deal. A bit too good. BND got suspicious then. Those suspicions increased when the renters started hiring workers for the farm. They hired Turkish and Arab immigrants from Bonn, curious selections since there's no evidence any of the employees have previous experience working on farms."

"BND paranoia strikes again," Bohler remarked. "But I admit it just might be justified. So you think those men might be terrorists?"

"No denying it's a curious mix of *Auslander* characters," Hahn stated. "After Black September Palestinians seized Israeli athletes at the Olympic Village in Munich and murdered the hostages in 1971, BND has tried to keep an eye on Arab immigrants. Much the same with the Turks—who comprise nearly a fourth of the population in Bonn. You both know this as well as I do. There's a rather large segment of right-wing Turkish Gray Wolves in Germany and left-wing radicals with the Turkish branch of the PLO and the so-called Turkish People's Liberation Party."

"That's right," Bohler said with a sigh. "As if we needed to import terrorists. It's bad enough we still have the German Red Army Faction, remnants of the Second June Movement and at least a dozen other German terrorist groups. Even the Baader-Meinhof Gang is still in operation. We'd hoped we'd heard the last of those fanatics in the seventies, but they resurfaced in 1981."

"Terrorists are like cockroaches," Katz declared. "You can exterminate them, but there always seem to be more to replace them. Until someone can figure out a way to rid the world of fanatics and extremists of virtually every type, terrorism will continue. However, it seems to me that in Germany most of the terrorist groups are left-wing, Marxist *Deutschlander* zealots, generally working with Palestinian groups."

"Of course," Hahn confirmed. "That's why BND became suspicious when the farm was rented by the Japanese and African 'agriculturalists.' As I understand it, the Japanese Red Army only has about thirty or forty members left. Apparently none of them operate in Japan anymore, but they still have cells scattered throughout the world. Most are supposedly in South Yemen with terrorist training bases stationed there. Nonetheless, JRA assassins have been known to participate in terrorist hits here in Europe, apparently working with local extremist groups. BND suspected this might be a variation, with the Japanese and their African partners posing as respectable humanitarians while using the farm to build a base for terrorists. Naturally, the Arabs and Turks make the situation even more suspicious."

"Let's not jump to conclusions, gentlemen," Katz urged. "These men might be innocent. Still, I'd like to know if the farm is located near the site where Skull's helicopter touched down in the Rhineland. If it's within a hundred miles or so, I think we should check it out as quickly as possible."

"Agreed," Colonel Bohler stated. "You and Karl can check with BND headquarters in Munich. I'm going to call in some of my men and have them ready if we decide to launch a raid on the farm."

"We'll do recon first," Katz insisted. "Still, it would be a great comfort to know you had a unit of crack GSG-9 antiterrorist commandos on hand. I can't call in my team since they're spread out in Belgium and France. Gary Manning is missing in action and in the hands of the enemy. I'm certainly glad both of you were available for this crisis. It's not a time I care to have strangers on a mission of such proportions."

"You can count on us, Yakov," Bohler said gently. "We've always been able to count on you, old friend. Only problem is I don't know if I can get more than a dozen GSG-9 commandos assembled in Frankfurt within less than eight hours."

"We've launched successful raids with far fewer men," Hahn stated. "It would be nice if we had a better idea of what the odds might be. My guess would be about thirty opponents. Any ideas about how to best handle the scum if the terrorists are located at the farm? They might have the hostages or the nuclear weapon you mentioned, or both.''

"We'll come up with something," Katz assured him. The Phoenix Force commander hoped he could make good that claim when the time came to carry out the raid.

PARIS IS KNOWN as the City of Light, but the famous capital city of France did not seem bright or cheerful that morning as Rafael Encizo stared out a third-story window of La Sûreté nationale. A blanket of fog draped the city with a somber gloom. The outlines of buildings were blurred by the mist, and all that was visible of traffic along the avenue de Suffren was moving headlights, like fireflies at twilight. The most famous symbol of France, the Eiffel Tower, was also party shrouded by the fog. It could have been a large antenna to a radio station in the heavy mist.

Encizo had been to Paris before on Phoenix Force missions, and it was not one of his favorite cities. Perhaps he would have liked Paris, and France in general, better if he spoke the language. The Cuban was the only member of Phoenix Force who did not speak French, and he vowed, for the hundredth time, that he would somehow work French lessons into his schedule in the future, although he knew he would probably never manage to since Phoenix Force seemed to have a mission almost every month. The fact he had been seriously wounded in France during a raid on an ODESSA Nazi stronghold did nothing to warm his feelings toward the country.

The depressing weather and the dismal results of their present mission had also brought an inner sense of gloom to Encizo. Old sorrows came back to haunt him as he stood at the window. Family and friends had been killed during Castro's takeover, and then during the disastrous Bay of Pigs invasion. Others had lost their lives during Encizo's pre-Phoenix days. The hardest blow had certainly been the death of Keio Ohara, one of the original five members of Phoenix Force. The tall Japanese warrior had been the youngest, yet his wisdom, gentle voice, immaculate manners and wiry sense of humor helped breach the age difference. The other men in Phoenix Force had tended to regard Ohara as sort of a kid brother. It had seemed cruel of fate to snuff out the life of the youngest first, and Encizo had felt the loss of Keio Ohara deeply.

Now Gary Manning was in the hands of Colonel Skull. Manning had been with Phoenix Force since the beginning, as long as Encizo, McCarter and Katz. They had shared so many experiences, risked their lives together and relied on one another for survival for the past seven years. Manning was closer than a brother. He was a part of Encizo, just as every member of Phoenix Force had become linked to his partners in a world apart from people who led more ordinary lives.

The world of Phoenix Force was clandestine. Their missions took them all over the globe, from Alaska to Mongolia, from Israel to Jamaica. Yet their actual world remained relatively small. They met with few people, seldom used their real names and made few friends. Only a handful of intelligence personnel in the world knew about their missions. Violence was commonplace in their experience. Incredible risks and tremendous acts of heroism were part of their regular duties. Yet they would receive no glory, no medals, no parades or official recognition for their work. It was often a dirty, ugly business, filled with distrust, deceit, terror and sudden death.

In such a world, the men of Phoenix Force could truly rely on little except themselves and one another. Their bonds had become extremely close and they knew one another as if all five men had shared a single skin. Encizo did not want to lose another spiritual brother. He knew Manning might already be dead or they might never know his fate for certain. If that happened, a part of Rafael Encizo and of the other three members of Phoenix Force would die.

"Monsieur?" Pierre Bertin called out with annoyance. "Would you mind? We need to discuss the business that has brought you here."

Encizo turned from the window and stared at Bertin's sour face. The Sûreté officer was a thin, waspy man with pinched features and a receding hairline that he tried to conceal by combing long strands of hair across his balding pate. He wore a single-breasted suit with exaggerated shoulder padding to try to make himself appear more muscular. The insecure Frenchman even wore elevator shoes. Encizo did not find anything about the man encouraging except Bertin's reluctant acceptance of the need to conduct the conversation in English.

"I guess we'd better talk to him, man," Calvin James told Encizo. "It's not going to be any fun, but Sûreté will need our help and we'll need theirs."

"We'll see about that, Monsieur Johnson," Bertin snapped, calling James by his current cover name.

"Yeah," Encizo stated as he walked from the window. "Let's see about it and get to work, damn it. We didn't come here so we could stuff our faces with French pastry."

"Let's all try to remain civil," Scott Bernelli declared, wishing the CIA had been able to supply another case officer with more seniority.

Bertin snorted derisively. "You people have opened Pandora's box and released the contents across Europe, and you want us to be civil!"

"Watch your mouth," James told him crossly. "This hallway isn't secure. Talk in the room. Okay?"

They walked through a narrow corridor to a soundproof conference room at the end of the hall. James wondered how many hours he had spent in stuffy little rooms with thick walls and reinforced metal doors since he joined Phoenix Force. The tough guy from Chicago had never cared for being locked inside high-security conference rooms. It was like being sealed in an overfurnished prison cell with a bunch of other men sucking up all the oxygen.

The room looked pretty much like every other one used for secret conversations. The floor was bare in recognition of the fact that microphones can be that easily hidden under a carpet. A metal table with a rectangular top and surrounded by ten chairs took up most of the space. Two black plastic ashtrays sat in the center of the table. The ceiling was cork with tube bulbs mounted above the table. Bertin closed the thick door and turned the latch.

"That's better," James said as he stepped closer to the Frenchman. "Now we can talk."

Bertin started to move toward the table, but James shifted into his way. The black man gazed hard into the face of the

Sûreté agent. Bertin squirmed uncomfortably, unable to hide his fear.

"Look, let's get things right," James began in a hard, even voice. "We've had a lousy twelve hours. We're not in a good mood, so don't tick us off any worse than we already are. One of us might lose his temper and knock your skinny ass across the room."

"Now, there's no need to threaten Monsieur Bertin," Scott Bernelli said quickly. "We're all on the same side."

"Hey, he's the one who wants to claim this is *our* fault," James reminded the Company man.

"Not you personally," Bertin explained, his voice sounding a bit unsteady. "Your government. The American government, which insists on trying to influence the foreign policies of Europe."

"We don't have time to listen to you complain," Encizo warned him. "Sûreté can either help us or they can explain to the French government why the United States is suddenly demanding payments still owed by France since World War II. Might also cut off some aid and pressure some nasty old U.S. corporations to reduce trade with France."

"You can't—" the Frenchman began.

"These two have authorization from the Oval Office," Bernelli said, shaking his head. "I wouldn't be surprised if they could do just about anything. Including influencing American policies."

"Sûreté intends to provide assistance," Bertin assured them. "However, I'm sure you know what happened when our soldiers tried to locate the terrorist helicopter after it landed in a forest about sixty kilometers from the Luxembourg border."

"The same thing happened in Belgium and West Germany," James told him. "Colonel Skull had people ready for his choppers to land. Son of a bitch had this well planned. Terrorists to carry out the operation, others to transport 'em and cover 'em when they reached their destination. It sure as hell is a mess. Does anyone have information about the vehicles that met the terrorists at the forest?"

"Information?" Bertin frowned. "What do you expect? License plate numbers? We don't even have descriptions of the vehicles."

"There must have been tire tracks," Encizo stated, recalling fundamental evidence-gathering tactics he had learned while working as an insurance investigator before he became a member of Phoenix Force. "The tracks can reveal what sort of tires were used. Large tires, large vehicle. Truck, car, whatever. How deep the prints are can also show how heavy the load probably was. That should give us a general idea of what sort of road machines the bastards have."

"I'll be damned," Bernelli remarked. "That makes common sense, but I didn't think of it."

"Let's hope Skull didn't consider it, either," James replied. The former police officer had noticed that many intelligence agents, especially those who had no previous experience in law enforcement, overlooked small details that the least practiced policeman would automatically think of. "We'll also need to check the lists of vehicles stolen within the past month and see how many fit descriptions of what the terrorists might be driving. There's a good chance they stole at least some of the vehicles. They're smart enough to change license plates and paint the cars different colors to prevent getting hauled over by the local police. Still, having an idea of the type and make of an automobile or truck might help us locate the vehicle or at least get an idea what they're using for transportation."

"I suppose that's a start," Bertin said with a shrug. "The present search is taking place in the general area where the aircraft landed. They destroyed the helicopter, you know. It was a German make, if that helps."

"Yeah," Encizo remarked, reaching inside a jacket pocket. "We already knew that and it doesn't help. Supposedly the bomb Skull has was built by a trio of French physicists he kidnapped some time ago. That means we're looking at a smaller group of people than the population at large. If Skull is telling the truth, it shouldn't be too difficult to find out who they were. If he lied about the physicists, it probably means the bomb isn't genuine."

"That would be a relief," Bernelli said, rolling his eyes toward the ceiling.

The French agent agreed with him without much of a show of enthusiasm. "But we can't rely on that. I fail to see how learning any details about the alleged physicists will help."

"If we can find out who they are, we might be able to contact other scientists who worked with them and learn some more details about how the bomb might be built," James explained.

"Possibly they could tell us about this, too," Encizo added as he placed the radio transmitter on the table. "It's one of the remote control units capable of triggering the bomb with a radio signal."

Bertin exclaimed with surprise, "How did you get this device?"

"From one of the terrorists we captured in Luxembourg," the Cuban replied simply. "An electrical engineer examined it and said it has an effective range of about two hundred meters. Simple transmitter that operates like the little pocket unit used for some answering machines—it beeps a high-pitched radio signal into a telephone to make the machine play back messages recorded while the owner was away from home. This transmitter sends a much stronger signal, of course. Maybe physicists could tell us if this thing could actually trigger a nuclear bomb. Unfortunately, we haven't been able to contact anyone so far who can give us a definite answer to that question."

"Got something else for you, too," James began, taking a small sheet of paper from his pocket. "It's a list I made while interrogating some of the terrorists who were under the influence of scopolamine. They supplied us with the names of some of Skull's undercover agents in Europe. The names on this list belong to double agents here in France. You'll notice a lot of them are members of police departments and the Sûreté."

Bertin's eyes bulged with astonishment. "Those terrorists infiltrated Sûreté? Unbelievable!"

"Skull managed to infiltrate CIA and the Soviet GRU, as well," Scott Bernelli stated. "Colonel Skull has set up his own intelligence network of traitors in at least half a dozen countries. I agree. It is incredible, but somehow he managed it.''

"Well, it's a sad fact, but there are always people who are willing to sell out their country if somebody offers them a good enough deal,'' James commented. "Money, power, whatever. To a lot of people loyalty has a price, and patriotism is second to ambition and greed.''

"This nightmare is getting worse every minute,'' Bertin muttered, shaking his head with dismay.

"And it's a long way from being over,'' Encizo said grimly.

15

The farm was located in a quiet grassy area in the west Rhineland. Few trees ringed the property, mostly Bavarian pines and cedar trees. The air was pleasantly scented with evergreen. Under different circumstances, the setting would have been relaxing and charming, even quaint.

Crops had been neglected and the barley waved high in the evening wind. Thistles and other weeds grew unchecked among the weaving stalks. Beyond the sea of barley stood the farmhouse and barn. Innocent structures, simple and practical with no ornamentation. The house was a plain two-story dwelling with a gray slate roof, a stubby chimney and windows that leaked little light through curtain-shielded glass.

Yakov Katzenelenbogen examined the house with the aid of Bushnell binoculars. Twilight cast sheets of dimness across the scene, but there was still ample light to observe the farm without the use of night-vision equipment. The Israeli lay on his belly among the barley, dressed in black night camos, a shadow among a steadily increasing blanket of darkness. His face was smeared with dark camouflage paint and his single hand was covered by a thin black glove. Even the trident hook device at the end of the prosthesis attached to his right arm was mat-black metal. The Uzi was strapped across his left shoulder and the SIG-Sauer pistol was sheathed in shoulder leather under his right arm. His belt was loaded with magazine pouches, grenades and a rather bulky sheath for the black metal ballistic knife at his left hip. The Phoenix Force commander was ready to charge through the gates of hell and take on whatever demons Colonel Skull had stationed at the farm.

Two sentries patrolled the property, marching the grounds in a monotonous pattern. Both carried Belgian-made FAL assault rifles with night-scopes mounted to the steel frames. A third guard was posted at the front porch of the farmhouse. Another covered the back entrance. Katz could not see the face of the barn, but he guessed a sentry was probably stationed at the hayloft. A beer truck with a canvas-covered top, a VW minibus, two medium-size cars and a tractor. The latter had probably been moved from the barn to make more room inside. There was no sign of the usual domesticated animals. Not even a chicken or a small dog stirred. The barn was being used to house human occupants.

Karl Hahn crawled to Katz's position. The German BND agent was dressed in a similar manner to the Israeli. A Heckler & Koch submachine gun was strapped to his shoulder and he carried a Walther P-5 autoloader in a shoulder holster. Hahn also had two canvas cases hooked to his belt. The German detached one case and handed it to Katz.

"There's a storm door at the back," Hahn whispered. "Must lead to the basement. Most likely place for the hostages to be, wouldn't you say?"

"If they're in there," Katz answered, lowering the binoculars to take the case Hahn offered him. "Is Bohler in position?"

"He's ready with the second squad," Hahn assured the Phoenix pro. "You want the basement? If they have prisoners, Gary might be one of them."

"I'll take the front," Katz announced. He decided not to take the basement because he might hesitate or be distracted by looking for Manning instead of dealing with the job with the cold, effective professionalism the tense situation demanded.

"The gas grenades are the same thing we used that time in Czechoslovakia?" Hahn inquired. "Puke gas with an additional chemical agent to make it more readily absorbed by the skin?"

"Dimethyl sulfoxide," Katz explained. "Cal came up with the idea of using it with vomit gas. It rapidly seeps through skin pores and increases the rate at which the other chemicals in the gas reach the bloodstream. DMSO is odorless, tasteless and harmless on its own, so it won't hurt any innocents inside the house, but it still makes the victim sick a lot faster than the gas would on its own.''

"I remember," Hahn assured him, recalling the time they had used the vomit gas in Prague. "I'll take the basement."

"Just be careful," Katz urged as he buckled the canvas pack to his belt. "Everybody has one of these protective masks?''

"And they've all taken the tablets with the antidote," Hahn confirmed. "If any of them failed to take their pills, we'll know when they start throwing up along with the terrorists. They know that they need both the antidote and the masks to protect them from the gas."

"Bohler's men are GSG-9," Katz said. "They've had the same training you've had, although they don't have even a fragment of your experience. I think they'll do a fine job."

"Of course," Hahn replied with a crooked smile. "I haven't been in combat since the last time I worked with your team. Most of the time BND has me sitting at a computer trying to patch into other computer systems at various embassies in Bonn or West Berlin. Not very exciting. I'm really glad to be working with you again, Yakov."

"I just wish the circumstances were different," the Israeli said. "We'd better signal Colonel Bohler that we're ready to move in."

"Right," Hahn answered. "If we don't do this quickly and if someone's timing isn't right . . .''

"Let's not try to think about that," Katz told him.

Colonel Bohler had managed to assemble a dozen GSG-9 commandos for the raid. Half the men remained with Bohler while Katz and Karl Hahn commanded the remaining six troopers. The crack antiterrorist soldiers were dressed in night camo uniforms and armed to the teeth. Like Hahn, they were armed with H&K MP-5 submachine guns and 9 mm pistols. In addition, three men carried H&K G-3 assault rifles equipped with telescopic sights. The other three had H&K M-69 grenade launchers, weapons that resembled oversize flare guns with a huge bore to launch 40 mm cartridge-style grenades.

Thanks to his fluent German, Katz had no trouble commanding the trio of GSG-9 troopers he led through the barley.

They crawled toward the front of the farmhouse while Hahn and three other commandos approached the rear. Colonel Bohler commanded six other GSG-9 warriors stationed beyond the tree line. They would advance on the farm and concentrate on taking out the enemy inside the barn.

The situation required drastic, ruthless tactics, generally acceptable only during a state of declared war. A war was indeed what they were faced with. Skull and his terrorist army had virtually declared war on the entire civilized world. The antiterrorist squad would respond accordingly. If Skull wanted a war, he would get his wish—and get more than his murderous minions could handle if Phoenix Force and its allies succeeded.

The first problem to deal with was dispatching the sentries. Katz's Uzi was equipped with a silencer, and so were the G-3 rifles carried by many of the German commandos. The long-range weapons were set on semiauto for greater accuracy. Two GSG-9 marksmen accompanied Katz. They shouldered their rifles in a prone position and aimed at the two guards at the front of the farmhouse. Through telescopes and cross hairs they zeroed in on vital points of terrorist guards.

The first rifle shot spit a muffled report, the muzzle-flash reduced to a mere flicker by the metal sleeve of the silencer. A sentry patrolling the grounds suddenly snapped back his head and crumpled to the ground without even uttering a groan. The 7.62 mm bullet had knifed through his skull and killed him instantly.

The other guard on foot patrol groaned, dropped his rifle and fell facefirst to the ground. The back of his skull was split open. Blood and brains spilled from the bullet-shattered cranium. A marksman with Colonel Bohler's team had taken out the man with another well-placed sniper round.

The second marksman in Katz's team fired his G-3 at the sentry stationed at the front porch. The terrorist had seen at least one of his comrades fall and realized the farm was under attack. He clutched his weapon and opened his mouth to shout a warning to the terrorists inside the building. The GSG-9 sniper triggered his rifle and a crimson bullet hole appeared in the sentry's chest, left of center.

A loud moan of agony escaped from the man's mouth as he fell back against a support post to the porch ceiling. Another sniper round struck the sentry in the chest. A third bullet smashed into his face. His nose vanished in a scarlet smear and two teeth fell from his upper mouth as the maxilla bone cracked. The sentry slid limply to the porch and tumbled down the steps to the ground below. His unfired weapon clattered on the risers and landed beside his corpse.

Yakov Katzenelenbogen hastily yanked open the canvas case on his belt and removed the protective mask. He used the steel hooks of his prosthesis to pull the straps over his head and fitted the mask onto his face. He heard the metallic whoosh of an M-69 as the third GSG-9 fighter in his team fired the launcher. The 40 mm grenade sailed from the barley field and crashed through a window near the front door. Billows of green fog appeared inside.

"Beeilen Sie sich!" Katz declared, his voice muffled by the filters of his protective mask. *"Schnell! Schnell!"*

The Phoenix Force commander charged from the cover of the barley and headed for the farmhouse, his Uzi poised across his artificial arm, muzzle pointed at the front door of the house. The two GSG-9 marksmen also donned their protective masks and followed the Israeli while the commando with the grenade launcher reloaded his weapon.

The door burst open and two men dashed across the threshold. One pulled his *keffiyeh* across his nose and mouth with one hand while he held a Skorpion machine pistol in the other. His companion was a tall blond man in green fatigues with a black beret on his tawny head. The second terrorist was armed with a Walther MPL subgun. Both appeared to be desperate to get out of the house and away from the noxious fumes that spread inside.

They were confronted by Katz, a bizarre figure dressed in black, head and face covered by the buglike lenses and filters of the mask. The Israeli's Uzi opened fire before either opponent could swing his weapon toward the Phoenix pro. The silencer-equipped submachine gun sputtered an angry salvo of muffled 9 mm rounds. The Arab terrorist triggered his Skorpion and blasted a useless volley of 7.65 mm slugs into the deep twilight sky before his bullet-riddled body tumbled down the steps to land beside the slain sentry.

The blond terrorist had also been hit by the Uzi blast, but the force of two parabellums to the rib cage did not bring him down. The gunman fell against the doorway, blood seeping from his bullet-torn side. He managed to stay on his feet and pointed the Walther subgun at the remarkable opponent who continued to advance on the house. The mask, the prosthesis with steel hooks for a hand and the silencer attached to the barrel of his Uzi combined to make Katz appear like a formidable opponent from outer space. The terrorist wasted a tenth of a second wondering if earth had been invaded by hostile aliens, then another burst of Uzi rounds terminated such concerns, as the high-velocity 115-grain bullets ripped him open from sternum to eyebrows.

Katz reached the porch and moved to the side of the open door. The sound inside the house could have been a repeat of the Tower of Babel, with a confusion of voices yelling in panic. Katz recognized a few choice bits of profanity in German and French and heard a voice in Arabic screaming to Allah for strength, all accompanied by sounds of coughing and choking.

The two GSG-9 marksmen continued to jog toward the house. They were delayed for a moment as they fired their G-3 rifles at figures that appeared at the second-story windows. Glass shattered, and a black man, clad in fatigue uniform and black beret with skull emblem, plunged through a smashed windowpane and plunged lifeless to the ground. Katz barely glanced at the dead man. Possibly one of the Africans who had rented the farm, he thought. Definitely another member of Colonel Skull's motley private army.

Another 40 mm grenade hurtled through the broken upstairs window to unleash more vomit gas inside the building. Katz glanced at the barn and saw that Bohler's team had also fired gas grenades into that structure. The GSG-9 colonel and his commandos rushed the barn. An explosion blew the doors apart to let Bohler's people charge through the impromptu entrance.

Katz assumed Hahn and his men were busy assaulting the rear of the house. Automatic fire erupted amid the confusion and heedlessness inside the dwelling. The Israeli ducked his head and dived through the doorway. He hit the door in a shoulder roll, collided with an armchair and kicked it out of his way to get a clear view of the room he had plunged into.

The chair slid into the path of a large bearded terrorist, who bellowed with anger at being momentarily held up. From Katz's vantage point on the floor the man looked like a shaggy mountain. The big terrorist used the barrel of an AK-47 to shove the chair out of his way. Katz promptly fired his Uzi. The silenced weapon coughed harshly and a trio of 9 mm rounds drilled into the terrorist's solar plexus to tunnel upward into his heart and lungs. The hairy behemoth collapsed with a great thud of deadweight.

The Phoenix veteran had seen men in a thousand battle-fields, but none had appeared more confused and disoriented than the ones staggering about the room in the green fog. Many were racked by convulsions as they tried to hold on to their weapons while vomiting uncontrollably. A couple of terrorists had managed to grab gas masks and slip the protective gear onto their heads and faces. However, the DMSO compound in the gas made the effort a futile gesture as the gas seeped into the pores of their skin despite the masks. The terrorists were doubled up in agony, clawing at the masks that trapped their vomit and threatened to drown them.

Some of the terrorists were unable to put up any sort of fight. They thrashed about on the floor, unable to control their bowels, their mouths hanging open as they continued being sick until their bodies were drained of strength. Other opponents fought off the effects of the gas with greater success, yet all staggered and moaned as their innards were racked with twisting fits of chemical savagery.

Katz was untouched by the treacherous fumes that drifted across the room like a sickly mist. He was not without problems, however, for the protective mask reduced his vision. He had already been forced to spray opponents with his Uzi to be certain he hit the targets. He figured he had probably burned up at least half the ammo in his magazine. The lenses of the

protective mask were clouded by the gas fumes and the heat
generated by the number of sweating, stumbling figures trapped
in a single room. He wiped a sleeve across a lens and glanced
up at a pair of legs that moved unsteadily toward his position.

Katz chopped the frame of his Uzi across the terrorist's ankles. The man cried out with surprise and yelped in pain as the
unexpected blow knocked his feet out from under him. He fell
to the floor, dazed and disoriented. Katz rammed the steel stock
of his Uzi into the man's wrists to break the opponent's grip on
a British Sterling subgun. The Israeli then hammered the frame
of his weapon across the terrorist's forehead. He hit the man
twice to make certain he would not get up for a while.

A terrorist let loose a Turkish curse and pointed his French
MAB pistol at Katz as he stared down at the Israeli through
tear-clogged eyes.

Katz immediately triggered his Uzi. The wave of 9 mm parabellums crashed into the Turk, then he was adroitly lifted off
his feet and hurled across the room. As he fell, the terrorist
fired his pistol, but the bullet blasted a harmless round in the
ceiling. The Turk slammed into a wall and slumped lifeless to
the floor, his chest oozing blood.

Another terrorist turned his weapon toward Katz. The Israeli pointed his Uzi at the gunman and squeezed the trigger.
The weapon did not respond. Katz had used up the last of his
ammo. The barrel of the terrorist's PPSh-41 subgun weaved
slightly as the killer aimed his weapon at Katz. Though the
man's clothes showed signs of his illness, his eyes burned with
energy born of desperation and sheer fury. Katz saw the enemy's face clearly for a moment, a dark Mediterranean face with
proud features. Sure that Katz was at his mercy, he managed a
sneering smile as he prepared to squeeze the trigger.

The Mediterranean features suddenly exploded in a volcano
of crimson and gray-pink brain tissue. Three 7.62 mm slugs had
crushed his face and blasted his skull like an eggshell struck by
a sledgehammer. The man toppled backward, the Soviet
subgun still clenched in his fists. His corpse hit the floor and the
impact jarred his trigger finger and unleashed a short 3-round
burst, which wilted another of the enemy.

A GSG-9 commando stood at the doorway with G-3 rifle in hand. Katz sighed with relief and made a mental note to find out which of his teammates had saved his life. The protective masks made it impossible to tell the commandos apart. Another German antiterrorist swung through a broken windowpane, landed feetfirst and fired his MP-5 chopper to blast an Arab who was about to pull the pin from a Soviet-made F-1 hand grenade. The Arab cried out and uttered a dismayed sound as blood and vomit rose from his throat. The grenade rolled from his fingers, pin still in place, as the terrorist fell to the floor in a quivering heap.

A black man, hidden behind a sofa, pointed a MAT-49 subgun at the GSG-9 trooper who had just wasted his Syrian comrade. He fired a half dozen 9 mm slugs into the chest of the German antiterrorist. The commando groaned beneath his protective mask and fell backward to tumble through the window he had used for an entrance.

Katz saw the African take out his teammate. The Israeli did not have time to reload his Uzi. With his left hand he drew the SIG-Sauer from shoulder leather and snapped off the safety catch. He aimed and fired in a single fluid motion. The 9 mm round slammed into the side of the black terrorist's skull. The impact sent the African spinning with a trail of blood, then the GSG-9 trooper at the doorway also nailed the African with a trio of 7.62 mm slugs. The terrorist's corpse collapsed across the backrest of the sofa.

Katz waved his arm at the commando at the door. "They're finished! That's it!"

The German marksman entered, followed by the other surviving member of Katz's temporary team. Only four terrorists in the front room were still alive. Two were unconscious, and one was immobilized by violent convulsions and dry heaves so that he could not get up from the floor. The fourth had been unable to pull his gas mask from his face and was choking in his own vomit. Katz slid the hooks of his prosthesis under the straps at the back of the man's head and yanked hard. The straps snapped and the mask fell from the terrorist's face. Katz shoved the man to the floor and jammed the muzzle of his SIG-Sauer into the base of his neck.

"Cuff these bastards!" Katz told the two GSG-9 troopers. "If any of them even looks like he might reach for a weapon, kill him!"

Katz let the German commandos bind the defeated opponents with riot cuffs while he retrieved his Uzi and shoved a fresh magazine into the subgun. The Phoenix pro watched the stairwell extending upstairs and glanced at the door that led to the next room. He heard shooting and explosions in other parts of the house and outside where Bohler's group was battling terrorists at the barn. According to plan, if either team finished with its opponents, it would bind the prisoners and come to the aid of the other two teams. If a team got wiped out, the surviving terrorists would surely come to the assistance of the enemy forces still locked in combat with the antiterrorist strike force.

Katz wondered how Hahn and Bohler were doing, but there was nothing he could do for them just then. The sound of footsteps above warned him that the battle was far from over.

KARL HAHN HAD HIT the rear of the house with his three GSG-9 commandos simultaneously with Katz's attack at the front. The BND agent's strategy was similar to the Israeli's. A marksman in his team had taken out the sentry at the back porch and M-69 grenades were fired through first-and second-story windows at the rear of the house. The three commando soldiers charged to the porch while Hahn ran to the storm doors.

Hahn knelt by the doors and placed a packet of plastic explosives at the hinges. Roughly the size of a pack of cigarettes, the packet contained an electrical switch, a nine-volt battery, a five-second timer and special blasting cap inserted in two ounces of explosives. It was a small charge, but Hahn wanted to blast the door, not bring the house crashing down. He flicked the switch.

Moving clear of the doors, he dropped to the ground and rolled close to the wall of the house. A bullet tore into the earth a fraction of an inch from Hahn's elbow as he slithered to the wall. Enemy gunman from an upstairs window, he guessed. His stomach was knotted with fear, but he was familiar with the emotion. The German pro resisted the instinct to ready his MP-5 and return fire. Wait for the packet to blow, he told himself as he covered his head with his arms. Five seconds could be a damn long time with the knowledge that he might be a target while he lay on his belly and waited.

The packet exploded. Splinters spewed from the storm doors, and debris showered Hahn's back and shoulders. A sharp wooden shard pierced the back of his left hand. Hahn gritted his teeth at the pain and tried to dismiss it as he quickly rose to his feet and unslung his MP-5. The BND agent swung the Heckler & Koch subgun toward the upstairs windows and triggered a fast volley. Glass shattered and chips splintered from the sills and frames. He hoped that would serve to discourage opponents in the rooms above from trying to take another shot while he hurried back to the storm doors.

One of the doors had been torn from its hinges and hung crookedly. Hahn yanked the pin from a gas canister and tossed it through the gap. If the hostages were in the basement, they would be stricken by chemical sickness along with the terrorists. Sick was still better than dead. Hahn hoped the protective mask strapped to his face would protect him from the gas. He slammed a boot into the broken door and kicked it out of his way before he charged into the basement.

The cloud of green gas fumes filled the basement. A single naked light bulb offered little illumination in the dense fog. Hahn realized too late the mistake he had made. The basement was smaller than he had anticipated. The gas created a smoke screen that prevented him from seeing more than vague shapes in the tiny room. Hahn shuffled forward, probing with the barrel of his MP-5, almost blind inside the mist-filled chamber.

Hahn heard the wretched sound of groaning and vomiting from a corner of the room. He moved toward the sound and saw the blurred shape of a man hunched over and trembling as he heaved relentlessly onto the hard stone floor. Hahn jabbed the barrel of his H&K blaster into the man's side.

"Hold it right there!" he ordered in English, hoping he had found one of the hostages—perhaps even Gary Manning.

Metal clattered on the hard floor as the captive raised empty hands. The son of a bitch had dropped a weapon, Hahn realized. The man slowly looked up, and lean features with tear-blurred eyes became visible. Atop that head was a black beret with a white skull emblem.

Hahn swore with disappointment.

Suddenly a powerful blow hit him between the shoulder blades. The force launched him against the terrorist and drove both of them into an old workbench. Hahn felt his arm brush a cardboard box. The container toppled to the floor. An assortment of metal nails spilled from the box. The nails scraped stone under Hahn's boots as he struggled to keep his balance.

The thin terrorist grabbed Hahn's wrists and twisted hard. The splinter in the BND agent's left hand stabbed deeper and weakened his grip. The MP-5 slipped from his fingers and dropped to the floor as yet another man appeared from the greenish fog. The second opponent was a medium-size man with a *keffiyeh* drawn across his nose and mouth in a vain effort to shield himself from the noxious gas. The Arab thug held a Walther P-38 in his fist, but with his vision obscured, he could not see clearly and was reluctant to use the business end of his pistol for fear of shooting his comrade.

Hahn whipped a knee into the first opponent's scrawny abdomen and tried to shove him against the Arab. The skinny terrorist groaned, but didn't topple as Hahn desired. Instead, the desperate man grabbed for the Walther P-5 autoloader in shoulder leather under Hahn's arm with one hand and clawed at the protective mask on Hahn's face with the other. The terrorist obviously thought he could achieve double salvation; protection from the stomach-churning gas fumes and a weapon to replace the one he had dropped.

The pistol slid from leather, but Hahn seized his opponent's wrist with both hands and twisted forcibly to push the barrel away from his own chest. The terrorist shoved Hahn's head backward with his free hand, his fingers tearing at the lenses of the mask, his palm rubbing against the filters. The BND agent ground a knuckle into the thug's ulnar nerve at the back of the hand fisted around the pistol. The gun fell with a clatter as the terrorist rasped through his teeth from the pain.

Hahn lashed a hard back-fist stroke to the skinny man's face. The terrorist staggered from the blow, a ribbon of blood creeping from his nose. The Arab quickly moved in and swung his Walther to slap the barrel across the side of Hahn's skull.

The BND agent's head seemed to burst in a blinding flash of pain that filled his eyes with white light. He fell back into a wall. His hand touched a long wooden object that felt like a pole of some kind. Vision returned, blurred and a bit disoriented, but enough to allow Hahn to see his Arab opponent point the P-38 at his chest.

Hahn reacted in the only manner that offered any chance of survival. A thin chance at that. He grabbed the pole and lashed out with it. The wooden shaft struck the Arab's gun hand as the terrorist squeezed the trigger. The Walther snarled and fell from the Arab's bruised fingers. However, the parabellum round from the weapon tore into Karl Hahn's stomach like a high-velocity red-hot poker.

The BND agent doubled up in agony. He felt his insides convulse as the bullet plowed into his stomach, after ripping open the lining. The pain was greater than any he had experienced in the past, yet he still held on to the pole and felt the wooden shaft connect with his opponent's thigh. Hahn looked at the pole in his grasp and saw the curved metal and wedge-shaped blade at the end of the shaft. It was a garden hoe, he realized.

Hahn screamed, agony mixed with anger and fear. He suddenly pulled the shaft with all the strength he could muster. The blade caught the Arab gunman behind the knee and the sudden yank tore his feet from the floor. The startled terrorist crashed on his back, winded by the unexpected fall. Hahn raised his arms, the hoe in both fists. He felt a burning pain, and blood oozed from his punctured abdomen. The BND pro's face was rigid with pain, his eyes squinted into slits. But he managed to swing the hoe and felt the blade strike his tormentor squarely in the chest.

The hoe shaft snapped in two from the impact. Hahn's rage and terror had contributed to his strength despite the condition of his bullet-ravaged body. The metal wedge of the hoe blade chopped into the Arab gunman's sternum. It cleaved through flesh and muscle to shatter the bone. Shards were driven inward to puncture the heart and lungs. The man's mouth opened in a cry of agony, but blood rose up into his throat to stifle the scream. His body twitched wildly, then he made a futile effort to pry out the hoe blade. It was his final attempt at anything.

The thin terrorist snarled something in a language Hahn did not recognize. Perhaps it was just a bestial roar as the man saw his comrade slain by the German commando. The thug reached down and scooped up the fallen P-5 autoloader. Hahn felt dizzy, doped up by the numbness of the nerve shock that began to rob him of his senses. The broken shaft of the hoe was in his fists, though, and he also realized that the surviving terrorist was about to open fire on him.

I'm dead anyway, Hahn thought as he lunged forward.

The Walther P-5 roared. Hahn saw the muzzle-flash, felt the bullet punch through his chest and burrow its way into his left lung. The pain was not as bad as he would have imagined. He had already endured so much a bit more hardly mattered. The BND agent collided with his opponent and both men crashed to the floor as the pistol cracked once more.

Another parabellum ripped into Hahn's flesh. This time the pain raked his whole body. Terrible agony that made his fingers claw the floor and his body tremble violently as blood spilled on the scrawny gunman beneath him. God, Hahn thought with astonishment, I've been shot through the heart....

Hahn was amazed that his mind was still surprisingly clear. The BND agent discovered that he had managed to ram the splintered end of the hoe shaft into the terrorist's narrow abdomen. The thug was already very sick from the effects of the vomit gas and the painful stab in the gut forced him into a wild convulsion on the floor.

The terrorist still held the Walther P-5, but Hahn scarcely noticed. His heart had almost stopped, and he knew he would be dead in another second or two. His fingers touched the nails on the floor. Gripping one between thumb and forefinger, with his muscles and spinal reflex commanding his actions more than conscious thought, the German commando struck. He lashed out like an enraged scorpion, the nail in his fist an improvised stinger. His fist slammed into the terrorist's face. The nail sank deep into soft tissue. The terrorist screamed and snapped back his head. Hahn glimpsed the head of the nail between the lids of his opponent's left eye. Blood oozed from the punctured orb as the terrorist placed a hand to the horrible wound.

Hahn swung the heel of his palm into the back of the terrorist's hand. The blow slammed the hand hard into the man's face and drove the nail deeper. It punched through the eyeball and bit into the man's brain, making him flop and thrash about in a final fit of agony. Hahn watched with a vague sense of satisfaction that he had managed to take out his own executioner before he died. Surprisingly, it did not seem terribly important as his vision dimmed and the last breath he would ever draw seeped out through the bloodied hole in his chest. The pain was gone. He just felt tired. A lifetime of worries, struggles, ambitions and dreams melted away. A final, eternal sleep seemed welcome and peaceful to Karl Hahn. He relaxed and allowed himself to drift....

KATZ'S UZI BLASTED a wave of 9 mm slugs up the stairwell and slashed two of the enemy with high-velocity fury. The pair executed a macabre dance as their bodies were rattled by the merciless hail of lead, then one terrorist flopped to the floor of the upstairs hall and died. The other, through the sheer determination of revenge, swung his Astra pistol toward Katz. The enemy swayed unsteadily and blood soaked his shirt, but the fire in his eyes revealed that he'd go out fighting.

Katz fired the Uzi. Another trio of parabellum slugs smashed into the terrorist's chest. The man recoiled from the impact and dropped his weapon. A puzzled expression appeared on his face. Death must not have been what he expected. The terrorist toppled forward and plunged down the stairs. Katz stepped aside and allowed the dead man to tumble awkwardly past him to the foot of the stairs.

"*Schweinhund,*" a GSG-9 commando growled as he kicked the Astra from the dead terrorist's fingers.

Katz reached the top of the stairs and glanced down at his companions. Three GSG-9 troopers had followed him up while

others covered prisoners in the room below. The raid seemed
to have gone in favor of Katz and his German antiterrorist
allies. Two men from Hahn's team had entered from the
kitchen at the rear of the house, and Colonel Bohler and two
of his men appeared through the front. The latter meant Bohler's team had taken out the terrorists in the barn.

The remaining opponents on the second story, however, still
presented a serious threat. Katz peered through the lenses of his
protective mask and examined the short hallway. It was unfur-
nished and had a bare wood floor. There were only three doors,
but potential death waited behind each one. Green mist drifted
from beneath two of the doors. Anyone inside the rooms ought
to have succumbed to the effects of the gas. But there was no
guarantee that all the fight was gone out of the terrorists.

Katz and a GSG-9 trooper moved to the first door while
other commandos approached the remaining doors, weapons
held ready. The Phoenix leader stepped to one side of the
doorway and his German companion stood by the hinge side.
Katz looked at the young commando. The man's face was covered by a mask, and the lenses and filters seemed to be his only
features. He held an MP-5, and nodded to Katz to signal his
readiness. The Israeli returned the gesture. Uzi cradled across
his prosthesis, Katz slammed a boot into the door and kicked
it open.

He immediately ducked back, clear of the entrance. A burst
of automatic fire snarled a violent welcome, but Katz and his
ally were not in the path of the attack. The West German
trooper swung the barrel of his subgun into the doorway to
trigger a short burst. A scream rewarded his effort. The
GSG-9 warrior jumped into the room. Katz thrust his Uzi in the
doorway to cover his companion. Orange flame exploded in the
room. The muzzle-flash blazed from the stubby barrel of an
Ingram machine pistol wielded by a stocky Asian kneeling at
the foot of a bed. The metal frame of the bed was empty. The
terrorists in the room had removed the mattress and used it to
cover the gas grenade that sputtered and burned under the improvised shield in a corner of the room.

Katz saw all that with a glance. He realized their simple tactics would reduce the effects of the gas, but would not spare

them from the noxious fumes entirely. He heard the loud groan
of agony as Ingram slugs smashed into the GSG-9 soldier who
had charged into the room. The Israeli immediately pointed his
Uzi at the Asian gunman and opened fire. The terrorist was
propelled backward by the high-velocity shove of three 9 mm
parabellums.

The Japanese killer groaned as he landed on the floor beneath a windowsill.

The terrorist tried to raise his Ingram, but his arms would not
respond. Katz shot him again. Three more parabellums tore a
diagonal line of ragged bullet holes in the gunman's barrel
chest. The man's head snapped back against the wall. Blood
spewed from his open mouth in a wide arc, and he shivered in
a final act of vain defiance before surrendering to death.

Katz followed his Uzi into the room. Another terrorist lay
dead on the floor, slain by the GSG-9 commando, who in turn
had been killed by the man Katz had eliminated. The small
bedroom was a microcosm of human butchery. Katz was glad
the protective mask blotted out smell, as well as the noxious gas
fumes. He knew the odors of such scenes all too well. The salty-
copper smell of fresh blood, the malodorous smells of fear and
death.

Suddenly the door swung forward and slammed into Katz.
He staggered from the unexpected blow as another man appeared from behind the door. The Israeli mentally cursed himself for making such a fundamental and careless error. The
terrorist had simply hidden behind the door and now rushed
toward the Phoenix commando, a pair of sticks linked by a
short chain in his fist.

The Japanese thug swung his *nunchaku*. A stick smashed the
frame of Katz's Uzi and struck the submachine gun from his
single hand. An angry, gaunt Asian face glared at Katz as the
terrorist lashed out with the *nunchaku* in a high arc aimed at
Katz's head. The Phoenix pro had encountered the unusual
martial arts weapon in the past and realized its deadly potential. The sticks whirled at almost one hundred miles an hour in
the hands of an expert, and a single blow could shatter bone
and rupture vital organs.

Katz ducked under the stick. It whistled overhead, narrowly missing his skull. The Japanese killer snapped his wrist and the *nunchaku* cut a fast figure-eight pattern to swing a diagonal slash at Katz's face, but the Israeli suddenly put up his prosthesis. Wood struck the metal limb. Katz snapped the steel hooks around the chain at the center of the *nunchaku*.

The terrorist still held one stick in his fist. The other hung useless, robbed of mobility by Katz's grip on the chain. Katz quickly took advantage of the opportunity and chopped the side of his hand across his opponent's wrist. The killer's fingers slipped from the *nunchaku* and Katz swung a kick at the terrorist's abdomen. With a groan of surprise and pain, the man stumbled backward. He tripped over the corpse of a slain comrade and fell heavily to the floor.

The *nunchaku* dangled in Katz's grip. The sticks swung against each other uselessly as the chain remained trapped in the steel hooks of the prosthesis. The Japanese killer glanced up at Katz, fear mixed with fury in his dark almond-shaped eyes. The terrorist groped along the floor and found the Ingram machine pistol.

Katz's hand streaked to the knife on his hip. He drew the weapon from the sheath and pointed the double-edged blade at his opponent. His thumb pressed the trigger at the black metal hilt and the powerful spring inside the hollow handle launched the blade. It shot across the room, struck the terrorist in the chest and pierced the heart. He stared up at Katz with astonishment and glanced down at the steel projectile buried in his flesh. A sigh escaped from the man's lips as he lay back and accepted death.

The battle was over. Katz gathered up his Uzi and stepped into the hall. GSG-9 commandos had managed to take two terrorists prisoner from the other rooms and marched them down the stairs at gunpoint. Katz followed them.

At the bottom of the stairs Colonel Bohler came up to him and placed his hand on Katz's shoulder. "No hostages and no bomb," Bohler declared. He sounded sad, as well as disappointed. "No sign of Colonel Skull, either. In fact, there doesn't appear to be anything here except the terrorists. Some of my men have a few other prisoners at the barn. I'm not sure how many we've got. Maybe they can tell us something that will help locate Skull.''

"I doubt it," Katz said, shaking his head. "These men were expendable. Skull wanted us to find them."

"What's that?" the colonel asked with surprise. "What do you mean? Why would he want us to find this base?"

"To see if we'd be afraid to attack it or if his threats to kill the hostages and detonate the plutonium bomb would prevent us from taking any action," Katz explained. "I thought this was too easy. Japanese and Africans renting a remote farm and hiring Turks and Arabs was the same as begging the BND to take an interest in this place. It was just a test to see how we'd react if we found one of his bases."

Bohler paled with anger and concern. "This is terrible. So many lives lost for . . . for a test run. Four of my men are dead, and one is wounded. I have even worse news for you, my friend. We found Karl in the basement. He's dead, Yakov."

"Oh, my God," Katz replied. The familiar sorrow at the loss of a comrade at arms squeezed his heart. "That's one more score we have to settle with Skull."

"I hope you find him," Bohler stated. "Sorry there isn't much more I can do. The raid will take a bit of explaining. The antiterrorist act authorizes search and seizure without a warrant when we suspect terrorist activities, but we overstepped those bounds. Still, it won't be too difficult. We certainly have adequate proof that the raid was justified. I hope Gary is all right."

Katz nodded grimly, still pained by the death of Karl Hahn. The idea that Manning might also be dead was even more distressing. "If Skull has killed him, I swear that sorry excuse for a man will have me to deal with personally."

"I know how you feel," Bohler assured him, "but you also realize it's dangerous to take these things personally. It can get in the way of your professionalism."

"You're damn right it's personal," Katz admitted. "I'll accept the added risk if it means I'll have a chance to take care of Colonel Skull myself."

16

Hal Brognola had been to the Oval Office several times in the past, but it was the first time he had met the vice president of the United States in the official headquarters of the White House. The head of Stony Man operations sat in a leather armchair, the usual unlit cigar stuck in his mouth, wishing he knew more about the man across the desk.

The slender middle-aged man with serious features and tranquil eyes was the acting executive in chief. The vice president looked tired, and lines scored his face deeply from the stress of the crisis that had unexpectedly placed him in the role of the top public official in America. He seemed uncomfortable seated behind the presidential desk. Perhaps the circumstances had thrust him into the position before he was ready to assume the office. The man was running a campaign for the party nomination as candidate in the next national election. Maybe the current experience might convince him to bow out, Brognola thought. The power and prestige of the presidency also carried with it an enormous burden of responsibility. If nothing else, the vice president was sure as hell getting some on-the-job training for the post he coveted.

"I'm not even sure who you are or what you do, Mr. Smith," the vice president remarked, tapping the end of a pen on the desktop as he stared at the mysterious visitor. "You certainly don't have the most original alias. 'Smith' isn't your real name, is it?"

"That's not important," Brognola replied. "You know the phone I used to arrange this meeting is a confidential line. It you become president on a more permanent basis, I'll share some more details concerning who I am and what I do."

"Super top secret?" The vice president shook his head. "Are you sure this is the time for keeping secrets from me? My security clearance is pretty high-level, you know."

"As former director of the CIA, I should certainly hope so," Brognola agreed. "But you must also know the Company hasn't got a flawless record for maintaining security. My organization is smaller, more specialized and the security is so tight even the President doesn't know any details that aren't absolutely necessary."

"On the phone you said you had information concerning the President and this wretched terrorist business in Europe," the vice president remarked wearily. "That's why I agreed to this meeting, Mr. Smith. I hope you're going to answer some questions we've got concerning the President's safety and efforts to rescue him—and the Soviet premier—from these terrorists. So far CIA and NSA haven't been too encouraging."

"Well, my people work in deeper cover than those better-known groups," Brognola explained. "They've also got more valuable connections with West European intelligence groups. I got a message from the unit commander of the team handling the mission in Europe."

"The men who tried to rescue the President and the other VIPs at Strassmacher Castle?" The vice president grunted. "From what I heard from my sources, they didn't do too well."

"They probably would have succeeded if KGB hadn't tried to charge in like a bull in a china shop," the Fed answered. He took the cigar from his mouth and stared at the unlit end. "Mind if I smoke this thing?"

"Will it help you talk faster?" the vice president replied dryly. "Frankly, if you don't have any progress to report, I'd just as soon not hear any excuses why your people haven't gotten results."

"They took out the terrorists who fled to West Germany," Brognola stated in a hard voice.

"Did they find the hostages or the plutonium bomb the terrorists are supposed to have?" the chief executive asked, his brow wrinkled with interest.

"I'm afraid not," Brognola admitted, snapping open a lighter to fire up his cigar. Only extreme stress made him light up, and he'd already acknowledged to himself that he could hardly be under greater pressure. "BND will pass on the details to CIA personnel in Germany, but the bottom line is the terrorist base in the Rhineland was just a decoy. Skull set them up to see if we'd hit the terrorists if we could locate them."

"How can you be sure of that?" The vice president frowned.

"We're not," the Fed confessed, puffing his stogie, "but the man who came up with this theory is the best in the business. He says they found a radio unit that was probably used by the other terrorists to keep in touch with the base. When Skull finds out the radio is no longer in operation, he'll know they've been taken out. Maybe Skull's people radioed them on an hourly level, maybe they called him or both. The terrorists who survived the raid will be interrogated, of course, but we may not learn anything of value from them. After all, Skull hung them out to dry so I don't think he'd supply them with important information."

"Radio unit," the vice president mused. "What about an estimate of an effective range for the radio frequency?"

"That's been taken into consideration, sir," Brognola replied. "My people are convinced the remaining terrorists are located in Belgium and northern France. It's even possible some of the terrorists may have crossed the border from France into Belgium to throw us off the track. Several vehicles were reported and logged in crossing into Belgium within two hours after the terrorist helicopter landed in France. The group remaining in France may be another decoy. On the other hand, Colonel Skull is very ruthless and clever. He may have already guessed we'd check the vehicle logs at the borders and assume we'll concentrate our manhunt in Belgium. The son of a bitch has second-guessed us pretty well so far."

"I find this 'Colonel Skull' business pretty hard to believe," the vice president admitted. "Sounds like something out of an old James Bond movie."

"Skull has taken advantage of that assumption for a long time," the Fed explained. "Nobody took him seriously because he sounded like a fictional villain. We have some idea who he really is. Henri Rikker, a Swiss national, disappeared about a year before Colonel Skull surfaced. Rikker was the son of one of the top bankers in Switzerland. Apparently he ripped off his old man's business and took more than twenty million Swiss francs when he vanished. It was a big scandal in Europe. Rikker didn't fit anybody's profile of a thief.''

''Wait a minute,'' the vice president began, his eyes wide as vague memories started to come back to him. ''I remember something about that. I was in Europe at the time. Rikker was supposed to be a brilliant scholar. History, languages, political science. No one figured he could handle embezzling a ton of money.''

''That's right,'' Brognola confirmed. ''Besides, he had also inherited a ton of money. Henri Rikker had about thirty-five million francs when he disappeared. If Rikker is Skull, we know what he did with that money.''

''He used it to build a private army of international terrorists?'' The vice president shook his head. ''Why? How could he do it? The man was an intellectual, as I recall. He wasn't a military expert or a political fanatic. I remember the stories that he was even a physical weakling. Sickly and pale with poor eyesight. Correct?''

''Pale and poor eyesight, for sure,'' Brognola confirmed. ''Henri Rikker is an albino. We think Colonel Skull might be an albino, too. Rikker isn't a physical weakling, although most people probably thought that. The info we dug up on him included private lessons in t'ai chi, sort of a kung fu style Rikker has been studying since he was fourteen. He's also knowledgeable about small arms, military history and tactics, although his physical condition made him unfit for military service. An albino's skin and eyes are extremely sensitive to light. All the t'ai chi in the world can't change that. The records also show that Rikker speaks French, German, English and Spanish fluently. It fits with what we know about Colonel Skull.''

''Incredible,'' the vice president said, still finding the story hard to believe. ''Why on earth would a man like that want to become a terrorist?''

''Hell, I'm not a shrink,'' the Fed answered. ''Offhand, I'd guess Henri Rikker probably experienced a lot of rejection as a child. His father was a big, healthy, self-made millionaire. Maybe he resented having an albino for a son. The kid was probably treated like a freak at school and maybe by his family. Rikker obviously turned to his studies to try to compensate for his physical problems and appearance. Maybe he hated his old man and hated the world in general. Take a look at what happens when men with inferiority complexes get power. Napoléon, Hitler, Torquemada—history is full of examples. Maybe all the Caligulas and Himmlers started off as bitter children looking for some way to get even.''

"Interesting," the vice president commented. "You may even be right. Let's say Skull is Henri Rikker and he decided to form his own terrorist army. From what I understand, his followers are all terrorists who got fed up with other groups they belonged to before. Disillusioned with old causes, disappointed with the way things were going with the previous outfits or just plain greedy and eager to get paid with something other than propaganda and promises. I still don't see the connection with Iraq."

"My people think Skull was hired by someone in the Iraq government who intends to assassinate his way to power and make it look as if the Iranians are the villains," Brognola answered. "After all, it's not too hard to convince people the Iranians are bad guys. After the new Iraqi government takes over Iran, they'll also take charge of the shipping lanes in the Persian Gulf. My guess is Skull plans to get a piece of that pie, as well. The oil fields in Iran will also be producing a lot more crude after the war with Iraq comes to an end and an opportunist like Skull gets into the picture. The worse thing is, I don't think Skull and his ambitious Iraqi pals will stop there. Maybe next they'll expand to Oman or Kuwait. With a stranglehold on Middle East oil and power in OPEC, they could become a real world power. I figure that's what Skull wants in the end. Godlike power over all us ordinary mortals."

"I've looked into the theory that some high-ranking Iraqi might be willing to try something this crazy," the vice president announced. "The name my researchers came up with is Ali-Rez Saddoon, newly appointed chairman of the National Assembly of Iraq. Ali-Rez and his brother, Nizar, are both known to be hawkish about the war, less than thrilled with the Soviet Union's involvement in their government and apparently interested in getting some sort of trade agreements going with countries that haven't been too eager to do business with Iraq in the past. A lot of people, including a number of Americans, would like to see Saddoon take over. Of course, many people thought Libya would improve after Khaddafi took power from King Idris and Cuba would become a sterling example of democracy after Castro took over."

"Well, we have an idea who the game masters are and what their ultimate goals might be," Brognola said thoughtfully. He watched smoke rise from his cigar and drift toward the ceiling, as if hoping to find some answers in the strands of gray mist. "But the solutions are still in the hands of the players in the field. My men are in France and Belgium already. CIA, Sûreté and Interpol are assisting them. The unit commander told me he was flying out from Frankfurt to Brussels as soon as possible. These guys are the best. If anybody can handle this mess and make everything turn out okay, they're the ones who can do it."

"Now I understand what your top-secret organization does," the vice president said with a thin smile. "You fellows are in charge of miracles. Right?"

"We come close to that sometimes," the Fed answered. He did not smile in return. "All I can say is they'll do the best they can and I've never known them to fail."

"I hope to God they don't," the vice president confessed. He turned to face the window. The view from the Oval Office was not as impressive as most imagined. The White House lawns and gardens seemed calm and undisturbed by the turmoils that shook the rest of the world. The Washington Monument towered above treetops in the distance.

"There's a lot at stake," Brognola declared, aware the remark was a vast understatement.

"The life of the President and the Soviet premier," the vice president stated grimly. "A possible nuclear disaster in Western Europe, the likelihood of breakdowns of relations between the United States and the Soviet Union...to say nothing of our relations with Europe."

He turned to face Brognola. "Yes, Mr. Smith. That's a lot. There would also be new problems with our relations with Iraq and probably with most of the other Arabic nations. We'll have to alert the Iraqi president to the threat from within his own government, but we don't have any proof that Saddoon or anyone else is plotting against his regime. They're bound to accuse us of trying to cause disharmony in Iraq and even charge us with assisting Iran."

Brognola thought of the recent Iran-Contra scandal, but he did not mention it. The vice president did not need to be reminded of that all too public embarrassment for the present administration. It would certainly resurface if events caused a deterioration in America's relations with Iraq. The United States had not been on good terms with the socialist-military rule in Iraq and had only reestablished relations since the Iran-Iraq war. That could all dissolve overnight if the situation continued as it had thus far.

"The Soviets still aren't convinced this business isn't our fault, and a number of politicians in this country are convinced the Russians are to blame," the vice president continued. "If this goes on, *glasnost* will be a faded memory by next year and the Cold War will be chillier than ever. I don't know how true the claims connected with *glasnost* might be, but I'd like to see it get a chance—to at least let it be clear the Soviets are the ones with shortcomings if things don't work out, and it can't be blamed on our lack of cooperation. Innocent lives could be lost, NATO could be damaged... God, there's no end to the things that might happen if this mess isn't straightened out soon."

The vice president sighed. "I suppose my rambling about foreign policy must sound a bit callous since the President's life is in extreme jeopardy."

"No," the Fed assured him. "I understand. I have to send good men, very good men, off to deal with missions that might very well cost them their lives. We've lost a couple of brave and noble warriors over the years. They died fighting battles most people will never know about, but because they made those sacrifices thousands of lives have been saved, entire governments salvaged and threats to our nation have been stopped cold. Still, I have to think about the mission, not the men involved. One of our people is also held captive along with the President and the premier and two other VIP hostages. We don't have the luxury to afford much time worrying about the lives of a couple of individuals, even if they are friends or world leaders. That's part of the price we pay for being in authority."

"You sound like you'd like to be in the trenches instead," the vice president remarked. "I think I might find them more comfortable right now myself."

"That's not the way the cards turned out for us, sir," Brognola said with a shrug. "Sometimes the toughest thing a man can do is wait and hope others will do what he isn't in a position to do. Personally, I have to go back to my own headquarters and be ready in case any word comes through."

"Good luck," the vice president told him. "So far your people have done better than anyone else. I hope their winning streak continues. By the way, I won't have that chair dusted for prints. Your true identity is safe, Mr. Smith."

"I appreciate that," Hal Brognola said with a smile. He did not bother to tell the vice president that he had coated his hands with a clear enamel, similar to nail polish, which temporarily obliterated his finger and palm prints by sealing up the ridges of his skin. The Stony Man head honcho also wore a small electronic scrambling device in his belt buckle just in case the conversation was being taped. No tape recording would be intelligible, let alone able to retain a recognizable voice print. "Good day, sir."

Brognola left the room. The vice president turned back to the window. Rain began to strike the glass as thunder rumbled outside.

NIKOLAY VASHNOV SAT in the back seat of the Citroën and peered out the rear window with a pair of night-vision infrared binoculars. The magnificent Arc de Triomphe stood within view of the car, but he had no interest in the colossal structure. The KGB agent was no stranger to Paris. He had formerly been stationed at the Soviet embassy in Paris and had spent three years in the city. Vashnov was familiar with the Arc de

Triomphe, which Napoléon had supposedly planned as a tribute to his victories. Vashnov wished he could have met Napoléon. The KGB agent suspected Napoléon had probably been
the last Frenchman with any real balls.

The perpetual flame to honor France's Unknown Soldier
burned at the base of the arch. Vashnov would not have objected if the entire French population had been nameless and
buried beneath a monument. He regarded the French as loathsome, greedy and treacherous people. Of course, he had little
use for anyone who was not of pure Russian descent. That
prejudice included the Ukrainians and Uzbeks of the U.S.S.R.,
as well as the many and varied ethnic groups within that empire. Vashnov considered them to be peasant farmers and near
savages, barely fit to shine the shoes of a true Russian.

Yet any nationality was better than American, Vashnov
thought as he trained his night-sight glasses on the Information Office on des Champs-Elysées. The two Americans he had
followed to the office were examples of why Vashnov held the
United States in such contempt: a black man who dared talk
back to a white Russian officer, and a Hispanic who seemed to
regard himself as equal to those of unblemished European
blood. A few Cubans and black Africans, mostly from Angola, attended the Patrice Lumumba University near Moscow,
but they knew better than to consider themselves the equals of
true Russians. To Vashnov's bigoted mind, that was as it should
be. The differences between races and ethnic groups seemed
obvious to Vashnov. He believed a division between these
groups always had to exist. Naturally, the KGB agent felt the
ruling class ought to be the one he belonged to.

"Comrade? How long must we sit here and wait? The
Americans are probably just asking for tourist information,"
Aleksandr Borgneff said in a bored voice as he sat behind the
wheel of the Citroën.

"These are not tourists," Vashnov replied, still staring
through his binoculars. "I told you what happened in Luxembourg. Don't you want to find the secretary-general? Don't
you want to expose these capitalist scum for their involvement
in this terrorism and kidnapping?"

"I wish you had some proof of these claims, Comrade Vashnov," Mikhail Pushkin, the third man in the car, admitted with a weary sigh. "Our chief of operations in Paris had better confirm your alleged secret mission directly ordered by Moscow."

"Your rank is too low to question my authority, Pushkin," Vashnov snapped. "I remind you both that I was formerly in charge of Morkrie Dela operations here in France. You two worked for me at that time. I am still authorized to order assassinations for the benefit of KGB security. If need be, I can put your names on a list for liquidation, as well."

Pushkin decided it was wise not to reply. He remembered Vashnov from the old days. The man was a fanatic, ready to blame anything and everything on CIA conspiracies. Pushkin felt that Vashnov was better suited for "black propaganda" than field operations. Still, Vashnov had managed to find Pushkin and Borgneff within minutes after arriving in Paris earlier that day. He clearly had connections with the Foreign Affairs Section, and his authority over the lower ranked Soviet agents was indisputable. Nonetheless, this impromptu mission raised many questions that Pushkin could not dismiss.

If Vashnov had actually been ordered to Paris by the Kremlin, then why had they failed to contact the KGB at the Soviet embassy? Why had Vashnov come alone if he had KGB and GRU personnel under his command in Luxembourg during the alleged terrorist action and kidnapping? Finally, the question of the two Americans' involvement puzzled Pushkin. If they had actually foiled Vashnov's efforts to rescue the premier in Luxembourg, as Vashnov claimed, they would have little reason to go to France to try to join the so-called terrorists. Vashnov insisted the pair might lead them to the terrorists' headquarters. Why? If CIA was responsible, they would certainly have agents in place already in France.

It was even possible—although Pushkin knew better than to mention this idea to Vashnov—that the Americans might be trying to locate and rescue their President from the kidnappers. This would suggest a third party might be involved. An enemy of both the Soviets and the Americans? Vashnov had been correct when he claimed the mysterious Americans had met with Sûreté before paying a visit to the Paris police. Interesting, but it did not prove the pair were part of some sinister CIA plot.

For now, Pushkin thought, it was best to go along with whatever Vashnov came up with. Later, Pushkin and Borgneff could file their reports—and their complaints—to their section chief. Until then, the best course of action was to simply follow orders.

Vashnov let out an excited little yelp when he saw Calvin James and Rafael Encizo emerge from the Information Office. "No doubt they met with CIA or some other Western espionage personnel. This conspiracy may involve the networks of all the intelligence organizations of the capitalists in Europe, as well as the United States."

Borgneff turned in his seat and glanced out a window. The sinister "CIA villains" did not impress him much. A tall slender black man dressed in a dark blue suit and a black turtleneck shirt and a muscular Hispanic fellow clad in a dark suit and a white shirt open at the throat. Neither man wore a hat or made any apparent effort to disguise his appearance or conceal himself as he walked from the Information Office to a yellow Toyota parked in front of the building.

"Now what?" Borgneff asked. "Do we follow them again?"

"Of course," Vashnov confirmed as he lowered his binoculars. "We'll follow them all night if we must until we get an opportunity to apprehend them and find out some answers by direct inquisition."

Vashnov reached into his jacket and removed a Makarov pistol. He fitted a six-inch silencer to the threaded barrel and screwed the device into place.

"And after we have our answers," he added with a crooked smile, "we'll terminate them both."

17

Gary Manning staggered through the corridor as Major Yas-nev prodded him along with the barrel of an AK-47. The walls and floor and ceiling were made of gray stone and mortar. A column of light bulbs had been strung along the ceiling and were powered by a rubber-coated cord. The light hurt Manning's eyes and he tried to avoid looking directly at it. His head throbbed and his legs wobbled unsteadily beneath him.

"American pig has trouble walking, eh?" Yasnev snickered as he shoved Manning again.

The Canadian Phoenix pro fell against a wall. Everything seemed to spin around him. He felt as if he was suffering from the worst hangover in the history of mankind since some smart ass in the ancient world discovered fermented grapes. Then Manning remembered he had not been drinking. He had been strapped to a chair and one of Skull's flunkies had stuck a hypodermic needle in his arm. Manning did not remember anything after that. He had no idea how much time had passed since he had been drugged or what had happened while he was under the influence of whatever the bastards had injected into his veins.

Yasnev herded Manning to a doorway. The room inside was darker than the corridor. The light within was tinted a soft crimson. Manning was glad to enter the room. The interior was shadowy and the only light came from a lamp over a desk. The skeletal face of Colonel Skull peered from behind the desk. The albino's red-pink eyes examined Manning without emotion as Yasnev led the Canadian to a chair in front of the desk. Skull's pale white head seemed to float above the desk, his black uniform blending into the shadows.

The terrorist leader placed a glass of water and a white saucer with two small yellow pills on the desk. Skull gestured toward the offering and leafed through some sheets of paper as he spoke without looking at Manning.

"Don't worry," he told the captive. "It's just for your headache. I understand scopolamine leaves one feeling a bit ill afterward. Go ahead. If I wanted to poison you, I would have ordered cyanide to be injected into your veins after they gave you the truth serum. I certainly wouldn't want you to mess up my office by dying in here."

Manning realized that made sense. He swallowed the pills and washed them down with water, draining the glass. He had not felt thirsty until that moment. All his senses were still numb. Skull raised a pitcher and poured some more water into the glass.

"Try to relax, Manning," Skull instructed. "Savor a few moments of civilized behavior. Enjoy it while it lasts."

"Maybe there would be more civilized conduct if there were fewer men like you," Manning said in a hoarse voice as he raised the glass to his lips. "What do you want now, you bastard?"

Skull stayed impassive and went on with his own line of dialogue. "I'm certain you're curious about what you told us while under the influence of scopolamine. One thing you obviously told us is your real name. You're Gary Manning and you're a Canadian citizen. That was a bit of a surprise. I didn't expect the Canadians to be involved in this business. I take it you must be working for the United States government somehow. Correct?"

"Didn't I answer that question when your boys drugged me?" Manning inquired, sipping the water.

"No." Skull sighed. "You gave your name, you mentioned you had formerly been a first lieutenant in the Canadian armed forces, attached to the United States Army Fifth Special Forces in Vietnam and you gave your service number. None of which interests me in the slightest."

"So fire the guy in charge of scopolamine highballs," Manning said, rolling his head to work the stiffness from his neck muscles.

"I don't think that's his fault," the albino said with a slight shrug. "It's obvious you've had some sort of posthypnotic training. Impressive. When the effects of any sort of mind-altering drug begin, your subconscious switches over to a cover story that has been planted there by hypnosis. That's rather sophisticated and specialized training. You're quite a character, Mr. Manning."

"Carlson," Manning answered. "My real name is Harry Carlson. Your people really messed up."

"Come now, Mr. Manning," Skull replied. "Some things even posthypnosis can't bury. Your real name, nationality, family background, names of close friends and so on. Still, I must admit we were unable to learn what organization you work for or how you learned about me or knew that I intended to launch the raid on Strassmacher Castle."

"I can't tell you that myself," the Canadian replied. "My head feels like it's full of cotton right now."

"That may be true," Skull said with a nod. "If it is, I suggest you wait for your head to clear and try to organize your thoughts carefully to tell us everything we want to know. If you cooperate, it really will be in your own best interest. Otherwise, the alternatives left to me will be very unpleasant for both of us. We could, of course, resort to torture. Major Yasnev favored that from the beginning. He'd be delighted to participate in inflicting physical agony to get you to talk."

"I figure he'd be delighted to do that to anyone for any reason," Manning commented as he glanced at the big Russian muscle man who stood by the doorway, AK-47 in hand. "I'm surprised GRU didn't recognize the fact that Yasnev here is a sick son of a bitch. How would you label him, Skull? Sadistic sociopath with psychotic tendencies?"

"Shut up!" Yasnev snarled as he moved toward Manning.

"No, Yasnev!" Skull ordered. "I don't want him harmed. Not yet, at least."

"I guess the Soviets didn't realize Yasnev was crazy because they've got so many paranoid nut cases in high command and they've had to order soldiers to do some pretty vicious things in the past," Manning continued, taking advantage of the opportunity to goad Yasnev. "The major here is the type who wouldn't object to dumping napalm on Afghan rebels or putting little bombs in toys so Afghan kids might get blown to bits when they picked up the goodies. I bet that's why he has that Stalin mustache. Yasnev would have fit right in with Stalin's policies of genocide in the Ukraine. Hey, Yasnev! Did you get mad at the premier when he publicly denounced what Stalin did? Is that when you decided to turn against the Soviet Union?"

"If he doesn't shut up..." Yasnev hissed through clenched teeth. His knuckles strained as he tightened his grip on the Kalashnikov rifle in his fists.

"Did the mean old secretary-general bad-mouth your hero?" Manning asked in a mocking tone. "Is that what pushed you over the edge to become a complete chest-beating brute?"

"That's enough, Manning," Skull warned.

"Does Yasnev realize he's as good as dead when this is over?" Manning asked, turning to direct the question to Colonel Skull. "He's expendable now. When he was a double agent inside GRU he was useful. Now, he's just a mad dog you'll have to get rid of to protect your own security."

"What is this?" Yasnev asked with a frown.

"He's trying to upset you enough to do something stupid," Skull explained with a deep sigh. "If he can convince you to try to take his head off with a butt stroke it might offer an opportunity to seize your rifle and disarm you. If that doesn't work, maybe he can put a germ of doubt into your mind about the value of remaining loyal to me. Painfully obvious tactics, Mr. Manning."

"I'm not in a position to argue with you," Manning declared with a shrug. His head was starting to feel better and the stiffness was beginning to vanish from his body.

Skull reached under his desk and produced a compact submachine gun. The terrorist leader snapped the folding stock of the weapon into place. Manning noticed the subgun resembled a cross between an AR-7 and a MP-40 Schmeisser. A long magazine extended from the weapon. Skull held the pistol grip in one hand and cradled the barrel in the other.

"I think you need to cool down, Major," Skull told Yasnev. "I'll keep our guest covered while you go find Major Hee and tell him to come here."

"You should not remain alone with this Yankee," the Russian began.

"I'll be fine," Skull insisted. "Put the handcuffs on Mr. Manning before you leave so there will be no room for doubt."

Yasnev muttered something in Russian and roughly pulled Manning's arms behind the backrest of the chair. He snapped a pair of handcuffs around the prisoner's wrists. Yasnev yanked on the short chain forcibly. Manning winced with pain. The Soviet brute chuckled with cruel pleasure and swatted his open palm across the side of Manning's skull.

"I'll look forward to doing some serious work on you later," Yasnev snorted as he gathered up his AK-47 and marched from Skull's office.

Manning heard the door slam. He looked at Skull. The terrorist mastermind seemed relaxed and calm despite the submachine gun he held. Skull did not point the weapon at his prisoner. Not that there was any need to threaten Manning with the firearm. The Phoenix Force commando knew there was nothing he could do at the moment, and he was not eager to attempt a suicidal charge.

"Interesting gun," Manning remarked. "A Swiss SIG MP-310, isn't it?"

"Yes," Skull confirmed. "It's a personal favorite of mine. Are you familiar with it? The MP-310 is a fairly rare firearm."

"First time I've seen one except in firearm books," Manning admitted. "Swiss weapons remind you of your homeland?"

"You are beginning to annoy me, Mr. Manning," the albino stated. "That's very foolish. I already warned you that failure to cooperate may force us to use torture. You really don't want Major Hee to demonstrate his knowledge of anatomy by using your pressure points and nerve centers."

"Major Hee is in charge of torture?" Manning inquired, stretching his legs because these were the only limbs he could move at the moment. "Yasnev will be disappointed."

"Yasnev would be too inclined to simply damage you or even kill you outright," Skull explained. "Major Hee will create excruciating pain and prolong it until your mind screams for the agony to end."

"I guess you guys have a lot of time to spare," Manning remarked, trying to sound more calm than he felt. "That's the problem with torture, Colonel. It takes time to do it properly. Hee might be able to make me scream my head off, but you guys will just have to guess how much of it is lies just to try to get him to stop."

"Oh, I don't imagine you'll break easily," Skull said, tapping his fingers on the steel frame of the MP-310. "Perhaps we'll try scopolamine again. Dangerous, of course. We'd have to use a bigger dose to try to break down your subconscious and that might kill you."

"Big deal," Manning said, and actually laughed. "You bastards are going to kill me anyway."

"Not necessarily," the albino replied. "When this operation comes to an conclusion, I'm going to be a very wealthy and powerful man. Governments will bend to my will. I will be a major force in the decision making for this entire planet. You could be part of that, Mr. Manning."

"Really?" The Canadian raised his eyebrows. "Just like Major Yasnev?"

"I don't think I'd force you two to work together," Skull said with a smile. "Look, Manning, I'm certain your first reaction to this sort of offer is to say 'hell no, I won't betray my country.' That's natural enough, but take advantage of the few precious hours I'm giving you to consider just how much you owe your country—whether that country happens to be Canada or the United States. Or perhaps you consider your loyalties to both. Regardless of how you look at it, your country—or countries—obviously don't give a damn what happens to you."

"Oh, I see," Manning said with mock seriousness as he solemnly nodded his head. "*You* really care about your men?

Seems to me you left a lot of them standing around without assistance so they could be slaughtered in order to buy your people a couple extra seconds during your escape from Strassmacher Castle."

"Don't be melodramatic," Skull replied, rolling his pale eyes toward the ceiling. "The men knew we were working on a tight schedule. If they failed to reach the helicopters in time, the rest of us couldn't wait for them. That was understood from the beginning."

"What about the poor bastard who grabbed one of the skids to the landing gear of a chopper and held on until he lost his grip and fell to his death?"

"I thought you were still unconscious when that happened," Skull said with a frown. "Overheard some of the men talking? Of course, that must be it. Most of the men speak French or German and you're fluent in both languages."

"Trying to evade the question, Colonel?" Manning asked.

"Not at all," the terrorist assured him. "If you'll recall, there were soldiers and various types of agents shooting at those helicopters. To open the sliding doors to a cabin in order to attempt to rescue the man would have endangered the lives of everyone on board the aircraft. There are risks. You should appreciate that."

"I still suspect you regard most of your men as little more than cannon fodder," the Canadian insisted.

"A man is worth what his abilities might be," Skull said without a trace of apology in his voice. "Just as any good commander tends to put his less valuable soldiers in the front lines, so I tend to put my men with lesser skills, smaller intellects and least long-term potential in the most risky positions during combat. I see nothing wrong with that."

"I don't imagine you would," Manning muttered.

"All my followers joined me willingly," Skull stated. "The terrorist organizations they were previously associated with were fanatical. Religion, politics, whatever. Victories were stupid and hollow. They seldom gained any land or acquired any financial reward. That certainly isn't the case with my terrorist-mercenary force. The men who survive this campaign will become quite rich. Wouldn't you like to be rich?"

"I don't think I'd like to be cannon fodder," Manning answered, shaking his head.

"No need to worry about that," the terrorist assured him. "A man with your ability and experience would be very valuable to my organization. Think about your choices, Mr. Manning. To be alive, wealthy and powerful is certainly better than the questionable status of being a dead hero."

"You're going on the assumption that you'll win," Manning reminded him. "I don't know exactly what you plan to gain, but you are obviously working some sort of international blackmail. You know, just about everybody is after your ass, Skull. The biggest and best intelligence networks and police organizations are already tracking you. Are you really so sure you can outthink all of them? Even if you get away with this, they'll still hunt you down eventually."

"If they find me they may keep me from winning, but they will still lose in the end," Skull insisted. "You remember the plutonium device? It is here at this base. If we're discovered— and I do realize that is possible—we will all die together and so will quite a few others. Thousands of others, including all those brave underpaid and overzealous dead heroes. A terrible waste. Let's hope that doesn't happen."

"Yeah," Manning said without enthusiasm. "I hope a lot of things don't happen, Skull."

MAJOR HEE ESCORTED Gary Manning from Colonel Skull's office. The big Korean was as physically intimidating as Yasnev, but Hee did not resort to the sort of bullying the Russian favored. Manning was not shoved or poked with Hee's submachine gun. The Korean obviously considered that method unnecessary, perhaps simply a waste of energy. Major Hee was clearly a man who chose to conserve his energy. Apparently Skull's henchman did not even care to speak unless it seemed necessary.

Manning was still handcuffed as he walked through the corridor to an opening at the end. He passed several doors, all made of seasoned oak, possibly centuries old. The Canadian and his silent escort emerged from the tunnel. A cobblestone square, roughly three acres, extended before the pair.

A five-ton truck, three jeeps and a small bus were parked in the square. The unit motor pool. Several men dressed in fatigue uniform stood outside. Though most of them wore the black beret and white skull emblem of the private terrorist army, an assortment of other headgear once again indicated that racially and nationally Skull had assembled a varied group. Manning was actually reluctantly impressed by Skull's ability to hold together such diverse peoples and apparently succeed in getting them to work in relative harmony. It was a stunning tribute to the power of greed and corruption. Clearly both traits were universal in man.

Yet, Manning knew, the same was true of determination, dedication and courage. Phoenix Force was also an international mix of professional warriors and he was certain his partners were still trying to find Skull's lair. He was less optimistic that they could find it in time. In fact, Manning himself was not sure where the hell the base was, and he stood right in the middle of it.

Stone walls, roughly fifteen feet high, surrounded the compound. These seemed old, perhaps ancient. The structure might have been a centuries-old fortress, now little more than an obscure ruin. The night sky was clear and did not have the blurred image of firmament above city lights and air pollution. The damp woodsy smell of a forest greeted his nostrils and the dark shapes of tall trees were visible beyond the walls.

A woodland area, Manning thought. Probably still in northern France. He tried to picture the map of France in his mind. The image was not as geographically detailed as he had hoped. Manning recalled that France was the largest country of Western Europe and more than a fourth was still forest and grasslands. That was a lot of territory to search, and there was no reason to believe anyone had any idea where Skull might be holed up.

"That way," Hee ordered, gesturing with the stubby barrel of an Uzi subgun to point to the east.

Manning had not seen much of the terrorist base until now, and he tried to observe as much as possible while he walked to the east wing. The buildings were block-shaped with stone frames and wooden shutters on the windows. A generator growled noisily behind a pair of wide wooden doors in a structure that had once been a stable. Black rubber cords extended from beneath the doors and stretched throughout the fortress like the tentacles of a giant octopus. Manning wondered if this was the only power source in the compound.

A radio antenna towered above a rooftop near the generator room. The shutters to a window stood open and Manning saw a bored figure seated at a transceiver with a headset over his ears.

Major Hee took Manning to a building at the east wall. A terrorist, armed with an FAL rifle, stood guard at the entrance. The man snapped to attention as Hee approached. Manning quickly glanced about, hoping to see some last bits of information about the base before Hee took him inside. The Canadian barely managed a glimpse before the major poked him in the ribs with the Uzi.

"Inside," the Korean ordered.

Manning obeyed. The interior was similar to the corridors at Skull's office. Hee marched the prisoner through a tunnel of stone walls. They passed three iron doors with barred portholes. A vague outline of a head moved behind the bars of one of these. Hee stopped Manning and forced him to face a wall. The Korean kept the Uzi pointed at Manning, while he pulled open another iron door.

"No tricks," Hee warned as he jammed the muzzle of the Uzi against Manning's tailbone. "I am not a wise choice to try any tricks with. Start to move and I'll shoot off the end of your spine."

Manning did not attempt to resist as Hee unlocked the handcuffs. The Korean would be a formidable opponent unarmed. Trying to take Hee when the major had a gun at his spine would be his last attempt at anything. Hee stepped back and ordered Manning to get into the cell. The Canadian entered, and the door was slammed shut. Manning heard Hee slide the bolt into place and turn a key in the lock.

The cell could have been worse. Naturally, the walls, ceiling and floor were made of stone. A bunk bed was placed near one wall with a mattress, blanket and pillow. There was also a small sink and a flush toilet. The captors had even supplied him a bar of soap, towel and toilet paper.

"Food will be brought to your cell in half an hour," Hee stated through the barred porthole in the door. "If you wish, you may have a book to read. We have publications in English, French, German, Spanish and Italian. You may also have a cassette player with some music tapes."

"How civilized," Manning told the Korean. "The food sounds good. I'll pass on the rest for now."

"Very well," Hee answered. "I believe the meal will be steak, vegetables, fruit and bread. If you are a vegetarian or have some religious opposition to red meat, something can be substituted for the steak."

"Steak is better than I expected," Manning admitted. "No bread and water diets. That's a relief."

"To be a prisoner is very bad," Hee said, revealing more compassion than Manning expected. "At least your food will be pleasant."

"Why the hell are you part of this, Hee?" Manning asked. "I can almost understand Skull. He seems to have a great need—no, a demand—for power. Yasnev is a mental case, and most of the others are probably disillusioned fanatics with lots of warped notions in their twisted little brains. You don't seem to fit in with them."

"I am an officer in Colonel Skull's army," the Korean stated. "How I became part of this does not matter. The reality is you and I came to be on opposite sides. That is all either of us need to know."

"And you don't care that this whole business is insane and Skull will never get away with it?" Manning asked.

"That is your opinion," Hee replied. "Many have believed Colonel Skull's plans to be mad, absurd and impossible to accomplish. Perhaps that is why great men succeed. They do not fear the impossible. Anyway, I have made my commitment and I must see it through. Do you want wine with your meal?"

"Coffee would be fine," the Canadian said, aware that Major Hee had changed the subject because the conversation was over.

"I'll tell the cooks," Hee promised before he moved away from the door.

Manning listened to Hee's footsteps in the corridor. The Phoenix commando examined the door. The hinges were on the opposite side of the door. He did not see any way to take the door off its hinges. Manning was not an expert at picking locks and he did not see anything he could use for a picklock. Even if he could manage to unlock the door, the bolt on the other side would prevent his escape.

"The food isn't bad," a familiar voice called out from the hall outside. "This book they loaned me is a bit of a disappointment. More sex and profanity than plot."

"Mr. President?" Manning replied, speaking through the bars in the door.

"Yes," the voice confirmed. "I'm in the cell next to yours. Glad to see you're still alive. I was afraid they might kill you. Are you all right?"

"So far," Manning answered. "Interrogation hasn't been too nasty, and they didn't learn anything of much value so far. Next session will probably be worse."

"Klaus Weiss is in another cell," the President explained. "I think he's asleep right now. The terrorists haven't treated us too badly, all things considered. They even have a supply of my medication. Still, I can't say I care much for this hotel. Maybe it would be better if I had an idea when we'd be checking out. Or if I knew if we'd still be alive when we leave."

"I've been only half-conscious most of the time," Manning confessed. "How long have we been here?"

"Two days," the President answered. "Well, you're the expert at this sort of thing. Any ideas about how we might get out of here?"

"I can't say much right now, sir," Manning told him. "Even if I had any ideas I can't discuss them because there may be microphones planted around here somewhere."

"There doesn't seem to be much we can do now," the President remarked grimly.

"Not yet," Manning was forced to agree. And in the silence that followed, both men faced the grim prospect that perhaps there wasn't much that anybody could do.

18

David McCarter had never been to Brussels before. Indeed, this was his first visit to Belgium. Yet the British ace decided that Brussels was a city he would like to spend more time in under more relaxed circumstances. The standard array of skyscrapers and modern monsters of steel and glass had sprouted from the cobblestone streets of Brussels. The twentieth century was getting ready to slide into the twenty-first and no major city could avoid the forest of monuments to the era that belonged to the future, as well as the present. However, McCarter appreciated modern architecture as well as the beautiful thirteenth-century Cathedral of St. Michael and the three-hundred-year-old Palace Royale, which also graced the streets of Belgium's capital.

The modern structures might lack the charm and personal details of the beloved buildings of the past, but McCarter liked the sleek, sturdy, practical traits of the new buildings. Such structures were like modern firearms, efficient and beautiful in their simplicity and lack of needless frills. The Briton appreciated cold steel and high-tech plastic that flawlessly fired factory ammunition more than he did antique weapons with iron barrels and hand-carved stocks that required muzzle-loading and flints to fire. McCarter was a pilot and he loved the old Spitfires on display in museums, but he would rather fly a modern Cessna or Bell aircraft. Modern architecture did not depress David McCarter in the least. He was not one to muse about the past ages when people supposedly lived in a more relaxed and less harrowing world. McCarter doubted there had

ever been a better time to live than the present, and the world
he had been born into suited him just fine.

Actually, the excitement and activity of modern Brussels
appealed to the Briton more than any notions about visiting the
Royal Palace or the Maison du Roi with all the historical costumes and celebrations associated with those sights. Shops and
boutiques were everywhere. Restaurants offered an assortment of Flemish and French gourmet delights. Nightlife in
Brussels rivaled anything offered by any city in the world. One
club along the rue Capitain Crespel was called Le Crazy. Any
place with a name like that was bound to intrigue McCarter.

"Leburton runs his illegal trade from a tavern called
Misschien/Peut-être," Edmond Quvey stated as he drove the
Volkswagen minibus along boulevard de Waterloo. "By the
way, the Palace of Justice is to our left. You may wish to see it
if you have the time later."

"I'm afraid we won't have time for sight-seeing, Inspector," Colonel Mauser answered. The Luxembourgian intelligence officer sat in the back seat, dressed in a raincoat and hat.
An overnight bag nestled between his feet. The pistol grip and
metal stock of a Sola submachine gun jutted from the bag.

Quvey nodded, a bit embarrassed. A member of the Belgian
branch of Interpol, Inspector Quvey was more accustomed to
hunting down smugglers and drug dealers than international
terrorists with VIP hostages and nuclear weapons. He would
have found his visitors' story hard to believe if a number of
Belgian soldiers had not been killed when they tried to inter-
cept the terrorist helicopter that had landed in Belgium less than
forty-eight hours before.

The Interpol officer had met with Colonel Mauser and David McCarter the morning after the incident. Mauser's authority and the Briton's Oval Office clearance had made quite
an impression on Quvey. He had also been surprised by Mc-
Carter's methods. The Briton explained that many of the terrorists had been armed with Belgian weapons. He suggested
that one of the big black-market arms dealers might be connected with Skull's operation. They had been trying to check
out local gunrunners, but so far the search had been in vain.

"You say this Leburton character is something of a veteran villain?" McCarter commented, tugging on the brim of a cloth cap. "Why haven't you blokes nailed him before?"

"Interpol and the Brussels police have come close from time to time," Quvey explained, glancing down at the briefcase at McCarter's feet. He knew the Briton had his KG-99 subgun and extra magazines stored in the case. "But Leburton is clever. He never handles the guns directly and always uses a go-between. A middleman. He also has been able to get witnesses to testify for him with ironclad alibis when deals were allegedly made with criminals and fanatic groups. The French Red Brigade is believed to be among his regular customers."

"Sounds like he might be the fellow we're looking for," the British ace remarked.

"We can't be certain your theory is correct," Mauser reminded McCarter. "The terrorists at Strassmacher Castle were armed with a number of Communist bloc weapons. The helicopters they used were made in West Germany. There's no proof Belgian gunrunners are involved."

"I'd say there's good reason to believe Skull would have connections with illegal arms dealers, forgers and assorted criminal types all over the bleeding world," McCarter insisted. "It also stands to reason that he arranged the purchase of a large number of FAL assault rifles fairly recently in order to have some of his people disguise themselves as Luxembourgian troops. The Luxembourgian military pretty much use the FAL as a standard weapon. Right?"

"The assault rifles made by our Fabrique Nationale d'Armes de Guerre are among the finest firearms in the world," Quvey stated. "The Fusil Automatique Légèr is sold worldwide. It is used by the military of numerous countries. Skull's people could have gotten the firearms from black marketeers in a dozen different countries."

"Possibly," McCarter agreed, "but this would be the most likely place to get them. Black marketeers generally get their weapons by stealing them from assembly lines—usually in parts that are smuggled out of factories—or by buying them from crooked soldiers or police who lift the weapons from military arms rooms. Besides, the Luxembourg tracking stations con-

firmed that the three Krumbacher LMY-17 choppers crossed
the border *from* Belgium before they headed for Strassmacher
Castle. That suggests someone pretty well connected with arms
deals and major smuggling operations had to be involved to get
that much equipment into your country undetected. The helicopters were probably taken apart after they were hijacked in
Germany and reassembled after they were smuggled into Belgium, but that's still a hell of a smuggling trick.''

"Leburton could do it," Quvey declared. "I don't know of
any other arms dealer who could have. Still, I don't see how
talking to him will help."

"There's the tavern," Mauser announced, pointing at an
orange neon sign above a shabby-looking building.

The legend Misschien/Peut-être flashed garishly over the
entrance. The tavern appeared to be a dump, a fact that was
well advertised by a thick layer of grime on the tinted windows. It was not the sort of place that encouraged most people
to seek it out. Quvey gave the place a probing look and parked
the VW in front of the tavern.

"Okay," McCarter began as he unzipped his black nylon
windbreaker so he could reach the Browning Hi-Power pistol
in a hurry. "Colonel, you stay here with the vehicle. The inspector and I will go in and see if we can find this damn gunrunner."

"Be careful in there," Mauser urged. "If Leburton and his
associates are connected with Skull's people, you two might be
walking into the proverbial lion's den.''

"Leburton is no fool," Quvey assured the Luxembourgian.
"He won't resort to violence in his own place. In fact, I doubt
that he'd do anything physical himself under any circumstances. He's an organizer, not a fighter."

"I wouldn't count on him being a pacifist," the Briton
warned as he gathered up his briefcase. "Let's go see what this
chap's really like.''

McCarter and Quvey left the minibus and walked to the
Misschien/Peut-être. The Briton considered the name of the
tavern to be the most idiotic he had ever encountered. Calling
a bar Perhaps did not sound any less stupid when the name was
spelled out on a sign in Flemish, Dutch and French.

The pair pushed through the door and entered the tavern. The interior was pretty much what McCarter expected. The bar was simple with a few stools and a rather bored-looking bartender. Only four customers sat at the bar and three others were clustered around a table. All had beer before them, which was the national favorite beverage of Belgium. The barroom smelled of cigarette smoke and dust. The bartender looked at the new arrivals as if annoyed that another pair of customers had come to bother him.

McCarter didn't understand a word of the Flemish Dutch spoken at first by Quvey and the bartender. After they had ascertained that the man spoke French, the Briton slapped his briefcase on the counter and stared at him unflinchingly.

"We've come to see Leburton," he announced in French. "Is he here?"

"I don't recognize you two," the barman said suspiciously. "You tell me who you are first."

McCarter unsnapped his case and opened it. Quvey sucked air through clenched teeth, afraid the British commando might remove the KG-99 and thrust it into the bartender's face. However, McCarter removed a different object from his case. He tossed the black beret on the counter, the white skull emblem facing up. The bartender's eyes widened.

"You show him this and tell him the colonel sent us," McCarter instructed. "And tell him if we have to waste time hunting for him we're going to be in a very bad mood when we finally catch up with him."

"I'll check in the other room," the bartender assured him, gathering up the beret. "Would you like something to drink?"

"Just get Leburton," McCarter insisted.

The bartender hurried through a doorway behind the bar. He was gone for barely five seconds. A short, portly figure with a round soft face and wavy black hair was with the bartender when he returned. The fat man looked at McCarter and Quvey with watery dark eyes. He turned to the other men in the tavern and informed them that they'd have to finish their drinks and leave. He soothed them by making a wry face and saying that the government wanted to look at his impeccable records.

Their resentment faded at that, and they started to file out with knowing grins.

The portly man turned to his visitors. "Come with me," he instructed, gesturing for McCarter and Quvey to follow him into the back room.

They entered the small, drab office, which had a wooden desk, some metal filing cabinets and two folding chairs. The chubby Belgian closed the door and turned to face his guests. "I'm Leburton," he confirmed. "What can I do for you?"

"Colonel Skull is interested in a new deal," McCarter replied. "A deal that will pay three million Belgian francs."

"That sounds very attractive," Leburton admitted, "but I'm afraid you'll have to tell this colonel that he isn't following the rules previously agreed upon concerning how I do business."

"Colonel Skull is in an awkward position right now," Quvey explained. "This is an emergency. We apologize for any breach of standard security...."

"Perhaps we can get around that problem," Leburton declared with a thin smile. He tilted his head toward the door and called out, "Raoul!"

The bartender entered. A .380-caliber Beretta pistol was clenched in the man's fist. Raoul pointed the gun at the ceiling, but his bent elbow was pointed at McCarter and Quvey.

Leburton's smile expanded. "I don't know what's going on here," the gunrunner stated. "However, there's a simple way to find out. If you fellows are police detectives, identify yourselves as such and you can leave. I won't even press charges against you for trying to entrap me. If you are associated with someone I know, then you'd better give me the name of someone who can explain this. Someone I know."

Quvey glanced at McCarter. His expression revealed his thoughts. *Now, what the hell do we do, smart ass?* McCarter raised his arms slightly and slowly approached, the briefcase still in one hand. Raoul slowly lowered the pistol to point it at the Briton's face.

"Easy," McCarter urged. "If you'll take a look inside this valise, it ought to answer all your questions. Fair enough?"

"Take the case, Raoul," Leburton said, arms folded on his flabby chest. "Let's see what they've got."

Raoul kept the Beretta pointed at McCarter and reached for the briefcase with his other hand. The British ace extended his arm and moved the valise toward the bartender's groping fingers. Raoul touched the case, and McCarter let go of it. The valise fell to the floor before the bartender could grab it. He glanced down at it. His reaction was natural, and he only looked down for an instant. Yet he was distracted long enough for David McCarter to grab the Beretta pistol with his left hand. Raoul pulled the trigger, but the weapon did not fire. The flap of skin between McCarter's thumb and forefinger was jammed between the hammer and the firing pin.

The Briton's right fist hit Raoul under the heart. The bartender grunted from the punch. McCarter rammed his head forward and the hard frontal bone struck his opponent between the eyes. Raoul tottered slightly from the blow and McCarter twisted the Beretta pistol hard. Bone cracked and Raoul cried out in pain. His index finger had been trapped in the trigger guard and broken by McCarter's sudden wrench.

"Just stay where you are," Quvey told Leburton. The Interpol agent had drawn a 9 mm FN Browning from his jacket and pointed the pistol at the gunrunner.

Leburton stiffened with fear and raised his hands to shoulder level. McCarter delivered another head butt to Raoul's face and yanked the Beretta from his dazed opponent's grasp. The Briton's right hand grabbed the bartender's shirtfront. He pulled Raoul forward to meet yet another head butt to his battered cranium.

Raoul began to sag. McCarter held on to the man's shirt and turned slightly to jam his hip into Raoul's abdomen. The Briton pulled sharply and sent Raoul hurtling over his hip. The bartender crashed to the floor hard and uttered a sound that was half moan and half sigh. His eyes closed and his body sprawled limp and unconscious.

"Son of a bitch has a head almost as hard as mine," McCarter muttered, rubbing his forehead with one hand. He held the .380 pistol in the other.

"Are you all right?" Quvey asked with genuine concern in his voice. The Interpol officer was afraid McCarter might have suffered a brain concussion, and he did not relish being forced to handle the situation on his own.

"Oh, hell yes," the Briton replied gruffly as he turned his attention toward Leburton. "I'm tired of playing games with you. Time to get some answers one way or the other."

"You two are police?" Leburton demanded. "Interpol? I'm not saying anything until I consult my lawyer."

"You aren't going to need a lawyer," McCarter declared as he pointed the Beretta at the gunrunner's face. "Just an undertaker. I'm convinced you've been doing business with Colonel Skull. That means you're either going to talk or I'll take you apart until you do."

"No!" Leburton exclaimed. "You can't do this! You don't have any proof—"

McCarter suddenly rammed the pistol into Leburton's soft belly. The gunrunner doubled up with a startled gasp. His mouth hung open and his eyes bulged. Quvey was almost as alarmed by the Briton's tactics as Leburton was. Actually, the blow McCarter delivered served to startle the gunrunner more than hurt him. McCarter just wanted to convince Leburton he was serious.

"Listen, you bastard!" McCarter hissed as he grabbed Leburton's hair and yanked back his head to jam the muzzle of the Beretta under his jaw. "We're not the police. We're not interested in arresting you or upholding the law or worrying about your goddamn rights. I don't give a damn whether this is legal or even moral. You're connected with international terrorists, and that's all the reason I need to blow your head off and never lose a second of sleep over it."

"You're bluffing," Leburton said, but his tone suggested he was less than certain of his claim.

"Really?" McCarter asked with a sly smile. "I guess we'll just have to do this the hard way."

His left fist suddenly swung into the side of Leburton's jaw. The gunrunner fell against the wall. He turned, touching his bruised face, which wore a shocked expression. Blood trickled from the corner of his mouth.

"Hard for *you*, I mean," McCarter added as he lashed a kick to Leburton's fat belly.

The gunrunner groaned, doubled up and fell to his knees. Quvey looked at McCarter as if he thought the Briton had gone crazy. The Phoenix pro ignored his companion's expression. He pressed the Beretta's magazine catch and allowed the mag to drop from the butt well, then pumped the slide to eject the .380 cartridge from the chamber.

"Here," he announced and tossed the pistol to Leburton.

Leburton caught the empty weapon. He looked up at McCarter with a puzzled expression. The Briton smiled as he drew the Browning Hi-Power from shoulder leather and took a nine-inch silencer from his jacket pocket.

"Good boy," McCarter declared, inserting the silencer into the muzzle of his Browning autoloader and screwing it into place on the threaded muzzle. "Now your fingerprints are on that gun. Your buddy Raoul probably left some prints on the cartridges when he loaded the magazine. So, if I kill you we can claim it was self-defense."

"What about your prints?" Quvey asked automatically, biting his tongue the second the words escaped.

"Hell," McCarter said with a shrug. "I picked up the gun without thinking about the prints, because I was so shocked and upset about having to kill Leburton in self-defense. You ought to see my grief-stricken, guilty, oh-my-God-I-had-to-shoot-him routine."

"You're insane," Leburton whispered as he threw the Beretta on the floor.

"And don't you forget it," McCarter answered. He pointed the Browning at the gunrunner. "Now, we know some of Colonel Skull's terrorists are hiding out in Belgium. Maybe Skull himself. So, where are they?"

McCarter squeezed the trigger. The silenced pistol coughed harshly and a 9 mm slug burst into the plaster of the wall less than three inches from Leburton's head. The gunrunner recoiled from the bullet hole with a frightened yelp. He fell back on his rump and stared up at McCarter with sheer terror on his face.

Quvey rasped an oath, astonished by McCarter's tactics. He'd had no idea the Briton would actually open fire on a helpless unarmed man.

"That's just to get your attention, Leburton," McCarter told the arms dealer. "It also shows you I'm pretty accurate with this thing even with a silencer. I can keep it up all night without making enough noise to attract the police. Of course, you'll start screaming pretty loud after I pump a bullet through your kneecap or elbow. You may even pass out after a couple rounds, but we've got all night. You'd be surprised how many times a bloke can be injured and revived before he finally goes into shock."

"You wouldn't . . ." Leburton said, his lower lip trembling with fear.

"Why not?" the Briton asked with a cruel smile. "I think I might start with your feet. Lots of nerves and such in the feet. Did you know more than half the 206 bones of the human body are located in the hands and feet? Put a bullet through a foot and it's bound to splinter some bones. Have to put a tourniquet around your ankle so you don't bleed too much. After a while you'll have four tourniquets tied around damaged limbs."

"I won't be part of this!" Quvey exclaimed. "You said nothing about torture!"

"Then take the bartender into the other room and keep out of my way!" McCarter replied sharply. "If you don't have the stomach for this, I don't want you here anyway. After I put a couple of bullets in the bastard he'll be easy enough to handle on my own. Of course, if I have to tear him up too much, we'll have to take the corpse somewhere and destroy it. Maybe stuff it in an industrial furnace or bury it under the cement of a building foundation. Can't very well explain self-defense if I have to shoot him through all four limbs and yank out half his teeth with a pair of pliers."

"You can't let him do this!" Leburton exclaimed, pleading with Quvey. "For God's sake! This is barbaric!"

"I saw the barbarians machine-gun good men at Strassmacher Castle," McCarter declared. "They opened fire from a helicopter you provided to Skull's army. Those same barbarians are holding two world leaders hostage and threatening to detonate a nuclear weapon somewhere in Western Europe. Those barbarians also have a friend of mine held captive and there's a fifty-fifty chance they've already killed him. I figure you're partly to blame for that. So I don't much care if I have to chop you to pieces. Why the hell should I mind? You sure as hell deserve it.''

"All right!" Leburton said quickly. "I'll tell you all I know! Skull isn't in Belgium. That's what I was told anyway. Koerner is in charge of the base here. Major Koerner. One of Skull's top men.''

"Where are they?" McCarter demanded.

"The base is in Luxembourg—" the gunrunner began.

"You lying sack of shit!" the Phoenix commando hissed. "We know they didn't slip back across the border from Belgium. The Luxembourgians have been watching the borders like hungry hawks in case the terrorists try to sneak in to throw us off the track. Doubling around and going to a place you've already been on the assumption nobody will look for you there is an old trick, but we've already considered it and have observation posts ready to spot the bastards if they try a stunt like that.''

"Mr. Masters!" Quvey said urgently, addressing the Briton by his current cover name. "Leburton might be referring to the province of Luxembourg. It's a province of Belgium that borders on the Grand Duchy of Luxembourg. Actually our province of Luxembourg is larger than Luxembourg the country.''

The gunrunner confirmed this with an anxious nod. "The province! I'm not exactly certain where the terrorists are based, but it is east of Rendeux. Koerner had one of his people meet him at Rendeux earlier this evening, in fact. He's decided to move his troops to another site. Apparently they're low on ammunition and explosives and want to purchase more. I don't know how long they'll be in the area or where they intend to move.''

"All right," McCarter said, lowering his Browning Hi-Power. "You and Raoul are coming with us. If you're telling the truth, we'll see to it your cooperation is taken into consideration if Interpol learns about your involvement and arrests you.''

Quvey smiled. Of course, Interpol already knew about Leburton. The inspector could have the gunrunner arrested any time in the future without letting his superiors know what sort of tactics McCarter had used to get his information.

"If you're smart," the Interpol officer began, "you'll turn yourself in to Interpol and make a voluntary confession. If you turn state's witness, things will go much easier for you."

"But if he isn't telling us the truth I can still pick up this interrogation where we left off," McCarter added. "On your feet, Leburton. Let's go."

19

Notre Dame is one of the most famous cathedrals in the world. To many it is best known because of Victor Hugo's classic novel about the hunchbacked bell ringer, but Notre Dame de Paris is also an architectural marvel and a monument to French history. The construction of the cathedral began in 1163, when Paris was still a Gallo-Roman village known as Lutetia. Nearly three hundred years passed before Notre Dame was completed.

At night the cathedral is bathed in floodlights to highlight the magnificent structure. From a distance, the visitor gets a ghostly impression, as if it were an ancient building one might glimpse in a dream. The famous tower, surrounded by several great steeples, is visible miles away. Notre Dame is enormous, built to accommodate congregations as large as nine thousand. It is certainly one of the most remarkable monuments to the faith that characterized the Dark Ages.

But Nikolay Vashnov barely glanced at the cathedral. An absolute atheist, and a man without an eye for beauty, Vashnov considered Notre Dame de Paris to be a prime example of how the proletarian masses had been neglected and exploited by the bourgeois forces of the Catholic church and French monarchs of the past. The fact that the present government had not converted the cathedral into a museum proved to Vashnov that the French were still bootlicking capitalist scum despite claims of socialist reforms. Vashnov was more interested in locating the yellow Toyota, the one Calvin James and Rafael Encizo had driven off in after they left the Information Office.

256   FIRE STORM

Aleksandr Borgneff and Mikhail Pushkin were pretty disgusted with their passenger. Vashnov was an annoying back seat
driver and constantly barked instructions at Borgneff. The
senior KGB officer kept ordering Borgneff to steer the Citroën
into different lanes and frequently complained that they were
either too far away to tail the Toyota or getting close and in
danger of tipping off the Americans.

The three Soviet agents had followed the car from the
Champs-Elysées district to the Ile de la Cité. The Americans'
car had driven onto Pont St. Louis and headed for the square
near Notre Dame. The Citroën pursued at a distance and arrived at a parking area near the cathedral.

"There!" Vashnov exclaimed, pointing at the yellow Toyota
parked among a number of other vehicles. "There! That is their
car! Those two Americans must be nearby."

Pushkin mumbled something in agreement, then shrugged.
"But why did they come here? This is a place for religious
people and tourists, not enemy agents."

"Maybe they want to pray for guidance for whatever mission they're on," Borgneff snorted as he steered into the lot and
maneuvered into a parking space.

"You idiots," Vashnov hissed. "They are obviously here for
a meeting with some of their coconspirators. Perhaps the leaders of the terrorists who kidnapped our secretary-general.
Borgneff, stay with the car. Pushkin, come with me. We will
find those Yankee bastards."

"How exciting," Pushkin muttered as he opened the glove
compartment and removed a French MAB pistol. "We may get
to see a pair of Americans taking communion."

"Just shut your mouth and get out of the car," Vashnov insisted. He draped a raincoat over his arm to conceal the Makarov pistol in his fist. "Don't forget, these men are dangerous."

Vashnov and Pushkin emerged from the Citroën. From behind the wheel, Borgneff watched the pair walk into the maze
of parked vehicles. The lone KGB agent sighed as his comrades crept toward the parked Toyota. Vashnov gestured toward one of the windows and peered inside, while Pushkin
placed a hand on the hood to see if the engine was still warm.

Of course it is, you fool, Borgneff thought sourly. The damn car arrived here about two minutes before we did.

The pair continued to head toward the cathedral. Borgneff shook his head and took a pack of cigarettes from his shirt pocket. After rolling down the window to avoid choking on smoke, he fired up a short black cigarette. He wondered if Vashnov was telling the truth. He knew there had been some sort of media blackout concerning the summit conference in Luxembourg. Apparently, both the Soviets and the Americans had enforced the prohibition on news coverage. Neither the premier nor the President had been available for questions, and nobody would comment about their whereabouts. Something was going on, but Borgneff did not know...

A sudden movement at the open window startled him. He turned his head and stared into the black hole of the muzzle of a silencer. It was attached to a Heckler & Koch P-9S pistol in the fist of Rafael Encizo. The Cuban stood at the side of the car and peered inside. Borgneff started to raise his hands.

"You understand English?" Encizo asked in a whispered voice.

"A... little," Borgneff answered nervously.

"You seem to understand *gun* all right," the Cuban warrior remarked. He kept the pistol trained on the KGB agent and pushed his empty hand into the air, palm out. "Put your hands against the inside of the windshield. Palms pressed against the glass. Better figure it out quick. Just do what common sense tells you."

The Russian was a bit confused. He placed both hands on the steering wheel. Encizo barked "No!" Borgneff tried again and jammed his palms against the glass as instructed. Encizo smiled and nodded. The KGB agent seemed relieved.

"We seem to be communicating," Encizo commented as he opened the car door and stepped back. He gestured with the H&K pistol. "Now, out of the car. Out!"

Borgneff obeyed, keeping his hands in clear view. Encizo pointed at the roof of the Citroën. The Russian placed his hands on it and assumed the spread-eagle position. Encizo grabbed a wrist with one hand and poked the H&K at the back of Borgneff's skull. He pulled the Russian's arm back and snapped on a pair of handcuffs. Borgneff did not resist as the Cuban pulled the other arm back and cuffed his wrists together.

"Good," Encizo told him. "You've been smart so far. Now let's see if you're packing any weapons or if you've got any ID."

He frisked the Russian and found a compact .25 auto in a jacket pocket. Encizo also discovered Borgneff's passport, visa and official papers. The Cuban was not fluent in Russian, but he could read enough of the Cyrillic letters to figure out what he had found.

"Cristo," he muttered. "You're with the Soviet embassy. I thought one of those clowns looked familiar, but I didn't get a good enough look to identify him. Vashnov got you to do this?"

"I do not understand," Borgneff said with a slight shrug.

"You will," the Cuban informed him resignedly.

VASHNOV DID NOT NOTICE Calvin James as the black commando crept up behind him. James ducked low behind a BMW, his Beretta 92 pistol in his fist. The Phoenix pro nearly groaned out loud when he recognized the KGB agent. He and Encizo had spotted the tail after they left Sûreté headquarters. They had allowed the Citroën to follow them until they decided on an advantageous spot to take out the guys shadowing them. The Phoenix pair had hoped they were some of Colonel Skull's people.

Hell, James thought with disgust. It was just Vashnov dogging their trail with his stubborn paranoid notions that the American CIA or another similar outfit had been behind the hit at Strassmacher Castle. Phoenix Force needed a KGB pain in the ass as much as a cancer patient needs a dose of the clap.

James watched Vashnov advance between a blue Le Car and an Italian sport vehicle with a canvas top. The KGB guy had not looked over his shoulder. James moved from the BMW and padded silently to the other two vehicles. He pointed the silencer-equipped Beretta at the Russian's back and stepped forward.

"Freeze, Vashnov!" he ordered in a harsh whisper. "Make a sudden move and I'll put a 9 mm navel between your shoulder blades. The weather has cleared up. Drop the raincoat and whatever you've got under it."

"That you, boy?" the Russian asked as he slowly raised his arms. The raincoat was still draped over one hand.

"I told you to drop it!" James hissed. "I'm not real eager to kill you, but it won't bother me much if I have to. Drop it or die, Vashnov."

The Russian muttered something under his breath and let the raincoat fall to the ground. He dropped the Makarov pistol on the wrinkled garment and slowly turned to face James. Vashnov held his hands at shoulder level, his expression hard, his eyes burning with anger but without a trace of fear. That made Calvin James very uncomfortable. Anybody who was not afraid when he looked into the business end of a gun was either crazy or had a reason to feel confident. In Vashnov's case, James reckoned it could be both.

"I thought those idiots might be following your car too closely," Vashnov commented. "That's how you guessed we were tailing you?"

"Actually, your driver was doing everything by the book," James explained. "A little too much by the book. When we noticed the same car keeping three or four cars behind on the road and yet showing up everywhere we went, we figured it had to be a tail. Didn't know it was KGB. Congratulations, asshole. You've managed to waste our time, as well as your own with this cloak-and-dagger stuff."

"So you say, black boy." Vashnov snickered.

"Jesus," the Phoenix pro said, sighing. "I keep running into bigots lately. Must be some sort of international, contagious insanity, or dim-wittedness going around. If you value whatever you've got left in that skull, then don't try anything. Get over by the car and spread 'em. I'll let you use the BMW."

Vashnov placed his hands on the roof of the car and stood with his feet apart. James kept his Beretta trained on the Russian and quickly glanced about. No tourists or security people were in sight. Good. They did not want any witnesses or pain-in-the-butt innocent bystanders to worry about. Another look confirmed that the other KGB agent wasn't in their immediate vicinity.

"Call your comrade," James ordered. "Tell him to get over here. And speak French, not Russian. I want to understand what you say."

"Perhaps I should say it in Swahili," Vashnov said with a snort.

"Perhaps I should smack you alongside of your head with this gun," James replied gruffly. "I'm not in a good mood so don't—"

"Halte là!" Pushkin snapped as he appeared around the front end of the BMW, pistol clenched in his fists.

"Son of a bitch," James rasped. He kept the Beretta pointed at Vashnov's head.

Pushkin stepped forward and aimed his French MAB autoloader at the black commando. James clenched his teeth and remained in his stance, weapon trained on Vashnov. The senior KGB agent chuckled and started to turn, but his expression turned to one of grim surprise when he discovered the silencer-equipped Beretta was still pointed at him.

"Drop the gun!" Pushkin demanded, still speaking French.

"Drop yours," James replied in the same language. "You shoot me and I'll still put a bullet in Vashnov's head. Maybe I'll live long enough to take you with me, too."

"I doubt that," Pushkin stated, raising his pistol to peer through the sights. The blade of the front sight bisected Calvin James's forehead.

"Kill him!" Vashnov commanded, fist clenched on the roof of the BMW. "Do it now!"

"Awful stupid for us to all die because of a misunderstanding," James declared. "Vashnov is full of shit. The United States isn't responsible for the terrorist attack on Strassmacher Castle. Neither the Americans or you Soviets were behind the attack on the summit conference. We can kill one another, but that won't help your premier or our President. The terrorists will still be running around with a plutonium bomb."

"He's lying!" Vashnov snapped in curt Russian. "Shoot him. That's an order!"

Pushkin heard the higher-ranking officer's command. His eyes remained fixed on James, pistol aimed at the black man's face. Pushkin swallowed so loud the other two men heard the gulp clearly. His KGB training demanded he obey Vashnov's order, yet he hesitated. What if the black man was telling the truth? Pushkin had had nagging doubts about Vashnov's claims from the start. Maybe the Kremlin had not sent Vashnov to Paris. Maybe the CIA was not involved with the kidnapping....

"Don't listen to Vashnov," James urged, guessing what the senior Soviet agent had probably told Pushkin. "He's a paranoid fanatic. Listen, *mon ami*. Let me handcuff Vashnov. Keep your gun on me if you want. After he's cuffed, I'll put down my pistol to show you I'm telling the truth."

Pushkin was confused. He was tempted to follow Vashnov's order to open fire, because he was accustomed to obeying orders without questioning them. Yet the American's suggestion did not seem unreasonable under the circumstances. Pushkin bit his lip, torn between which action to take.

"Damn you, Pushkin!" Vashnov spit out the words.

"Shut up and let him think!" James barked. "After the first shot is fired none of us will have a chance for second thoughts. I'm going to reach for the handcuffs. If nobody starts shooting before I cuff Big Mouth, then I'll make the first gesture of disarmament—"

Vashnov suddenly whirled and swung both fists at Calvin James, taking the Phoenix pro by surprise with the desperate move. James's attention had started to shift toward Pushkin and he had failed to keep a close enough eye on the other, unarmed KGB agent. Vashnov had taken advantage of that and had managed to jump his captor.

A fist chopped down on James's wrist and struck the Beretta pistol from his hand. Vashnov's other fist rocketed into the American's face. The punch knocked James backward into the side of the Italian sports car. He instinctively lashed out a karate kick in retaliation, and his foot smashed into Vashnov's belly. The Russian grunted breathlessly from the blow.

James swung a kick with his other leg, aiming at Vashnov's bowed head. The KGB man jammed a forearm into James's calf to block the kick and thrust a fist in the direction of his crotch. The Phoenix fighter swiftly swatted a palm to his opponent's arm to check the attack and slashed the side of his other hand at the Russian's neck. The karate chop missed its target and struck Vashnov above the left eyebrow.

Vashnov's head recoiled from the blow, left eye closed and mouth twisted in an expression of pain. James quickly hooked his left fist to the side of Vashnov's head. His knuckles stung from contact with the Russian's hard skull. Vashnov stumbled and nearly lost his balance. James raised a hand and prepared to deliver a blow to the KGB agent's neck. Vashnov suddenly swung a hammer fist to the American's lower abdomen.

James felt as if he had caught a cannonball in his gut. He started to double up from the blow. Vashnov quickly shoved a hand on the top of James's skull to push his head down, then slammed a knee into the Phoenix pro's face. James tasted blood and the blow propelled him back against the BMW. Vashnov moved back, yanked open his jacket and reached for the handle of a dagger in a sheath at the small of his back.

"Pushkin!" he exclaimed as he drew the double-edged steel from its scabbard.

Vashnov glanced away from James to see why the hell Pushkin had failed to come to his assistance. He saw the reason and nearly dropped his knife. Rafael Encizo stood behind Pushkin with his H&K pistol pointed at the man's head. Pushkin had dropped his gun and held his empty hands above his head. Encizo looked at Vashnov and nodded polite greetings.

"Drop the knife, Vashnov," the Cuban ordered. "Stalemate's over. You lose."

James had glimpsed the blade in Vashnov's fist and reflexively reached his left hand inside his jacket to grab the Jet-Aer G-96 fighting dagger clipped to the Jackass Leather rig under his right arm. He drew the knife as Vashnov turned to face him. A crooked smile slithered across the Russian's lips.

"Well, black one," Vashnov remarked, "let's finish our personal business. One way or the other, there will be a winner tonight. The loser will be dead."

The Russian did not wait for a reply. He lunged at James's face. The black man weaved his head away from the deadly thrust and slashed the G-96 at Vashnov's knife hand. However, the Russian's lunge had only been a feint. His arm had already moved clear of James's knife swing. The Soviet's dagger struck out at the Phoenix pro's left wrist in an attempt to disarm James and cripple him in the process.

An experienced knife fighter who had first learned to handle a blade as a kid in Chicago's South side, James was expecting such tactics in a duel of cold steel. He jumped back from Vashnov's dagger and quickly switched the Jet-Aer knife from his left hand to his right. Vashnov saw the exchange and swung his blade at James's right hand, hoping to take out his opponent's weapon before the black warrior could manage a countermove. James recoiled from his enemy's blade, but the knife snagged his shirtfront before he could move clear. Sharp steel slit the fabric and James groaned in pain as the blade cut flesh at his right rib cage.

Encizo cursed under his breath and quickly chopped the butt of his pistol into the deltoid muscle of Pushkin's shoulder. The Russian cried out in surprise and pain. Encizo adroitly kicked the agent's feet out from under him, and the man fell to the pavement. Encizo would apologize later for this unprovoked and seemingly unnecessary roughness. The Cuban simply had to get Pushkin out of the way in a hurry. He could not risk trying to aim and fire at Vashnov while Pushkin was still in a position to grab his gun arm and attempt to take the H&K away from him.

"Damn!" Encizo growled. James and Vashnov were too close together for him to try to pick off the Russian knife artist. The silencer reduced accuracy, and Encizo could not risk hitting his partner by mistake.

James swung a left hook to his opponent's jaw. Vashnov staggered away from the black man. He slashed his blade in a wild figure-eight pattern to keep James at bay. The American stayed clear of the whirling steel and waited for the enemy to make the next move. Blood stained his shirt and the cut on his chest burned, but James had been cut before. He knew it was a shallow wound. It would not kill him unless he allowed it to distract him while Vashnov was still trying to polish him off.

Vashnov ran his tongue along the ribbon of blood on his split lip. He had bit himself when James punched him. The Russian glared at his opponent, but he controlled his anger, aware that rage makes a man careless. Vashnov waved the knife in a high circle to get James's attention and swung a kick for the knife hand.

James quickly slashed his blade across Vashnov's shin above the foot. The Russian yelped in pain and swung his dagger at James's face. The Phoenix fighter dodged the attack and lunged with his G-96. The steel point pierced the biceps muscle. The KGB agent screamed from the agony of the knife thrust. His arm quivered and the dagger fell from his trembling fingers. The Jet-Aer was still lodged in the Russian's upper arm, the blade buried in muscle and jammed into bone.

Vashnov was not a quitter or a coward. He snarled like a cornered beast and grabbed for the handle of the knife stuck in his arm with his good hand. James whipped a back fist to his opponent's face. Vashnov fell back into the BMW, a crimson flow gushing from the nostrils of his broken nose. Calvin James immediately raised a knee and launched a side kick. The bottom of his foot slammed into Vashnov's chin. The Soviet spy's head snapped back and connected forcefully with the roof of the car. His eyes closed and he uttered a slight moan as he slid to the pavement.

"You okay?" Encizo asked James, although the question might have been directed to Pushkin as he once again covered the KGB agent with the H&K.

"Yeah," James assured him. He knelt beside Vashnov's unconscious form and yanked the knife from his arm. The black commando reached for the first-aid kit attached to his belt and prepared to bandage the wound. "Unless you want to include the fact I'm pretty pissed off."

"I know what you mean," Encizo replied. He turned to Pushkin and added, "Thanks to your comrade over there, we've been fighting each other instead of trying to find Colonel Skull. So neither your people nor ours are any closer to solving this mess, and we don't have a hell of a lot of time before Skull's deadline expires. When that happens, the President and the Soviet premier are dead meat, and God knows how many others will die before Skull figures he'd had enough revenge for not having his plan succeed."

"Hey, man," James remarked as he tied a bandage around Vashnov's wounded arm. "If we can find the son of a bitch we can really disappoint him all to pieces."

20

The trio of Guerreaigle H-1 helicopters cut across the predawn sky above the miles of grassy farmland below. The West European gunships were relatively new additions to the Belgian military. Roughly based on the design of American Bell choppers, each GH-1 was equipped with a brace of 7.62 mm machine guns, a .50-caliber Gatling gun and four rocket launchers. The carriage of each could accommodate sixteen troops.

The gunships traveled in a triangle formation. The craft at point scanned the ground below with heat detectors. The device operated in a manner similar to radar. Waves traveled forward at the speed of sound and bounced off objects in the distance. The sensors picked up the returning waves and fed data into a small computer on board the lead chopper. The computer produced an image of the objects from several miles away. Multicolored shapes appeared on a view screen. The device registered different levels of heat, translated into colors that ranged from pale blue to bright red. The rainbow figures could reveal a camp fire twenty kilometers away. The screen could locate humans or large animal life within ten kilometers in any direction and, based on body heat, even indicate if the living forms were inactive or involved in some level of physical exertion. It could differentiate between a hardworking farmhand and a teenager with overactive hormones.

Yakov Katzenelenbogen and David McCarter were among the passengers on board the lead gunship. The Phoenix Force commander had arrived in Brussels the night before and had met with McCarter, Colonel Mauser and Inspector Quvey when they returned to Interpol headquarters with the gunrunner-turned-informant Leburton. Although Katz had told them the good news about taking out Skull's headquarters in West Germany, he also informed them that Skull had probably sacrificed the base simply as a means of testing his opponents. The news of Karl Hahn's death was a personal blow to McCarter. The BND agent had been a sort of part-time member of Phoenix Force. Hahn had been a warrior brother and he would be sorely missed by his comrades at arms.

The other passengers comprised nine Belgian soldiers, including the pilot and copilot, and two Americans who operated the heat detectors. The latter belonged to the United States National Security Agency. They were experts in the new school of espionage. Spy versus spy was no longer a game played by agents in trench coats with miniature cameras and microfilm. Most modern espionage relies more on electronic surveillance devices, computer taps and other high-tech contraptions that could have been included in Orwell's *1984*.

Katz had been involved in espionage most of his life, but agents like Victor Collins and Timothy Jarred were a new and different breed. They did not even call themselves agents. They considered themselves to be electronic and technical engineers employed by the United States government. They spoke in hi-tech jargon that was often unintelligible to Katzenelenbogen. The Israeli spoke six languages fluently and a smattering of a dozen others, yet the other two's references to "modes" and "inputs" baffled Katz. They generally tended to discuss people as if they considered human beings to be the same as their machines. Katz wondered at times if a new generation of intellectuals was being created—as cut-and-dried as step-by-step computer programs, but unable to appreciate the difference between flesh and blood and plastic and metal alloys? Would they regard the human mind as no different from microchips and wiring?

Collins liked to talk about his machines and rambled on about the technical marvels involved in the construction of the heat scanner and computer detector. He was a thin, balding man who seemed out of place dressed in a borrowed fatigue uniform that was too large for his slender frame. Jarred was a replica of Collins, a few years younger and with more hair, and fewer of his teeth appeared to be capped. Both men were products of an "attitude mode" that emphasized push-button "input." They conversed with each other a great deal, but only spoke with the others when necessary. Katz heard one of them complain that he was disappointed in the last Woody Allen film he had seen, and the other claimed that at least Allen's movies were not as misleading as Wall Street. Katz was not certain if "Wall Street" referred to the stock exchange or the movie by the same name.

"The screen has just registered the presence of several vehicles approximately ten kilometers to the northeast," Collins announced as he looked up from the computer terminal. "The heat levels suggest these are internal combustion vehicles, ranging from three to seven meters in length. High probability these are two automobiles and four trucks."

"Vehicles appear to be headed west, in our direction," Jarred added. He adjusted his horn-rimmed glasses as he consulted a printout sheet from the machine. "Approximate rate of travel, 50 kilometers per hour, or about thirty-five miles, if you haven't gone metric."

"Does that thing tell you how many individuals are in the convoy?" McCarter asked as he glanced over Collins's shoulder. The colors on the screen seemed blurred to the Briton, and he could tell little by looking at the shapes.

"The dark green here," Collins began, pointing at the screen, "probably means body heat of several people inside the larger vehicles. We'll be able to tell more as they get closer."

"What do you think?" McCarter asked Katz, taking a pack of Players from a pocket.

"I don't think you should smoke," Jarred declared, glancing up from the printout sheets. "The surgeon general has strongly denounced smoking and has labeled it as a definite health hazard."

"So is hunting down bloody terrorists," the Briton replied gruffly and stuck a cigarette in his lips. "Besides, I wasn't talking to you, mate."

"Leburton said the terrorists planned to move to another location," Katz mused. "The convoy could be them. That gunrunner told you Skull wasn't among the group here in Belgium?''

"He didn't think so," McCarter replied, taking a lighter from his trouser pocket, "but Leburton's information was sort of secondhand. Mentioned somebody named Koerner was apparently in charge. Major Martin Koerner, although Leburton wasn't sure whether that was the bloke's real name.''

"One of the terrorists at Strassmacher Castle mentioned Koerner before," Katz reminded the Briton. "That CIA traitor, Mamer, also mentioned him. Said he was supposed to be the son of a Nazi war criminal who had been raised at ODESSA strongholds somewhere in the Mato Grosso.''

"You really shouldn't smoke around this equipment," Jarred insisted, looking at McCarter as if the Briton intended to sabotage his precious machine. "Computers are very sensitive to smoke.''

"Oh, for Crissake," McCarter muttered, leaving his cigarette unlit.

"Never mind," Katz said. "Let's radio Mauser and your Interpol friend, Quvey, and tell them about the convoy. We won't jump to any conclusions. We don't want to attack an innocent group of trucks carrying live cattle to an auction or a bunch of kids on a hayride.''

"Do Belgian kids go on hayrides?" Collins asked.

"Shut up and play with your computers," McCarter snapped. "We'd better assume the vehicles below are the enemy. I'm a bit worried about charging down on those blokes when they might have that bomb or the hostages.''

"Koerner might have some of the hostages," Katz answered. "But Skull wouldn't want the bomb out of his sight. From interrogating members of Skull's army, we know a couple things about Skull. One is the fact he's probably a genuine albino. Our friends in Washington even have an idea who he really is. That means he isn't Koerner or one of the other second-in-command types with a clever makeup job. Another thing we know is Colonel Skull is a battlefield commander. He was in one of those helicopters at Strassmacher Castle. The man's no coward. If Leburton is right, Skull isn't in Belgium and neither is the bomb.''

"We'll be putting the hostages at considerable risk," the British ace commented.

"They already are," the Phoenix commander said with a sigh. "You know how these things go, as well as I do. We'll do what we can to minimize the risk to the hostages, but the top priority has got to be stopping the terrorists. If they get away with a stunt as outrageous as this, God knows what they'll try next."

"I know, I know," McCarter said, and for once he really did seem to be in full agreement. "Still, we've never had a situation quite like this one. Two world leaders and one of our teammates are among those hostages."

"That bothers me as much as it does you," Katz assured him. "One thing in our favor is the fact Skull's people aren't fanatics or motivated by any demented hatred against any particular political group. They won't be inclined to kill the hostages as long as they think the prisoners will still help protect them. We've noticed since we first encountered these terrorists on board the *Sea Venus* that Skull's followers aren't suicidal and they aren't too long on loyalty."

"Not surprising, I suppose," McCarter remarked. "After all, they've pretty well turned against their countries, their former political convictions and probably just about everything else. Why would they have any great loyalty toward Skull?"

"Convoy is getting closer," Collins announced, still watching the screen. "The body heat of the passengers now registers orange. High probability human life forms. Still difficult to estimate a precise number."

"You chaps watched a lot of *Star Trek* when you were kids, didn't you?" McCarter inquired, shaking his head.

"Leave them alone and let them do their jobs," Katz told his British partner. "The rest of us had better be ready to do ours."

The Belgian troops were armed and ready for action. Most were members of the *corps de parachutistes*. The paratroopers had received plenty of training with NATO headquarters located in Brussels, as the Belgian military is very serious about training. The paratrooper unit had been trained as antiterrorists, although Belgium had not suffered nearly the degree of terrorist activity as many of the other nations of Western Europe. As well as NATO, the Common Market and the Benelux Union also have headquarters in Brussels, which meant terrorists could target Belgium for increased operations at any time. The paratroopers were kept in peak condition in case this possibility became reality.

The Belgian antiterrorists were well armed with FAL assault rifles, Browning 9 mm side arms and an assortment of grenades and fighting knives. A few carried grenade launchers or rocket launchers. The troops wore woodland-print camouflage uniforms, helmets and parachutes. Katz and McCarter were equipped similarly as a precaution in case the chopper was attacked in midair. Clad in the same type of uniform as their Belgian allies and armed with their standard weaponry, the Phoenix pair positioned themselves near the sliding doors with the paratroopers and waited.

THE CONVOY TRAVELED the seldom used dirt road below. A British Land Rover led the vehicles, followed by four large beer trucks, big five-ton rigs with metal trailers and the name of a popular brew painted across the sides. A Citroën brought up the rear of the convoy. There was nothing sinister in the appearance of the convoy. Beer trucks were hardly unusual in Belgium. No weapons were displayed, the men in the Land Rover were dressed in blue coveralls and caps, and the vehicles moved at a steady even pace, neither racing nor crawling along the country road.

The setting would have been quite peaceful and pleasant under different circumstances. The sun rose gently in the early-morning sky. A slight breeze barely stirred the surrounding oaks and pine, and the grassy meadows stretched into the distance with no sign of motion except for a few quail that scurried along the ground in a follow-the-leader line.

The tranquillity ended abruptly as the three GH-1 choppers appeared above the treetops. The driver of the Land Rover turned to his companion and said something. The other man gestured for the driver to keep going and gathered up a walkie-talkie to report the aircraft. The helicopters changed formation, breaking up the triangle pattern and spreading out to hover in a horizontal line in the air. Giant mechanical birds of prey, the gunships remained suspended above the trees.

A voice from an amplifier called out from one of the craft. It echoed in the morning sky and ordered the vehicles below to come to a halt by authority of the NATO Defense Forces and the government of the kingdom of Belgium.

When there was no response from the convoy, the nearest GH-1 opened fire from a machine gun mount. A short volley of 7.62 mm rounds tore into the road roughly twenty yards ahead of the Land Rover. Far enough to prevent damage from a ricochet, but close enough to get the meaning across. The convoy could either stop or risk being chopped to pieces by the firepower of the gunships.

The Land Rover came to a halt. The truck behind it nearly crashed into the back of the lead vehicle. The other rigs also stopped. The Citroën in the rear pulled alongside the last truck. The car door on the passenger side opened, and a figure clad in blue-and-white pinstripe emerged with a bullhorn in hand.

Two Guerreaigle choppers descended below the treetops, headed for clearings large enough for landing. The third craft continued to hover, maintaining a bird's-eye view of the convoy below. The amplified voice once again bellowed from the floating chopper.

"All persons in the vehicles will now step into the open!" the voice ordered in rapid French. "Throw down your weapons and raise your hands above your heads!"

While the man in the pin-striped suit raised his bullhorn and blasted out a reply that led to a longer exchange laced with indignation and surprise, a door at the rear of the last truck in the convoy opened. Two men slipped outside. One carried a metal tube, nearly five feet long with funnel-shaped flared ends. The other had four rockets, each a foot and a half long, secured to a pack strapped to his back.

The other two helicopters had managed to land in separate clearings as the debate continued. Katz and McCarter were the first men out of their chopper. The Phoenix pair hastily removed their parachute packs as Belgian troops hurried from the open cabin doors.

"The bastards are stalling for time," McCarter growled, working the bolt of his KG-99.

"That's what it sounds like," Katz replied with a solemn nod as he braced the frame of his Uzi across his prosthesis.

"Inspector Quvey is the bloke using the loudspeaker," the Briton commented. "Poor chap probably never guessed he'd wind up in a mission like this. Still, he volunteered. Said he thought Interpol ought to be represented. Since he already had clearance and he'd helped me find Leburton, he seemed a natural choice."

"He's probably doing the job best suited for him," Katz replied. "Interpol personnel aren't really trained for this sort of mission. Quvey should stay clear of any fighting, just as those two NSA computer jockeys should stay back with their machines. They'd just get in our way on a battlefield and be more of a threat to themselves than the enemy."

"We won't be much of a threat to them ourselves if we don't get closer," McCarter said as he glanced at the trees that blocked their view of the road.

"We know where they are," Katz stated, taking a walkie-talkie from his belt.

McCarter and the paratroopers headed into the trees while Katz contacted Colonel Mauser via the transceiver. Mauser was aboard the other GH-1 copter that had landed, but Katz was not certain where the craft had set down or how far away it might be from the convoy.

"Unit Two, this is Unit One," the Israeli announced. "Do you read me, Unit Two?"

"This is Unit Two," Mauser replied. "Read you loud and clear, Unit One."

"We're approximately half a kilometer from the convoy," Katz stated. "Difficult to say for certain. Too many trees."

"Unit Two is a bit closer than that," Mauser replied. "Looks like we'll reach the enemy first."

"Be careful," the Phoenix Force commander urged. "Remember the strategy we planned earlier. Timing is important and—"

The violent whoosh of a large projectile cutting through air suddenly interrupted Katz. He had heard the sound many times before and knew what it was even before the noise of an explosion confirmed his suspicions. A fireball burst across the early-morning sky. Chunks of metal and assorted debris hurtled downward. Burning bits of plastic and rubber fell along with charred remains of human beings.

The third helicopter had exploded in midair. Inspector Quvey and all the others aboard the GH-1 had been blown to pieces. The sound Katz heard an instant before the explosion had been a round from a rocket launcher. The terrorists had decided to take the offensive.

Katz hooked the walkie-talkie on his belt and hurried after the others. McCarter and most of the paratroopers were already through the tree line and headed toward the convoy. Flames crackled overhead. Burning wreckage from the exploding helicopter had set fire to the leaves and branches of some of the trees.

Another type of fire was also in progress. Terrorists had emerged from the trucks and set up two mounted machine guns. The weapons rattled out rapid-fire bullets at the tree line. They had seen the helicopters descend and had a general idea where the strike force would come from. The two men armed with the Soviet-made RPG rocket launcher and the stash of projectiles for the weapon had reloaded the launcher. Major Koerner himself stepped from the rear of the third truck and opened a button-flap holster on his hip. The holster was unusually large and nearly reached Koerner's knee. The terrorist commander drew the pistol from leather. His side arm was a vintage Luger P.08 with an eight-inch barrel.

"Fire for effect!" he ordered, shouting at the machine gun teams. "Make it difficult for the enemy to advance toward our position! Do not use the rockets unless you have a clear target!"

"They may have rocket launchers, as well, Major," Kevin O'Shea, a former IRA bomb thrower said nervously as he clutched an American-made M-16 rifle in his ham-size fists.

"But they'll be afraid to use the rockets," Koerner replied. "If they were willing to simply blast us to oblivion they could have done that by firing down on us with the gunships. They are afraid of harming the hostages and they can't be sure whether we have the plutonium device. They're not going to fire any missiles at us when there's a possibility it might detonate a nuclear explosion.''

The sudden whoosh and the cometlike trail of a hurtling projectile abruptly proved Koerner had guessed wrong. The rocket sailed from the tree line and crashed into the Land Rover at the front of the convoy. The driver and passenger had abandoned the Rover when the shooting started, but they had chosen to duck behind the vehicle for cover. It turned out to be a fatal decision. The pair were torn apart when the missile exploded. The Land Rover burst into a thousand pieces. Wreckage and burning petrol shot across the road and fell in all directions.

Several terrorists were struck by flying shrapnel, and their screams were heard above the chatter of the machine guns. Burning gasoline claimed other victims. Some terrorists fell back and dropped their weapons to beat at flames that ignited their jackets. One man was drenched in burning fuel. He screamed in agony and ran into the middle of the road, his body ablaze. His hair vanished in a hideous halo of flames and fire danced wickedly across his torso.

"Gott!" Koerner rasped as he held the Luger in both hands and aimed carefully.

Major Koerner was a crack pistol shot. He favored the old Luger because it was a weapon he had grown up with, the personal side arm of his late father. Yet he knew the weaknesses of the Luger. It was a delicate weapon, apt to jam if fired repeatedly for a short period of time. Nonetheless, Koerner appreciated its accuracy. He was accustomed to the sights of the weapon and the pull of the barrel. He also liked the toggle-top action that reduced recoil. The Luger might not be the best choice for rapid fire or sustained shooting, but Koerner seldom missed with the P.08.

Now he triggered a single shot. The 9 mm parabellum got the burning terrorist with a head shot and put him out of his agony.

The Phoenix Force pair and their Belgian allies quickly took advantage of the shock effect of the rocket. The terrorists would be shaken and a bit disoriented for a moment. Colonel

Mauser's team attacked first. The Luxembourgian intel offi
cer signaled for his men armed with grenade launchers to open
fire. They canted their weapons high to launch the 40 mm shells
in high arcs above the grassy turf.

The grenades exploded on impact about twenty yards from
the convoy. The blasts tore up large chunks of earth and
shrapnel showered down on the terrorists, but the explosion
caused little damage to Skull's forces. The grenades were in
tended to keep the enemy off balance and more concerned with
staying alive than fighting. More grenades were fired closer to
the convoy. These burst into columns of thick green smoke. The
smoke screen reduced the terrorists' vision as the strike force
closed in.

The dense green cloud also made the terrorists less visible for
Katz, McCarter and their allies, but they had a better idea
where their opponents were located than the terrorists did. The
best marksmen among the Belgian paratroopers aimed their
FAL rifles at the shapes among the smoke. They fired 3-round
bursts, taking out opponents as they drew closer. Particular
effort was taken to dispatch the enemies at the machine gun
and the pair with the RPG launcher. Several rifles fired at those
positions simultaneously. The screams that blended with the
chatter of automatic fire announced success. The fire from the
mounted machine guns ceased. Either the gunners had been
killed or they had been forced to flee for cover.

Crouched low, David McCarter and three paratroopers
charged toward the convoy, weapons held ready. The terrorists
returned with an assortment of automatic rifles, submachine
guns and pistols, but their aim was poor due to the smoke gre
nades. But some bullets still struck flesh, and a Belgian trooper
next to McCarter suddenly doubled up with an agonized moan,
dropping his FAL and clutching his blood-spewing abdomen.

The British ace saw the soldier go down, but he could no
help him. More bullets sizzled all around McCarter. A stray
round even creased the skin above his elbow, but he barely no
ticed the burning sting of the shallow wound. The thrill of
combat filled the Briton with excitement and fear. Every time
he went into battle it was like going on the scariest roller coaster

of all time. The ride might kill him, but that was why it was the greatest.

McCarter held his fire, aware that his KG-99 was a short-range weapon compared to the FAL rifles carried by the Belgian paratroopers. He allowed the soldiers to take the offensive as they drew closer. The troops continued to fire at the terrorists. More enemies fell among the fog of green smoke. The terrorists also returned fire. McCarter heard another paratrooper cry out somewhere behind him. The Briton snarled with anger and frustration as he yanked an SAS flash-bang grenade from his belt.

"You bastards!" he shouted and yanked the pin from the grenade. "I got somethin' for you bleedin' sods!"

He hurled the grenade as hard as he could. It landed near the fiery remnants of the Land Rover. The concussion grenade erupted with a furious blast. The shock threw several terrorists to the ground and literally tossed some of their companions into the air. A number of opponents were rendered unconscious by the blast. Others howled in pain, hands clutched to their heads as blood oozed from nostrils and ears. The truck near the explosion trembled from the force of the concussion blast.

McCarter had used the concussion grenade instead of a fragmentation blast to avoid blowing up the gas tank of one of the trucks. He and his companions did not want to explode the larger vehicles because at least one of them probably hid the hostages. McCarter glimpsed Colonel Mauser and his team closing in from the opposite side of the convoy. Despite the thick smoke, the Briton recognized Mauser and the Sola submachine gun the Luxembourgian officer carried. The Sola is a rare 9 mm weapon, out of production since the late 1950s. It was similar to German MP-40 Schmeisser subguns, but the Sola was actually a Luxembourgian weapon. McCarter wondered why Mauser had chosen to bring such an obsolete submachine gun into the battlefield.

Perhaps Mauser used the Sola because he was good with the weapon. The Luxembourgian colonel accurately blasted two terrorists beside the first truck with controlled 3-round bursts. Belgian paratroopers with FALs provided backup for Mauser. The colonel was a brave man and did not hesitate to charge into

the heart of the battle although the enemy continued to return
fire with furious desperation.

McCarter saw a trio of terrorists swing weapons toward his
position, and threw himself to the ground as the gunmen
opened fire. Bullets slashed air above his prone figure. One
terrorist suddenly dropped his subgun to slap both hands to his
bullet-shattered face. A paratrooper had taken out the man
with a well-placed FAL slug. The Phoenix fighter fired his
KG-99 at the remaining pair. One terrorist doubled up with three
9 mm bullets in his stomach. McCarter blasted another trio of
parabellum rounds in a diagonal slash across the chest of the
other enemy triggerman. Shot through the heart and lungs, the
man opened his eyes with astonishment and slid lifeless to the
ground.

The Briton scrambled to the trucks while more terrorists
cursed and tried to train their weapons on him. As he ran,
McCarter fired his KG-99 and nailed another opponent with a
dose of high-velocity death. The man collapsed as others prepared to open fire. Yakov Katzenelenbogen and a Belgian
trooper came to McCarter's rescue. The Israeli hosed the terrorists with Uzi rounds while his companion fired an FAL rifle
at the gunmen.

Bodies jerked and convulsed from the impact of bullets. Four
more terrorists fell. Two others retreated behind the rear of a
truck, one clutching a wounded shoulder. Only one living opponent remained in the open. He swung his Skorpion machine
pistol at Katz and the paratrooper. McCarter triggered his
KG-99 and blasted a trio of parabellums into the side of the
gunman's skull. The man's head exploded in a grisly shower of
blood and brain matter.

Katz rushed to McCarter's position and covered his partner
while the British warrior hastily swapped magazines to reload
his KG-99. Shooting continued all around them. Screams and
moans of agony mingled with the reports of automatic weapons and pistol shots. The smoke was beginning to thin as the
wind blew the artificial fog away from the road. The combat-
ants on both sides had greater visibility.

The two assassins armed with the RPG rocket launcher had
discarded their large, awkward Soviet blast machine and spare

ockets. The launcher could not be used against enemies at such
close range without killing their own people, as well. The terrorist pair had drawn side arms and had run for cover at the
rear of a truck. One of their number, O'Shea, was already stationed there, trying to aim his M-16 around the edge without
exposing himself as a target. The Irish gunman was not having
much luck. Every time he poked the barrel of his rifle from
over a Belgian trooper opened fire on his position. The Irishman had to duck back again and again as bullets sparked
against the steel frame of the truck.

"*Cristo!*" one of the terrorists cried out as a slug ripped into
his right thigh while he darted behind the truck for cover.

His companion fired a H&K pistol at the paratrooper. A
9mm round raked the soldier's rib cage. The Belgian commando was knocked backward by the impact. He triggered his
FAL rifle, but the barrel rose as he lost his footing and the
rounds blazed high above the top of the truck. The terrorist
fired his pistol again and drilled two bullets into the paratrooper's stomach and solar plexus. The soldier crumpled to the
ground, moaning, bleeding and dying.

"I got that bastard!" the pistol-packing terrorist announced with an Oklahoma drawl. He spun the H&K on his
trigger finger in a cowboy spin. "Gimme that M-16 and I'll pick
off some more. Just like back in Nam."

"You were never in Vietnam, Jake," the Spanish terrorist
rasped through clenched teeth as he tried to plug up the bullet
hole in his thigh. "You're only twenty-six years old. What age
were you when you fought in the war? Thirteen?"

"You callin' me a liar, José?" the American demanded,
glaring at his comrade. "I ain't in the habit of takin' shit from
greasers—"

"Shut up, both of you!" O'Shea snapped, furious with the
two lower-ranking terrorists. "There's no bloody time for this
idiotic bickering! Here!"

The Irish terrorist shoved the M-16 toward Jake. The American took the rifle and O'Shea removed a Soviet F-1 hand grenade from his belt. He inserted a finger in the ring and tilted his
head toward the corner of the truck closest to the heart of the
battle.

"You fire at the bleeders to keep them occupied long enough for me to try to locate an effective target," the Irishman declared. "I don't want to toss this thing around the corner without seeing what I'm throwing it at. Could blow up half a dozen of our own people if I did that."

"Just make it quick," Jake replied, putting the stock of the M-16 to his shoulder.

José moved out of their way, dragging his wounded leg while squeezing the artery to try to stop the bleeding. O'Shea knelt near the corner of the truck, the F-1 blaster gripped firmly in both hands. Jake stood beside the Irish terrorist and swung the rifle around the edge. He started shooting before he could even see what the weapon was pointed at. The American was less concerned about the lives of his comrades than he was about his own.

Some of the wild 5.56 mm rounds tore up dust a few inches in front of Katz and McCarter. The Phoenix Force commander immediately swung his Uzi toward the rifleman and opened fire. O'Shea pulled the pin from the grenade a split second before he leaned forward, just in time to catch a 9 mm parabellum through the forearm. The Irishman cried out as his fingers popped open and the grenade hit the ground. Jake fell across O'Shea's neck and shoulders. He was deadweight—literally. The Uzi burst had blasted three rounds into his chest. Jake's heart had exploded and a parabellum had severed his spinal cord before punching an exit hole between his shoulder blades.

"¡Madre de Dios!" José exclaimed. "The grenade! Where is it?"

"Sweet Jesus Christ!" O'Shea gasped as he tried to push Jake's corpse out of the way. His forearm was shattered and he could use only one arm as he tried to disengage himself from the dead man.

José spotted the grenade. He limped forward and reached for it. The terrorist's fingers nearly touched the F-1 when it exploded. The blast sent chunks of all three men hurtling from the rear of the truck. The explosion also smashed open the radiator of the next truck and snapped the hood latch. Water spilled from the rig and the hood popped up. A series of low crack-

formed in the windshield and steam spewed from the engine within.

"God," McCarter rasped, shielding his eyes from the glare with a cupped palm.. "I hope none of the hostages are back there. Or the bloody bomb."

"Let's find out," Katz replied. He jumped to his feet and headed for the trucks.

McCarter followed, glancing around for other terrorists. Colonel Mauser and his team were exchanging shots with opponents at the opposite side of the convoy. The Luxembourgian's section had also lost members, but the terrorists were definitely suffering more casualties. Of course, they outnumbered the commandos so they could afford to loose more men.

Katz moved to the rear of the first truck. The doors stood open. The Israeli felt something sticky and soft under his boots. He tried to ignore it and did not look down to see what he had stepped in. Katz knew what it was and he had no desire to look at it. The mess underfoot was caused by the remains of the terrorists who had been blown apart by the grenade. The Phoenix commander kept his eyes on the truck and pointed his Uzi at the open doors. The big trailer was empty.

A Belgian paratrooper ran to the rear of the second truck to search for hostages or the sinister plutonium weapon. He ran right into a burst of submachine gun rounds. The terrorist gunman leaned out from the doors of the trailer and fired his Ingram M-11 in one fist. The paratrooper collapsed, his chest torn open by a line of bullet holes. His assassin did not get a chance to gloat, for Colonel Mauser hit the terrorist with a salvo of Sola slugs. Even one of the shots was enough for instant death.

Mauser approached the truck from one side while McCarter closed in from the other. The Briton reached the end of the trailer first and quickly peered around the edge. He saw somebody near the door with an AK-47 tucked under one arm and both hands clutched around a F-1 grenade. McCarter switched the selector on his KG-99 from full-auto to semi.

"Hey!" he called out as he pointed the subgun at the terrorist.

The man looked up from the grenade and stared at Mc-
Carter with surprise. The Briton shot him between the eyes. The
terrorist fell sideways from the threshold, the grenade still
clenched in his fists. The dead man landed on the ground, but
his fingers had pulled the pin from the grenade in a last reflex
action.

McCarter barely noticed the dead man fall as another terrorist suddenly poked a pistol around the edge of the doorway
and opened fire. The Briton jumped back the instant he caught
sight of the gun barrel. A bullet screeched past his head, and
McCarter ducked behind the rear tires of the trailer rig, his
heart racing from the near-lethal encounter.

Colonel Mauser swung around the corner, Sola chopper
pointed toward the terrorist pistol man inside the trailer. The
Luxembourgian officer nearly opened fire, but he spotted two
figures seated on a bench inside the truck. Mauser noticed the
pair appeared to be chained to the bench. He realized they were
almost certainly hostages. Mauser held his fire, afraid a burst
of automatic fire would cause ricochets that might harm the
prisoners within the metal walls of the trailer.

The terrorist suddenly saw Mauser and swung his pistol toward the Luxembourgian. Mauser stepped forward and lashed
out with his Sola. The long barrel smashed across the gunman's wrist and struck the pistol from his hand. Mauser's free
hand snaked forward and snared his opponent's belt to yank
hard and pull the terrorist off balance. The man fell forward
and landed on top of Mauser. Both of them toppled heavily and
dropped across the corpse of the terrorist McCarter had previously shot in the head.

The grenade exploded beneath Mauser and his opponent.
The explosion blasted both men into oblivion. McCarter was
bowled over by the shock wave. His head swam for a moment,
the world flashing from dark to light and his ears ringing from
the effects of the blast. The Briton shook his head to clear it and
rose to his feet. He glanced down at the bloodied remnants of
Mauser and the terrorist. The bodies had muffled the explosion and absorbed most of the blast, including virtually all the
shrapnel. If they had not been literally atop the grenade,
McCarter would have been killed or seriously injured.

Merely bruised, the British ace moved forward and peered inside the trailer. The two hostages looked back at him. The Briton recognized the thin, pinched face of Andrew Thornton. He had voted against the guy when he ran for Parliament in the most recent election in Great Britain. The man next to Thornton was even more familiar. The round-faced middle-aged man with a balding head and a vivid birthmark was recognized by half the people in the world. The secretary-general of the Soviet Union looked at McCarter through the fogged lenses of his metal-rimmed glasses.

"I'll be damned," McCarter whispered as he climbed inside, wincing from a bruise at his left shoulder blade. "We were hoping we'd find you blokes."

"Thank God!" Thornton exclaimed, struggling with his chains. "We've been rescued! What are you? SAS? I knew Her Majesty's government wouldn't let one of its own remain a captive to these terrorist brutes."

"Can it, mate," McCarter said gruffly as he knelt near the two VIP prisoners. The Phoenix pro kept his attention trained on the opening of the trailer, KG-99 pointed at the gap. "You two appear all right for now," McCarter said with relief, then looked more closely at the men for confirmation.

The premier nodded, but did not say anything. Thornton said, "I suppose so."

"Are the other hostages in the remaining trucks?" McCarter asked.

"No," Thornton answered. "Their leader separated us when we got off the helicopter. They stuck the premier and me in a great, dirty truck and drove us off to God knows where. Had us in a cell—"

"There's still a battle going on," McCarter told the M.P. "No time for a chapter from your biography. What about the bomb and the President of the United States, that German fellow Weiss and the chap who jumped aboard the chopper when it took off at Strassmacher Castle? You know what happened to them?"

"Skull still has them, I reckon," Thornton answered. "That's the albino. Calls himself Colonel Skull. Ever hear of such nonsense?"

"On election day when you got a seat in Parliament."
McCarter snorted. "So they're all still alive? Including the fellow who got on the helicopter to try to rescue you people?"

"You're bloody rude," Thornton said, sniffling. "That man a friend of yours or something?"

"Answer my question!" McCarter snapped. "Is he still alive?"

"As far as I know he is," Thornton said quickly, startled by the anger, near desperation, in McCarter's voice. "I think they're all still alive. I don't know. Skull and his henchmen have them."

"All right," the Phoenix fighter said, his tone more gentle than before. "You two relax and we'll get you out of here as soon as possible."

McCarter headed toward the doors. Thornton nearly called after him, but decided not to. The premier mentally sorted through his limited English vocabulary for appropriate words.

"Good luck, friend!" he declared. "Go win!"

"I bloody well hope so," McCarter replied with a nod.

MARTIN KOERNER and two terrorists, a short man in a cap and a tall turbanned Sikh ran for cover behind the Citroën. The man in the pin-striped suit lay dead near the front fender. The driver was slumped over the steering wheel, the window next to him punctured and cracked by bullet holes. His skull had stopped the projectiles after they passed through the glass.

The terrorist major dived onto the hood of the car and slid across to the other side. A Belgian paratrooper fired his FAL rifle and drilled three 7.62 mm rounds between the shoulder blades of the thug dressed in coveralls. The man screamed and fell forward. His skull crashed into the front of the Citroën, the forehead shattering a headlight. His body fell heavily to the ground where it twitched slightly and lay motionless in death.

The Sikh terrorist dropped to one knee by the nose of the car and returned fire with a British-made Mark V Sten gun. The weapon chattered a furious volley of full-auto fury, but the paratrooper ducked behind a truck. Bullets whined against the metal trailer rig. The Sikh fired another salvo. Koerner punched him on the arm to stop the man from burning up ammo uselessly.

The major's thoughts were gloomy as he moved to the rear of the car and peered carefully over the top. His men had been virtually wiped out. The strike force had hit swiftly and skillfully. Although the terrorist mercenaries under Koerner's command had far outnumbered them, the strike force comprised better-trained and more-motivated fighting men. Koerner's people had been no match for them. The terrorists had killed many of the enemy, but there was no doubt which side would be victorious.

Koerner had no illusions about his own fate. He was as good as dead. If he tried to run they would cut him down. If he stayed put behind the cover of the Citroën they would eventually take him out. A single grenade or rocket would do the job. All that remained was for Major Martin Koerner to try to kill as many opponents as possible before he died.

The paratrooper cautiously stuck his head around the edge of the truck and brought the barrel of his rifle up to attempt to fire at the Citroën. Koerner triggered his Luger. A 9 mm slug split the paratrooper's forehead, and the soldier died on his feet.

Katz had checked the rear of the last convoy truck and found it empty except for one mangled and bloodied terrorist who had crawled inside and bled to death. The Israeli heard shots being exchanged by the two terrorists at the car and some of the Belgian troopers. That seemed to be the only portion of the battle still in progress. Katz moved around the end of the truck and waited for one of the terrorists to present a target.

The Sikh stood up next to the hood and fired his Sten chopper at some paratroopers along the convoy. Katz immediately opened up with his Uzi. The Sikh gunman spun about from the impact of three parabellums to the face and head, and then fell across the hood of the Citroën, his face bathed in flowing crimson.

Katz retreated behind the rig, not a moment too soon. A bullet streaked past his head, barely missing his left temple. Koerner clucked his tongue with disgust when he realized he had failed to hit Katz. The terrorist major scanned the battle-

field and peered through the sights of his Luger for another
target.

McCarter leaned around the front of the cab of a tractor
trailer rig. He held the Browning Hi-Power in both fists. The
Briton saw a single gunman, armed with a pistol, positioned
behind the Citroën. The terrorist was making the most of his
cover and barely exposed himself when he took aim with the
Luger P.08 and fired at a target. If McCarter was going to take
him out, accuracy would be needed more than multiple firepower. The Browning had been McCarter's favorite weapon for
nearly two decades. He had participated in Olympic competi-
tion with a Browning, had qualified in the finals but had been
ordered to Oman by the SAS before he could participate in the
deciding competitions. There was no gold medal at stake this
time. The Briton's accuracy with a pistol was now a matter of
life or death.

He aimed quickly, relying on years of training and experience and the highly tuned instincts developed in countless battlefields. Koerner spotted McCarter and trained his Luger on
the Briton's head. Clear target, the terrorist thought. This time
he would nail his opponent dead center. Koerner's finger
squeezed the trigger.

McCarter fired the Browning a split second earlier. The
115-grain parabellum smashed into the fingers clutched to the
butt of the Luger. Koerner cried out as the 9 mm slug crushed
bone in the ring fingers of both hands. The bullet struck the
butt of his pistol and drove his arms backward. The Luger
snarled as the barrel jumped upward. Koerner saw the muzzle-
flash burn overhead and bitterly realized the shot was fired
harmlessly into the sky.

The Luger fell from his grasp. Koerner glanced down at the
pistol. The butt had been smashed, walnut grips shattered and
the magazine well badly dented. Blood oozed from his hands.
The ring fingers had been severed at the second knuckle. Bits
of metal and wood had pierced his palms. Several bones in his
hands had been broken by the force of McCarter's bullet. The
Luger P.08 was wrecked. It was a delicate gun and no doubt
ruined by the destructive force of the 9 mm round. Koerner
could not pick it up anyway. His hands were useless, chunks of

bloodied flesh that delivered jets of agony through his nervous system.

"Freeze!" Katz ordered as he approached the wounded major, Uzi pointed at Koerner's chest.

"Kill me," Koerner rasped, his voice taut with pain. "Go on. Kill me."

"Why should I do you any favors?" the Israeli asked as he lowered his subgun. "Try to run and I'll chop you down at the kneecaps. You're going to answer some questions for us."

"Perhaps I will," Koerner admitted as he leaned against the side of the car, staring at his butchered hands. "But you may not like what I have to say."

=== 21 ===

"You Americans have certainly made a mess of things," Pierre Bertin complained as he stroked his suit jacket with a lint brush. The French intelligence officer barely glanced at the other men in the conference room. "Terrorists running all around Europe. Gun battles with KGB agents in the heart of Paris. Lunatics kidnapping world leaders and a nuclear bomb somewhere here in France. Monstrous!"

"Oh, shut up!" Scott Bernelli snapped. The young CIA officer thrust an index finger at Bertin and glared at him with raw anger. "You've done nothing but bitch since we arrived. I'm sick of hearing it, and I'm sick of your snotty remarks about America. So just stuff it!"

"Is this the same bloke we met back in Italy?" David McCarter commented, surprised by Bernelli's vehemence.

"He's been slowly losing patience with Bertin," Rafael Encizo explained with a shrug. "After you've been around the guy for a while, you'll understand."

"I think I understand already," McCarter assured him.

"Yeah," the Cuban was forced to agree. "But we have to work with Bertin and Sûreté. Personality clashes are a luxury we can't afford right now."

Bertin had responded to the CIA agent's remarks by spitting out a combination of English and French that was difficult to follow in either language; in his anger he kept switching as though he could not decide which language would serve him best to insult the CIA man.

"Calm down, calm down, both of you," Encizo urged, stepping between Bertin and Bernelli. "We're all on the same side."

"And you two have a lot in common," McCarter added. He leaned back in a chair and popped open a chilled bottle of Coca-Cola as he spoke. "You're both members of government intelligence outfits. You're...well, your names both start with the same three letters. You both wear suits—"

"Shut up and drink your Coke," Encizo growled. He did not need McCarter's "help" as a diplomat, a role that had never suited the fiery Briton. "Let me talk to them."

"Okay," Bernelli said with a sigh. He turned to Bertin and gestured with open palms held up. "I was out of line and I'm sorry. But you pissed me off."

"Let it drop," Encizo insisted. "Bertin, knock off the crap about how we Americans screwed up. I haven't heard you complain about the Soviets, and their security was violated, as well as the Americans at Strassmacher Castle. Besides, we were not part of the security forces that let Skull's people get in."

"You let them get away," the Frenchman said with a sniffle.

"Why you little bastard!" McCarter snarled as he banged the bottom of his Coke bottle on the tabletop. Cola foamed up from the mouth of the bottle and oozed down the sides. "We're risking our lives to try to find these terrorists while you sit here in this safe office and pass judgment on us!"

"Don't start!" Encizo told his partner. "We're getting close to wrapping up this mission. Let's not have any more hostility among our allies."

"Mauser and Quvey were our allies," McCarter stated. "Not to mention Karl Hahn. They all laid their lives on the line and they're all dead. So are a lot of other good men. There may be a few more die before this is over."

"Frenchmen have died, too," Bertin reminded him. "They were killed by the terrorists when they crossed the Luxembourg border and first arrived on French soil. Do you think I don't care about this mission? If Skull sets off that plutonium bomb it will be in my country. I am as concerned as you are."

"You have a funny way of showing it," Bernelli muttered. "You bawled out Johnson and Santos when they captured those three KGB agents."

"What's this?" McCarter asked with surprise. "I heard Bertin mention something about gunfights with the KGB in Paris, but I figured it was just exaggerated rot."

"It's exaggerated because no one was shot," Encizo explained. "But Vashnov and two other KGB guys followed us around Paris and planned to either kill us or kidnap us. We spotted them, jumped the dummies and captured them. Johnson had to use his knife on Vashnov, but the bastard is still alive. He's been deported. Flown back to the Soviet Union where I don't think he'll get any warm greetings. He won't be a problem anymore, but his little stunt certainly got in the way of our progress here in France."

"Yes," Bertin agreed, tapping a cigarette on the crystal of his wristwatch. "Yet we have made some progress. We know some of the terrorists crossed the border into Belgium. The fact that Kenver and Masters found the Soviet premier and the British member of Parliament proves that. This suggests the enemy are probably still in the northern part of the country. Probably somewhere in the Metropolitan Department of Meuse, Ardennes or Marne."

"Metropolitan departments." Bernelli sighed and shook his head. "You make it sound as if those are portions of a city instead of what amounts to entire states here in France. You can't even be sure Skull hasn't moved south or west by now. Those sons of bitches in Belgium were headed for a new site when Kenver and Masters cut 'em off on the road."

"Do you know why they moved from their original base in Belgium?" Bertin inquired. "Was this a security precaution or was there some other reason?"

"There was a reason," Yakov Katzenelenbogen announced as he entered the conference room. Calvin James followed right behind him and closed the door. "You ought to lock and bolt this thing. These meetings are absolute top-secret. We don't want some file clerk wandering through the corridor and overhearing our conversation."

"It's secure now," James declared as he bolted the door.

"You interrogated the prisoner you brought from Belgium?" Bertin asked eagerly.

"His name is Koerner," Katz answered, moving to the table to slump into a chair. "He was Colonel Skull's second in command. At least that's what he thought. Koerner knew that the terrorist base in Germany had been put out of operation after they stopped sending radio signals to Koerner's group in Belgium. He realized the terrorists in Germany had been set up by Skull. They had been sacrificed to throw us off the trail and cause us to waste time. Koerner figured his base might be in jeopardy as well, so he tried to move to a new location. He didn't make it."

"Did you give Koerner scopolamine?" Bernelli inquired.

"Yeah," James answered. "Not sure it was even necessary. Koerner figures Skull either sold him out or would have before everything was over. He might be right, but Skull made a mistake."

"Bloody glad to hear that," McCarter commented. "Since the bastard doesn't seem to have made too many so far."

"He made a big one with Koerner," Katz stated as he fired a Camel cigarette with his Ronson lighter. "Skull must have assumed Koerner would never be taken alive. Considering the man's personality, that's an understandable assumption, but it proved incorrect. Koerner knew details about Skull's operation that none of the lesser flunkies were aware of. Among other things, Koerner told us about the Saddoon brothers. Ali-Rez Saddoon is the chairman of the National Assembly of Iraq. He and his brother, Nizar, hired Skull. At the end of the week they intend to assassinate the president of Iraq and anyone else who stands between Ali-Rez and the office of supreme command of the country. The Soviet premier has already contacted the Soviet embassy in Baghdad. They're in touch with the Iraqi president by now. Saddoon and his coconspirators will be arrested on suspicion of plotting to overthrow the government and murder the present leaders of the country."

"Well, that will rob Skull of his ultimate victory," Bernelli said, clearly disappointed. "But that doesn't help us locate Skull's base here in France or the President and the damn bomb."

"There's still some hope for that," James declared. "Koerner also said that his base in Belgium was transmitting signals to an unknown radio base in France. Just beep-beep coded junk that nobody else would think much of. Now, the base in Germany had probably been doing the same because the plan called for all three outfits keeping in radio contact. Considering the effective frequency range, Skull's headquarters must be in northern France."

"Just as I said!" Bertin declared with a smile.

"Great," McCarter commented. "That's still a hell of a lot of country to try to cover."

"First thing we need to do is blanket the northern departments with radio scans by Sûreté and the military," Katz began. "Anything that sounds remotely like a signal. Anything that can't be explained by regular radio transmissions should be tracked and investigated. CIA and NSA can help, too. They should be familiar with equipment for tracing the source of radio transmissions."

"Of course," Bernelli confirmed. "Anything we can do, just ask."

"What about checking on stolen vehicles that fit the tire tracks the terrorists left when they escaped from the site where the chopper landed?" McCarter asked. "Or look into the arms dealers in major French cities. A gunrunner in Brussels was my lead to Koerner's outfit."

"We've already looked into those possible leads," Encizo answered. "Apparently none of the vehicles were stolen, or the terrorists managed to disguise the tracks well enough. Sûreté and various police departments have been checking out illegal arms dealers, but no luck so far. France is almost ten times the size of Belgium. It's a lot harder to hunt people down here. We might get lucky, but I'd say that's a long shot in this case."

"Does Koerner have any idea where Skull might be located?" Bernelli asked hopefully.

"Not really," Katz answered. "Colonel Skull claimed it was necessary to maintain security so he didn't tell Koerner where his base was set up. All we can do is try to pursue the possibilities we've already discussed and any others that might come up."

"*Zut!*" Bertin exclaimed. "That is all?"

"Well," James began in a weary voice, "I might try to hypnotize Koerner and attempt to probe for any subconscious information he might have. I doubt if that will do any good, but it's possible Koerner may have heard or seen something that might help us and that he genuinely doesn't remember. Scopolamine can, and generally does, tap into the subconscious anyway, but hypnosis would allow us to cross-check."

"Let's not leave anything neglected," the Phoenix Force commander replied. "We'll also need to assemble the best antiterrorist squad or skilled commando teams available and have them on standby, ready to go into action at a moment's notice. We may be able to get assistance from the West German GSG-9, the Belgian paratroopers, the British SAS and the American Delta Force. The British and U.S. governments sent teams to Luxembourg Ville after the Strassmacher incident."

"You think it's wise to call in anybody else?" Bernelli asked. "Seems to me that might jeopardize security. Maybe GSG-9 and Belgian troops who have already been involved in the mission, but I don't think bringing SAS or Delta Force in is a good idea."

"French troops should handle this," Bertin insisted. "This is our country, gentlemen. Let us defend it."

"This is an international crisis and everyone is involved," Katz declared. "However, I am inclined to agree with both of you, but for somewhat different reasons. We'll need all the help we can get to locate Skull's lair. The French authorities are better suited to handling that role simply because they know their own country more intimately than the groups I mentioned, especially the Delta Force personnel from America. Besides, a bunch of extra foreigners poking around is more apt to alert Skull."

The Israeli crushed out his cigarette in an ashtray and continued. "When we find the base, stealth and strategy are going to be more important than enormous firepower or troop strength. Too many men in a mission of this sort could ruin our chances of catching the terrorists off guard. We have to assume Skull will kill the hostages and detonate the plutonium if he knows all is lost."

"Hell," McCarter said with a snort. "If he sets off that nuclear fireplug he won't have to kill the hostages. We'll all go up together. Judgment day for everybody involved."

"You sure know how to cheer us up," Calvin James said with a sigh.

22

Gary Manning sat up on the bunk when he heard a key turn in the lock. The face of a black African terrorist peered through the barred window. Manning heard the bolt slide back. He got to his feet as the door opened. The African stood at the threshold with a .38 Smith & Wesson in his fist. A grim-faced blond gunman stood next to him, a Skorpion machine pistol held loosely in his hands.

"You have an appointment with Major Hee," the black terrorist said solemnly. "Step forward, very slowly. Stand facing the door, feet apart. Then place your forehead to the door and put your hands behind your back. If you resist, Jurgens or I will shoot you in the leg and you will still be taken to interrogation."

"You mean I'll be taken to the torture chamber Hee has set up," Manning replied as he moved toward the door.

"You had a choice," the African said with a shrug. "Perhaps you still do. You will talk eventually. If you are wise, you will spare yourself a great deal of pain."

Manning considered the odds of jumping the two armed terrorists. Even if he failed to overpower them, a quick bullet in the heart or the brain would be better than a slow painful death from torture. However, the black gunman had told the truth. They could easily shoot him in the leg if he tried anything. The Canadian faced the door and put his arms behind his back.

"Help...me!" a voice groaned from the next cell. "My heart! My chest is...it's crushing me...."

"The President!" the blond terrorist exclaimed with alarm.

Manning glanced over his shoulder. Both men had turned their heads toward the President's cell. The distraction offered Manning the only chance he was apt to get to take action. The Canadian whirled and quickly slashed the side of his hand across the African's wrist. The .38 revolver fell from the black man's grasp. The man yelped as bones popped in his wrist. Manning's other hand balled into a fist and shot into the terrorist's face.

The punch propelled the African back out the doorway of Manning's cell, across the corridor and into the wall. The Canadian Phoenix pro was a powerful man, and desperation contributed to the power behind each blow. The blond gunman cursed and swung his Skorpion toward Manning's lower limbs. The Canadian lashed out a boot and kicked the Czech subgun from the terrorist's grasp.

The blond terrorist immediately responded with a fast left hook to the Phoenix pro's jaw and drove his other fist into Manning's stomach. The brawny Canadian barely grunted from the punches. He was charged with adrenaline, and it would take more to stop him. Manning grabbed the terrorist's shirtfront and shoved him into the doorway. The man groaned as his spine slammed into the hard edge.

Manning drove a knee into his opponent's abdomen. The terrorist gasped and the wind was driven from his lungs. Manning next rammed an uppercut to his solar plexus, making him double up with a wheezing, half-choked sound. The Canadian hammered the bottom of his fist between the man's shoulder blades and wrapped an arm around his neck to grip him in a firm front headlock. Manning turned sharply and hauled his opponent into the doorway.

The Phoenix commando charged into the corridor, still holding the blond gunman by the neck. He rammed the terrorist's lower back into a wall and whipped a knee under his jaw. The terrorist fell unconscious just as his African comrade, somewhat recovered, grabbed Manning by the back of the collar and punched him in the kidney.

Manning hissed in pain through clenched teeth and quickly delivered a back elbow stroke. The elbow smashed into the African's mouth. His head snapped back from the blow, blood spilling from split lips. Manning swung a hammer fist into the black terrorist's gut and slammed another elbow strike to his opponent's breastbone.

The Canadian whirled and lashed a back fist across the African's face. The terrorist fell sideways into the opposite wall. Manning swung a boot to the man's torso. The African doubled up from the kick and received a hard uppercut to the jaw. The blow lifted the black thug off his feet and he landed unconscious on the stone floor.

"I hoped you'd do something like that," the President of the United States whispered from the porthole to his cell door.

"You're okay, Mr. President?" Manning asked, moving to the door. "So you just faked a heart attack to distract them?"

"A minor acting part," the President said with a chuckle. "I'm a little rusty, but I guess I was convincing enough. I thought you'd be able to handle those two if you could get them off guard."

"Find the keys!" Klaus Weiss called from his cell. "Get us out of here!"

"Keep it down," Manning urged. "There are more terrorists outside."

Weiss repeated quietly but in an urgent tone, "Please, look for the keys."

Manning found the fallen .38 revolver and Skorpion machine pistol. He stuck the revolver in a back pocket and slipped the sling to the Skorpion over his shoulder. The Canadian inhaled deeply. It felt good to be out of a locked little room. It felt even better to fight back after being pushed around by his captors. He was finally armed and on the offense once more. The odds were still overwhelmingly in the favor of Skull's forces, but at least Manning had a chance. If he died, it would be as a ram rather than a sheep.

The Canadian dragged the unconscious terrorists into his cell. He stripped off the blond one's clothes and tossed them in a corner. The terrorist was roughly the same size as Manning, and the guy's uniform would fit well enough, Manning reckoned.

He removed the African's boots and belt. Manning added the holster and spare ammo for the .38 to the pile of clothing and found a single key attached to a ring. There was nothing else of any value to Manning in the African's pockets. He did not need the passport, wallet or a small metal disk that appeared to be a good luck charm of some sort.

The terrorists were beginning to regain consciousness. Manning knew the smart thing to do would be to kill them both, but he was not a murderer and he could not justify the killings in cold blood. This sense of morality, the belief that there are lines that cannot be crossed if one is going to fight evil without becoming part of it, made the men of Phoenix Force different from the barbarians they fought.

Manning did the best he could to neutralize the pair without killing them. He unlaced the African's boots and pulled the black man's arms behind his back. Manning tied the man's thumbs together with one of the laces. He wound the lace around the thumbs to reinforce the slender cloth cord. Manning pushed the man's fingers inward, toward the palms, and used the remaining length of the lace to tie the little fingers together. It is very difficult to untie knots without using one's thumbs and binding the little fingers would further reduce the man's ability to use his hands.

The other terrorist opened his eyes and groaned. Manning punched him on the point of the chin. The man's eyes closed and he slid back into dreamland. Manning used the other bootlace and tied him up also, relying on the same method. He hauled the unconscious enemy troopers to the sink and toilet. Manning used the African's own belt to tie his ankles together with the pipes to the sink between his legs. The black man started to wake up. Manning let him be and removed his own shirt to tear off three strips of cloth.

"Scream for help and I'll kick your head in," Manning warned. "I'm not sure it makes much difference whether you shout or not. Nobody seems to have heard our little fistfight and rushed to your rescue."

"Wha...what are you doing?" the African asked with a wince of pain from his split lips as he spoke.

"You'll see," Manning said and proceeded to tie the other man's legs. With that done, Manning knelt beside the African and prepared to gag him.

"A moment, please," the black man said quickly. "I ask that you do not gag Jurgens. He may choke to death while unconscious."

"All right," Manning agreed. "I probably shouldn't, but I don't want a possible murder on my conscience. If you don't know what a conscience is, look it up in the dictionary some time. It's something that would have disqualified you from ever joining Skull's terrorist army."

"Do my reasons matter?" The African sighed. "I appreciate your mercy. You could have killed us. I am almost sorry you will never leave here alive."

"Sure," Manning said as he stuck the knot in the black man's mouth and tied the gag into place.

Manning discarded the third strip of cloth torn from his shirt and moved to the pile of clothes he had set aside. He donned the terrorist's uniform and checked the pockets. He found a pair of handcuffs and a key for them. Manning had not used the cuffs on either man because he might need them later. Manning added the revolver holster to Blondie's belt, which also held two spare ammo pouches for the Skorpion machine pistol.

At last, he emerged from the cell, carrying the Czech subgun under his arm and the S&W revolver holstered on his hip. He pulled a black beret with the white skull emblem onto his head, closed the cell door, locked it and shoved the bolt into place.

"Good God," Weiss whispered from his cell. "What has taken you so long? What are you doing? Get us out!"

"Try to calm down, Klaus," the President urged. "This gentleman is doing the best he can."

"I don't have the keys to the other cells, Mr. President," Manning informed the captive world leader. "I'm not sure where they might be, either."

"Then try to get out of here and get help," the President replied. "You might be able to escape from this place on your own. You're young, well trained, and you have had experience with this sort of thing. Weiss and I would slow you down. You'll do better on your own."

"But, Mr. President . . ." Weiss began desperately.

"I'd like to get out of here too, Klaus," the President assured him. "But there's more at stake here than your life or mine. These terrorists still have a nuclear bomb. Colonel Skull is trying some sort of international blackmail. He may also still have the Soviet premier held captive. This incident is like a powder keg. It has to be stopped, even if that means we have to die here."

"I'll be back, Mr. President," Manning promised.

"Good luck, son," the President replied.

Gary Manning headed down the corridor to the entrance of the cell block. He pushed the thick iron door, but it refused to budge. It was locked from the outside. The Canadian cursed under his breath, swallowed hard and pounded a fist on the door.

"Open the door!" he demanded, hammering on the door with his fist.

"You have the prisoner?" a voice at the opposite side of the door inquired.

Manning started to explain in an aggravated and impatient voice. "The stinking pig put up a fight. We had to beat him senseless. Jurgens was hurt. Open the door, damn it! They will both bleed to death if you do not hurry!"

There was the scraping sound of the bolt moving. Manning sucked in a deep breath and hoped the sentry was alone. The Canadian had heard only one voice, but there could be two or three guards outside. The door began to open. Manning stepped to the side and waited, his Skorpion machine pistol clenched tightly in both fists.

A single terrorist stepped across the threshold, a small, dark man with olive skin. He was armed with a Belgian FAL rifle, whose sling was over his shoulder. Obviously he did not expect to use it.

"Hold it," Manning said in a sharp whisper as he pointed the muzzle of the Skorpion at the man's face. "Don't say a word and no sudden movements. I'll blow your head off if I have to. Now, close the door."

The sentry turned slowly and pulled the door shut. Manning clipped him behind the ear with the steel frame of the Czech machine pistol. The man moaned softly, as if glad to be

knocked senseless, and his body began to sag. Manning caught
him and lowered him to the floor.

The Phoenix pro took the FAL rifle. He smiled at the familiar feel of the frame and barrel of an old friend. The FAL was
Manning's favorite assault weapon. Accurate and deadly with
a big 7.62 mm caliber for reliable knockdown force, the FAL
had always served him well in the past. There was no time to
spend adjusting the sights and, of course, he could not fire a
few practice rounds at a firing range with the newly acquired
rifle, but he felt more confident with the same type of firearm
he had used so effectively many times in the past.

He hastily confiscated the unconscious man's spare mags for
the weapon and tied the man's arms behind his back, using the
sentry's own belt. It would not hold the man for long, but
Manning realized time was running out anyway. Major Hee was
probably already wondering why Manning had not been escorted to the Korean's chamber for "interrogation." It would
not be long before Hee or Skull himself sent someone to investigate. One or both terrorist leaders might even check on it
personally.

Manning opened the door a crack and peered outside. The
square in the center of the terrorist compound looked much the
same as it had when he saw it before. In the bright afternoon
sunlight two men were inspecting the trucks and jeeps to make
certain they were in good condition. Three other terrorists stood
around in the square, but none seemed interested in the cell
block.

The Canadian slipped the strap to the FAL over one shoulder and the Skorpion over the other. He opened the door,
stepped outside and closed it. Manning slid the bolt into place
and glanced about the compound, trying to formulate a plan
of action.

The crumbling old fortress where Skull had set up his base
was not particularly large, but it was big enough to house at
least thirty terrorists. There could be twice that many opponents in the compound. He knew that the ancient stone buildings were deceptive. The corridors within extended
underground and contained more chambers than they appeared to from the outside. The plutonium bomb could be

anywhere, and there was no time to spare hunting for it. Manning was unsure he could deactivate the bomb even if he found it. He would have to concentrate on targets he could be certain of.

The monotonous hum of generators drew his attention to the stone structure nearby that housed the great black octopus with its rubber-cable tentacles that extended throughout the base. The radio antenna rose from the second story above the generator room. Manning recalled the radio operator he had formerly seen at the window. Though the shutters were closed, the communications section was no doubt on duty twenty-four hours a day. The Canadian strolled toward the building. He hoped he looked nonchalant as he shuffled along the edge of the square toward the rumble of the generators and the antenna steeple that beckoned him.

Manning found a door to the generator room. A pair of bored terrorist mercs sat at a card table, playing chess. One man wore a *keffiyeh* and the other sported a shaggy red beard. They sipped tea as they considered the board. The Arab glanced up and nodded at Manning, barely looking at the Canadian. Apparently the two were in charge of maintaining the generators. They were accustomed to the grumble of the diesel-powered machines, and they must have been used to people coming in and out because neither of them showed any interest in Manning. The redheaded man did not even bother to glance up from the chess game.

Given the guard's lack of inquisitiveness, the Canadian commando could only assume that they were used to people dropping in, but as to why anybody would bother visiting that area he had no idea. There was nothing especially fascinating about the generators themselves, which were ugly, squat machines with loud gears, whirling turbo-wheels, fueled by a large black tank of smelly diesel. Then Manning noticed a large red chest attached to the main cable of the generators by an umbilical cord of black rubber.

Manning walked to the chest and raised the lid. It was filled with crushed ice and stocked with an assortment of bottles. Beer, soft drinks, even milk were stored in the chest. That explained why the other terrorists would visit the room without having any business to discuss with the two mechanics. Manning selected a bottle of Coca-Cola, probably because it reminded him of David McCarter. God, he wished that crazy Briton and the other three members of Phoenix Force were by his side.

With the unopened bottle in his hand, Manning glanced about the room. The terrorists still ignored him, all their attention taken up by their chess game. However, an AK-47 and a Sterling machine gun were located near the teapot and hot pad. The pair were not harmless maintenance workers. They were careless because they took their role in the operation for granted. If either man bothered with a second glance at Manning, the Canadian would have a fight on his hands.

Then he saw a flight of stone steps leading to the second story. Manning quietly walked to the stairs. The chess players barely noticed him as the redhead debated how best to move his king out of check. Manning ascended and when he reached the head of the stairs, he stepped into a narrow, drab corridor. There appeared to be only two rooms in the second story, although a wooden ladder stood at the end of the hall. Manning glanced at the ceiling and saw a square-shaped wood door above the ladder.

The crackle of static drew Manning to one of the doors. The door was open. Inside, a thin man sat at a desk. His dark hair was so short it appeared as though his head had been shaved recently and his face had a pinched and underfed look. He wore a radio headset, and a large transceiver radio was mounted on the desk in front of him. The man was puffing on a cigarette as he casually leaned back in his chair with a French paperback in one hand.

"Excusez-moi," Manning began as he slipped the FAL rifle from his shoulder and stepped into the room.

The man looked up with surprise. He removed the headset and placed it on the desk. Manning smiled and stepped closer and suddenly swung the buttstock of the FAL into the terrorist's ratlike features. The man's head was jarred violently by the butt stroke, and he toppled out of the chair to land on the floor in a senseless lump. Manning closed the door and knelt beside the unconscious figure, then took the handcuffs from his hip pocket and quickly cuffed the man's hands behind his back.

Manning sat at the desk and examined the radio. It was a powerful set, with a frequency range that could broadcast just about anywhere in Europe. He adjusted the dials and turned up the frequency level as high as it would go. Manning picked up the microphone and switched it on.

"*Levez-vous, Phénix,*" he spoke into the mike, as loudly as he dared. He repeated the message in English. "Rise, Phoenix."

Manning readjusted the settings and repeated the message in English and French. He switched settings several times to try to transmit the message to as wide a range as possible. He translated it into German, as well and said it repeatedly in all three languages. Manning spent less than two minutes with the radio, but it seemed as if it had taken much longer. The Canadian knew the terrorists would soon discover he had escaped from the cell block. The stress tightened his stomach and raked his spine with fear.

He left the microphone on and allowed the radio to transmit the background noises as he scanned the room. The Canadian found three portable field radios in the commo room. Each was battery-operated and equipped with a backpack carrying case. He grabbed one and switched on the power to be certain it worked. Manning had to put down the Skorpion machine pistol in order to slip the radio backpack harness over his shoulders. He placed the other two field radios on the floor and smashed in the control panels with the butt of his FAL rifle.

Before he left the room, he decided to make some use of the Skorpion. Though he was a powerful man, carrying the radio, the FAL rifle and the Czech subgun would be too great a burden if he needed to move fast. He pulled back the Skorpion's wire stock and braced it against a wall. Manning jammed the frame of the Czech weapon along the edge of the desk.

"I never realized before how much I appreciate bootlaces," Manning muttered as he knelt beside the unconscious radio operator and quickly unlaced one of the man's boots.

He tied one end of the shoelace to the Skorpion's trigger. Manning put the selector switch in the fire mode and moved to the door. He held on to the lace and carefully stepped from the room and pulled the door almost shut. Manning reached inside and tied the bootlace to the inside of the doorknob. He carefully closed the door and turned toward the stairs.

The man with the red beard suddenly galloped up the stairs, and there was a troubled expression on his craggy face. He carried the British Sterling submachine gun in his fists. Manning immediately bolted down the stairs and met the startled terrorist at the halfway point. The Canadian lashed out with his foot and kicked the surprised gunman in the center of his bearded jaw.

The terrorist fell backward and tumbled down the stairs in a graceless roll. Manning ran down the corridor to the ladder and quickly climbed the rungs to the trapdoor. He shoved it open and hauled himself onto the roof.

Manning sprawled on his belly across the tar-patched shingles. The FAL rifle was in one fist as he tried to flatten himself on the roof. The bulk of the field radio between his shoulder blades made the effort futile, but his luck was holding. A thick chimney stood beside him, effectively blocking him from the view of a sentry positioned on the west wall of the compound.

How long that luck would hold seemed doubtful. The square below had burst into activity. Terrorists dashed about the motor pool and charged into the doors of the aged stone structures of the centuries-old fortress. Manning realized his escape had been discovered. He recognized the tall, muscular figure of Major Yasnev among the men in the square. It was a strong temptation to aim the FAL and put a bullet in the big Russian's chest, but Manning could not afford to draw attention to his position. Not if he wanted to stay alive.

The sun felt like a burning white spotlight, determined to betray him to the enemy. A sentry stood watch by the east wall, a Kalashnikov rifle canted across his shoulder, and Manning was in full view if it occurred to the man to look at the roof. For the time being, the guard's attention was on the square below.

Manning lay motionless, although his nerves trembled with tension, muscles ached to take action—any action, rather than lying still like a helpless target for the enemy. Sweat beaded his forehead and started to form little rivulets along his body. In his mouth was the taste of salt and copper, rather than the sour taste of fear.

Suddenly automatic fire erupted inside the radio center beneath the rooftop. Someone had opened the door to the commo room, yanked the bootlace tied to the Skorpion machine pistol and triggered the weapon. From the sound of gunfire, the tactic had startled at least one terrorist badly enough to make him open fire as well, without taking time to see what he was shooting at.

Manning quickly swung his FAL rifle toward the sentry on the east wall. The man's attention was drawn by the sound of the bullet choppers in the radio section. Naturally, he looked at the outside building and saw Manning on the roof. The guard swung the AK-47 from his shoulder and pointed the Soviet death machine at the Phoenix warrior.

The Canadian triggered his weapon first. The FAL snarled a trio of 7.62 mm slugs and the terrorist sentry buckled from the impact of all three. The high velocity projectiles tore into his chest and sent him tumbling from the wall.

Metal whined against stone and ricochets wailed as the bullets bounced off the chimney. The west wall guard had opened fire on Manning's position, but the chimney had protected the Canadian from the enemy volley. Manning thrust the barrel of his rifle around the side of the chimney and returned fire. The 3-round burst missed the guard stationed along the wall. However, one bullet hissed within inches of the terrorist's head. The sentry recoiled in terror and jumped back. Unfortunately for the terrorist, there was no place to jump to. He cried out as he unintentionally leaped from the top of the wall and fell fifteen feet to the cobblestones below.

Manning scrambled across the roof toward the wall. Voices shouted from the square. He had obviously been spotted by some of the enemy. The Canadian had to move, though he wasn't sure there was anywhere to go. Manning headed toward the wall because there seemed to be no other option.

The edge of the roof was about eight feet from the wall surrounding the compound. Manning did not hesitate. He ran to the lip of the roof and leaped for the wall. The FAL dangled from his arm by the sling and the field radio on his back felt as if it might wrench his spine as he dived for the wall. Manning's hands lashed out at the top of the stone barrier. His palms slapped down on the hard surface, and his fingers clawed for a handhold.

Manning gripped the top of the wall. His boots hit the stone side of the wall and pushed. He hauled himself over the top and swung his body to the other side. He dangled from the wall, his body suspended full length, hanging from fully extended arms. When a bullet chipped the stone an inch from his fingers, he gasped with surprise and alarm and let go of the wall.

The Phoenix commando dropped to the ground outside the fortress wall. Because he had hung at full length by his hands, the distance to the ground was only six or seven feet. The impact traveled up through his feet and jarred his legs and groin. The Canadian sucked in a short mouthful of air through clenched teeth and turned away from the wall.

The forest surrounded Skull's base. He ran for the trees and heard a babble of shouts rising from within the wall. Major Yasnev snarled an obscenity in Russian as he saw Manning dash to the forest. The GRU double agent had emerged from the trapdoor to the roof and from that vantage point watched the fugitive escape. He aimed his AK-47 at the fleeing figure and opened fire. Manning darted into the tree line and Yasnev saw bark splinter from the trunk of an oak as the Kalashnikov rounds struck the tree instead of the Canadian.

"He took off into the forest!" Yasnev shouted to the men in the square below. "The Yankee bastard has a rifle and one of the radios!"

Colonel Skull towered in the center of the square amid the confusion, pale and immobile. His face was tense, the muscles taut across his jaw. Skull turned toward his terrorist mercenaries in the motor pool. Fifty men, nearly all of the remaining forces, stood before their leader. The sunlight reflected on the polished bill of his black uniform cap and the dark glasses that protected his eyes from the merciless brightness of daylight.

"What the hell are you idiots waiting for?" he snapped. "Find him! He's only one man, damn it! Hunt him down and shoot on sight! Don't come back until you can bring me his corpse or what's left of it!"

23

The tall, athletic stranger raised his bushy blond eyebrows as Pierre Bertin met him at the door to the conference room inside Sûreté headquarters. The Frenchman frowned as he glanced at the badge clipped to the man's suit jacket. The newcomer glanced beyond Bertin and saw Yakov Katzenelenbogen in the room. He slipped past Bertin and entered. The Sûreté agent protested, but the man had already moved inside and embraced Katz like a long-lost brother.

"Gray!" he exclaimed, then spoke to him in enthusiastic Russian.

"I'm fine, Viktor," Katz replied in English, a bit embarrassed by the informal greeting. "I trust things have gone well for you?"

"*Da,*" the other man replied, breaking the embrace. "Yes, I am a colonel now, although I cannot tell you what department I'm with. KGB must keep some secrets, you know."

"Gentlemen," Katz announced, "This is Colonel Alekseyev of the Union of Soviet Socialist Republics."

"I'll be damned," Scott Bernelli whispered with astonishment as he stared at the KGB field officer. "You guys are really friends?"

"Oh, yes," Alekseyev replied with an amused smile. "Gray and his team worked with me fairly recently. It is top-secret, of course, but I can tell you it concerned the best interest of both the United States and the Soviet Union. I realize we are on opposite sides, but we had a truce of sorts at the time. KGB and Gray's commando unit worked together for a common goal. It was quite a mission. Was it not, Gray?"

"It was indeed," Katz agreed. "By the way, I'm calling myself Kenver. Please try to remember. We don't want to confuse these other fellows any more than they already are."

"I am more disturbed by this flagrant disregard for security than confused by the presence of a Soviet spy," Bertin declared, shaking his head. "I can't believe you authorized a high-ranking KGB agent to enter Sûreté..."

"The secretary-general of the Soviet Union has personally ordered me here," Alekseyev stated. "Not as an enemy of your country, but as a friend who wants to help you locate the President of the United States, the terrorists who kidnapped him and the alleged nuclear weapon they have in their possession. Gray... Kenver can tell you I am an honorable man."

"I trust Viktor as much as I could ever trust anyone in the KGB," Katz commented. "Which might not be saying much, but under the circumstances, KGB wants this matter settled as much as we do. If the President isn't found alive and well, a large portion of the West will always believe the Soviet Union was responsible for the kidnapping and the bloodshed and terrorism connected with it. With *glasnost* in progress, at least for now, the U.S.S.R. wants to maintain friendly relations and certainly doesn't want to be blamed for something it did not do."

"I would not have described it quite that way," the Russian said with a shrug. "Still, that is fairly accurate. I've often wondered if the mission we did together in the past was the secret foundation of *glasnost*. Remember that missile reduction was part of what both our governments promised if both sides cooperated on that little covert operation?"

"I've wondered about that, too," Katz admitted. "But I guess we'll never know for sure. I asked the premier to try to send you to Paris, Viktor. So far KGB hasn't been much help."

"Please," Alekseyev groaned. "I know Comrade Vashnov caused trouble for you. You must also know that I want only to help. Tomorrow we may have to kill each other, my friend. Today we are allies. It is a strange world, is it not?"

"Very," Katz agreed. "Can you help us, Viktor?"

"I am not certain," the KGB agent admitted. "However, one of our listening posts detected a strange signal in the northern

Metropolitan Department of Marne. A brief radio message that said 'Rise, Phoenix' in French, German and English. We have no idea what it means, but our Department Eleven personnel recorded it in case it was a covert message.''

"This may be very important, Viktor," Katz replied, anticipation in his voice. "Was the KGB able to track the source of the radio signal?"

"Of course we have some very fine equipment for that," Alekseyev answered. "Since it was in three different languages, I found the message of particular interest and asked our people to trace it. The frequency seemed to be coming from a forest area in Marne. One of our agents in place, who has been stationed in France for several years, believes it may be coming from some old ruins. A fortress that was probably built four hundred years ago during the Thirty Years' War. KGB had some interest in it as a possible safehouse at one time because it is a neglected site, largely ignored and seldom visited."

"My God," Bernelli said tensely. "Do you think this could be it, Kenver?"

Suddenly, the door burst open to slam into Bertin with such force it nearly bowled the Frenchman over. Calvin James and David McCarter charged into the conference room. The pair were excited and barely noticed Bertin curse as he rubbed his bruised arm.

"Sorry, mate," McCarter said, "but you shouldn't stand so close to the bloody door."

"I was just about to lock it," the Frenchman muttered. "And I wish I had."

"Man, we got some news....'' James began. He stopped in midsentence and stared at Alekseyev. "Viktor! Nice seeing you, man. Anyway, a ham radio operator picked up a signal from somewhere in Marne."

"Bit of freak luck," McCarter added. "The radio buff thought this was strange, because it was just two words repeated in English, as well as French, so he contacted a police department and told them about the message."

"Rise, Phoenix?" Katz inquired.

"How?" James knitted his brow, but then turned toward Alekseyev. "Don't tell me the ears of the KGB are everywhere, huh?"

"Perhaps this will make up for what Vashnov did," the Russian colonel said with a shrug.

"I'm not mad at Vashnov anymore," the black man assured him. "Not since I cut him up a little when he crowded us too much here in Paris. Got nothing against you, Viktor, but I'm still not going to put an 'I love the KGB' bumper sticker on my car."

"I don't care how we got the information," McCarter stated. "CIA, KGB or a bleeding ouija board. The French coppers couldn't get a trace on the radio signal. Were your people any luckier?"

"It's almost pinpointed," Katz supplied the answer. "KGB even suspects a certain old fortress as the point of origin. That might be where Skull is located."

"Yeah." James grinned. "But Skull wouldn't have sent that message. It means Gary...our partner is still alive."

"He might not be if we don't get moving," McCarter commented. "Where's Sanchez?"

"You mean Santos?" Bernelli asked.

"Hell, it's not his real name either way," the Briton growled. "You know who I mean. Where the devil is he?"

"At the American embassy checking with the NSA personnel stationed there," Katz answered. "Bernelli, contact Santos and tell him to bring Collins and Jarred with their fancy computer set and heat detectors."

"Not the two NSA eggheads again," McCarter snorted, rolling his eyes toward the ceiling.

"They may have less personality than a department store mannequin, but they're good with those machines," Katz insisted. "They did fine in Belgium and we can use them now. They're not battlefield material, but we won't use them for combat. Santos and the computer chaps can probably get to the airfield ahead of us. Tell them to meet us there, Scott."

"I'll call Major Mazarin and tell him to get his Parachute Legionnaires ready," Bertin announced as he reached for a telephone. "They are probably as eager as you to go into combat against the terrorists. They are all a little crazy. Especially Mazarin himself. He was formerly one of the commanding officers of the foreign legion stationed in Corsica. I am certain you are familiar with their reputation.''

''The French foreign legion is legendary,'' Katz confirmed. ''I don't care if Mazarin has to be put in a straitjacket between missions as long as he does his job. We'd better be on our way.'' Katz turned to the KGB officer next. ''Viktor do you have a detailed map of the Marne Department with the scan readings of the radio signals?''

''Naturally,'' the KGB agent confirmed. ''If you can supply me with appropriate clothing and weapons, I'll be happy to assist. I can handle myself in a firefight.''

''I know, Viktor,'' Katz replied, ''but you don't have authorization from Moscow to charge off into battle, and I'm a little reluctant to take you. If anything goes wrong, the KGB could wind up being blamed because you participated. If you get killed, the Kremlin might blame us—or at least the CIA and Sûreté—for purposely putting you in danger. We're all bending a lot of rules as it is. Probably best if you sit this one out.''

''A shame,'' Alekseyev said with a sigh. ''Perhaps next time. I just hope we never wind up on opposite sides in combat. You take care.''

''Until we meet again,'' Katz said with a nod.

''I don't suppose you'd agree to let me join you,'' Scott Bernelli asked hopefully. ''I've been part of this from the beginning and I'd like to see it through to the end.''

''Sorry, Scott,'' the Phoenix Force commander told him. ''You're more use to us back here than in the front lines.''

''Well, I got off on the wrong foot with you guys...'' the young CIA agent said, stumbling on his attempt to apologize.

''Forget it,'' James said with a shrug. ''You've done okay, so don't worry about it.''

''Come on, come on,'' McCarter said impatiently. ''We got to do some hunting down.''

''Yes,'' Katz agreed with a solemn nod. ''Let's finish it.''

24

The jeep rolled across the uneven ground, forced to maneuver cautiously between the thick trunks of oak and pine trees. A terrorist mercenary stood in the back seat, elbows braced on the roll bar as he peered through a pair of binoculars. An H&K machine gun was mounted to the bar, an ammo belt attached to the chamber.

Another terrorist sat next to the driver, cradling an automatic rifle in his lap. The man behind the wheel tried to concentrate on driving, aware that the other two would search the forest for the armed fugitive. Two dozen other troops were also hunting for the escapee, six in jeeps and the others combing the forest on foot. Yet the driver could not resist glancing about fearfully from time to time, concerned that the resourceful lone opponent might be lurking behind the next tree or bush and take them by surprise.

The birds were silent. Their songs ceased as the terrorists drew closer. Only a few creatures moved furtively among the branches. But the hunters of human game paid little attention to the small creatures, except for one tense gunman who nearly opened fire when he saw a squirrel jump from one branch to another. The terrorist uttered a nervous chuckle and continued to scan the forest.

Suddenly, the man stationed at the machine gun mounted on the roll bar groaned when a projectile slammed into his chest with a solid thud. The report of the single rifle shot barked from a cluster of bushes ahead of the search party. The binoculars fell from the terrorist's fingers and landed in the lap of the man beside the driver. He glanced up at the face of the lifeless gunman, who was draped across the bar. Blood seeped from the dead man's punctured heart.

Another shot erupted, and a bullet punched through glass in the windshield. The terrorist next to the driver recoiled against the backrest of his seat. The driver stared at his comrade's face, his eyes wide with horror. A 7.62 mm slug had smashed into the man's left eyebrow. The eye socket had cracked and the orb popped from the bloodied cavity, suspended by the thick cord of the optic nerve. The bullet had tunneled into the terrorist's brain and split open the top of his skull. The black beret atop his head was stained crimson.

The driver cried out in terror and revulsion. He ducked low behind the steering wheel, fearful he would be the next target of the unseen marksman. The jeep rolled forward and crunched against the trunk of a large oak. It came to an abrupt hált, and the vehicle shivered from impact. The driver was seized by violent tremors, but he was relieved to still be alive.

A Swedish terrorist on foot pointed his Valmet rifle at the bushes. "Over there!" he shouted.

An Iranian gunman swung his AK-47 toward the target as the Swede opened fire. The Valmet and the Kalashnikov blasted full auto rounds into the bushes. There was a general confused shouted exchange among the terrorists and some of them ran toward the gunfire to assist their comrades.

The Swedish and Iranian gunmen advanced slowly, their weapons still trained on the bush. They had not seen or heard anything to suggest they had hit anyone hidden behind the bushes, but no shots had been fired at them, either. The pair moved closer, using the trees for cover as they advanced. They avoided the jeep, which seemed to be the favored target of their unseen opponent.

A slight movement suddenly caught the attention of the Swede. He turned toward a sturdy oak with a thick trunk quite some distance from the bushes. An arm became visible in a blur of motion accompanied by a whipping sound. The Swedish gunman glimpsed an object hurtling toward him. He instinctively ducked, but he was not the intended target. A baseball-size rock slammed into the Iranian gunman. The man's head was jarred violently by the unexpected blow, and his feet shot out from under him. The Iranian killer hit the ground, blood leaking from his red-dyed turban.

The Swedish triggerman dropped to one knee and brought his Valmet around to track the enemy when he appeared. Manning suddenly showed himself around the trunk, a Smith & Wesson revolver in his fist. The Canadian triggered his handgun before the terrorist could fire his weapon. Two .38-caliber slugs plowed into the chest of the startled gunman. The Swede triggered his Valmet as he felt the slugs crash through his breastbone and ribs. The automatic rifle blasted a trio of rounds into the tree, but Manning had already ducked behind the trunk. The terrorist's heart stopped, pierced by bone fragments. He tasted the bitterness of failure before he tumbled to the ground and died.

Gary Manning slid the .38 into the belt holster and gathered up the rifle sling he had removed from his FAL. He held the ends of the shoulder strap in one fist and placed a rock in the center. Manning swung the improvised sling and whirled it like a propeller. He spotted another terrorist headed toward the jeep.

Manning lashed out with the sling and released one end. The rock catapulted forward. It rocketed toward the startled gunman. The terrorist tried to duck, but the attack was too sudden, too unexpected. The rock struck him in the chest. The impact knocked the man off his feet and dropped him, badly winded on his back.

Another member of Skull's private army rushed toward his fallen comrade. The man was at a loss to understand what had happened. He had heard no gunshot, seen no muzzle-flash of a weapon and there was no arrow, spear or other projectile sticking from the flesh of the fallen man. The terrorist did not pay much attention to the eight-ounce stone next to the dazed man.

Manning decided the terrorist was not close enough to effectively take him out with the sling or the revolver. That was why he had hit the other opponent in the torso instead of the head. Too far for an accurate throw, even with the sling. He draped the strap over his shoulder and raised his rifle. The Canadian marksman lined up the sights and triggered the FAL. He fired one shot. The weapon was on semiauto. Faced with so many opponents, he needed to conserve ammo and did not want to resort to full-auto unless necessary.

One shot took care of the terrorist who had stepped beside the dazed fellow on the ground. The 7.62 mm slug hit him above the left ear. The man's skull burst and his corpse fell across the body of the stunned terrorist. Manning was tempted to rush forward to collect more arms and ammunition from his vanquished opponents, but he realized other pursuers would arrive any second. He headed deeper into the forest and hoped his tactics would stall them for a few moments. Manning needed every microsecond he could get. His life and the lives of many others depended on it.

MAJOR YASNEV RODE in a jeep, AK-47 in one hand and a two-way radio in the other. He shook his head with disgust and uttered a string of obscenities as his vehicle approached the scene of the brief battle. A single glance told him at least four of his people had been killed or seriously injured. Two others appeared to be close to nervous breakdowns and a jeep had been disabled, its nose jammed against a tree. Yasnev noticed that the other terrorists seemed more apprehensive as they moved into the woods. The fugitive had gotten the better of the hunting party, and he was still at large.

"Stop the car!" Yasnev told his driver. "The jeep is useless among the trees."

The vehicle came to a halt and Yasnev stepped from it. He gestured to a group of terrorist mercs who had recently arrived at the scene. They all seemed a bit rattled, their behavior disgusting. Damn cowards, he thought. They were very brave against unarmed opponents or when they had an overwhelming advantage in numbers and firepower. Now one man had outtricked and generally bested some overconfident dolts, and the morale of the rest seemed about to fall apart.

The survivors of the encounter told the others what had happened. They both claimed the fugitive had struck from nowhere and disappeared like some sort of supernatural demon. Yasnev wanted to cut out their stupid flapping tongues. Manning had probably spared them in the hope they would tell such tales to the rest. Psychological warfare combined with hit-and-run tactics. Very old tactics, and still effective.

"Move that jeep!" the Russian ordered. "The radiator may have been damaged, but it was not traveling fast enough to be wrecked when it struck the tree. It should still run."

"What shall we do then?" a flunky inquired as he climbed behind the wheel. The man looked at the two corpses in the jeep and shivered.

"Get those bodies out of there and don't be so damn squeamish!" Yasnev snapped. "You're supposed to be soldiers, but you act more like a gathering of old women. Take both jeeps, circle around the forest and make certain the bastard doesn't reach the road."

"The American is a devil in human form," a Syrian gunman said, shaking his head with despair. "He has already killed half a dozen of our comrades. Perhaps Allah favors his cause more than ours—"

"Perhaps you would like me to send you to your Islamic God, you ignorant Arab savage!" Yasnev hissed. "We're hunting a man. He's clever, he's resourceful and he's well trained, but he's just a man. I myself gave him more than one sound beating, and lightning didn't streak down from the sky to strike me dead for it. Now, gather up the weapons of the dead. Don't leave anything lying about that he might use against us."

Yasnev raised the walkie-talkie and switched it on. A voice spoke from the radio before he could transmit.

"Rise, Phoenix," the fugitive's voice said. It repeated the message in French and German. "Rise, Phoenix."

"Damnation!" the Russian growled. "The son of a Yankee whore is using the field radio to try to send some sort of code signal. He probably used the main radio back at the fort before he smashed the other field sets and stole the one he has with him."

"Every major intelligence network with a listening station in Europe is probably scanning every broadcast on every radio frequency with a range over twenty kilometers," a Greek terrorist said grimly. "If they haven't already tracked the message to this general area, they soon will if that American keeps sending it."

"All the more reason to find him," Yasnev declared.

"Perhaps we should go back and tell the Colonel," the Syrian suggested.

"Skull has the main radio," the Greek reminded him. "The radio has been monitored nonstop since this mission began. Skull has certainly been told of this message already. He knows what it means, as well as we do."

"Then we should leave here immediately!" a French terrorist exclaimed. "The devil with this American. Let's get out of here before the police, the military and God knows what else swoop down on us!"

"No!" Yasnev insisted. "We find the pig and we kill him before we go back. As for leaving, that is for the colonel to decide. If we stop the American now, there may still be a chance the enemy have not determined the site of our base. But if they have, then it is probably already too late to run."

"Then Skull will detonate the plutonium bomb?" the Greek asked, a slight tremor in his voice.

"None of us would survive if the enemy attacks with full military strength," Yasnev said with a shrug. "Believe me, no one wants any of us to stand trial. They'd be afraid to simply imprison us. Even if they did decide to put us in maximum security, we would never get out. Probably would not survive the first year. Execution, death in a locked cell or a quick flash of light and oblivion. What difference does it make?"

"Not much difference to us," the Frenchman had to admit. "But it will certainly matter to all the other people who will die, as well."

"I know," Yasnev said with a sneering smile. "If it is to be the end of my world, then let it be the end for as many others as possible as well."

THROUGH THE COURSE of the next few hours, the search continued. Manning set a few booby traps and demolished a number of the enemy with an improvised grenade fabricated partly from the innards of the radio. But he could hold out for only so long, he knew. The hunters were getting closer, and their

circle was slowly shrinking in around him. Manning headed for
some thick underbrush and burrowed into the cover of dense
foliage after reloading his FAL with the last magazine in his
possession.

Suddenly, a loud roar of great blades cutting air erupted
somewhere in the distance. The roar of engines accompanied
the chopping sound as the noise drew closer. Manning recognized the familiar sound of helicopters. He tried to peer
through the ceiling of leaves and branches, but the cover was
too dense and he saw little except the vague form of a helicopter above the treetops.

Did it mean his message had been received by friendly forces?
Perhaps the other members of Phoenix Force themselves had
learned of it and come to his assistance. Manning did not let his
hopes get too high. The aircraft might be taking part in regular military maneuvers. Maybe it was merely some type of forest ranger patrol. Reports of gunshots might have reached local
authorities. If the choppers were loaded with policemen prepared to take on a few poachers, the terrorists would cut
through them as if they were made of soggy cabbage.

Maybe the cavalry had arrived, but maybe not. Manning
would have to fend for himself until he knew for sure. He almost hoped the helicopters were not comrades in search of
Colonel Skull's headquarters. The terrorists still had the plutonium device. Having met Skull, Manning had no doubt that
Skull would use the nuclear weapon if his insane mission
seemed doomed to fail.

"I hate it when I feel I ought to start praying," Manning
whispered to himself so softly that the sound did not get past
his clenched teeth. "But I'm not sure what I should be praying
for."

MAJOR YASNEV ALSO HEARD the helicopters and gazed up at
the sky as the whirlybirds approached. The Russian recognized the aircraft as American-made Bell gunships. Two choppers in view and probably more on the way. Yasnev took the
walkie-talkie from his belt and switched it on. The radio whistled harshly, a high-pitched shriek that made Yasnev recoil. The
noise made his ear ache. He pressed the transmit button.

"Unit One to Headquarters!" he nearly shouted into the walkie-talkie. "Come in, Headquarters!"

The whistling continued without regard for his efforts. The Russian uttered a short oath and angrily threw the radio to the ground. Two fellow terrorists were startled by the GRU officer's behavior. They stared down at the shattered bits of plastic and metal that had formerly been the walkie-talkie.

"What is wrong, Major?" a confused Turkish trooper asked. He did not like Russians in general and Yasnev in particular, whom he regarded as a brute unfit to command a flock of diseased sheep, let alone men.

"Everything is wrong, you idiot," Yasnev replied curtly. "We haven't found the American, but we've discovered the bodies of several of our comrades, killed by the fiend. Now, these damned helicopters have appeared. Military gunships, in case your inept education and limited experience doesn't include aircraft. Those helicopters are almost certainly armed and probably contain dozens of enemy troops. As if that isn't bad enough, the damn radio doesn't work, either."

"It sure ain't gonna work now that you broke it," a tall black terrorist, originally from Jamaica, commented.

"Didn't you hear that noise?" Yasnev demanded. "That was some sort of radio-jamming that overrides wavelengths. Probably a type of microwave transmitted across this area by the helicopters."

"They cut off our communications," the Turk said grimly. "We cannot warn Colonel Skull or seek his help."

"Skull will see the helicopters before they can reach the fortress," Yasnev replied. "As for his helping us ... we'll have to help ourselves for now...."

As he cast a glowering glance at his companions, the Russian suddenly spotted Gary Manning among the dense bushes. He swung his AK-47 toward the Canadian's position and opened fire. However, Manning had seen Yasnev as well, and already ducked for cover behind a tree trunk. Yasnev spit out an angry expression in his native tongue, aware that he had missed his target.

"Pin him down, mon!" the Jamaican declared as he took a grenade from his belt. "If I get close enough to lob this egg then those trees ain't gonna be enough protection for him!"

"All right," Yasnev agreed. "We'll cover you."

Manning's FAL snarled. Bullets whizzed through the air near the three terrorists. The Turk cried out as a slug tore through his right thigh. Yasnev darted behind the trunk of an oak and stayed low as projectiles hammered his cover.

The Jamaican had thrown himself to the ground and stayed on his belly, afraid he would catch a bullet if he raised his head. The Turkish terrorist crawled to the flimsy shelter of some bushes. Blood poured from the wound in his leg, but he still held his G-3 assault rifle. The Turk and Yasnev opened fire simultaneously. Twin streams of rapid-fire rounds shredded the foliage where Manning was stationed. The Jamaican yanked the pin from his grenade and rolled on his side to hurl the explosive at their elusive opponent.

The grenade landed far short of its target. It exploded more than thirty feet from Manning's position. He ducked his head and leaned against the tree trunk as clods of earth pelted the area. He realized the attempt to take him out with the grenade had failed because he was out of range for the hand-launched minibomb.

Manning still had one F-1 blaster left, but he was faced with the same problem as his opponents. The Canadian touched the sling draped over a shoulder. An idea struck like a lightning bolt inside his head. He gripped the ends of the sling in one hand and placed the Russian hand grenade in the center. He pulled the pin.

He spun the sling quickly, aware that he had scant seconds to carry out the plan or he would blow himself to bits. Enemy bullets thrashed the foliage surrounding him, but Manning leaned forward and swung his arm through an opening. The sling snapped forward and the grenade rocketed toward the enemies' position.

The grenade flew faster and farther than if it had been thrown by hand. It sailed over the terrorists' heads and exploded above them. The blast ripped the Turk apart with a shower of shrapnel. Yasnev was bowled over by the explosion and tumbled down a grassy knoll, his AK-47 nowhere in sight. The Jamaican screamed as shards of metal and splintered wood from a nearby tree pierced his buttocks and lower back.

"Oh, hell!" he bellowed and raised a Sten gun with both hands. "I kill you, mon!"

Manning fired his FAL and shot the Jamaican in the head with a 3-round burst. He stepped forward, rifle in hand. The Jamaican and the Turk were obviously dead. Yasnev was on his hands and knees. The Russian shook his head and started to rise. Manning jogged closer and pointed his FAL at the major.

"I owe you a few lumps, Yasnev," Manning announced as he approached. "It won't take much to convince me to kill you."

"Yankee pig," the Russian spit, but he raised his hands.

"I'm Canadian," Manning informed him. The Phoenix pro stood six feet from Yasnev and aimed the FAL at his opponent's chest. "Slowly, use one hand to unbuckle the gun belt."

Yasnev lowered a hand to the buckle. His Makarov pistol was on his hip in a button-flap holster. The Russian realized an attempt to reach for the handgun would be fatal. He pulled open his belt buckle and slipped off the belt. He extended his arm, the belt in his fist.

"Put it down," Manning ordered.

Yasnev suddenly slashed the belt across Manning's rifle. The holstered Makarov struck the FAL barrel and knocked it away from the Russian. The rifle spit out a 3-round burst, but missed Yasnev by almost a foot. The major charged forward and quickly chopped a forearm across Manning's wrists. The FAL fell from the Canadian's grasp.

Manning whipped a knee into Yasnev's abdomen. The big Russian groaned from the blow, but retaliated with a short, hard punch to Manning's jaw. The Phoenix fighter was dazed by the impact, and Yasnev grabbed his shirtfront and sleeve. He turned sharply and hurled Manning over his hip in an adroit judo throw.

The Canadian grabbed Yasnev's shirt as he fell to the ground. The landing jarred Manning's spine, but he held on to Yasnev and yanked his opponent down with him. Yasnev had to bend over forcibly. Manning rolled onto his shoulders, bent a knee and slammed it into the side of Yasnev's startled face. The Russian groaned and tumbled sideways from the blow. Manning rolled away from his opponent and jumped to his feet.

Yasnev also rose quickly, his fists raised as he squared off with the Canadian commando. Manning waited for his opponent to make the next move. Yasnev did not disappoint him. The Russian feinted a left jab and suddenly swung a kick toward Manning's groin. The Phoenix crusader shifted a leg and blocked the boot with a thigh muscle. Yasnev's left jabbed a hard blow to Manning's breastbone, and the side of Yasnev's hand chopped the Canadian across the collarbone.

Manning doubled over from the karate chop and Yasnev tried to drive a knee into his opponent's face. Manning jammed both palms into Yasnev's knee to block the attack and rammed his shoulder into the Russian's belly. Yasnev gasped breathlessly, and Manning suddenly thrust both arms between the major's legs.

The Canadian straightened his back and heaved Yasnev off his feet. The Russian flipped head over heels and crashed to the ground hard. Just as he rolled over and started to rise, Manning stepped forward and lashed out a boot. The heel slammed into Yasnev's mouth, splitting a lip and breaking two front teeth. The Russian collapsed on his belly, stunned by the hard kick.

Manning straddled his dazed opponent and sat down on the small of Yasnev's back. He grabbed the Russian's head and yanked hard. Yasnev struggled vainly as Manning slipped his fingers under the major's jaw. Yasnev clawed at Manning's hands, trying to break the grip. Gary Manning hauled back with all his might. Yasnev's upper torso bent back in a sudden bow, his lower spine held down by Manning's weight. Bone cracked at the lumbar vertebrae. Major Yasnev uttered a feeble moan and his body went limp. Manning had broken his back.

The Canadian warrior rose from the still body of Major Yasnev. He gasped to catch his breath and walked unsteadily to his fallen FAL. Automatic fire erupted somewhere nearby. The roar of the helicopter rotor blades sounded closer, as well.

Manning gathered up his rifle as two figures approached from the east.

"Gary!" Calvin James exclaimed. "God, I knew you were still alive! You just had to be, man!"

Manning lowered his rifle as the black commando and David McCarter approached. Both wore green-and-brown camouflage-print uniforms. James carried an M-16 rifle and the Briton held the Barnett Commando crossbow in his hands with the KG-99 hung from a shoulder strap by his right hip. They also had an assortment of grenades, ammo pouches, pistols in shoulder leather and other gear. At that moment, Gary Manning thought they were goddamn beautiful.

"Well, you've been busy, mate," McCarter commented, glancing at the corpses nearby. "Came across a bit more of your handiwork farther back. Hell of a way to mark your trail."

"Are the others here?" Manning asked. "Yakov and Rafael?"

"Yeah," James confirmed. "They're helping some French paratroopers dust a few terrorists riding around in jeeps. I think there are more running around in the woods, but they aren't goin' anywhere. We've got a heat sensor set up that will hunt 'em down no matter where they hide."

"Skull and the rest of his men are in an old fort about four kilometers from here," Manning said quickly. "He still has the President and a German diplomat named Weiss. He still has the plutonium bomb, too. I don't know how we can get to him before he uses it . . . ?"

"There's no time to waste talking about this," McCarter declared. "Come on. Let's get back to the others at the chopper and you can fill us in along the way."

"It might be the last story you ever get to hear," Manning remarked as he followed his partners through the forest.

25

Colonel Skull stood at the entrance to his temporary head-quarters building. The SIG MP-310 submachine gun hung from a strap across his shoulder. He gazed up at the sky, the dark glasses concealing whatever emotion might have been displayed by his pink-red eyes. A helicopter circled the compound. It remained more than a mile from the fort, beyond effective range of conventional aircraft weapons. Skull knew the gunship was not alone. At least two more roamed the afternoon sky.

"This is the end, Major," he said softly, speaking to Major Hee. The Korean stood beside his commander, silent and motionless as a stone figure. "The plan did not work, and now there is only one course of action left."

"Yes, Colonel," Hee replied with a solemn nod.

The Korean glanced down at the radio transmitter in Skull's hand.

"It was a high-risk plan, of course," Skull continued, his thumb inching toward the red button of the remote unit. "I see now some mistakes I made. Involved too many people, leaving a lot of room for error and too many enemies to deal with."

"Life itself is a gamble," Hee said with a slight movement of his lips that might have been a smile. "It was a good gamble, Colonel. You almost won."

"Perhaps," the terrorist leader said with a shrug. "No one will really win. I suppose a stalemate is better than losing."

"Men are remembered as much for what they try to do as for what they actually accomplish," Hee stated. "Most never attempt the big gambles so they never lose or win. Whatever judgment we may face—by history or by whatever gods may run the universe—none can fault us because we did not try.''

"You talk about this as if it was a noble undertaking," Skull said with a slight laugh. "Well, you've been a good aide and second in command, Major. Thank you for that."

"I've no complaints, sir," the Korean assured him. "Should I tell the men?"

"That they're about to be vaporized by a nuclear explosion?" Skull shook his head. "Why upset them? Not all of them have your fatalism and belief in the ultimate justice of karma. Nor do they have my willingness to end the constant disappointment and disillusionment of life. It's a damn cheat. Maybe death will be more honest. However, the others will probably be frightened and alarmed."

"You're right," Hee agreed. "There is no reason to tell them."

"That's it then," Skull stated, his thumb on the button.

"Goodbye, Colonel," Hee said and closed his eyes. He bowed his head and waited for the flash of all-consuming heat before facing the ultimate mystery of death.

"Goodbye," Skull answered and pressed the button.

Nothing happened.

Skull stiffened and pressed the button again. Still nothing. Hee opened his eyes and looked up at Skull with surprise. The terrorist leader glared at the remote unit in his hand, and muscles in his jaws constricted from anger.

"This doesn't work," Skull hissed as he dashed the radio transmitter to the ground. "Whatever they're using to jam radio communications is also blocking the radio signal from the remote. Clever bastards, but not clever enough. We'll have to detonate it manually."

"Very well," Hee replied with a nod, although he did not seem very pleased about that necessity. "I'll take care of it, Colonel."

"We'll also have to—"

Skull's statement was cut off by a sudden tidal wave of machine gun rounds. Bullets raked the outer walls of the fortress. A sentry at the east wing twitched and staggered from the wall, his chest and abdomen riddled with bloodied holes. The man fell from his station as the machine gun continued to chatter out murderous sprays of high-velocity slugs.

The helicopters had suddenly opened fire, hammering the fortress with tremendous firepower. The immediate purpose, though, was to disorient the terrorists and keep them pinned down rather than kill them. Two jeeps, confiscated from the terrorists stationed in the forest, raced to the walls of the enemy stronghold. David McCarter drove one vehicle with Katz and Encizo for passengers. A French parachute legionnaire handled the steering wheel of the second jeep. Calvin James and Manning rode with the paratrooper.

Skull's guards at the wall and entrance had already ducked for cover from the fury of the gunship machine guns. The copters had to cease fire when the jeeps reached the walls to avoid blasting the Phoenix Force commandos by accident. Manning directed the paratrooper to pull up to the east wall. The French soldier stopped the jeep and Manning and James jumped out.

The Canadian demolitions expert carried a canvas case over one shoulder and an FAL rifle over the other. He also carried a French MAB 9 mm pistol in shoulder leather. Manning glanced up at the wall and recalled the positions of buildings inside Skull's fortress. It was almost impossible to judge the exact location of the cell block from the outside. He had little time and had to rely on instinct as much as memory. The Canadian opened the canvas container and removed a disk-shaped object that was no larger than an ashtray.

Manning placed it against the wall and turned the dial attached to the plastic circlet. He motioned for the others to get down and dashed for cover behind the jeep. The C-4 plastic explosives roared a half second later. James raised his head first and smiled at the large hole blasted through the wall. It was roughly six feet high and four feet wide. A perfect porthole into Skull's compound.

"You're a goddamn genius with explosives, man," James commented, impressed by his partner's expertise.

"I just hope I made the door in the right place," Manning replied.

James headed for the gap in the wall, his M-16 at port arms. The Canadian charged after him. James cautiously poked his head around the improvised doorway. The hole led directly to a corridor inside the compound. Several doors lined the walls of the hallway. James noticed the doors were made of thick metal and equipped with heavy bolts, as well as locks. He also saw two figures dressed in fatigue uniforms and black caps with the sinister skull emblem. The terrorists were doubled up in the corridor, stunned by the explosion. They coughed and half choked on rock dust but both had managed to hold on to their weapons.

The black warrior from Chicago almost opened fire on the guards, but he was reluctant to shoot inside the corridor. The chance of ricochet rounds was too great. It was unlikely a ricochet might hit one of the hostages because it appeared to James that the VIP captives were still in their cells. But it was a chance he was unwilling to take.

James ran into the corridor and rushed the two dazed opponents. He slashed the barrel of his rifle across the wrist of the closest terrorist and chopped a Beretta M-12 subgun from the man's grasp. The other terrorist gunman uttered a word of surprise or rage in a language James did not recognize. The man started to swing his Star PD autoloader at the black commando, but James managed to strike out first with the buttstock of his M-16. The hard plastic edge stamped into the thug's forearm. The terrorist's hand popped open and the .45 pistol fell from the triggerman's quivering fingers.

The first opponent lashed a fist at James's face. The Phoenix champ raised his M-16 like a steel bar and blocked the punch. The terrorist's forearm bounced painfully from the rifle frame. James drove a knee into the opponent's lower abdomen and followed with a short butt stroke across the startled face.

The second opponent lunged for James, who caught the movement from the corner of an eye and unleashed a high side kick. The bottom of his boot smashed into the terrorist's face. His nose mashed into a broken, bleeding pulp, the man was flung against a wall. James thrust the buttstock of the M-16 under the man's sternum. The terrorist groaned as if he might throw up, then he slumped unconscious to the floor.

Hands seized James from behind. The first opponent still had some fight left. He grabbed the barrel and stock of James's M-16 and forced it against the black man's chest, then attempted to bring the frame up under James's chin. If he could yank the rifle across the commando's throat, he could easily throttle the American warrior.

James did not intent to cooperate. He pulled down on the rifle to keep the weapon at bay and snapped a back kick between his opponent's legs. The back of James's heel crashed into the terrorist's testicles. A choked gasp was the response, and James thrust both arms overhead, the M-16 still in his grasp. But despite his pain, the terrorist also held on to the rifle with extended arms. The Phoenix fighter suddenly dropped to one knee, making the enemy hurtle forward and sail over James's bowed head to crash-land on the hard stone floor. His skull kissed the pavement, and the man moaned softly before he passed out.

"I hope you're on our side," a voice remarked, a voice that was familiar to James, who had heard it in speeches on numerous television broadcasts.

He turned toward one of the cells and saw the face of the President of the United States behind the bars of the porthole. James sighed with relief. The man from the Oval Office was still alive. Just then Gary Manning came up to James, and the President smiled as he saw the Canadian's face.

"You did it," he said with a nod.

"A lot of other people helped, Mr. President," Manning replied as he opened his canvas case. "Stand back from the door. I'm going to blast the lock."

"Thank God!" Klaus Weiss exclaimed from the next cell. "We're rescued! At last, we are saved!"

"Not yet, fella," James muttered. He moved toward the end of the corridor to cover the door there, and it was none too soon. Several terrorists had heard the explosion that had blasted an opening in the wall to the cell block. Three men rushed to join the two sentries stationed by the entrance of the

prison. The guards waited until reinforcements arrived before
they opened the iron door to the cell block.

Calvin James was waiting in the corridor. He fired a 3-round
burst. One opponent fell backward, all three M-16 slugs in his
chest. The others jumped back from the doorway. James fired
another trio of 5.56 mm rounds at the threshold. The door was
hastily slammed shut.

Manning stepped away from the President's cell. The result
of his handiwork, a small glob of plastic explosive that was
mixed with a buffer gel, was jammed into the lock. The pencil
detonator in the glob burst, and the compound exploded. The
blast was little louder than a firecracker, but the explosion tore
the lock apart. A split second later another explosion blew the
lock to Weiss's cell door.

"Okay!" Manning exclaimed as the doors to the cells swung
open. "Let's get out of here!"

Klaus Weiss emerged from his cell, glanced about and headed
toward the hole in the wall at the end of the corridor. The
President seemed equally relieved to be free, but he paused to
turn his attention toward Manning.

"What about the nuclear bomb?" the President asked.

"Skull can't detonate it with the radio transmitter," Manning explained. "A microwave scrambling device has blan-
keted the area so no radio waves of any sort will work. We can't
simply blow the fort to pieces because we might set off the plutonium weapon in the process. So we have to find it and make
certain the terrorists don't set it off manually."

"But how can you find it in time?" the President asked.

"We don't know where it is," Manning answered, "but we
know where it isn't. The bomb isn't here. It isn't in Skull's
headshed or the commo section, and they wouldn't put it in the
mess hall or kitchen area...wherever that might be. That could
make the men too nervous. It wouldn't be in the billets, either.
The men would not be able to rest or relax much with that thing
in clear view. Skull's smart enough to appreciate the psychology—"

"Hey!" James shouted, still watching the entrance. "Can we
talk about this later, man? Shit's going be coming down on us
any second now."

"Right," the Canadian agreed. "We have to get you out of here, Mr. President."

"You're in charge right now," the President replied. "Let's go."

Manning, the President and Weiss hurried through the improvised opening in the wall. James followed, his M-16 covering the corridor as he backed out. The President and Weiss were loaded into the back of the jeep. Then the Phoenix warriors stood back from the doors of the jeep, and gave the driver the go signal. The driver stepped on the gas pedal. As the jeep bolted toward the forest, Manning raised his FAL rifle to watch the top of the wall for enemy gunmen. The helicopters continued to patrol the sky above, and those inside them saw the jeep head for the trees. A flare was fired from the cabin doors of one craft. The flare burst in a bright green light above the fort. Since radio contact was impossible, the flare signals had been arranged in advance. The green light alerted the other choppers and the Phoenix Force trio by the east wing that the President had been rescued.

James pointed his weapon through the gap in the wall and triggered the M-203 attachment. The grenade launcher fired a 40 mm shell through the corridor and exploded the entrance of the cell block. The blast seemed to rock the foundations of the fort.

"That should take care of the dudes at the door," James remarked as he jacked the pump to the M-203 to eject the spent cartridge casing. "Just hope the ceiling didn't fall in."

"Let's find out," Manning replied and stepped into the gap, but he couldn't advance because the corridor was filled with flying rock dust from the blast.

"Damn," James muttered as he joined Manning. "Better let this stuff settle a bit first. Hope the other guys are doin' okay on their own."

DAVID MCCARTER HAD HURLED a grappling hook up to the top of the wall and climbed the rope, followed by Rafael Encizo and Yakov Katzenelenbogen. One by one they descended on the opposite side of the wall and paused to take stock of the situation.

The Bell gunships had resumed machine gunfire on the fortress. The fire was concentrated on the outer walls and spared the sections near the positions where Phoenix Force penetrated the base. The hail of bullets was intended to keep the terrorists busy while the commandos infiltrated Colonel Skull's stronghold.

"Attention!" came the voice of Major Mazarin over the loudspeaker from one of the choppers. "You are surrounded. We have enough firepower to destroy your entire base! None of us want that! Let's see if we can negotiate some sort of terms. Send out one man, unarmed, to talk to us. Maybe we can work something out!"

Mazarin's offer, Katz knew, was made largely to keep the terrorists off balance. It was also an attempt to delay the last drastic act left to the terrorists—setting off the bomb. Mazarin was stalling the enemy so Phoenix Force would have a chance to find the bomb and the hostages.

Katz, McCarter and Encizo moved to the side of the building containing the generator and the radio room. The motor pool was deserted. No one wanted to stay outside with limited cover while the gunships dominated the sky. The tactics seemed effective as the terrorists were kept busy with the gunships and the explosion at the cell block and were not concerned about the possibility of intruders at the west wall. Apparently, the Phoenix trio had gone unnoticed.

McCarter kicked in the door to the generator room. Katz dived inside, his body close to the ground, then he tumbled forward in a shoulder roll, Uzi in his left fist, cradled by the prosthesis. Two men saw the Israeli and swung their weapons in his direction. One of them suddenly dropped his subgun and staggered backward, his hands clutching the short shaft of a crossbow bolt that jutted from the center of his beard.

The Briton burst into the room, his Barnett crossbow in one hand and his KG-99 in the other. The remaining gunman, an Arab, shifted his AK-47 toward him. Katz opened fire in a kneeling stance. The silencer-equipped Uzi sputtered a short trio of coughs. The Arab collapsed, his skull cracked open by three 9 mm slugs.

Another terrorist leaped for the cover of the generators. McCarter snap-aimed his KG-99 and triggered a short burst. The silenced weapon burped harshly and the terrorist cried out as he fell against a wall. He dropped his Sterling chopper and held up his arms in surrender. Bloodstains marked his lower rib cage where at least one parabellum slug had pierced flesh.

"Cuff him," Katz instructed curtly as he moved to the stairs.

Encizo entered and pulled the door shut. He noticed the green flare burning above the compound. The explosion at the cell block had blown away the iron door and sent the bodies of four terrorists hurtling across the square. The Cuban peered out the crack at the door and scanned the grounds.

"They got the President out," Encizo announced. "The green flare is up."

"Mark up another point for our side," McCarter commented as he bound the wounded terrorist's wrists with a pair of riot cuffs.

Encizo's eyes widened as he saw a heavily muscled Asian march across the motor pool. The man carried an Uzi submachine gun and his features were stern, a mask of determination. The Cuban unslung the H&K MP-5 from his shoulder.

"You remember the description of Major Hee?" Encizo asked.

"The Korean," McCarter replied. "Skull's aide."

"I think I just spotted him," the Cuban explained. "According to Gary's description of the fort, it looks like Hee has just left Skull's headshed and he's pretty serious about wherever he's going."

"Might be headed for the bomb," the Briton said, eagerly sprinting toward the door.

"I'm going after him," Encizo declared. "You'd better stay here. Yakov might need you."

"But..." McCarter began, but he realized there was no time to argue. "Be careful."

"I'll do my best," the Cuban assured him as he opened the door and slipped outside.

Katz descended the stairs and saw Encizo duck out. McCarter told him what happened. The Israeli glanced outside, but did not see Encizo or Major Hee in the motor pool.

"The radio room upstairs is deserted," Katz stated. "Nothing here but the generators. We'll put them out of order. Cut off the electricity—let's shake them up a bit more."

"They're pretty shook already, I reckon," McCarter replied.

"If Gary and Cal can get through the cell block to the inside of the compound, they'll go after the billets next," Katz continued. "That might be Hee's destination also. You go outside, stay low and be careful. Either Rafael or the other two will need backup. Be ready to help either way."

"What are you going to do?" McCarter asked, setting down his crossbow to hold the KG-99 in both hands.

"I'm going after Colonel Skull," the Phoenix Force commander declared grimly. "I'm going to personally make sure that he doesn't get away."

MAJOR HEE STRODE to the wooden doors of the small bay area near the motor pool. He pushed open a door and entered the eight-by-twelve room within. Two terrorist guards stared fearfully at him. The room was bare except for a small table, two folding chairs and a single light bulb in the ceiling. In the center of the room stood the ugly gray steel vessel of the plutonium device.

"You men may leave now," Hee told the guards.

"You're going to detonate this thing, aren't you?" one of the terrorists demanded sullenly. "The radios don't work, so Skull can't trigger it by remote control. He sent you to do it instead."

"It is time for you to leave," Hee insisted.

"This is insane, Major!" the other guard declared. "We've already lost! What point is there in suicide?"

"If we surrender now..."

"We will be dishonored," Hee stated. "At least our deaths will mean something."

"*Merde alors!*" The gunman raised his compact MAT-49 submachine gun and pointed it at Hee. "You are as mad as that albino! We were all crazy to get involved in this scheme, but at least we know it is time to accept defeat and try to bargain with the authorities to save ourselves!"

"Put down your gun, Major," the other one ordered, pointing his Skorpion machine pistol at the Korean. "We'll kill you if we have to."

Hee shook his head and slowly unslung the Uzi from his shoulder. The Korean lowered the submachine gun to the floor and raised his hands, but the gunmen were still nervous as they kept their weapons trained on the major. They knew Hee was a deadly martial artist who could kill them both with his bare hands if he got the chance. They did not intend to give the Korean such an opportunity.

"The message from the helicopter said we can negotiate terms for surrender if one unarmed man leaves the compound," one of them remarked. "You or I could go."

"If they don't shoot you before you get a chance to talk to them," his companion replied, his attention fixed on Major Hee. "I think we should first find out how many still want to die for Colonel Skull and who will side with us for survival."

"But how can we—" the French gunman began.

The door burst open with a clang. The man who had been interrupted swung his Skorpion toward the figure at the threshold. Rafael Encizo triggered his MP-5 before the other man could open fire and three 9 mm rounds smashed into the gunman's face and throat. The man toppled backward, his face drenched in a crimson flow.

The other gunman started to turn, his weapon swinging toward Encizo. Major Hee swiftly seized the guard's MAT-49 with one hand and lashed out a powerful karate chop with the other. The blow struck the man in the left temple, making the bone cave in. Hee held on to the MAT-49 subgun and pulled it from the dead man's grasp, then spun about to face Rafael Encizo.

The Cuban fired his Heckler & Koch blaster. A trio of parabellum slugs slammed into the Korean's chest. The impact took Hee off his feet and dropped him to the floor hard. The French machine pistol fell from his grasp and skidded across the stone surface.

Encizo barely glanced down at the three bodies, he was so transfixed by the firepluglike casing of the plutonium bomb. The Phoenix fighter sighed with relief. He turned toward the door and reached for a canvas case on his belt. It contained three flares labeled green, red and yellow. The red flare would be the signal that the bomb had been located.

"Haai-ya!" a voice screamed behind Encizo.

He whirled and saw Major Hee charge toward him. The Cuban raised his H&K chopper as Major Hee thrust a heel-of-the-palm stroke. The Korean's hand struck Encizo's forearm and knocked the MP-5 from his hands. The force of the blow staggered Encizo and sent him stumbling backward.

Hee attacked. The three bullets that had made holes in his shirtfront did not seem to even slow him down. There was only a slight bloodstain on the fabric from the trio of high-velocity slugs. The Korean swung a roundhouse kick for Encizo's head. The amazed and physically stunned Phoenix pro managed to raise a shoulder to protect his cranium. The karate kick struck like a sledgehammer and sent him flying into a wall.

Encizo yanked his H&K P-9S pistol from shoulder leather with his right hand. Hee's fingers closed around the Cuban's wrist like the steel jaws of a bear trap. The Korean shoved Encizo into the wall and pumped a knee into his abdomen. The Phoenix commando felt as if his innards had been ruptured. His left shoulder ached and his right wrist seemed destined to shatter in the Korean's powerful grip. Hee held on to Encizo's wrist, forcing the pistol toward the ceiling. His other hand rose to deliver another deadly karate stroke.

Rafael Encizo ignored the throbbing pain in his left shoulder and snapped his elbow up in a hard *empi* uppercut. The blow caught Hee under the chin. The Korean's head bounced from the stroke, but he immediately responded by seizing the Cuban's shirtfront with one hand while with the other he maintained his hold on Encizo's wrist.

Hee threw himself backward and landed on his rump and left thigh. His right boot caught Encizo in the midsection as the Cuban was hauled forward with Hee's abrupt movement. The Korean straightened his leg and sent Encizo hurtling overhead in a judo circle throw. The Cuban lost his grip on the H&K pistol and heard it clatter on the floor an instant before he slammed into the stone surface. The hard landing seemed to drive his backbone into his lungs. The Cuban rolled away from his opponent and climbed to his feet.

Major Hee had already gained his feet and immediately attacked once again. A tae kwon do front kick to the stomach doubled up Encizo with a painful gasp. The Korean raised a hand and prepared to deliver a lethal chop to the seventh vertebra at the back of Encizo's neck.

The Cuban suddenly shifted away from Hee and pulled the Cold Steel Tanto from its belt sheath. The side of Hee's hand smashed into Encizo's already bruised left shoulder. The pain shot through him like a fire in his veins, but Encizo struck out with the big steel knife and drove the point into his opponent's belly.

Major Hee groaned and jumped back from Encizo. The Tanto wobbled, the tip buried in the Korean's shirt. Encizo stepped away, trying to gulp air into his lungs. Hee gripped the handle of the Tanto knife and yanked the blade from his belly. A small droplet of blood marked the steel tip.

The bastard is wearing a bulletproof vest, Encizo realized. Major Hee drew closer, the Tanto knife in one fist. The Cuban nearly groaned aloud. The Korean terrorist was already beating the hell out of him, and now the son of a bitch had a knife, as well. Hee closed in, blade held ready in one hand and the other hand open, slightly cupped, ready to strike with deadly force that nearly equaled that of the sharp steel. The Korean's expression revealed nothing. He had not even broken sweat during the fight. Encizo seriously wondered if the Major Hee might be some kind of karate-trained robot disguised as a man.

Hee thrust a fast stroke with the Tanto. Encizo dodged before he realized it was a feint. The Korean lashed a fast kick to Encizo's legs and clipped him at the ankles. Encizo's feet were swept out from under him and once again he landed on his back. Hee flipped the knife and grabbed the handle in an overhand grip. Clenching it in both hands, he swung his arms like ax handles, determined to drive the Tanto blade through the Cuban's chest.

Encizo managed to roll away just as the knife descended. Steel struck stone with incredible force. The blade snapped and broke in two. Encizo quickly swung a back fist into Hee's face.

The Korean fell back, blood oozing from a nostril. He is human, Encizo thought with relief. And if he can bleed, he can die.

The Cuban rose from the floor, drawing his Gerber Mark I fighting dagger from a boot sheath. Major Hee stood and raised his hands in a combat stance. Encizo stepped back, the Gerber knife hidden behind his right thigh. Hee advanced.

Suddenly Encizo raised the Gerber knife in his fist. The Korean saw the weapon and prepared to fend off the blade. Encizo's arm snapped forward and he hurled the dagger with all his might. The Gerber rocketed toward the floor. Hee screamed with pain and glanced down at his left foot. The hilt of the Gerber bobbed near the bootlaces. The blade had pierced his instep.

Rafael Encizo charged forward. He chopped the sides of both hands across Hee's forearms to prevent him from striking first. The Cuban rammed a knee into the knife slit in the major's belly. Hee might not have suffered a serious wound in his abdomen, but the cut would still be more vulnerable than any other point of the Asian's torso.

The Cuban's fists swung forward, thumbs extended and anchored by the second knuckle of each index finger. He stabbed the thumbs into the sides of Hee's neck, violently jabbing the nerve centers and carotid arteries. The Korean's face contorted in pain as he screamed a *kiai* and thrust a ram's head punch at his tormentor.

The blow missed, for Encizo had stepped from the path of Hee's attack. The Cuban swiftly drove a heel-of-the-palm stroke to Hee's face. The major's head recoiled from the blow, and Encizo slashed the side of his hand across his enemy's exposed neck as hard as he could. His thyroid cartilage crushed, the terrorist grabbed his neck with both hands. His windpipe was ruined, and he uttered some ugly gurgling sounds as he sank to his knees. Encizo stepped back and watched Hee fall on his face—dead.

The Cuban warrior walked unsteadily to the door, his head spinning, back and shoulder throbbing and stomach about to turn over. He took the flare from the pouch, checked to be certain it was red and opened the door.

THE RED FLARE by the bay area signaled the location of the nuclear bomb. It also served to inform Phoenix Force that the rest of the base was virtually open season for them. Calvin James fired a thermite grenade into the vehicles in the motor pool. The trucks and jeeps exploded in burst of chemical flames.

David McCarter rushed to a barracks and lobbed an SAS flash-bang grenade through a window. The concussion blast shattered glass and burst open the door. A bloodied body tumbled outside. The Briton charged into the building and fired his KG-99 into three stunned opponents inside.

Four unarmed terrorists emerged from another building, which had served as mess hall and kitchen. They held their arms high in surrender. Gary Manning pointed his FAL at the trio and ordered them to get down on their stomachs and extend their arms in front of them, palms up.

Three more terrorists gave up. The others were already dead or seriously wounded. The battle was over, and Colonel Skull's private terrorist mercenary army was defeated, nearly wiped out by Phoenix Force and its allies.

However, Yakov Katzenelenbogen's expression was grim as he walked from the headquarters building to join his teammates at the center of the square. The other four men covered the prisoners while Katz ignited a yellow flare to signal for Mazarin to land his chopper. The other helicopters would remain in the air, transmitting the microwave jamming device until they were certain the bomb had been deactivated.

"Did you find Skull?" McCarter inquired, glancing at Katz's face.

"I found his office," the Phoenix Force commander explained. "Skull was not there. His desk had been moved forward. There's a trapdoor in the floor and it leads to a tunnel. Colonel Skull has escaped."

"Bullshit!" Manning snapped. "Let's go after him."

"You know better, Gary," Encizo informed him. "A tunnel is the easiest thing in the world to booby-trap or mine. Skull has a head start. He'll get to the opening first and blast the tunnel for sure in case anyone followed him."

"We left a jeep outside," Katz remarked. "If it wasn't blown to bits, I'm going for a ride."

"You got an idea where the sucker went?" James asked.

"Well, hell," McCarter said. "Let's go find him."

"The rest of you stay here," Katz ordered. "There's still a nuclear bomb that has to be taken care of, and the safety of the President is still a major concern. I'd hate to find out we over looked a terrorist when he fires a sniper round into the President. I'll look for Skull on my own."

"You know, this is personal for all of us, Yakov," Encizo reminded Katz. "We've all got a score to settle with Skull."

"Yes," Katz replied with a thin smile. "But I'm unit commander and I'm pulling rank. This one is mine."

26

Some of the rocks in the pile at the foot of the ridge loosened, wobbled unsteadily then tumbled forward. A pale white hand was extended from the resultant gap in the stone heap, and more rocks were shoved aside until the space was large enough for Colonel Skull to climb out from the camouflaged mouth of the tunnel. He made certain his dark glasses were in place. The tunnel had been pitch-dark, but once again he stepped into the daylight and the boiling sun that rode the sky above the tops of the surrounding pine trees.

Skull placed his SIG MP-310 submachine gun against the rocks and brushed dirt from his black uniform. He had not expected to have to use the tunnel. He had been prepared to die with the others when the bomb exploded, but he had seen the red flare in front of the bay area and guessed what it meant. Major Hee had failed to get to the nuclear weapon to detonate it. In the end, all his men had failed him.

He could find other men, Skull knew, men who would be ripe for recruitment when he rebuilt his army. It would be difficult and would probably take years, but he had nothing else to do. Eventually, the authorities might find him. They would either put him on trial or kill him on sight. Yet there was still a chance he could rise from the ashes of defeat and come back stronger than before.

Skull gathered up the length of cord that extended into the tunnel to an explosive pack set more than half a mile away. A timer was attached to the cord. Skull set the dial for one minute and tossed it into the tunnel. If anyone had followed him, they would soon be buried under a ton of earth.

He reached for his submachine gun, then yanked back his hand in alarm as clumps of earth were suddenly flung from the ground, inches from his hand. Bullets ricocheted on stones, accompanied by the roar of an automatic weapon. Skull retreated from the MP-310. He turned slowly. Yakov Katzenelenbogen had stepped from the edge of the ridge, Uzi braced across his prosthesis.

"Reach for it again," Katz invited, stepping closer. "Next time I won't aim at the ground."

"How did you find me?" Skull asked as he raised his hands.

"The tunnel is very old," Katz answered. "Probably built about the same time as the fortress itself. KGB had considered using the old fort as a safehouse at one time. The Russian agents who evaluated the site didn't remember too much about it, except the tunnel. They recalled that it extended from the fort to the base of this ridge, three and a half kilometers away."

"KGB?" Skull began, slowly walking toward Katz. "So you're one of the Soviet knights of the Sword and Shield of the Committee for State Security?"

"Take another step and I'll cut you in half," Katz told him. "I'm not working for the KGB. In fact, I'm working for the United States, but bringing you down was something of a group effort."

"I didn't think you Americans could manage to cooperate with Europeans and Russians so well," Skull admitted. "You came alone?"

"I wanted to do this personally," the Israeli answered. "No need for this to be a public execution."

"Oh, I see," Skull said, apparently unalarmed. "You're going to kill me. So why don't you?"

"There's no doubt you deserve to be executed," Katz stated, "but if I killed you now, while you are unarmed and making no effort to attack, that would be murder. Better that you stand trial. Better for the whole world to see that Henri Rikker is a bitter, warped lunatic."

"Henri Rikker is dead," Skull said stiffly. "He died the day I was born."

"Just like a phoenix rising from the ashes?" Katz said with amusement. "It's not going to happen again. Not for you, Rikker."

The charge inside the tunnel went off with a roar that was like the bellow of a monstrous underground beast. The explosion surprised Katz and his attention turned toward the sound. Colonel Skull immediately took advantage of the distraction and lashed out a kick to the Israeli's Uzi. The edge of his boot slammed into the frame of the weapon and struck the submachine gun from Katz's single hand. Turning in a circular manner, Skull hooked his hand into the side of Katz's face, and stamped the heel of his palm in the Phoenix warrior's cheekbone.

The blow sent Katz hurtling backward. His spine connected with the trunk of a pine tree. The Israeli's head ached from the impact of Skull's blow. T'ai chi ch'uan. Katz recalled the file Brognola had wired to Phoenix Force concerning Henri Rikker. The albino had been practicing the ancient Chinese martial art for nearly three decades.

Skull's hand streaked toward Katz's face, the fingers arched like the talons of a bird of prey. Katz ducked and weaved away from the tree, and Skull's tiger-claw stroke connected with the tree, making chips of bark fly into the air as the nails raked the wood.

Skull immediately shuffled toward Katz, moving sideways in a kung fu horse-straddled stance. He hissed like a serpent and snapped a kick for the Israeli's groin. Katz chopped the hooks of his prosthesis across his opponent's shin to block the kick and drove his left fist under the rib cage. Skull groaned and staggered slightly from the punch.

Katz thrust the end of his artificial limb into Skull's midsection, the blow aimed for the solar plexus. It missed the target by a fraction of an inch. The terrorist leader grunted from the blow, but instantly grabbed the prosthesis in both hands. He pulled the arm forward and raised it upward to pivot under the arm.

Skull yanked hard. It was a move taught in several martial arts. The idea was to lock the wrist and elbow and force the opponent off balance, who either goes down or his arm is broken. However, this time Skull was attempting the technique on a man with an artificial arm. The albino pulled with considerable strength. His training in breath control, concentration and moving with his entire body flowing with the direction of a stroke allowed him to harness all his potential power. Yet he noted in surprise that Katz did not hurtle into the air or scream in agony as his elbow snapped at the joint.

Katz felt the harness straps snap and the prosthesis pull loose. The pain was little more than unpleasant. Skull still held the prosthesis, limp and useless inside the Israeli's sleeve. Katz turned quickly and hooked his left knee into the opponent's gut. Then he swung his right shoulder and smashed the end of his stump into his opponent's face.

Skull fell backward from the unexpected blow. The prosthesis slipped from Katz's right sleeve and fell to the ground as he pursued his enemy. The Phoenix commander drove the heel of his left hand in a hard uppercut stroke to Skull's breastbone. The blow struck with surprising force. The Israeli had been an amputee for almost twenty-five years. His left arm had developed considerable strength to compensate for the missing limb. Skull was lifted off his feet and flung to the ground.

The terrorist knew how to break his fall and rolled backward onto his knees. Katz stepped forward and lashed a kick at Skull's face. But the man was swift with his hands and caught the foot at the toe of the boot and the back of the heel. Skull twisted the ankle hard, and Katz was thrown off balance.

The Israeli hit the ground and Skull pounced, hands poised like twin claws, determined to tear his opponent apart. Katz pivoted on the small of his back, braced himself with his shoulders on the ground and kicked out with both feet. One boot slammed into Skull's chest and sent him hurtling backward once more.

Katz got to his feet and started to reach for the SIG-Sauer pistol in shoulder leather under his right arm. Skull lunged forward and swung a roundhouse kick for the Israeli's head. Katz countered with a rising forearm block, the autoloader in his left fist. Skull's ankle struck the forearm hard. The pistol popped from Katz's fingers and Skull quickly thrust the stiff fingers of his left hand into the Israeli's solar plexus.

The fingertips stabbed like knives. Katz gasped in agony as the blow seemed to tear inside him to attack his heart and lungs. Skull's other hand shot toward Katz's face, index and middle finger poised in a V-shape, tips aimed at the Israeli's eyes. He intended to poke Katz's eyeballs out of their sockets, perhaps stab the fingers right through the cavities into the brain.

Katz bobbed his head and Skull's finger jab struck his forehead. The fingertips poked the frontal bone forcibly, but Katz hardly noticed. He swung his left hand forward and raked his fingers across Skull's face. The dark glasses snapped off the bridge of Skull's nose. Katz gripped the glasses in his fist and tossed them aside.

Colonel Skull cried out, and started to back off, peering about for his glasses.

Katz panted heavily, his entire body raked with bruises and his chest still aching from the blow to his solar plexus. He gazed at his opponent. Skull squinted shortsightedly, covered his eyes with one hand and slashed out with the other. He was obviously handicapped. Under different circumstances, Katz would have felt sympathy for Colonel Skull's plight. But the terrorist had felt no mercy for anybody and therefore deserved none.

Katz swung his booted foot in a kick that got his opponent between the legs. Skull doubled up with a wheezing gasp of agony. He grabbed his injured body with one hand and blindly thrust a spear-hand stroke with the other.

The finger stab missed as Katz stepped around his opponent. The Israeli grabbed the end of his empty right sleeve in his single fist and swung it like a noose over Skull's head to close it around his neck as Katz pulled hard. He planted a knee at the small of Skull's spine and increased the traction. The stump of his right arm jammed between Skull's shoulder blades as Katz bent the man backward.

Skull struggled. He tried to throw his opponent off his back, but it was impossible to get leverage against the knee anchored at his spine. He reached overhead and clawed at Katz's head. He could not find the Israeli's face to gouge at the eyes, and Katz's short hair did not offer enough to grip and pull. Soon

the resistance grew more feeble as oxygen was cut off to Skull's
brain.

Katz felt the body go limp, but he held on and continued the
stranglehold. The fiend had to die, because as long as he lived
he was a threat to the entire world. Katz pulled on the sleeve
until the fabric tore at the shoulder, and at last he let go. He was
exhausted and sickened by the vengeful emotions that had
welled up inside him during the battle. It had had to be done
and it was done. What bothered Katz was realizing that he had
wanted to do it.

Even the best of us are still part savage, regardless of what
cloaks of civilization we drape ourselves in. Katz understood
this. Justice had been found not in a courtroom but on the
battlefield. The need for such justice was the reason Phoenix
Force existed.

THE PRESIDENT of the United States had just completed his
first speech since returning to America. He had spoken about
the kidnapping, but gave few details about his rescue. He emphasized that the terrorists did not represent any government
or nationality. They were apolitical anarchists who had threatened world peace and civilization in general. The President
praised the efforts of the police, the military and the intelligence networks of Luxembourg, West Germany, Belgium and
France. He officially thanked Interpol, GSG-9, Sûreté, CIA
and NSA and recognized the assistance of the Soviet KGB
which, officially at least, had cooperated fully with American
and West European counterparts to deal with the crisis.

Of course, Phoenix Force was not mentioned, nor was its
major role in the mission acknowledged. The elite commando
team could not function if it did not maintain tight security.
The President concluded his speech with a moving comment
about the good, brave men of so many nationalities who had
lost their lives during the incident that had nearly set Western
Europe into total turmoil.

Yet, the President insisted, something positive had emerged
from this experience: the proof that nations can work together
to deal with emergency situations. That served as encourage-
ment, and summit conferences to discuss reduction of nuclear

arms must continue to be held so men of all nations can strive to make the world a better place for all.

Hal Brognola switched off the television set and turned to the five men seated at the conference table in the Stony Man War Room. The Fed picked up a computer printout sheet.

"Aaron gave me this just before you arrived," he announced. "It's a confidential report from Iraq. The Saddoon brothers were arrested yesterday, along with several other Iraqi officials who were involved in the conspiracy to assassinate the present leaders and overthrow the government. Evidence against them was pretty strong, thanks to Koerner's testimony. I think they still have capital punishment in Iraq."

"So the last bit of the mission is taken care of," Gary Manning remarked, sipping black coffee as he listened to Brognola. "I have to admit, this one was a real ball-buster."

"We almost got everything busted," Rafael Encizo added. "Including our heads."

"Oh, what the hell!" David McCarter said cheerfully as he popped the tab of a Coca-Cola can. "We did it, and everything worked out in the end. Pretty well, anyway."

"I think it was an incredible mission even by Phoenix Force standards," Brognola declared, chewing on a cigar as he spoke. "You guys rescued VIP hostages, including the leaders of the two biggest superpowers in the world, you stopped a potential nuclear disaster that could have killed thousands of innocent people and you put one of the worst terrorist outfits in history out of business."

"Does that mean we're going to get a raise?" Calvin James inquired with a slight grin.

"I figure you guys deserve at least a three-month vacation and all the money you want to spend while you're on R and R," the Fed stated. "But something has come up."

"Another mission?" Manning groaned. "Already?"

"Yeah, I know," Brognola said, bobbing his head. "You guys don't have to take it. I mean, I'll understand if you decide to pass on this one after everything that's happened. Still, it's pretty important...."

"All right, Hal," Yakov Katzenelenbogen began with a weary sigh. He glanced at his partners and knew what the answer would be for every one of them. "Let's hear what you've got for us this time."

"Gotcha!" Brognola said as he punched Katz on the arm. "There *will* be something down the line, but for now, I want to rest my eyes. Be off!" The head Fed looked at the men sheepishly, then as they started filing out, he added, "Just check in with me after a couple of weeks. Will I ever have something for you—so keep your carcass in one piece!"